"Beguiling and unsettling"
—Kirkus Reviews

"Fun, fast-paced fairy goodness"
—Peadar O'Guilin
Bestselling author of The Call *and* The Invasion

Aionios
Books

Fallen Princeborn

STOLEN

Jean Lee

Fallen Princeborn: Stolen
(Book 1 of the *Fallen Princeborn Series*)

For information, please address:
Aionios Books, LLC, P.O. Box 1010, Carlsbad, CA, 92018, USA.
AioniosBooks.com

This book is a work of fiction. Names and characters are the product of the
author's imagination. Any resemblance to actual persons, living or dead, or to
actual events is coincidental.

Book design by Gerardeen M. Santiago

Published 2019, by Aionios Books, LLC.
Printed in the United States of America.

ISBN-13: 978-1-949428-00-1 (Paperback)
Library of Congress Control Number: 2018957888

For my daughter,
Born the spring before this story came to the page

Contents

PART 2

Fallen Princeborn
STOLEN

Prologue

Sure was nice of that storm to wash so much of the blood off. Sure was nice of that trucker to pick him up after that storm. He could be... a dirty, worn out farmhand, fired after butchering the wrong cattle. Easy story to spin in these parts.

He waits in line for his bus ticket with quiet patience. He looks down at the newspaper stack next to the ticket counter. The folds of his claylike face smooth as he reads the front-page headline:

6 Found Butchered in Bus on County Line: Hearts Missing

CLINTONVILLE, WI. Waupaca and Outagamie County officials are collaborating to investigate the suspicious deaths of six people in a bus found ten miles north of Highway 76.

The bus was discovered by an Amish farmer on Tuesday morning when his dog brought home a human hand severed above the wrist. After he contacted the police, Johann Stukkler and his dog, a retired search-and-rescue Belgian Malinois, led several members of the Waupaca sheriff's department to an old school bus hidden behind a makeshift screen of tree branches and brush.

Despite the vehicle's broken, rusted frame, the bus engine and tires showed signs of recent use.

The bus's interior left many members of law enforcement "speechless."

1

He steps outside to wait for the bus and the evening stars to arrive. Street lights buzz to life one by one. Mosquitoes buzz right along with them, always on the hunt for fresh blood. One lands right on his thumb. His eyes glow like candles lost in bottomless caves as he raises his thumb to within a foot of his face. His forefinger hovers just above the mosquito's twitchy wings.

He thought for sure he'd picked a safe spot to hide that bus. But now, it'll have to be some months before he can go back to that farm in the middle of nowhere to see his new friend from over the old stone wall.

His finger moves just a little closer, just barely touching the greedy mosquito's body. His eyes flicker.

It's all about patience.

Part I

I've had enough of childhood
I've had enough of graves
—Pete Townshend

So Much for Plans

Charlotte breathes in as she steps down, the last passenger to get off the bus. Her nose tells her that the bus has leaked its gasoline all over the highway, that the man with the fry pan ears hasn't bathed in days, and that a predator killed its prey somewhere in the surrounding forest two, if not three, days ago. A sickly raven lands on their lopsided bus and hops alongside her as she passes the trio of older women who introduced themselves as the Sweenil sisters. They are tsk-tsking Wisconsin road conditions. Charlotte adjusts her headphones, trying to tune them out.

"Those pot holes." Saucy Sweenil teeters on pumps made for a woman thirty years younger, her red dress short enough to show everyone just how high varicose veins can go.

"You'd think our driver'd look for these things!" says another Sweenil sister, her hair dyed a garish blue, her puffy pink cheeks framing a tulip mouth.

Charlotte turns away to roll her eyes and focuses on the woods lining either side of the highway. Wild berry bushes mingle with elms and maples—it's nearly impossible to see a few feet beyond those green walls. Gold and orange already gild a few treetops—autumn's not far away. Kind of pretty, but claustrophobic too.

5

"Betcha ten we see a driver in ten minutes." Jackpot Sweenil's layers of goldish baubles bounce against her neck flab.

"I'll see that bet and raise you five!" Blue Hair Sweenil ups the ante.

Charlotte turns up "I Am the Sea" and weaves herself between Studchin and her sister, who has, of course, latched herself onto the hot young bunch of musicians "sooooo close to breaking out. A music prof at Lawrence knows a guy who's got a cousin—"

"Yeah." Bubble pop. "That's where my sister's goin'." Only Anna would use bubble gum for punctuation.

Charlotte rolls her eyes and continues to walk, pretending not to hear her sister. Headphones are useful like that. She passes Twitchy, who's using his chewed-up fingernails to scrape the smile off the badger logo on the bus's BADGER MIDWEST EXPRESS sign. The raven cackles.

Studchin pitches a rock at the raven. Feathers fall from its wings as it rolls, stricken, across the roof and then stagger-hops, the screech-scratch of its claws raising goose bumps on Charlotte's arm. The raven's violet eyes narrow (*Can ravens glare?*) and it stares at Studchin with its wings outstretched like a pathetic vampire cape. The harsh staccato cackle in its throat pries its beak open wider and wider until it finally flaps its cape-like wings and lifts itself off the bus, flying for the sunbeams strangled by the treetops.

"Gah, that is too creepy." Air suck. Bubble pop.

Charlotte waves the feathers away from her face and smells berries mixed with ash.

Charlotte's eyes flick from Anna to the raven, watching it fly. Its beak remains downward as though smelling the gasoline trail. As it passes over the end of the fuel trail, it executes a neat chandelle and then dives into the trees.

Air suck. "No wonder Uncle Mattie hates birds. He'd say that qualifies as an 'ominous omen.'"

Something sparks on Charlotte's shoes.

Air suck. Sigh. "Could you just talk already?"

Charlotte bends over. No feathers lie on the ground. Only ash. "Do you see this?" She points down as she shucks off her headphones, draping them around her neck.

"'Oh, hi, Anna, how are you holding up?'" Anna loves making her Charlotte impersonation sound like that vicious crone of a librarian from Bismarck Central.

"I mean it. Where are the feathers your boyfriend knocked off that raven? There's only ash everywhere."

"Boyfriend? Does this mean I FINALLY get to date?"

"No."

Anna sticks out her tongue. "'C'mon, Anna, we never do anything together anymore. Let's visit family, Anna. It's just for a week, Anna. NOT! Because it's really *forever*, Anna. Because I'm a bitch who hates our mom and because—'" she stops when Charlotte stops looking at her.

The sheet metal on the back of their bus has large cuts like an angry child would make with scissors slashing at paper. Charlotte crawls closer and sees more gashes underneath.

Anna hunches down and gives judgment. "So we ran over someone's barbecue grill. Big deal."

The scent of something old and male wafts from Anna's left armpit. Charlotte doesn't even bother to hold out her hand. "Give it to me."

Bubble pop. Glittery eyelashes bat at Charlotte. "Whatcha mean?"

"Give. It. Back."

A breeze picks up Anna's bright-red hair and sends her berry shampoo scent up the road alongside the gas. "Fi-ine." She stretches her arms, letting a man's worn leather wallet fall to the ground. "Uncle Mattie would be proud."

Charlotte's skin grows hot as she pinches the wallet between thumb and forefinger. "Whose is it?"

Anna bobs her head toward Potential Homicidal Maniac.

Of course. Charlotte stands up and cocks an eyebrow, nostrils still flaring. *No wonder Uncle Mattie would be proud.*

Studchin and his other band members whistle for Anna to join them. Their clearance-aisle cologne rolls across the street to the sisters. "They're idiots, you know that."

"*They* are following *their* dream instead of their stupid sister's. Maybe I'll be a roadie on their next tour." Anna turns on her smile and skips over. Charlotte curses under her breath, but doesn't try to get Anna back. Pudgy grunge wannabes don't smell like much of a threat, not compared to the rusty odor on Mumbles, with his "Lizzy likes pink things" song on repeat, or the peculiar sanitizer-and-vomit bouquet around Potential Homicidal Maniac.

"Best get away from there, both of you," Maisy the bus driver says as she hobbles over, her once Pepto-Bismol pink uniform now so coated with dirt and grease that her nametag fittingly reads "Ma."

"Both of—?" Charlotte looks to her side and sees Potential Homicidal Maniac lurking a step behind, his face a mashed-up pile of clay. Charlotte takes two slow, deliberate steps back because a quick, jerky movement would be perceived as skittish and would make her look weak. And she is not weak.

Maisy groans at the sight of the marks and lies down, scooting her body halfway under the bus. "This under-carriage is a mess. Can't imagine what got in there."

Charlotte's chest prickles. Eyes stare at her from some-where. The feeling comes from way off, in the distant trees where the gasoline trail ends. The world is unsettling itself:

8

she feels it beneath the pavement. "Did we run over someone's grill?"

"Dunno, but it sure did a number on us."

A distant bleep-bleep from inside the bus.

"Sounds like someone mighta gotten my SOS. Stay away from here, okay? Fumes'n'all."

Charlotte extends her hand and hoists Maisy up from under the bus and watches her hop-hobble to the front of the bus and up the steps. Then Charlotte reaches for her necklace, one relic of her father she'd rescued from her mother's purge, and breathes.

Like headphones, oversized clothes disguise, camouflage. Conceal. So, secure in the knowledge that Potential Homicidal Maniac cannot see her muscles, or even the cuts on her knuckles from her last fight, Charlotte steps forward and thrusts his wallet out to him. "You lost this." The cuff of her plaid shirt reveals only her calloused fingertips.

Potential Homicidal Maniac studies Charlotte's exposed fingertips and then takes the wallet without a word. His unkempt graying hair blocks his eyes as the breeze shifts and brings new smells. Oil. Rust. Smoke and ashes. Are they near a dump? The trees cling to the roadside, sheltering them from what lies beyond. A few branches rustle, marking a corridor where the raven disappeared.

"Something's out there," he says.

Charlotte flinches. She didn't think Potential Homicidal Maniac could speak, let alone with a radio voice. "Like what?" The vision of rotting prey fogs her senses. Surely there are bears, wolves, cougars, coyotes, all eyeing them hungrily from their hiding places.

"Dunno. Something," his freak-huge hands stuff themselves into worn coat pockets, "unfriendly."

Fat help you are. Charlotte squints at the tree line and then drags her gaze back to see Maisy emerging from the bus.

"Good news, folks! Help is on the way!"

Potential Homicidal Maniac follows Charlotte to join the others grouping around Maisy, who's saying something about a tour bus coming back from a job. Only Charlotte notices the world shifting—the tremors in the air and deep rumbles beneath the road.

A sharp cackle comes from overhead. The raven is back, its violet eyes shining. It circles them once, twice, then lands on their bus.

Charlotte's chest prickles even more. What does that raven want? No one has food out here. No signs of roadkill. And it keeps staring at certain people, like Mumbles and Jackpot Sweenil. And Anna.

Charlotte grabs her necklace again. Tucked beneath her shirt, a few inches below the base of her neck and just above her heart, a diamond-shaped red pendant the size of a half-dollar dangles from a thin silver chain. At the pendant's center blooms a six-petaled white rose surrounded by silver leaves. Her dad never did explain why he wore something so feminine under his uniform. Charlotte figures it came from his mom, who had died long before she was born. Now it's hers. Well, theirs. She shares it with Anna sometimes. Otherwise, *from firstborn to firstborn*, Dad said. Usually its cool touch calms her.

But not this time. There's a click somewhere deep inside Charlotte's heart, and a Voice, quiet and light, peeks out and whispers: *Stay here. Don't go.*

"I can't," Charlotte says aloud.

"Excuse me?" Saucy Sweenil teeters forward, her breasts doing their damnedest to escape their confines.

Oh shit, that wasn't her. That was INSIDE me. I'm hearing voices. "I can't sneeze," Charlotte says, quickly starts shaking her head, pulling more air in, and in—

The Voice pokes a rib bone. *I know you're listening. You know I'm right.*

"Am not—ah-CHOO!" Spit and snot erupt. Charlotte tilts her head to either side and thinks, *There. Voice gone.*

"Ahem." Saucy Sweenil rights herself just before she bursts her dress and then whisks out a Kleenex. Her lips squish together as she says, "Young ladies do not spew out bodily fluids." A few flakes of tangerine lipstick float down and dot her chest.

Charlotte wipes her lips with her sleeve—she doesn't want to laugh at the seventy-something in a minidress. Not loudly, anyway. "Whatever you say, ma'am."

The lady clucks her tongue and clicks along down the pavement to join her sisters, which suits Charlotte just fine. Life is hectic enough, with keeping track of Anna and preparing for college. The last thing she needs is a voice telling her not to go where her own dreams are waiting to come true. *Next I'll be seeing ghosts and goblins and rescuing dudes in distress.* Charlotte tightens her hold around the pendant. *Just get to Appleton, to Aunt Gail. Relax. Be safe.*

Anna's bubble-laugh floats over and pops above Charlotte. Charlotte maneuvers through the Sweenils to see Stuchin's pal Henna Neck put a hand on Anna's hair. Even from this far, her eyelashes sparkle like a fairy sat on them.

A green bus thunders and belches a black fog of smoke as it approaches. Only Charlotte sees the raven watch the bus as intently as the others do. Its brakes sound terrible, and the E in the old SCENIC TOURS sign is peeling off as if to flee before anything else can happen to it. The bus groans as it halts, then regurgitates a burly man with chalky white skin.

Tufts of thin red hair dapple his scalp and arms.

Maisy comes forward and wipes the grease off on her pants.

"You must be Maisy." Burly Man holds her hand like an old friend.

Air suck. "Who let him out of his cave?" Bubble pop.

"Hush." Charlotte hisses.

"You'll save my bacon if you can get them to the Appleton station tonight." Maisy opens the luggage bay of the broken-down bus and starts handing out bags. "I've got to stay with the bus until a tow arrives."

"Not a problem at all, ma'am," Burly Man says with a tilt of his blue sunglasses. "I got plenty of time, folks, to help you get to where you got to go. I love a trip to Appleton—know just the route to see the prettiest, quietest countryside in the state. Jamie, get yerself out here and load up!"

A lanky black-haired man—barely, judging by the state of his acne—plows Charlotte over to reach the baggage compartment.

"Sorry." He cackles. His sunglasses match Burly Man's.

Charlotte sidesteps to regain her balance and then eyes the tour bus, its wheels covered in grass and mud. Not easy to come by on dry paved roads.

Don't go, the Voice in Charlotte's heart whispers again.

Apparently, sneezes don't evict weird voices.

"Thanks, Jamie!" says Burly Man as Jamie begins to load the bags. "Now you just come on up, ladies and gentlemen, and we'll take you right where you wish to be," waving them all toward the bus.

That's all Jackpot Sweenil needs to hear—she and Sweenils Saucy and Blue Hair climb in. Twitchy follows, holding a newly scraped C from the SC NI TOURS sign. No one but Charlotte hears a tense, quick sniff coming from Jamie every time he lifts a bag into the bus. With Anna's, the sniffing doesn't seem to stop. Charlotte grabs her own backpack from the pile and reaches for Anna's, which is clenched in Jamie's pocked fingers. "I'll take that."

"No need, miss." His smile puts a chain-smoker's teeth to shame.

"Yeah, there is. Give it."

Bubble pop. Teeth click. "Charlie, just let him do his job."

Charlotte yanks the bag strap hard. Jamie's body whips forward, his sunglasses flying, backpack smacking Potential Homicidal Maniac in the ass as he boards the bus.

Noxious sigh. "Nice one, Charlie. Gah, don't you trust anybody?"

Charlotte takes a breath, heaves the packs onto one shoulder, stoops to pick up Jamie's sunglasses, and then holds them out to him. "Sorry about that. Here."

Jamie blinks bright violet eyes. "Thanks." He cackles. Sunglasses back on, he whips the last bags into the hold. The luggage door moans like a dying animal as he pushes it shut.

Don't go. Stay here.

Charlotte's hand presses the pendant into her sternum as if to cover whatever's cracked open inside her. It's all she can touch—Anna's out of reach, she and every other passenger, their bodies floating about behind dimmed windows. Does no one else smell the old oil and neglect, like meat burned down to nothing? The way Jamie stands by the door, hands clasped behind him, grinning like a choir boy, all pleased with himself, Charlotte knows, freakin' *knows*, someone's pulled an Ed Gein and made the bus seats out of bodies.

"Sweetheart, you've got to board, okay?" Maisy calls from the coach. "You can't stay here with me. It'll take days to get the bus fixed."

And you know you're oversmelling it, Charlie, just like earlier with the bears and shit. It's just an old bus, is all. But Charlotte continues

13

to hesitate.

"Hurry up, Charlie, let's go!" her sister calls from a window. "They've got food in here. And it's all posh, come on!"

Jamie's grin grows.

It's just a bus. Charlotte decides, and tucks the necklace away. *DON'T GO.*

Happy to Help

"So what's your name?" Charlotte asks Burly Man as she boards.

"Today you call me Mr. Smith, sweetheart," he says with a wink.

Jamie cackles again. He even bobs his head.

Stop it, Charlie. People are not birds.

Charlotte sees seats of soft leather, new carpet, a bathroom, a table piled high with cakes and fruit and cans of soda. Yet all she *smells* is rot and blood. She shakes her head again and again, as if whatever gunk had died in her nose just needs to be blown out and smeared on Studchin's seat.

Bubble pop. "I'm not even gonna ask." Anna sticks her gum to the windowpane and rips open a cake wrapper. "Why are you looking at me like that?" Chomp.

Charlotte swallows down her bile. "Sorry. Just. It smells expired."

"Gah, you and your nose." Chomp.

"That's right, you just help yourselves, folks." Mr. Smith glances at them via the rearview mirror.

The Sweenil sisters can't shut up about "that nice man's generosity." The three of them tick their heads side to side like chickens.

"Just feel these seats!" says Blue Hair Sweenil.

"We are lucky ladies, lu-cky!" adds Jackpot Sweenil.

"My favorite coconut cake! I was just wishing for one a minute ago." Saucy Sweenil licks her lips.

"Young lady, you mind moving?" asks Jackpot Sweenil.

Don't sit down. Get your sister. Get out, insists the Voice.

Jackpot Sweenil's cough feels like a polite shove to get the hell out of the way. "Young lady, if you don't mind."

Should that table be blocking the rear emergency exit? Charlotte eyes the obstruction, then shrugs before wedging herself into the seat next to Anna, who had chosen the seat next to the side emergency exit, clearing the narrow aisle to accommodate the bulk of sister Sweenil. *Just cram yourself in, Charlie. That's it. It's just a bus. These guys have uniforms and everything. You'll get Anna to Aunt Gail's, you'll get you to college, and this will all just be... whatever this all is. Not Bismarck, that's all that matters.*

"Any problems?"

Charlotte does her damnedest not to stare up into Jamie's nostrils as her knees press into the empty seat ahead of her. "No."

Chomp. "Moh."

Jamie's stare travels down Anna's face to her chest. Oily sweat shimmers over his acne.

Anna turns away and gags.

Charlotte thrusts her arm around Anna and glares up at Jamie. *Get your freaky-ass eyes off my minor sister.* "So how much for whatever my sister took?"

"Oh, that's compliments of the company. On account of the unexpected change of plans."

Henna Neck and Frost Tips lunge for the table again, Studchin calling for "more of that custard stuff!"

"The bus company?" asks Charlotte, puzzled.

Jamie's grin close up reveals bits of weird yellow leaves, like the guy had forgotten to brush his teeth after that spinach last week. "Shu-ure," he drawls.

"We ready?" Mr. Smith whistles a batch of notes. "Off we go! Now what's that Sinatra song about luck?"

That sets the Sweenil sisters all atwitter, and soon the entire bus settles into quiet conversation and chewing.

Anna shoves Charlotte's arm off and yanks her head-phone cord. "Off, you ass. Jeez."

Charlotte digs through her backpack for a Tootsie Pop, her sugar of choice on hard days. *Dammit! Had the last one when we left.* She sighs and searches for her phone instead. Get online, check a map. Stop that damned prickle in her chest. "Anna, where's my phone?"

Anna kicks her own pack while wiping her hands on the seat in front of her. "Battery's dead. Sweetie Smash Challenge while you had to—" bubble pop, finger wiggle "—air-practice, or whatever."

"What about your phone?"

"I had to say goodbye to my friends somehow." Chomp. Sniffle. "Not that you care. Bet you didn't even say goodbye to Mom." Slurp.

Who cares if I said goodbye? Jack Shit, that's who. Whatever. Charlotte bites back the snark and hides in her headphones again. She starts "The Real Me," thinking, *The bus SMELLS old and gross, but nothing FEELS old and gross. Give me two seconds and I'd be out cold, it's so damn comfortable.... Dad's pendant, it's warm. Or I'm warm, probably a stupid fever because of course THAT would happen the night before I can finally change my life.... And then there's Anna and her shit-for-giggles. Gah, I do not need Sweenil wrath or ol' Burly Smith on my case because of her.*

At least food has settled Anna down. Now she's content to walk that quarter from Uncle Mattie up and down the fingers of her right hand. Then flips to her left. The quarter continues its deliberate tumble from pinky to ring to middle to forefinger to thumb and back again. Up and down. Then down and up.

Like practicing scales on a piano, observes Charlotte.

"Nice moves." Studchin's face betrays a lack of skills with a napkin.

"Thanks. My uncle taught me."

Charlotte does a quick passenger check: Potential Homicidal Maniac sits as far from Anna as possible. Twitchy is de-threading his own coat. Mumbles starts singing "Lizzy likes locked things." The Sweenils argue over who won that Waters Meet Bingo tournament. Mr. Smith sings too softly for her to hear.

Black feathers fly across their window. Violet flashes, a cackle rumbles.

Charlotte spins 'round and stares at the back of the bus.

Jamie is gone.

"Where is he?"

Anna bats those damn glitter-lashes at Studchin one more time before asking, "Who?" Slurp.

"The crazy acne boy with the bags. Where is he?"

Anna opens another cake. "Probably bathroom. Why, wanna ask for his number?"

"What's this about numbers?" Studchin's breath reeks of mouse turds and sugar. "Cuz I've got one, if you want it."

Charlotte's chest burns beneath the pendant. It's burning like hell, she's going to pass out—

"Can you see the real me, can ya? Can ya?"

What the—? Who the—? Who has the audacity to sing a Who song OVER The Who? Charlotte swivels around in her seat, trying to locate the source. Not Studchin, he wouldn't know good music if a chorus of show girls sang it from a Jacuzzi of custard. Not his bandmates and, thank god, not Mumbles.

Potential Homicidal Maniac? Nope. Dead silent, head still.

It's Mr. Smith, singing right along with Roger. But how can he hear what she's listening to on her headphones, from that far up front? Charlotte shakes her head and stares at the back of Burly Man's head. He stares right back at her from the rearview mirror. Not even the Sweenils notice him singing. No one but Charlotte, always Charlotte.

"Charlie?" Slu-urp. "What's going on?"

"Shut it."

"Char—"

"Can you see, can you see the real me?"

"SHUT IT." To Anna or to Mr. Smith—Charlotte doesn't care. *Get away from my music, my head, my sister. Get away.*

Ash-wind pulls on Charlotte's nose. Black, green, black, green, black: the raven's circling again. *Get AWAY!*

"Can you see the real me, Preacher?"

"I mean it, where is that Jamie guy?"

"I don't know, Charlie. Why do you care?"

"Dude, what is up with your sister?" Studchin to Anna.

"Can you see the real me, Doctor?"

Ash chokes, feathers fly, song deafens, eyes glitter—

"Can you see the real me, Mother?"

Charlotte sees Mr. Smith's fingers drum along in perfect sync with the song.

And he stares right back. His teeth are painted, ablaze in his smile.

"Can you see the real me me me me me me?"

The raven strikes.

Dreams Delayed

The bus swerves back and forth. Impossible to manage, about to capsize.

The raven shrieks with human cries, its body flattened on the windshield, trapped in a glass spiderweb.

The Sweenil sisters screech. Everyone but Charlotte screams with the raven. Compelled by the raven.

Mr. Smith hits the brakes again and again.

Charlotte wraps one arm around Anna and braces them both with the other: "Cover your head!"

Anna screams on, hair flying around her face.

A final squeal of the tires.

Then silence.

Charlotte holds Anna away from her, hands on either side of her face. "Anna, are you okay? Anna!"

Cough. Double blink of baby-blue eyes. "Not so loooud."

Mr. Smith turns around like they've just completed a routine scenic tour. "Is everyone all right?"

The raven twitches and falls out of sight, taking the entire windshield panel with it. Unfazed, Mr. Smith doesn't bother to look.

"Land a' jumpkins!" Jackpot Sweenil laughs nervously and readjusts her sunhat. "Haven't rocked that much since the State Fair of '79!"

Her sisters nervously giggle in agreement.

Studchin and his mates bemoan the damage to their musical instruments trapped under the snack table.

Twitchy stares at his pile of threads in despair before picking them up, one at a time, placing them in a row, one at a time.

Potential Homicidal Maniac slowly wipes Fry Pan Ears's nosebleed. He sniffs the blood.

Charlotte hears herself jabbering in her head. *Anna's fine. I'm fine—fingers all accounted for. Audition still a go.* If only her chest would stop burning and, *This Jamie... guy, and the Burly Smith—it's all fucked up.* Doesn't matter where they are: Charlotte's got to get herself and Anna out. Now.

Clank. The side emergency door swings open.

Charlotte doesn't see Mr. Smith scowl and ask himself, "What's that doin'?" She just shoves Anna out despite her protests and follows.

"Great idea, sweetheart." Mr. Smith's voice follows them out, all polite and nice, like the raven never hit them in the first place. "Let's step out, folks, and bunker down for the night."

Charlotte hears no one ask why they should have to bunker down here of all places: a farm. No, a forest. A farm and a forest? The highway cuts through the farmland: a small wheat field to the south, golden hisses in the breeze. To the north stands the farmstead, complete with barn, tractor, an old well, a giant tree, and a farm... castle? Three stories tall, all clay and stone, with battlements on top. *That cannot be common in agricultural architecture.* Trees surround everything, as if some giant were trying to hide his farm playset from his annoying sister.

21

"Where are we?" Charlotte scans their surroundings.

Gum wrapper. Bubble pop. "Motel, duh." Anna points to another building on the farmstead, partially obscured from the highway by the giant tree. In stark contrast to the farm-castle, this one is a long, low wooden structure, painted a crisp robin's egg blue with bright-yellow shutters and doors. Even the gravel dust kicked up by the bus can't dampen its colors. "At least we're not stuck in the bus for the night." Bubble pop.

Charlotte swivels her head from the Smurf house, then back to the bus, with its fine tires and obviously fine brakes. *Just a bus. Yeah, a bus totally capable of driving. Totally capable of going to a real town instead of stopping here, in the middle of nowhere, but no, we have to overnight here because of a "raven"?*

And there's the little bastard, crimson and hobbling along. Un-be-lievable. Still alive. "Well," *to kick, or not to kick?* "That's convenient," Charlotte mutters aloud. But no one hears her.

And no one sees the raven. Why should anyone else see a bloody raven (which really should be dead) dropping bits of glass and feather in the grass? Where Charlotte can see the feathers pfft!—turn to ash?

Mr. Smith stands next to the bus engine and directs every-one's attention to the farmhouse, where a petite woman is waddle-running down the drive. Her hands are covered with oven mitts, her hair in curlers.

"Well hello there!" booms Burly Smith.

Yeah, have them all look at YOU, not the raven.

"Why Mr. Smith, is it really you?" The woman pulls a mitt off and warmly shakes his hand, then everyone else's.

But Charlotte's attention is still on the raven. Which she

sees collapse at the foot of the old tree. Where a gray squirrel hurries down its trunk and takes the raven in its paws. To help it sit.

Help it sit? What the—? A hand grabs Charlotte's and she jerks, ready to break the wrist attached to the offending hand, and—*Oh, it's just—*

"—Mrs. Blair, but please call me Joanne."

At least Charlotte remembers her manners for once and shakes the woman's plump hand.

"My husband will be out in a minute to help with bags," she calls to group. "You two girls can stay at our house," this to Charlotte and Anna. "We have a daughter who's right about your age." She nods and smiles at Anna. "JENNY!"

A small girl with glasses and long blond bangs, clothes spotted with dirt and grass stains, peers around the corner of the blue motel and stares at the raven and nurse-squirrel.

Jenny can do what no adult can: she SEES.

"Jenny, there you are!" Mrs. Blair sweeps her hand in the air, and an invisible string yanks the girl out of her hiding place. "Now, this time we have two sweet girls to take care of. Isn't that nice? Won't this be fun, Jenny? Why don't you set them up in the house?"

Charlotte sighs. She'd take a castle over the Bates Motel any day.

Anna snatches her duffel before Jenny can reach it. "I got it, kid." Bubble pop. "Our packs are still on the bus, Charlie. Be a dear, will you?" Her tone is squishy and sour. She walks toward the castle like she knows where to go.

Jenny hoists Charlotte's duffel, visibly shaking under its weight—no, she's hiding behind it. And she's peeking at the source of chattering from the old tree. There the raven perches, glass shards all shaken off but still sparkling and bloody.

23

Is blood supposed to sparkle that way?

The squirrel skitters down from the tree, scampers toward them, and stops five feet away. It stares at the girl, chatters *at her*, actually moves toward her. The stench of want, obsessive want, saturates the air.

Jenny shakes like she's about to piss herself.

Charlotte's chest burns (*like that last fucking night with Uncle Mattie*), and she will never, ever let someone else know that pain. Her pendant hums with her wild heartbeat.

Smith's laughter transforms into burly static.

The Voice in her heart speaks: *Get the squirrel away from the girl.*

To kick or not to kick. No question here. Charlotte swings her leg for the goal, connects, and damn but that squirrel could have traveled a solid thirty yards if not for the old tree. Its shriek-chatter ends as it falls, limp and still.

Nice aim, congratulates the Voice.

Thank you kindly. "Go on, before we both get lectured on cruelty to animals." She nudges Jenny, who looks up at her like some starstruck groupie before bolting for the castle.

Charlotte puts her headphones on, even though that freak-duet between The Who and Burly Man drained the last of her MP3 player's battery. Instead she listens to the Sweenil Sisters' Choir....

"How *awful!*"

"Never met such a horrible girl!"

"The poor defenseless creature!"

Studchin and bandmates join their a cappella chorus.

Whatever. So long as she can get her packs and be away from this damn bus forever and ever, she doesn't care.

Charlotte hops up the steps, and freezes. *This, this cannot be the same bus.*

All the leather, all the posh, is gone. Seats of bent metal and moldy, slashed upholstery. Sunlight penetrates rusted holes in the ceiling. Some windows lack glass. Splatters of molded crusts and maggoty cores everywhere.

A single spot of bright-pink color on all the rust and broken glass: Anna's gum.

Now the world doesn't just unsettle—it plunges off a cliff. Charlotte cannot breathe.

"Looking for something?"

Charlotte swivels around, stumbles back, and coughs. The ash-air strangles with fingers Charlotte can't pull off.

Mr. Smith slides his blue sunglasses down his nose: his violet eyes stare wide and cold at Charlotte, ready to flood her, drown her.

Out of his eyes! the Voice in her heart shakes her from the inside out.

Charlotte blinks, fixes her stare on the wiry dark hairs now poking out above Smith's ears.

"You looking for these, I bet." Smith leans to the side, revealing Jamie, that stupid smirk on his pocked face, the backpacks in his hand. "I just never know where you're going to turn up, Jamie, now do I?" Then back to Charlotte: "Do you still want his number, girlie?" Wink.

Jamie cackles. His skin is covered in cuts, many of them not even scabbed. They're welling up slowly, red pools and white pimples, a candy-cane face.

"What did you do to our *first* bus?" Charlotte accuses, slowly and deliberately backing up.

"I don't think I like your tone." Mr. Smith smiles, baring his painted teeth: they're pointed. "Looked like an accident to me. Looked like Sweet Maisy ran over one of them barbecue grills. Happens all the time out here, on these here roads, girlie."

"Why did you bring us here?" Charlotte's voice cracks under the weight of the question and the adrenaline hammering her temples.

Smith steps forward until only a couple seats' worth of space separates them. "Something off about you." Sniffing, his nostrils flaring. His lips move with words Charlotte cannot understand. His eyes reach for, around, beyond her.

Charlotte continues to move backward, stepping on wrappers, a maggoty core. She doesn't question the missing snack table because, really, what's the point? "Answer me: Why are we here?" Continues retreating until—

Thud. A wall. Just the back wall of the bus. Like there had never been an emergency exit at all.

A new heat emanates from her chest and father's pendant. Not an "ow" burn, but a spark to ignite her senses. *See Jamie's weak posture, know his poor response, weigh his body.* Imagines ramming Smith with shoulder and elbow, sending him crashing back into Jamie, their blood browning with the rust.

She is not weak.

She will bring her fists, her all, to this.

She will not give in.

She will not die here.

Smith frames his pasty teeth up in a smile and retreats a step. "Easy, sweetheart. I don't have the means to kill you all here and now. Toss those out, Jamie."

That means some passengers are never meant to get away.

Smith had eyed Anna. Jamie had sniffed her.

Charlotte crooks her arm back, loading—

"Whoa, hold on." Dark pupils pulse behind Smith's blue-tinted lenses. "A truce is all I want from you. You'll get to your school and your new life—"

How the hell does he know?

"—And I'll get back to mine, and we'll all be happy." He

holds his hands up in surrender, smile still in place but now strained.

Charlotte's eyes catch something glowing beneath the kerchief tied on his wrist, but there is no time to study it: the seams of his pant leg start to rip, and more dark hairs poke through.

WHAAA?

Smith registers Charlotte's bulging eyes, her gaping mouth, and chuckles like Uncle Mattie would whenever Charlotte warned him to leave their mom alone. "I think we're done here," he says, and waves a hand, blood trickling down his nose (*Why the hell is he bleeding?*)—and something else: a violet fluid, lit but flickering, like a bulb about to die. "C'mon, Jamie, let's finish unloading before anyone else starts nosing around."

Clank. The emergency exit zaps back into existence.

Charlotte shoots through it, running for the farm-castle before she can think any more about whatever is passing itself off for a bus driver.

Watched

Jenny slams the door behind Charlotte and bolts it. The two crumple to the floor, quivering.

"Jennifer, for the last time, mind that door!"

"Yes, Mom."

Charlotte's breaths jackhammer against her chest. She counts to calm down: One. Two. Three. Four.

Bubble pop. "Whatcha do, run to Aunt Gail's and back? Gah, you're such a drama queen." She twists her hair around one finger of one hand while her other hand flutters inches from the antique weaponry hanging on the wall. "So kid, these guns here look pretty old. They worth anything?"

Jenny wobbles herself to an upright position and peeks through the window before answering, "Old as the house, I think."

Charlotte inhales. Tomato, and oil, and body odor, and grass, and dust. Unlike the bus, this time her nose matches her other senses: the dated furniture she sees, the creaking oven door she hears, the worn carpet she feels under feet and fingers. Despite its castle-y exterior, this is still a home.

Splashes of red, yellow, and blue inch across the floor as the last rays of day creep by a stained-glass window depicting a sleeping dragon in an underground cave. Some knights stand

28

over it, swords drawn and pointed to shining stars. Charlotte approaches to touch the glass with quivering hands. Its smooth coolness calms her senses, just like her pendant. "This is pretty cool."

Mrs. Blair calls from the kitchen, stirring a pot of tomato bisque. "The window? Oh, I know. So old, so romantic. You're welcome to look around. You'll find so many amazing little treasures tucked away in each room."

Charlotte scans the room and turns toward Anna, who's studying how those old guns were mounted. "No kidding."

"We've still got a few minutes until supper's ready. Care to make a wish in the wishing well outside? Everyone does it. Sort of a tradition for all the guests."

Tongue click. "Even for runaways?" Anna flicks her quarter singing into the air.

"We're not runaways, Anna."

Anna catches the coin and begins to walk it. "Whatever." Bubble pop.

Better prove it, Charlie, and quick. "Seriously, we're not runaways. We're going to our aunt's place in Appleton," Charlotte pulls out her money bag and walks into the kitchen, "and I want to pay for the room and a phone call."

But Mrs. Blair waves it all away. "No worries, dear. What matters is that you and your sister are safe from all the goings-on out there at night. Our nearest neighbors are a good twenty-minute walk from here, and Bear Creek is a half-hour drive. When it's dark and there aren't many people around, wild things tend to take over." And with that she pats Charlotte out of the kitchen to join Jenny and Anna, who sit by a bay window facing the barn, the driveway, the old tree. And the well.

"Shh." Jenny beckons Charlotte to approach.

Charlotte's chest prickles, but she holds her tongue and joins them to look out the window.

"One at a time, folks, no need to rush." Jamie stands near the well, and a pretty old one it is too. Moss and flowers blanket nearly every stone.

No one seems to notice Jamie's been gone at all.

The Sweenil sisters poke each other for change, and soon everyone has quarters whether they wanted them or not. Twitchy gnaws on his before flipping it into the well. Henna Neck and Studchin argue over which wish is better: to get a contract or to get laid. Potential Homicidal Maniac stares at Jamie and then deliberately lets his coin fall to the dirt. It catches sunlight—and something else. A moving something, a liquid moving something. It slithers out of skirts and pants, thread-thin but bright—*look DOWN, people!*—and trickles *up* the stones to the flowers. Their violet buds pulse. Bloom.

The HELL? Charlotte's jaw drops open.

Mumbles flips a coin into the darkness. "Lizzy likes locked things, Lizzy likes locked things…"

"That Doer hussy's beat me five years in a row. I need all the leg ups I can get."

"Jackpot, language!" tsk-tsks Saucy.

"Let her be, Sally. That woman's a tramp and you know it!" intervenes Blue Hair.

Jamie goes still and stares straight through the window at Anna. His irises pulse like the well flowers. Then he bows with a sweeping gesture toward the well, dead-spinach grin sprouting.

Baby blues go vacant, then awake. Air suck. "Come on Charlie, let's each make a wish and see whose'll come true." Bubble *pop*.

Charlotte scowls, daggers at Jamie, silence at Anna. *One shot, please, just to break that fucking smile off his fucking face.*

"It's all in good fun, right, Jenny?" Mrs. Blair hands her daughter a tray laden with grilled cheese sandwiches and crocks of soup while she grabs another tray. "Young lady, why don't you join them out by the well? Now's the time to make that wish. Go on with you."

Charlotte thrusts a hand out to stay Anna—

But the girl pulls a jeté and pirouette from God Knows Where to cross the room as Charlotte does some bad parkour maneuvers to catch her. She trips over the couch, rams the chair with her knee, and nearly falls on her face. Grabbing Anna's arm, Charlotte huffs, "No, thank you, ma'am. Anna and I will call it a night."

Indignant air suck. "Come on, Charlie, even music nerds like you risk a little somethin' now and then."

"You two sure you don't want to go out?" Mrs. Blair asks, gesturing at the screen door with the point of her chin. "Takes just a second."

Back off, woman! "Yes. We're sure. We need to call Aunt Gail, anyway, before she steals the Flight for Life helicopter to hunt us down. Maybe Jenny can show us the phone?"

Bubble pop. Eye roll. "Why should Aunt Gail care?"

Charlotte hisses, "*Shut up*, of course she does." To Mrs. Blair: "I have a deadline to check in, and we're about ten minutes away from it. So you enjoy yourself, or whatever."

With Jenny leading the way, the girls clatter up the stairs, bags and food tray in tow. A short hall meets them at the top.

Jenny sets their tray down on top of a bureau inside the last room, a small space filled with fabric, sewing notions, and an antique black-and-gold sewing machine. One window opens out to a backyard where a neglected red-and-blue plastic playset sits, swings hanging askew and slide tilting off kilter. About fifty yards from the house-castle, an old stone wall separates the Blair farm from the forest beyond.

Charlotte sets their packs down in the corner. The fabric reminds her of Aunt Gail's craft room and its never-ending scraps of color. It smells normal enough, at least compared to the scents from the bus. "Thanks, Jenny. This is perfect."

"Give me a minute to... arrange things." Jenny's voice wavers as she scurries out and in with sleeping bags and pillows. She never really looks at them, or at the window.

Anna plucks a grilled cheese sandwich from the tray and flops down on a green sleeping bag. "Better than hay in the barn, I guess." Chomp.

Charlotte just shakes her head. She sips soup while watching the sky darken outside. Curious how the wall seems to play hide-and-seek among the forest's shadows, almost like parts of it vanish altogether.

Jenny returns from one final trip for some peanut butter brownies, lemonade, and supper for herself. But this time, Jenny hesitates in the doorway. Well, Anna, preoccupied with cursing over her charging phone's lack of reception, certainly wasn't going to let the girl feel welcome in her own house, so Charlotte says, "Look, we're not lepers. And we didn't even tell you our names, did we? Sorry to be rude. That's Anna moping over there, and—"

"And that's Charlie." Slurp. Burp. Anna stiffens her back and spreads one hand across her chest. "'*MY* name is Charlie, and *I* am the grrrandest musician in the world, and I'm going to drag my sister *ALL* over the country because *I* don't have any friends.'"

Charlotte glares. "Yeah." Softening her tone, she turns to Jenny, "Call me Charlotte. Sure you wanna come in?"

Jenny's fingers shift a bit under the tray. Charlotte sees papers. Forms from her folks? No, that's something Mrs. Blair would do with them, surely. This is something else. By the look in Jenny's eyes, it is *definitely* something else. "Oh, just give me that and sit down." Charlotte nudges Jenny with a gentle kick at the ankles as she takes the tray, papers and all.

Jenny sits down and passes the plate of brownies and some lemonade to Anna. Sugar addicts know their own. "Sure is nice having company. We usually just get hunters and hikers. Buses don't have kids. Not that I remember, anyway."

"I'm not a kid. I'm going to college," says Charlotte as she dips her sandwich—and her dirty-blond braid flops right into her soup. *Awesome. Bus funk, evil-freaky bus funk, and now tomato. The latest and greatest in hair care.* "Crap. Where's the bathroom again?" Charlotte hesitates at the door.

Jenny points toward the stairs. "Last door on the right."

Anna gnaws on a crust until she hears the bathroom door close. "So, this place. It's pretty old, huh?" Slurp.

"Mom thinks this is some outpost from the Civil War, but Dad says it's probably older than the state. It's not on the historical landmark list or anything. But it's so weird, being like this out in the middle of nowhere, so I think traders built it. Like an outpost or something."

Anna sits up straighter and then slides in closer. "Don't suppose there's hidden treasure anywhere."

Jenny shakes her head.

"Damn. Worth a try." Anna scoots back and rests her head on her knee, eyes focused on the wad of gum stuck to her plate. Anger puckers the skin around her mouth.

"So why is your sister dragging you along?"

Slurp. "Charlie doesn't want me left back in Bismarck

because Mom is…" Sigh. "She never got over Dad dying." Chomp. "People deal with stuff in their own way, you know?" Anna pushes the food aside to walk a quarter along both hands. "Grandma can be nice, in her own way. Uncle Mattie can be fun too, if you're into his games." Anna holds the flashing coin before her eyes. "He taught me how to take what I want when I want it."

"Yeah, and you've visited the Bismarck East Police Station how many times?" Charlotte interrupts from the doorway.

Anna flips the quarter at Charlotte's face.

Charlotte catches it.

Silence.

Jenny stares for a long second at Charlotte's scabbed knuckles. "When we went camping, I used that sleeping bag," Jenny points beneath Anna. "But we don't go anymore. Camping. Because of, well, stuff around here. But it's okay, because I know how to get away in the trees and find the nicest places, like this little glen near the Wall. I made friends there. With wolves." Jenny's braces morph her teeth into crazy little lights. "D's my favorite. He's got one blue eye and one green eye, and he lets me snuggle against his fur. When it's dark, my dad can never get a good aim on him because he's all black. He's—" Jenny stops when she sees Anna's face has screwed up in a skeptical expression. "Sounds crazy, doesn't it?"

"Y-yeah. I mean no. Well, yeah, it does." Anna forces a smile. She never smiles, not for free. She must *really* pity this girl. "But I've never been the outdoorsy type, so whatever." Meal finished, she reinserts her gum.

Charlotte leans against the wall, puzzling over the pieces of Jenny in her head—nearly pisses herself over a squirrel, enjoys social time with wolves, is antsy around sewing equipment—and shrugs. Nope, she doesn't get it.

Jenny locks eyes with Charlotte. "I'll take the dishes back down and get you some extra blankets." Jenny leaves the room, and the papers. Crayon pictures of a squirrel, a raven. An orange something. *More* somethings.

Door now closed, Charlotte throws her shirt on the pictures, before Anna notices them, and rummages through her duffle for pajamas. The tank Charlotte wears shows her wiry frame —too little food at Grandmother's—and her muscles—too many fights at school. But it's Charlotte's skin that always makes Anna go quiet: pinkish-white splatter marks cover her left arm and her chest.

Bubble pop. "What is…"

Charlotte covers herself. "What is what?"

Air suck. "Nothing." Bubble pop. "This school of yours. It's really worth all this hassle? You go there and you'll become a world-famous pianist?"

"Not world-famous, but, I don't know. Hook up with an orchestra, professional gigs, get my name out." *To finally be away from the squalor and the belts and, just, all of it. Be a nomad, follow the road music gives me. And if this sister of mine can just see reason for two damn minutes, she'll know life away from pills and shoplifting, and actually like it.* Charlotte turns to see her backpack open. "Anna, for once could you just ask?" *No, the money's still there.* Music. Books…

The picture—

Happy days. Charlotte straddles the flannel piles and sits down next to her sister. The left side of Anna's body hardens, but Charlotte doesn't stop tracing the four smiling faces with her finger, smudging the faded photograph even more. Curly red pigtails, which means Anna was only four. Charlotte's hair looks healthier, lighter in color, like corn silk, long and straight behind the headband, her sleeveless dress revealing tanned skin. Her eyes are just like their father's, as sparkling green as a Christmas tree. Their mother's smile beams real and true.

There were no smiles after the shooting.

"Look, I know what I'm asking you to do is a big deal. I'm asking you to try a new life. It's just..." *because Dad died and Mom half-died. Because Grandma likes to pretend we're dead and Uncle Mattie's... It's all shit, Anna.* "I just think a new life will be so much better for you, when you're with people who aren't going to teach you how to steal and won't numb themselves with pills and won't sit in a rocking chair surrounded by decaying baby things, babbling lullabies.... You think I wanted to leave Mom there?"

Anna wraps an arm around Charlotte and leans against her shoulder.

Is this affection? Charlotte hugs back. "I had to get you out of there first. Then I can go back and get her."

"Promise?" batting her baby blues.

"Promise."

Tinkle-clink. "Good." Anna pulls back and waves their father's pendant in the air. "You get this back when I see Mom."

Charlotte stiffens. *You little bitch. Like. Hell.* But before she can say anything—

Jenny knocks and enters with crazy-looking quilts that would have made Aunt Gail proud.

"Crap, I forgot to call Aunt Gail!"

Jenny's eyes drop to Charlotte's shirt, where the pictures hide.

"Actually, Anna, you call her. There a phone up here she can use, Jenny?"

Jenny's face brightens. "Sure, in my room. There's a computer too, if you need to chat with anyone."

"Really? You don't care? You guys got dial-up, or—"

"Cable. You did notice we have plumbing and stuff, right?" Jenny giggles. "Come on, I'll help you get on the internet and stuff."

Anna laughs a little, a first in days.

"Call Aunt Gail before anything else, please." Charlotte hands Anna the number and waits for the two to leave. Then she shoves some flannel piles aside to make space for the pictures, a ton of pictures: the squirrel, the raven, and an owl. Orange bird. A nasty-ass badger. Raccoons, even. All of them have the same eyes, a mix between dark royal and lavender.

Jenny returns, softly shutting the door behind her. She drops to the floor next to Charlotte and plunks a tattered notebook on top of the raven. "Okay, let's really start this. I saw your missing windshield. The raven do that?"

Shee-it, let's start this is right. "Yeah, and your squirrel friend looked like it was nursing him."

"You saw that too!"

"Why doesn't anybody else?" And Charlotte spills all the beans, from the ashy feathers to the rusted SC NI TOURS. Even Smith.

Jenny sifts through her notes while she listens. "People with animal-ish parts... I didn't think of that. But why not? The animals act like people."

"Do you..." Charlotte pauses. "Do you think Jamie and raven could be the same... thing?"

Jenny raises her head just high enough to look over the sewing table and out the window. Night has come. "Yeah, I do. Wonder what Mr. Smith turns into."

Charlotte tugs her hair back and rebraids it away from her face. It's all she can think to do, apart from screaming, which doesn't seem like a smart idea. "How can you treat what I just said as normal?"

"Because of my life, that's why." Jenny starts to shake, and her story erupts, each successive word overtaking and swallowing the previous word in an uncontrolled free fall from her mouth. "This room used to be my brother's room. He went away six months ago. Don't look at me like that, I didn't say he died. I said he *went away*. But no one remembers him. Not Mom, not Dad, no one at school. Just one morning his room is this, whatever this is, Mom barely sews, and every little piece of him from the planet *is gone*."

Jenny grits her teeth to the point Charlotte thinks the girl could break her braces. "Those animals weren't always like that. Like the owl—he'd just watch Sammy and me sometimes, but he never scared us. Or those raccoons. Even the squirrel used to just hang out by the Wall, you know, and leave us alone. But one day I heard screaming in the barn, and I thought something was trapped. This brown squirrel, totally normal, had given birth in the hay. Okay, no big deal, right? But the babies…" She stops.

Both turn toward the door. Charlotte hears faint clicks of a keyboard. Anna's still occupied. Good.

"They had the biggest, weirdest purple eyes, like the color wouldn't stop moving, kinda like a lava lamp. And they, it sounded like they could, say 'hungry.'"

Charlotte slowly spread the pictures out with her fingertips. "Newborn animals. Talking."

Jenny turns away. "I know. Stupid crazy."

"No." Charlotte holds Jenny's hand. Being with Smith and Jamie for one day is bad enough, but Jenny's been in this hell forever. "Not any crazier than a nasty caveman bleeding that sparkly purple stuff and willing doors to vanish. Actually, I think that sounds more nuts."

Jenny flips through her notebook for doodles and clipped pages from photocopies of horse births, bird births, even a cow birth. "The sparkly stuff! That was mixed with the afterbirth—I could see it. I ran and got Dad, and he went in and got rid of them. Shot them. And then," her arms flop once about her, "this. Sammy's gone. And this, this is all there is. Like he never was."

Charlotte doesn't notice how her own fists clench, or how her eyes narrow into the distance, fixed on a fight she wants so badly to start with Jamie, Smith, and any of their furry freakin' friends. "Retaliation."

Jenny shoves her fingers beneath her glasses to rub her eyes. "Now they just keep showing up. Dad's shot more of those things this year than since I was born." She pauses to listen to sounds of truck wheels on gravel—Mr. Blair and Mr. Smith have returned with a new windshield. "He always keeps his rifle by him, no matter where he is. Cleans it every day. Before, he only took it out in November for deer hunting, cleaned it before and after, and that was that. Now it's like his third arm."

She draws herself up and moves to the window. Charlotte follows. "And since those squirrel babies in the barn, some animals have been acting really, I dunno, weird. Scary. I used to run around the yard, playing and stuff, until things like possums and foxes would sit *together* on the Wall just... watching me. And you don't pet a possum, you know? So what's one doing walking up to me with its mouth open? Dad came with his gun and handled it. Then foxes started scratching the doors of our house like dogs, trying to get in. Dad and his gun again. Then the birds started flying into windows. Oh, not where Mom was—or even Dad was—but always where I was. And Dad would go out with his gun." Her voice cracks when she adds, "They're so little but their weird blood just gets everywhere."

Charlotte tugs down her sleeve and uses it to rub away the snot dripping down Jenny's lip. "But the wolves are different. They don't come after you."

Jenny nods. "That's why I dragged you into the house so fast. The ones like the squirrel use the old oak tree to watch everything on the farm. But they don't, at least the squirrel doesn't, come inside the house or over to that glen past the barn where D and his pack stay. Thanks for earlier, kicking the squirrel, I mean. But he's going to be after you now, just as bad as me."

"Can't be any worse than Burly Psycho Magic Bus Man." *What hell did I drag Anna into? Dammit, Dad, I am so sorry.* "I've got to get us out. You, Anna, and me."

Jenny flops the notebook open to more pictures and torn pages. Her face shows a fatigue Charlotte knows too well. "Can't. At least not right now. They're worse at night. Just listen." With trembling fingers, Jenny unlocks the window.

Charlotte reaches out with her ears. Her nose tags along. Silence and animal smells are completely absent. Not a cricket. Not a bird. Not even a bat. Only the faint smell of ash, as if Nature itself can't bear to linger in a place like this. "That's messed up."

"I used to think this was normal, until I slept over at my cousin's place up north." Jenny bites her tongue to hold back disgust, fear, the lot. "But here, none of this is how the *normal* world works, is it?" She shrivels. One wave of flannel and she could vanish into the past too, along with her brother Sammy.

Charlotte takes Jenny's shoulders and holds them up, back. "You've survived way more than most people I'd call normal ever could. That takes courage. Perseverance. Wherever your brother is, he's proud of you. I know it."

Tears spill on the moonlight reflecting in Jenny's glasses. "Think so?"

"Know so."

Chattering. Outside.

Charlotte looks out to see the full moon blanketing the woods in pale light. The Wall glows but for its shadows, and one in particular: a tiny shadow moving swiftly along the stones. The squirrel.

It stops. Faces them.

Jenny's body seizes.

"Shit—" Charlotte blinks.

"Where's my Charlie? My badge could use a shine."

Charlotte blinks. *What the—? Dad? No—*

The squirrel, chattering.

Charlotte pulls the window shut and hugs Jenny to her chest. "Breathe with me, kid, one, two. Breathe with me, okay? Come on, he's gone," she lies, afraid of the squirrel's chatter because it shouldn't be able to create ghosts out of wishes and dreams—

A howl, long and furious. A swift black shadow runs along the Wall's edge. It leaps into the air toward the Wall and —with a streak of violet and shadow—is gone.

Charlotte waits for the squirrel to return, or that wolf, but nothing comes. Even the stars seem to move and search the Wall, their light transforming the clouds into fleeing ghosts.

Jenny whimpers when Charlotte tucks loose strands of hair behind her ear.

"Mr. Smith and your dad are out there now with a gun. They're looking around."

Mr. Blair cocks his rifle and walks along the Wall.

Mr. Smith stops to look up at the house. He slides his glasses down.

Applause fills Charlotte's ears. She blinks.

"We are pleased to introduce Miss Charlotte Aegir, our most accomplished concert pianist."

The applause switches off short.

Charlotte blinks again and then sees Mr. Blair and Mr. Smith walking back to the garage.

"What's going on?" Jenny asks from inside the room.

Don't tell the kid how fixated they are on this room right now. Swallow that scream. "They're going back into the garage. Looks like one of your wolf friends chased the squirrel over the Wall."

Jenny's face breaks from relief. "D can't do much in the day, but at night he chases the nightmares away." She puts her head to the floor and listens. Television voices keep talking. The hall floor doesn't creak. Mrs. Blair never heard them.

"But where do they go? Where do they come from?"

"The Wall." Jenny crawls to one side of the sewing table while Charlotte positions herself on the other. Together, they can just see different pieces of the Wall exposed by moon-light. "My parents have never gone over it, and they've never talked about anyone living back there. It's not marked as a nature preserve or conservancy or anything. It's just… there. It's been there as long as this farm. Longer."

"Some wall, if it can't keep them in."

"I don't think it's about keeping them in so much as keeping *us* out."

Autumn so often brings traces of smoke in the air from those who burn leaves or have final campfires. This evening there is a smell in the air, but it's not leaves: it's thick. Sticky. Persistent.

Hate.

Jenny pulls another sheet from her book, a page ripped

out of a literature textbook. Jenny's circled the four-line refrain over and over and over:

Come away, O human child!
To the waters and the wild
With a faery, hand in hand,
For the world's more full of weeping than you can understand.

"Yeats. 'The Stolen Child.' You think..." Charlotte has to pause, because to say this is even possible... No, she couldn't let this be possible. "You think those animal things are fairies?"

"What else is there? Death doesn't take away everything that person ever was to everyone else. I mean, you don't just... *forget* someone after they die. And *animals* don't act like that, and *flowers* don't glow like that. Just because people make *wishes*. I KNOW I am not crazy, even though the counselors say so and my parents say so." She hiccups, "But everyone just wants me to shut up and take pills."

Charlotte snorts. "Yeah, because that's a surefire way of bringing you back to reality." *Because that worked so well for Mom.*

Jenny holds up page after page of notes and sketches: a boy kite-flying, a boy tree-climbing, a boy playing with G.I. Joes under the kitchen table. "I dream of Sammy every night. Meds just make the dreams fuzzy and hard to understand. Those fairies make my dreams *hurt*. They make me want to follow them, because I know they can lead me to Sammy. When I'm with D, they're not... I don't know, dreams any-more. They feel like normal memories, things I can just pick up in my head like I was trying to remember what I ate for lunch the other day."

Charlotte slips the poem back into Jenny's book and holds up one of her sketches of D. He does not look snuggly. "So what does that make D?"

"I don't know. He never chases the owl off, or those other ones. Just the raven and that squirrel. So maybe some of these fairies aren't all bad."

The door swings open and Anna floats in, oblivious to the frantic shuffling of papers and furtive looks. "Your father's back." Tongue click. "Aunt Gail says to call her before we board. And hi. And lovey loves to Sweet C." She says the last bit with her squishiest voice.

Charlotte tosses a pillow at her sister's legs, but she doesn't mock in return.

Jenny stands up and brushes a few brownie crumbs off her pants. "Thanks for letting me hang out. Everyone's always so geared for that well—I don't get to talk to guests much."

"What is the deal with that thing, anyway?" Bubble pop. "Please tell me you at least haul a bucket of quarters out of there every year."

Jenny squints her eyes, hugs her papers just a little bit closer. "From the wishing well? It takes all the quarters because it really works."

Tongue click. "Uh-huh."

"I'm serious." And Jenny's smooth face and moonlit glasses say yes, she is pretty damn serious.

Anna pings her quarter into the air. "C'mon then, Charlie, let's both make a wish and see if we head east or west in the morning."

"Hold on." Charlotte plucks the quarter from flight and pinches it lightly between her fingertips. She turns to Jenny. "How do you know it works?" *Please don't mention glowing flowers.*

"Whenever things get real slow around here, Mom'll throw a coin into the wishing well and wish for more people.

44

Within two days a bus *always* breaks down."

Anna's mouth hangs open—although not enough for her gum to fall out. "You're playin'."

"Nope. She wishes, and there's a bus. It never takes more than two days, and it's always a bunch of people."

Air suuuuuck. Bubble pop. "How many times has that happened?"

"For as long as I can remember. I know Mom says everyone that comes here uses it, but I don't know what they've wished for. I just know it fills the motel for Mom and gives Dad a twelve-point buck every year."

One of the lamp's bulbs flickers and dies. Moonlight overtakes the room, save for the corner, where the hurricane lamp barely lights the floor. Cheers and commentary on the Packers' latest preseason game echo up the stairs from the television.

"Guess I'll head to bed. Thanks for listening." Jenny adds a small hidden smile for Charlotte and closes the door.

Anna waits until the soft pads of Jenny's slippers fade out of ear shot, then says, "That Jenny is a weirdo. Don't get me wrong, she's nice and all, but still—that was weird. And she got you all weird too."

Charlotte tosses the quarter back. "She didn't get me weird, Anna. This whole day got me weird." *And scared shitless, but you don't need to know that.* "Only kid stuck way out here, I don't blame her for telling stories to get attention."

Air suck. "She's not really a kid, she's twelve. Saw it on her homework. That's old enough to know what's make-believe and what's not."

Charlotte gives Anna the stink eye before rolling over. "You're fourteen. Fourteen does not mean you know what's real and pretend all the time either." She listens to Anna

45

crawl around and mess up the sleeping bag before settling in.

A metallic ting in the air: flipping the quarter again. "Like you know." Tongue click.

"Well, I have something of an idea, yeah."

Bubble pop. "Whatever."

Chattering. That squirrel. Back on the Wall again.

Freak fairy thing.

Chattering.

SHUT UP.

Air suck. "Think it works?" Bubble pop.

"What?"

Eye roll, sigh. "The well."

"No." *Dammit, Jenny, now you've put more ideas into Anna's head.*

"Come on. You gotta admit it's pretty weird that her mom just has to wish for customers and," bubble pop, "a bus breaks down?"

As if on cue, heavy creaks and quiet mutterings come down the hall: the Blairs are on their way to bed.

"Not a semi, not a car, but always a *bus* of people?" continues Anna.

Smith told Charlotte he wasn't able to kill everyone right away. Maybe that wasn't about timing, but about the number. *If they can erase people from the planet, who's going to notice a passenger or two missing from a bus full of people? And they've been doing it for years. Years!* "I don't know. Maybe the Blairs have something going with a few drivers." *Get Anna to Appleton. Get set for college. Get Mom. Get Jenny? Yes, this kid's suffered enough.*

Anna runs her fingers up along the assortment of flannel fabric remnants stacked by her sleeping bag. "We're sleeping in these people's sewing room, Charlie. Whatever they got going on with bus drivers isn't exactly making them rich."

Their father's pendant slips out from Anna's sweatshirt and shimmers in the remaining lamplight. Charlotte's face softens when she sees it. "Would be nice to have a piece of good luck tomorrow," she says, eyes on the white flower.

But Anna tucks it away. "I said when I see Mom again, and I meant it. Don't need you double-crossing your own promises."

Charlotte grinds her teeth and forces herself not to argue. "Just don't go outside making your own surprise plans either."

Bubble pop. "Fine." Anna watches the squirrel run up and down the Wall, chattering away. Its movement seems to leave a faint purple afterglow. She can't decide if the phosphorescence is real or a trick of her eyes. The squirrel is a rich gray in the moonlight, dark like ashes after the fire's completely out.

She looks down at her sister. Charlotte's body, always tensed for an ambush for whatever reason, has finally begun to relax.

The squirrel gets louder.

Anna blinks.

"There's my special girl." Coin flip. **"I've got a surprise just for you, if you can sneak out of there."**

Anna swallows her gum. Uncle Mattie must have followed their bus, and now he's waiting, just for her, calling for her.

Air suck. "I need to pee."

"Mmmph."

"Back in a sec." Anna silently whisks her phone and Charlotte's sneakers off the floor—her own boots would be impossible to slip on without Charlie hearing the leather squeak.

Down the hall, through the dark living room, and out the door.

Everything is silver and navy and white: the ghost of a barn, the long snake of a motel, the waves of grass in the field across the street, and the distant Wall shadowed by the trees. The well stands in the middle of the gravel drive, smack dab in the middle of the farmstead. It looks innocent enough —just old heavy stones like the castle and the Wall. Why did Jenny make such a big deal of it before?

"Uncle Mattie?" Anna's whisper carries and almost echoes back.

Night and damp cling tight to her neck. She feels a sudden urge to call for Charlie, but bites it back. "Uncle Mattie?"

He stands by the well, funky glasses and all. **"Make a wish, little girl."**

Anna picks up a pebble and drops it in. She counts to fifteen before she hears a splash.

Steps behind her.

Anna pivots in her sister's sneakers and opens her mouth to tell Charlie she's going to go back to Bismarck with Uncle Mattie, so piss off. But her tongue knots in place.

Three people from the bus are shuffling like zombies up the drive: one of those old ladies, Sweeney-something. That cute guitar player with the chin stud. And another guy, the one always singing about Lizzy.

Two more shadows appear behind the others. Anna recognizes the driver Mr. Smith and Jamie. They smile and start singing badly:

> **"Wish for sleep**
> **Sleep and dream**
> **Dream your wish**
> **Your life we'll keep."**

She should scream for Charlie. Her quarter falls with a weak ting on the ground. She turns to scream to Uncle Mattie for help.

"Close enough."

She blinks.

The squirrel sits on the well just inches from her, quarter in its paws. Its eyes are violet and silver in the night.

Charlotte stirs in her sleep, dreams again of the concert halls, the spotlights daring her to sweat, the calls for an encore. Anna in the front row, beaming with pride. Aunt Gail next to her, tears flooding the laugh lines at the corners of her eyes. Her mother, healthy and beautiful, her spirit no longer broken.

Her father, no longer riddled with .38 caliber bullets.

All is bright and glorious and perfect. And then the usher steps forward—

"Wait, where are you taking me?" Anna's voice from outside the concert hall.

From *outside*—?

Her father turns to dust. His badge glitters on the seat. Her mother's body crumples and her eyes glaze over with white powder. Aunt Gail continues gazing upon Charlotte with those tears in her eyes as though the concert has never been disturbed at all.

Then silence and nothingness.

5

Anna Erased

The morning smells like maple syrup and mud. Charlotte unburies herself from the sleeping bag and mangles the phone until its 7 a.m. alarm finally shuts off. She rubs the grit from her eyes, gets up, then rummages for some clean underwear.

Outside, an engine roars to life. "Sounds like the bus is fixed," she says to no one. "You want the bathroom first or—" She pauses, forgetting... *something.*

There should be someone there, in the corner, where the flannel remnants are stacked so neatly. Right? Or no. Bubbles float through her memory and pop just out of reach.

The Voice in her heart reaches out and cups one bubble, guiding it down and into Charlotte's chest. It pops a flash of red and baby blue.

Baby blues.

Red.

Remember.

The picture!

Charlotte dumps all the clothes and sheet music and books, chucks her headphone cord out of the way. Her hand shakes as it lifts a small wallet-sized photo: her mother's beaming smile. Her father's glowing eyes. And Charlotte herself, tanned and healthy—

Pigtails. There should be red pigtails in this picture. Baby blue eyes.

This family is missing someone. Just like this room is missing someone. The other sleeper, the one Charlotte spoke to without thinking, the one who should be here blowing bubbles and fluttering baby blues.

Her name is Anna.

Charlotte's ribs snap shut like a bear trap over her heart and she stumbles forward, clutching the sewing table—the world spinning, unreal, all of it unreal, as she hears Anna's snark inside her but cannot find a single hair, not even a bit of glitter. *Yes, glitter, she… she liked makeup. LIKES makeup. She —Oh sweet god I forgot my own sister's name.* Her whole body shakes. She counts breaths of stale air until she's able to sit upright on the edge of the sewing bench.

The Voice in her heart pries her ribcage open. Air and heat churn through her. *Their magic is most thorough. But they have also underestimated you.*

Her eyes are steely as they focus on the wishing well outside the window. *I have been whipped, I have been burned, I have been beaten down. You bastards do not know the SHITstorm you have unleashed.*

Charlotte throws a set of clean of clothes on and stuffs her bag. She searches for her shoes. They're not by the door, not in any corner, not in her bag, not under the desk. She even scatters the flannel remnants everywhere. Nothing under there.

She pounds down the stairs to hear quiet chitchat in the kitchen: Jenny and her mom eating breakfast. Turning toward the bay window, Charlotte cracks her neck, squints, sees Saucy and Blue Hair Sweenil nodding in thanks to Mr. Blair as he serves them coffee and cinnamon rolls. Henna Neck and Frost Tips argue over how the drums should be loaded. Fry Pan Ears and Potential Homicidal Maniac stand guard by their luggage while Twitchy plays Eenie Meenie Miney Mo with SC NI TOURS sign letters. Bus driver and seven passengers, including Charlotte. That would make nine. Sounds right… sort of.

Baby Blues. Berry shampoo. *Sister*—she has a sister.

"Why good morning, Miss Charlotte! I hope you slept well." Mrs. Blair ushers Charlotte into the kitchen and sits her next to Jenny. Everything's sunny yellow and sky blue: the walls, the cupboards, the tablecloth. Even that stupid little sunshine happy face of a napkin holder on the table. "My husband's seeing to the other guests, making sure nothing gets left behind. Buses don't come by often, you know."

Jenny gives a half smile and keeps chewing.

She told you a story last night. Charlotte's chest warms with every steady heartbeat. *Remember.*

And the old, strange energy hiding everything in bubbles begins to dissipate. Charlotte picks up on the smell of ashes beneath the waffles and bacon, of pain beneath the warmth of the kitchen.

Mrs. Blair pours a single cup of batter into a waffle maker. "Care for some breakfast?" Her smile is bright, her hair neatly curled. She slept well.

Jenny guzzles her juice and asks, "Did you need to call your aunt so she knows you're back on the road?"

"Just me?" Charlotte's hands tremble on the table top.

Jenny stares at Charlotte—at her disheveled braid, her shirt buttoned askew, her open fly—and then pushes away her juice glass as her lips barely form: "Oh no."

"That sounds like a fine idea, Miss Charlotte." Mrs. Blair hums while shaking the orange juice carton. "I've got a phone right here on the counter."

"No!" Jenny and Charlotte shout in chorus.

"I mean, she should have some privacy for a personal call. Right, Mom? Right. You can use the phone in my room."

They both charge up the stairs.

Neither says a word until Jenny's door is shut and locked.

Charlotte walks straight to the window, ignoring the extensive collection of wolf sketches covering the walls, and slips her fingers between the blinds to slit them open. No sign of Smith so far. "The driver. Where is he?"

"Mr. Jamie? Dad said he was on the b—*ow! Let go, let go!*"

But Charlotte does not let go. She's absolutely sure of *that* memory: of Burly Man shaking Maisy's hand, of a raven screaming in the windshield. "Jamie wasn't the driver. *Smith* was the driver." Her eyes spark like someone set a Christmas tree farm on fire. "Where. Is. Smith?"

"It was just the one bird-guy with weirdo glasses!"

"And my sister?"

Jenny stops breathing, her mouth agape.

The girl really doesn't remember. *But I do. The baby blues and the red hair, and, and the gum, and her stupid, stupid eyelash glitter, a waste of money, so of course she stole it—I REMEMBER.* Charlotte resists the urge to body-slam the girl to the floor. She grabs Jenny by the shoulders instead, shaking her. "You had to tell her about that stupid well. You had to—"

Two tears slide down either side of Jenny's face. "I'm sorry."

Charlotte lets go and turns away, inhaling and exhaling loudly through her nose. "Aunt Gail. I have to call her."

Jenny almost drops her old rotary Snoopy phone, fumbling with its tangled spiral cord as she hands it to Charlotte. "She's not gonna say what you wanna hear."

A warmth emanates from the Voice in Charlotte's heart and surrounds her body, hugging her.

"I know." Charlotte can barely focus as she dials, her senses in a downward spiral like a baby bird knocked out of its nest.

"Hello?" Sweet and sleepy.

"Aunt Gail? It's Charlie."

A loud exclamation of happiness. "Good morning, Sweet C! When do you hit the road?"

"Uh…" Charlotte unspools a string of verbal nothings. "It depends. On… how long it takes for… Anna… to get ready."

"Anna?" The way the "An-" and the "-na" comes over the line, it's like Aunt Gail has never put the two sounds together before. "Is she another girl who came on the bus with you?"

A tiny red droplet splashes on the floor. Another makes a path down Jenny's lip. Her teeth are cutting her lower lip, deep. *How many times did Jenny put herself through this with cousins, friends? Her own damn parents?*

"Girls, the bus is leaving in a couple of minutes!" Mrs. Blair's voice echoes up and down the hallway.

"Y-yeah, Aunt Gail. She's another girl who came with me on the bus." Charlotte wipes the blood off Jenny's chin using her own sleeve.

"Oh, how nice you had someone to travel with. I didn't much care for your going all that way all alone." Aunt Gail yawns. Charlotte imagines her in Brewer pajamas, kicking off the handmade quilts and tussling with her shoulder-length gray hair. Had Maisy's bus not broken down, Charlotte would have been there to say good morning, to bring her a cup of coffee, and to talk to her about Anna's anger and how to deal with it, like Anna was some sort of problem that had to go away.

Had to go away—Charlotte's eyes squeeze shut against her guilt.

"Just give me a buzz when you see the Fox Valley Mall, okay? Then I'll know when to get scootin'."

"Sure." What else is there to say? *I'd love to get on the bus, Aunt Gail, but it's run by a nasty fairy who's kidnapped the niece you don't remember. Fuck the scholarship. Fuck the future. I'm going to bring her back or die trying.*

They-They *will*-will *not*-not *have*-have *her*-her. The Voice in Charlotte's heart echoes her, and the echoes become the bellows to her inner fire. Charlotte straightens her back. Stronger. Reforged. New.

"Charlie? You there?"

Such a chance to say it may not come again: "Just wanted to say that I love you, Aunt Gail."

"Oh, Sweet C, I love you too. It'll be so nice havin' you over, child." A pause, followed by clinks and clanks in the background—she's getting her own coffee. "Not fearing the worst, are we? You're not exactly driving a busy road, you know."

A cynical smile plays across Charlotte's face. "Never know, though, right? Bye."

"Bye, Charlie! See you soon!"

Charlotte thrusts the phone into Jenny's lap.

"Girls!" from below.

"Coming!" Charlotte pops the lock and opens the door.

But Jenny does not move from her bed. "What are you going to do?"

Charlotte looks over her shoulder and says: "I'm going over."

Over the Wall

Charlotte shuttles in and out of the sewing room, throwing her bags down the stairs and thudding closely after.

In the kitchen, "Sorry to keep you waiting." Drinking some orange juice, *I hate orange juice.* Swallowing it, *Ugh. Don't spit it on Mrs. Blair.*

"You kids today," Mrs. Blair tsk-tsks as she minds the timer on the waffle maker. "Down to the last minute, forgetting your things everywhere. Why goodness, dear, you even left your sneakers outside." Sugary air emanates from the waffle maker.

Charlotte wants to vomit. "My sneakers?"

"Yes, dear. They're outside by the well."

No heartbeat. No breath. "Oh."

Mrs. Blair pulls out the waffle, flaky and just a touch crispy. When Charlotte refuses it, Mrs. Blair begins to pull it apart with her fingers. "Well, never mind it, they're safe and sound. Be sure to check them, though. Don't want to find a little mouse or some other woodland dearie making a home in your shoe!" She smiles, pops a piece of waffle in her mouth, and says, "Oh, and no need to worry about paying me, Miss Charlotte. You just put that money toward your college tuition."

"Um, thanks." Charlotte grabs the remaining bit of

waffle and shoves it in her mouth lest she speaks her mind, which has very few polite words at that moment. *Hang on.* "I never mentioned going to college."

"Why of course you did," says Mrs. Blair as she pours another cup of batter. "During supper last night. And Jenny told that silly story about her pet raccoon."

And you talked about hunters and their frostbite. Why is this all so clear?

"And then you talked about becoming a concert pianist. Course, I thought you said something else—" Mrs. Blair winks at Charlotte.

You covered Jenny's ears, all shocked over my language until Mr. Blair spelled it out. This, this happened?

"PiaNIST! Goodness, I just laughed till I cried!"

Remember… the Voice in her heart tickles her memory.

Bubble pops. Bubble pops. Shoo out Mrs. Blair's chatter and I see them: baby blues. Bubble pops. Quarter walks. Glitter. Red hair, angry face, so angry. I'm so sorry, I just wanted you safe and this girl Jenny, she tells me things, shares pictures and poems and, good GOD, the fairy freaks.

This—whatever she should call it—this isn't loss. Her father's death, that was a loss. Shot and killed, buried with honor. Remembered. Even though Mom, Grandma, and Uncle Mattie pretended he never existed, they couldn't deny it. Records exist. His sister Gail exists, his partner, his Navy comrades. Charlotte remembers him, and Anna—yes, Anna would too, if not for… Anna's not a loss, but *lost.* Erased, like Jenny's brother.

But Charlotte is not Jenny. This time, Smith, Jamie, and all those other freak-fairies aren't dealing with a scared little girl.

"Funny, how my shoes got out there. Since shoes need feet in them to wander off."

"Not always." Mr. Blair's solid figure guards the doorway leading to the yard. He holds his rifle in one hand, barrel pointing down. "Farms with woods like this one get lots of critters. Cats. Mice. Raccoons." His eyes drill into Charlotte's. "They like taking things that don't belong to them."

Hold the goddamn phone. The rifle always loaded. Killing those squirrel babies. Does he KNOW? "So what do you do about 'em?"

Mr. Blair harrumphs and limps across the living room. "I watch my own very, *very*, carefully. Anything else, not my responsibility." There: pain, in his voice.

Charlotte hops the coffee table and thrusts herself between the screen door and Mr. Blair's big—very big— muscular body. "Hold on a second, Mr. Blair."

Mr. Blair quirks a brow at Charlotte and then heaves his bad leg past her and walks out of the house, but not toward the bus. Instead, he goes around the back, by the window with the knights and dragons beneath the stars. Its colors glow in the morning light despite summer's dirt and cobwebs. He turns and looks straight at Charlotte.

"Jenny thinks you don't know anything. But that's not true, is it, sir?"

Mr. Blair's loaded rifle leans faithfully against his leg. His voice clings to the gravel beneath their shoes. "My family has lived on this land for generations. Whatever happens is meant to happen. What we remember is truth."

"So what Jenny remembers—"

"Jennifer doesn't *remember*. She dreams. Big difference." His large hand, its creases mapped out with dirt and oil, grips Charlotte's shoulder hard.

She shakes free. *OFF, old man. I have cracked ribs and broken jaws of boys as big as you.* "I. Remember. And so. Does. She."

Mumbled small talk around the corner. Jamie's cackle.

Neither Charlotte nor Mr. Blair moves.

"Dad?" Jenny appears with Charlotte's bags, plus an extra leather satchel. Sunlight reflects in her glasses as her gaze shifts from her dad to Charlotte, then back to her dad.

Pain ebbs and flows between father and daughter. Mr. Blair coughs, again and again, and uses his clean hand to wipe his eyes. "Oh, girl. We've got it hard." If that's for Jenny or Charlotte, Charlotte can't tell, but it doesn't matter. Neither of them is crazy: this man knows he lost his son, and he *still* has to deal with them to protect his daughter. With fairies for neighbors, something must have gone down a long time ago, and from then on, no Blair's had a choice but to live here.

Jenny sniffles and nods quickly. "I found your shoes."

The flowers stand like sentries above the moss at the base of the old stone well. Neither shoe shows any signs of blood, scratches, or scuff marks. They were simply left behind.

Charlotte puts them on.

"Looks like some stuff needs loading." Jamie sounds awful, and looks it. His cuts and burn marks are pus filled and smell of burned flesh. Little pockmarks speckle his head, neck, all exposed skin. "Don't want to forget anything, do we?"

That's not acne. Not tufts of hair either. Those are feathers. *Can't keep the person-suit on forever, huh? No wonder you're so eager to load up and go.*

Jamie's cackle halts at the sound of a rifle cock.

Mr. Blair stands directly behind Jenny and towers over that sick excuse of a bus driver. "Best take off. I've got some hunting to do with my girl."

Jenny gives her dad a genuine smile and says, "Just gotta help Charlotte with her stuff. Customer service!" She hands Charlotte one of her bags, tugs at the satchel strap weighing her left shoulder down, then leads Charlotte past Twitchy, who's deeply intent on claiming the U and one S of SC NI

TOURS for his own.

"Would you just stop that?" Saucy Sweenil bats Twitchy with a knitting magazine before stuffing it into her canvas tote.

But Twitchy gets his letters: the bus sign now reads EN C O RS.

"Good morning, ladies! I don't know about you, but I'm ready to burn some rubber!"

"Oh, these horrible country mornings…" Fry Pan Ears whines to himself as he half-stumbles up the steps.

"Sis, get in here!" Blue Hair calls from the bus window above them. "The contest registration starts in six hours!"

"Oh, yes. But let's hit the hotel first so I can assemble my opening night *ensemble*." Saucy Sweenil twirls around Charlotte and Jenny and does what Charlotte assumes is a samba, mamba, tanga, whatever. "Oh, you two will be missing a treat. I was quite the swinger in my day."

Charlotte smiling politely and thinking, *Lady, spin around me one more time and you'll suck face with the gravel.*

Frost Tips and Henna Neck wolf-howl from their window-seats.

"Now now, down boys." Saucy gives a royal wave to her admirers. "Don't you go waking up that monster from last night."

"Monster?" Charlotte wraps an arm around cringing Jenny.

"Wolf last night."

Everyone, even Jamie, turns to face Potential Homicidal Maniac rooted by the back of the bus. His eyes look like candles lost in bottomless caves. "Ran past the window."

Saucy Sweenil titter-laughs and bends down to Jenny. "You didn't hear it? Land a' jumpkins, that surprises me! But you and your parents must be familiar with all sorts of ghoulies and beasties. Isn't that so, Mr. Blair?"

A noncommittal monotone. "Wolves like hanging around

60

this time of year."

"Dude," Frost Tips nudges Henna Neck's seat, "remember that shaman guy at UW Superior? He said wolves make excellent power animals. They can even grant wishes."

"Yeah, and then they rip your heart out of your ribcage," Henna Neck says as he tests his phone's ringer volume. "That guy was a nutjob. Let it go, dude."

"Would you *please* keep it down!" Fry Pan Ears's face fills the window in front of Henna Neck's seat.

The bus goes quiet after that.

"*Bud?*" Mrs. Blair hollers from the kitchen window. "The stove's acting up again!"

Mr. Blair looks at his daughter, at Charlotte, at Jamie. He looks *down* on Jamie. "If you'll excuse me. And my family."

Jamie croaks, but says nothing.

Saucy Sweenil makes one final sweeping gesture toward the farm. "And so, it is time to bid farewell to this little adventure. You girls ready to follow me in?" Saucy looks pointedly at Charlotte.

"Girls"—the word sounds so normal, so right. Charlotte swallows and tries again, just one more time. "Oh, this isn't my sister. This is Jenny, she lives here. Is my sister on the bus?"

"Girl, don't you be a pest, now," Jamie drawls—and flips a quarter at Charlotte.

She instinctively catches it an inch from her face. Familiar, but all wrong. *Don't you cackle at me, Bird Boy. You'll get yours before the sun sets, I swear.*

Cackling. "Well, how many sisters does this bus need? Two's plenty in my book. Now, are you ladies coming or not?"

"Land a' jumpkins, I'm coming, I'm coming," Saucy wheezes as she waddles up the steps.

Jamie smiles like the smug bastard he is. "Are *you* coming?" he asks Charlotte. More tufts pop out of his skin. The faded

61

Scenic Tours uniform may bear his embroidered name, but the shirt now looks two sizes too big on him, turning him from lanky to sick. "Not forgetting anything?"

Charlotte thrusts her hands her pant pockets. "Let's see." She looks down. "Forgot to zip my pants." Fixes that. "Forgot to brush my teeth." Runs her tongue across her pearly whites. "Didn't forget my shoes, as you can see. Nope, I do not intend on leaving anything behind. Not," she takes one step toward Jamie, "one," another step, "thing." And she licks her lips and slowly makes an "O" with her mouth. Spit bubble pop.

For a moment, Jamie looks like he's about to puke, but then he fixes his glasses and smiles his pus-yellow teeth. "Well then. Guess it's time to go our separate ways." He throws his fingers up in salute. "For now."

At last Potential Homicidal Maniac comes forward to board. His gaze rolls slowly from Charlotte to Jamie to Charlotte: "For now."

Jamie follows him on board. The door cuts off his cackle.

"For now," Charlotte says to the dust cloud and then reaches down to take her bags. Then to Jenny: "Where to?"

Jenny points to the tree line to the north, past the barn. "We're just a couple of minutes from where you can cross the Wall without anyone seeing."

And there it stands, extending from east to west, dividing the farmstead to the south from the woodlands to the north: blue and gray rocks of all sizes piled together. But unlike the well, which has the same kinds of stones, the Wall doesn't have a speck of moss or flower growing anywhere on it, not on the stretch Charlotte can see. It's even got a bit of shine to it, as if workers just finished it this year and not centuries ago.

"First let's see if D's around. If he isn't, you'll have to go over by yourself."

They turn east, walking a short distance along the Wall, and after a minute they arrive at a small glen of maples dotted by past sap taps. The air is cool for an August morning.

A single long growl fills the space between the trees.

Then another.

Then another.

Then another.

Then another.

"*That's* D?" Charlotte whistles.

D's pack enters the glen, five strong, but damned if Charlotte knows what D needs a pack for. One eye the color of grass, the other the color of a clear blue winter sky, he has to be the size of a small horse. His black coat shimmers with broken pieces of morning. The pack blocks their way to the Wall.

Charlotte tucks Jenny behind her and stands on the balls of her feet, fists out, ready for—

Jenny gives an exasperated sigh and walks around her. "D, this is a friend. Please. We have to help her."

Only D comes forward to meet Jenny. Although the other wolves perk their ears up when she opens her satchel, no one moves until after D licks Jenny's face. Laughing, she pulls out a plastic grocery bag and dumps a number of steaks onto the ground.

Bet her folks would be thrilled about that.

The gray wolves yip and trot to a corner with their own hunks of steak and leave nothing for D. Yet he does not seem to mind. He remains with Jenny, his muzzle in her hand or up against her neck. "I missed you too. I was so worried when Charlotte said Dad tried for you again. This is Charlotte." Jenny moves her head so D and Charlotte can look eye to eye, nose to nose.

Charlotte senses the canine, yes, but there's another layer. Not ashes, like Jamie and Smith, but a burning, like a fire still going. "Hi, D."

D doesn't seem to like what his nose takes in.

"Look, I'm sorry I didn't shower. Can we move on?"

Jenny says, "D, Charlotte's in trouble. They took her sister like they took Sammy."

D snorts as if to say, "Go on."

Charlotte opens her mouth, ready to do so. The photo shines in her mind: a family of three. Who's missing again? So clear a second ago, by the bus with Jamie. Those bubbles again, popping in her mind—

The bubbles!

Remember, a soft reminder from the Voice in her heart.

Yes, I do, I do, I do. "My sister. Smith and Jamie, the bus people, fairies, whatever they are with those glowing purple eyes, they did something to her. Please, I have to get her back."

His green eye fills with pity, but the blue eye smolders with an old anger. D barks at his pack. They snatch up the last bits of meat and flee further into the woods. He nuzzles Jenny, then leads them both to the Wall.

Up close, it stands about ten feet tall, just enough that no person can jump or look over it. Charlotte pushes at some stones—not one loosens. The smallest pebbles fit just so among the others. And damn, they're warm. Each rock feels like those rocks she'd ring around her campfires in summer. Smells like them too: comforting, inviting, a big hug waiting.

"You never tried to go back there and look for Sammy?"

D nips at Charlotte's hand and snarls.

Jenny takes off her glasses before tears can stain them. "No… I don't know. I guess there's this part of me that knows I can't bring him back."

D whines and rubs his head against her chest.

Jenny continues to sob. "I don't know what will happen when you go over. You might disappear from my head. You might disappear from everything." Her little frame shudders as she shrugs off the satchel and hands it over. "Some water, trail mix, a hunting knife, matches…"

Charlotte's eyes pop. She never once thought about how *long* this could take. This place might be the size of a state park —of a whole state. "Thanks. I know Smith is expecting me, but hopefully not armed. Good thinking, Jenny!"

"How do you know he's expecting you?"

"My shoes. Remember Smith said there was 'something off' about me? They took Anna but left me because I wasn't fooled like everyone else, and they knew it."

D continues to sniff the air around Charlotte, and he slowly nods in affirmation.

"My shoes by the well. They didn't take those when they took her—that was an invitation. Bait." Charlotte checks her satchel and tightens its leather strap across her torso. A loose strap could get her caught by a branch and therefore by Smith.

Jenny watches Charlotte's hands as Charlotte reworks her braid. "But *I'm* not fooled like the grown-ups, and they took my brother. So why are they trying to trap you and not me?"

Charlotte gives the Wall a final inspection before turning back to Jenny. "Guess we won't know until I go over." She takes a red hair band off of her wrist and slips it around Jenny's. "Here. Do not take it off. Embed it in your brain that you cannot take it off no matter what. Hopefully, this will be enough of a trigger to remind you of me. So you won't completely forget."

Jenny's soft hands tremble inside Charlotte's calloused ones. "I won't take it off, promise. I hope you find her." A fresh wave of sobs rocks her hard. "I'm so sorry… Sammy, I wish

65

I could have—"

D whimpers by Jenny's neck.

Charlotte embraces her. "Don't. You've been fighting them long enough. You just stay alive, stay near your dad. He knows, even if he can't talk about it. I promise to send D back when I can." Charlotte rests her head on top of Jenny's. *Don't look up, kid. Don't see how scared I am.*

It is time, says the Voice in her heart.

Damn straight.

Charlotte stands at the base of a tree with a thick branch hanging over the Wall. "Ready when you are, D."

He closes his eyes and grunts softly. He takes a couple of steps back, haunches taut, and leaps to the top of the wall with ease. A final snort, a flash of black, and D's over.

Trees, so many damned trees. From her place atop the wall, Charlotte pauses to survey the land before her. There is a break ahead, perhaps a clearing. And a flat, reflective surface, perhaps a roof. There. Charlotte will go there first. There, and wherever else she needs to go until she finds her sister.

Wait: something catches her eye, wedged between the stones at her feet. A single red hair. Shiny. Long. It smells like berries.

I am coming.

"Charlotte?" Jenny's voice floats up the Wall, delaying Charlotte's descent.

"I'm all right." She sounds like someone's covered her in a dozen blankets.

"Jennifer Rachel! Get away from there!" her father cries, with a sharp cock of the rifle.

"Be careful."

"Don't forget me. ..." Charlotte's words are low, slow,

lumbering and thick, like mud flowing down over the stones.

"GET AWAY FROM THERE!"

"I won't!" Jenny calls to Charlotte just before her father wrenches her away from the Wall, his grip so tight around her wrist that Charlotte's red hair band leaves its imprint on her pale skin.

Follow the Silver Squirrel

Thud. *Ugh-umph!* Of all the rocks in the Wall, Charlotte lands near the sharp one, scraping her wrist.

Charlotte spreads her hand across the stones. Here the Wall feels new and rough, like her high school parking lot. Cigarette smoke and broken glass, football sweat and salted blood. As if Charlotte's memories have been distilled here to simmer in the hate-filled warmth beneath the rocks. But the Wall can't know Charlotte's hate: she's never been here.

"Don't forget me," she calls back to Jenny one last time, lingering at the base of the Wall. *Please don't, kid. Please.* She hears no response.

D is waiting for her. He paws her hip to turn her around.

Trees are trees are trees.

"Too damn ordinary," Charlotte whispers to herself. She maneuvers sl-ow-ly to study one: Will it throw apples? Grab her with its roots? No. Just a tree. Fat and tall, and shaped exactly like all the others she can see.

A quiet tree.

Not a bug, a bird, a rodent in the vicinity. Charlotte closes her eyes to hear the buzz of mosquitos, cicadas, anything. Perhaps a distant car speeding down the highway by the Blairs' farm.

Nothing.

And the branches—Charlotte tilts her head up—weave together with the other trees. No wonder she saw nothing from Jenny's house, or even from the top of the Wall. The trees form a hunter's blind. Peek through its opening, pick off the prey. One. By. One.

One strip of land is clear. But it isn't wide, maybe only six feet across, and it begins not far from where Charlotte stands by the Wall. There, D sniffs the ground and waits for her.

Charlotte observes the long blades flattening beneath her feet as she walks. On this path, much of the grass is already trampled, mixing with dirt and shifting underfoot. Charlotte crouches on all fours to sniff and search.

A little grunt. D's green eye is curious, the blue eye impatient.

"What? My nose works too." She rubs some grass away. "Though not right now. Too intense."

In the grass and in the air, away from the salt and creosote aroma of the Wall, she's bombarded with fruits and flowers: jasmine, lavender, apples, strawberries, star flowers. If scents were audible, these would be screaming. No way can Charlotte detect ash, let alone Anna's shampoo and bus funk.

She looks to D. "When I was standing on the Wall, I saw some kind of structure. Does this path go there?"

D nods.

"Right, then." Charlotte pulls the hunting knife out of the satchel and ties its leather sheath to her left leg. Weapon's now at the ready. The stupid scratch on her wrist starts to itch. "We'll start there."

D swings his head pendulum-style as they walk.

Charlotte's neck and shoulders tighten in response to the strangely intense smells and the even stranger silence. "So what's with a road leading to a wall?" her natural voice sounding unnaturally loud here.

D looks up at her.

"Not talkin', huh?" she lowers her voice to a husky whisper.

D grunts.

"Bet you know a lot of stuff you aren't telling."

He licks his chops, even does a fine imitation of wolfish laugher.

Then, from the distance, a roar. A deep. Building. Tree-shaking. Knee-buckling. ROAR. A mouth that can roar like that will be attached to teeth, a throat, a gut. An appetite.

"ANNA!" Oh God, does that thing have her?! Charlotte hunches forward, prepared to fight or flee.

But D hauls himself up onto his hind legs and lands his front paws on Charlotte's shoulders, saliva flying from his tongue as he shakes his head.

"What do you mean? Whatever-that-was doesn't have Anna?"

Trust him. The Voice in her heart is urgent and sure.

"Charlie!"

ROAR.

Charlotte pushes back on D's neck as she struggles to look around him. She heard that—she knows she did. And there —there! Almost out of sight, but not quite, behind the trees, Charlotte spots curly red hair, baby blues. Bubbles pop.

D whines and scratches at her hip to push her back to the road, but Charlotte's not listening to some overcautious dog. She *sees*, she *hears*.

"Charlie!"

Charlotte mouths, "Anna."

The Voice in her heart tries to tell her, *It's not real.*

Damn you! I remember.

A coin sings through the air. Charlotte snatches it mere

inches from the ground. It hisses in her palm. Disintegrates. Transforms. Grows tendrils, snaking around her hand, hunting for blood and there's that freakin' scratch on her wrist ready to oblige—

LET GO.

D bats the "coin" from her hand. It sparks and decays into the ground, just another bit of dirt on the forest floor.

Breathe, Charlie. Another whatever-it-is. It didn't get you. But they know you're here now, and they're sure as hell gonna do their damnedest.

Chattering where Anna's voice came from. But there's no Anna, only a squirrel, silver furred. He stands between the trees, a violet flash and silver shimmers among the shadows, too animated for this world of green stillness.

D snarls. His lips peel back to reveal long, eager teeth.

Can I kick him first? "Wait, D, no!"

Too late—D gallops, it scurries, Charlotte follows. It taunts D from branches and tree trunks, always just out of the reach of D's snapping jaws. They move too fast for Charlotte to see where they're running, to get her bearings, deeper and deeper into the strange land—

Until the green stillness vanishes in an air of ash and sulfur.

Charlotte slides to a stop on dirt—not the grassy dirt from the green stillness behind them, but dirt-dirt. Gray brown, and bone dry. Trees lining this gray-brown circle bend inward, toward the earth, in mourning or in worship.

There before Charlotte, in the midst of this ashen, unholy circle, stands a tree of night—no, darker. Like a witch's hair, coarse and tangled. Reflecting no light. Ropes of black marble roots emerge from the ground to form twisted slender trunks, each measuring two to six inches in diameter. These individual trunks coalesce and writhe upward, weaving together to become one central, squat, massive trunk as wide as that damned Scenic Tours bus. Charlotte's eyes trace the leafless branches as they taper off the trunk and snake upward in prayer to a cold Medusa sky.

SHIT, IT MOVED!

A reflexive swipe at her leg, and Charlotte's in her fight stance with hunting knife poised at the ready—*wait, no. Only the squirrel.* It slips in and out of the tangled roots at the base of the tree, sniffing and chattering all the while. Then its paw presses on a slender flake of marble bark. Pop pop pop pop: four marble ropes peel off the trunk, leaving a gaping hole, a black, toothless maw in the giant trunk. The four ropes twist into a single bundle as they peel downward, slithering on the dirt away from the trunk, and reach out toward Charlotte.

The bark tongue taunts Charlotte, a splash of blood on its tip.

Or is it?

She reaches for it with her knife blade. But D bites down on her satchel and pulls her back as she struggles forward. She has to know what that red is. It's not just red, but white too, and it's... familiar, somehow.

"Get off, D, I'm serious. Off!" A good yank and her satchel's free of D. She falls, bracing herself on all fours.

The tip of the bark tongue lies just inches from her face. No blood on it at all, but a necklace. Hers. Her father's. Dangling, almost within reach.

D clamps down on the cuff of her pants, and his growl says he's not keen to let go.

Don't go. The Voice in her heart sounds pretty firm about it.

Aloud to D, to the Voice: "Look, if she's down there, then that's where we need to go."

"Charlie, hurry up, supper's on the table!"

Dad?

The Voice insists: *It is* not *real.*

The bark tongue retracts a few inches back toward the tree's black mouth—the pendant still within reach. But D digs his paws into the dirt, anchoring Charlotte in place. A few more inches, her pendant almost at her fingertips, Charlotte can't lose it—

"Charlie, come on, what are you waiting for?"

It is NOT REAL.

"What am I waiting for?" she echoes the disembodied voice, giving it credence, validity, reality. So she continues to strain against D's teeth, to reach. The tongue's sliding a bit farther away again. *Dammit!* So close now, she's in the marble tree's shadow. Where it's freezing, her icy fingers numbing, but she doesn't care. The tongue is retracting completely into the black mouth, all but its tip. She can smell Dad's gunpowder and his special-recipe chili, and a laugh, Anna's laugh…

"I'm so hungry, Charlie! Get down here!" A profusion of bubbles popping.

Anna—let go, dog! Charlotte kicks at D with her free foot.

D releases her pant cuff to howl at her, but she doesn't care. She ignores the Voice in her heart—

NOT REAL. NOT REAL!

—And rips the pendant off the bark tongue before it slips completely into the waiting mouth.

Charlotte doesn't realize D's howls have morphed into words, his paws into hands: "I said *away!*" A strong *hand* wrenches her away from the door in the tree trunk and throws her several feet, away from the gray-brown dirt, to land on the edge of the green stillness.

Charlotte rolls to her knees, *en garde*, brandishing the hunting knife.

Before her stands a tall young man with a sharp face and lean build, dressed in tattered black. Wavy, chin-length black hair frames his almond eyes: the left green as grass, the right blue as a clear winter sky.

"D?"

He holds out his long olive hands, clenching and unclenching his fingers, staring at them as if he's never seen them before. He rakes both hands over his face and through his hair. Then he looks down as he lifts one foot at a time. Only when he finally turns his attention away from his body does he see Charlotte crouching on the ground, eyes wide. "I said away," he snarls, brushing past Charlotte and away from the marble tree.

The scratch hurts like a wasp sting. Charlotte rubs her wrist against her pants to try to assuage the pain. Over her shoulder, "Wait, where are you going? We can't leave them" —*Gah, don't talk crazy to the dog*—"here." She turns back to the tree, still transfixed. "We can't leave them down there."

D's shaky hand hauls her backward until she nearly trips on a tree root. "Not. Here." His voice is guttural, rusty, and his face twists in concentration. The rhythm and depth of his breaths keep changing, as if he's unsure whether to breathe from his nose or from his mouth, or in through one and then out the other.

Trust him. The Voice in Charlotte's heart is clearer now that her dad's pendant rests in her hand.

But why should she trust him? She doubts Jenny's seen him as a person—she had given Charlotte no indication of this. Even D doesn't seem familiar with his human form. Not like Jamie at all.

Which, Charlotte admits to herself, is a big check in D's favor. "Why not here?" She quickly wraps the pendant's broken chain 'round her wrist and knots it tight. The scratch immediately stops stinging.

D touches his mouth and stretches his jaw before

74

answering. "Had you entered the Pits that way," pointing at the black tree, "you'd already be dead." He turns his head just enough so the blue eye fixes all of Charlotte in its visual field.

Charlotte feels D's focus train on her pendant and the scratch on her wrist. *Back off, Toto, I know what I'm doing.* She covers her right wrist with her left hand.

"I know someone who may be able to help you enter another way."

"Please tell me it's not a raven."

D laughs like he barks: short bursts, full of feeling. "No. Jamie is the least of your problems."

Charlotte puts the knife back in its sheath and follows D away from the clearing, back into the green stillness.

The intense fruit and flower smells return, but Charlotte can handle them now. The air even starts to feel more... normal. The tree branches are no longer so uniform, and their leaves twitch in the breeze. Some flowers bloom in the scraps of sunlight on the forest floor, and even the occasional berry bush wraps 'round a tree trunk. The stillness, that bizarre silence, is gone.

"Who are you? What are you, really? Why do you care so much about Jenny?" she asks as they walk on.

"My name is Dorjan. I am an exile, thanks to some —how would Jenny say it—'loudmouths' of my kind." D continues to feel out the shape of his mouth as he speaks. Words must feel strange on the tongue after barks and howls. "The girl Jenny's desire to protect her brother, her own, runs very deep. I suppose," he smiles as his fingers trace the foliage around them, "she is my friend. Ergo, the exchange of names. Or first initial, on my part."

"Well, I guess 'D' is a whole lot easier to scrawl on the dirt with a paw." Charlotte chuckles as she walks a couple of steps behind the wolf-man. "Wonder what she thought of you writing at all."

Dorjan guffaws. "Considering I had just chased off Jamie and Campion for the first time, she thought quite well of me, actually."

They stop at the edge of an oval clearing. But compared with the clearing with the marble tree, this one is huge, about the size of the Blair farm, and no coldness, no ominous air hangs over it. Charlotte at last feels the sun again, and somehow, the "real" world doesn't quite feel so far away anymore. Nor does Anna's rescue seem impossible.

To Charlotte's left, on the western side, stands what she saw from the top of the Wall. The reflective surface shines diamond bright atop the roof of a gothic mansion. Three stories tall, built of wrinkly gray stones, its latticed windows encased in thin white frames like the rims of an animal's eyes. The central edifice runs approximately the same length as each of its two flanking wings, which splay open at an obtuse angle on either side like a giant's hands ready and waiting to trap a fly. A stone portico, with a gray slate roof supported by stone columns, wraps around its entire perimeter, almost like a moat.

But the roses are what really disturb Charlotte. The bushes are trimmed—not a sign of sickly branches or overgrowth. The red and pink blooms sparkle as though recently watered. *Too damn picture-perfect.* Someone cares about them. A lot. Takes time to nurture and protect them. *If flowers get that kind of attention around here, what do fairy-freaks get?*

Shit. "What *is* this place?"

"The center of it all, really."

Charlotte turns to Dorjan and then looks over his shoulder

76

to the eastern side of the clearing. "And what about that?"

An arrangement of branches, each protruding three or four feet out of the ground, forms a circle twenty feet in diameter. She squints: no, not branches. Roots. Stark white, thick, yet dry and diseased, they gather together and twist around a center point, then plunge in a downward spiraling tunnel, drilling deep into the ground—a static whirlpool of wood and earth.

Dorjan does not look back. The ice of his blue eye could freeze a little girl easily enough. "Leave it."

But Charlotte walks around him, just for a few steps, for a closer look. She *feels* something, little needles prickling her toes, neck, head, trying to find a way in. Then, faint echoes of… tinkling piano keys, bubble-gum punctuation—?

Not this way! the Voice kicks her gut.

"Heart's fire, don't you listen to ANYone? I said leave it!" He steers Charlotte around and away from the static whirlpool and back toward the clearing's edge, but not where they came from. Instead, they walk a bit further down, to where two pillars mark the end of a grass road and the entry point to the clearing. Each pillar is topped with a stone eagle, its wings outstretched, poised for flight. The base of each pillar is littered with broken remains of other statues: jaws, legs, claws.

"On either side of the clearing you can see grass roads." He sweeps his hand from the south side of the clearing to the north side, where two more eagle pillars stand. "The Southern Road ends at the Wall separating the River Vine —what we call this land—from the Blair farmstead. The Northern Road takes you past the Orchards and into the Wild Grasses. That is likely where my pack is staying, and where you should go if you must flee, since it will take you to the northern end of the Wall."

77

"Why can't I go back to the Bl—"

"Because I will not risk Jenny's life by allowing you to lead harm to her," Dorjan snaps at Charlotte. "She has suffered enough, don't you think?"

Charlotte's hand moves to the knife strapped to her leg. "Down, boy."

Dorjan eyes her hand hovering over the knife hilt and scoffs. "Don't insult me. I've ripped hearts out of ribcages faster than you can pull your puny blade out of its sheath."

Charlotte's scowl must be pretty clear: Dorjan's look softens. But the flares behind his eyes never die. "A strong spirit. I see why they took an interest in you. And the longer they focus on you, the longer Jenny is left alone and I can hunt those responsible for her brother."

Charlotte nods. *Now THAT, I get. Okay then, Dorjan, we'll follow your rules. For now.*

Dorjan moves on as though she's said as much aloud, leading them away from the pillars and on toward the mansion.

Charlotte takes one last look at the white strangeness. "It's almost like a tree." *Almost, but warped to blazes. Whatever did that was wrong, very wrong.* "Where's the rest of it?"

Dorjan bites his lip and continues walking, eyes straight ahead. "Part of the Pits. These days." He stares at the stone fortress with an inscrutable expression.

Okay, well, aren't you the little chatterbox. Charlotte follows him, trying to identify the scent he trails in his wake. Among his strange smells, Charlotte recognizes something familiar. Not fear. Not quite that. More like apprehension. "So where the hell is the 'safe' entrance to these 'the Pits'?" Charlotte fills the air with impatient quotation marks. "Because at least the black tree thing had a door."

"The only other entrance to the Pits is within Rose House."

Inside? With the obsessive rose gardener? Oh goody. "Inside *Downton*

Abbey, you mean? So can we go through the front door, or do we have to use the servants' entrance?"

"Y-yes, n-no… uh, through the main entrance, of course." He cocks his head, unsure of how to respond. "Inside Rose House is a door leading down to the Pits," he repeats, on surer footing. "And like the black tree, it is also guarded. But don't worry," he winks, "I have an 'in' with the keeper, as Jenny would say." He looks at her wrist. "He could give you something for your injury too."

But Charlotte brushes him off. "It's fine. The inflammation's gone, so no big deal."

Seeing it from the other side of the clearing was intimidating enough, but now that Charlotte stands on its portico, she has a nagging feeling that she's stepping into a Venus fly trap. The wings of Rose House flank outward, but who knows if it's like that marble tree, with its grasping tongue and gaping mouth? Maybe these wings will fold over and slam shut.

Rose House has already deceived Charlotte one way: what she took for wrinkles on its stone walls aren't wrinkles at all. Someone, from who knows how long ago, carved vines and rosebuds into the stones, from the ground behind the living rose bushes up to the second floor. Charlotte takes a closer step, pressing her left cheek up against the wall in order to closely examine the ornate relief work of tiny thorns and flowers. Her finger traces one curlicue tendril and follows it from one window to another and up, out of reach. Shadows rim blooms slightly open, full and rich, wilting and broken —all stone. Exquisite, yet hard and cold.

BANG. Charlotte leaps back, knife out, eyes darting.

"Are you always this skittish?" Dorjan asks, bemused, with his hand on a large rose-shaped iron knocker attached to a heavy door of old wood, polished dark beneath a wrought iron grillwork of vines.

Don't you run, Charlie. One, two, three, four. Remember why you're here. Hold the pendant. Remember. She slips the knife back into its sheath and leans against the wall next to the door. "Kinda had to be."

Charlotte crosses her arms while Dorjan knocks again, and tilts her head up. All the carving on the stones, all the pretty flowers—yet this place looks so *strong*. "What do fairies need a fortress for, anyway?" she whispers to the air.

The Voice answers: *To fight the darkness that lives underground.*

"What did you say?" Blue and green eyes flash at her.

"I asked, 'Who's the keeper?' Some wolf ears you've got."

Dorjan raises an eyebrow, but answers, "A friend." He looks up at the windows, then at her. "I hope."

A gaunt man with short, peppered hair and a neatly trimmed beard opens the door. He is dressed in a clean white shirt with rolled-up sleeves, a black vest, and dark pants with boots, old but clean. A leather bracelet with a Celtic knot pattern fits snugly over his right wrist. Not quite Dorjan's height, but that doesn't matter because Charlotte smells something Dorjan lacks: authority. Although that gardening basket he's holding—not a booster in the power department.

The gaunt man looks down at Charlotte's knife, then up at Charlotte, then finally at Dorjan.

Dorjan smiles broadly. "Hello, Uncle."

Enter Rose House

Uncle? Another freak-fairy type. Looks kind of old for a guard. Might explain why the fairies are wreaking havoc past the Wall.

"You needn't be rude."

Charlotte's eyes bulge and dart. "I didn't say anything."

The man's dark eyes glitter a bit, but not like Smith's or Jamie's cursed purple sparkles. More like... mischievous.

Dorjan pushes Charlotte gently inside and tilts his head toward the forest. "We must talk, Uncle, away from prying eyes and ears."

The man says nothing as he shuts the door behind them.

They walk into a small reception hall with a polished wooden staircase running up along the left wall. From where Charlotte stands, she sees three archways leading out of this hall, each bordered by stained-glass flowers of red, blue, or green. The red-flowered arch on her right leads into someplace full of gilded, swirly wallpaper and crystal. Gold embroidery on old-school Victorianish chairs surround a formal dining table which gleams like one big mirror—not a smudge or fingerprint on it.

Charlotte's lip curls at the ridiculous glamour.

At the opposite end of the reception hall, the green-flowered arch opens to a room containing a potbelly stove and some shelves with pots. Kitchen. Not interesting.

The blue-flowered arch to Charlotte's left leads to the homiest room by far: one furnished with a simple square table with two plain chairs. This room's only concession to décor is a tall glass vase of fragrant lilacs resting on the wood table. A small fire burns in a hearth that's big enough for a person to sit in. The mantel is lined with various tins and tiny vases, each filled with a few buds of different flowers. Two armchairs with faded blue cushions face the fireplace, each with its own little end table. It's… pleasant, actually. Lived in.

Last of all, she notes a little door set under the stairs. Could be a closet. Or a way to a basement, underground.

Charlotte feels the uncle's eyes on the back of her head, like her brain's a book to thumb through.

"You swore to a life of four legs until your name could be cleared," the uncle says, his speech lilting.

"Yes, I know, but this is different. They are breaking rules, even their own, over her."

Tempting as it is to ponder their Irish heritage and fairy connections, along with that cryptic statement, Charlotte ignores them and slides ever so discreetly toward that stair-well door. Of course, it has a big rusty lock on it.

Both Dorjan and his uncle stand in silence by the front door.

Are they watching me?

Her mind becomes a flip-book: Anna's face—*flip*—Smith's —*flip*—Mom's—*flip*—Dad's—*flip*—"STOP. Get out of my head," knife in hand, "now."

Their stare breaks. Dorjan approaches her like *she's* the dangerous dog. "I promised to help, Charlotte, and I will."

"Help?" The uncle hangs back. A new scent grows from him: curiosity.

Beats animosity.

Charlotte backs up until her heels touch the door beneath

the stairs. *And now I will not move from this spot until you open it.* "My name is Charlotte. The fairies took my sister, and I'm going to get her out of—what did Dorjan call them—the Pits? Underground. I need to go underground now. Please." At least she remembers to be polite.

The uncle holds his chin and runs a finger across his lips. "Fairies."

What is with you, old man? "Yeah. Fairies." *Don't look at me like I'm fucking nuts. Stop sharing looks with your damn nephew and HELP ME. Did you catch THAT flipping through my brain?!*

"There's no need to insult—"

"Let her be, Dorjan. Our behavior's not helping." He steps forward. "My apologies, young lady."

Still, her hand grips the knife's hilt. The moment he smells off, she'll be ready.

"My name is Arlen, and I am keeper of Rose House. Dorjan, get some tea and apple bread. Don't sulk. You can have some too."

"Tea, are you kidding me? We don't have time for any goddamn tea, we have to—" Charlotte lets out a small yip as she's silenced by a strong, young grip on her right biceps from the emaciated old man. He leads her under the blue-flowered arch to the parlor and sits her in one of the two armchairs by the hearth. Charlotte scans the room and briefly registers a narrow wooden door opposite the blue archway.

They're dawdling, the two of them. She should go alone, and she knows it, but... she can't. She is simply too, damned, scared. And that, more than anything, shames her. "Please," she sobs. "Please, help me."

Steam whistles from a cast iron kettle hanging in the mouth of the fireplace in front of her. Against the wall between two latticed windows, a long, worn sideboard is set with a silver tray holding a delicate rose-patterned porcelain tea service.

"I will do what I can," says Arlen. "But unless you want me to 'flip through your mind,' as you put it, you must tell me everything yourself, and that can happen only after we steady your nerves."

Charlotte's thumb strokes the pendant again and again as she describes the raven's attack, Smith's trick with the bus, and the shoes by the well.

While she speaks, Arlen selects a tin and two vases, each containing different tiny purple flowers. He silently chops the flowers and adds them to the kettle.

"Anna didn't want to come along, never did. But I *know*," she smacks her armrest, "she would not just leave me and take off in the middle of nowhere, not willingly. It's like Jenny's brother all over again."

Arlen sets the tea tray on the square table. "Jenny's brother?"

"Braammel Bear." Dorjan comes in with a bowl of jam and half a loaf of apple bread, setting these on the table. The other half loaf is in his mouth, which he unstuffs to say again, this time more coherently, "Samuel Blair. The son of the border family. I tell you, Uncle, someone must stand up to them. If the Bloody Prince can't be disturbed, we must be the ones to act." He can't sit fast enough to dip his bread into the jam and gnaw on it.

"Dorjan!" The uncle snatches the untouched half loaf away and slices pieces for Charlotte.

"Sorry, Uncle. It's been far too long since I've tasted your baking. Where did you get the apples? I thought the orchards were barren."

"They are. Devyn found an orchard to the north some time ago and steals when he can."

"That old curmudgeon, bless him."

A strange spring floral scent fills the air. "Here, I think

this will help." Arlen fills each cup with a yellowish liquid. Bits of green leaves and purple petals settle at the bottom. "It's lavender and rosemary. Drink up. I assure you, it's not a sedative."

Charlotte accepts the cup. She needs their help, and they're offering—dawdling, but offering.

It's okay, the Voice in her heart assures her.

I'll hold you to that.

The drink hits her like a caffeinated Vitamin C booster shot. Her limbs twitch. She's ready to chew bubble gum and kick ass, except that her sister has all the bubble gum. "So the fairies like darkness and they like being animals. What do they need my sister for?"

Arlen places a slice of bread in her hands. His fingers linger a moment longer than necessary. "You keep calling them fairies. Why is that?"

"A poem Jenny showed me, about fairies who tempt children to run off with them." She does her best to recite the refrain.

Dorjan smiles through his jam mess of a face. "That's Jenny—as brilliant as Eos herself."

Arlen sits in the other armchair, opposite Charlotte, and sips his tea slowly, all the mischievous sparkle gone. When he fixes upon Charlotte again, her stomach hardens: he bears the same expression as Dad's partner did when he came to the door ten years ago. "We are not speaking simply of fairies and folk tales. We are speaking of that about which man no longer knows anything at all. Ancient, real, and powerful."

Dorjan's eyes drift toward the fire as he sucks the last of the jam off his fingers.

Charlotte spins her finger to spool the air. "Whatever. Just tell me what I need to know so I can get my sister out alive."

"That is my point, Miss Charlotte. I doubt your sister lived past dawn."

He is wrong. The Voice is resolute.

The cup shatters in Charlotte's hand. Blood trickles down every finger and threads itself through the chain on her wrist, staining the white petals of her pendant. "No."

"I am sorry, child." New lines appear on Arlen's face, like grief itself is aging him.

"No!" Charlotte flies out of the chair, out of the room, into the reception hall and straight for the door under the staircase.

Dorjan anticipates her and lunges to intercept.

"Get the HELL out of my way, Dorjan! She is *not* dead, I *know* she's not." Charlotte throws him into the wall and pins him as he did her. "Open, the damn, door, NOW. Or your blood's joining *mine* on this floor."

Quiet, fast, strong: Arlen's arms wrap around Charlotte to hoist her off.

She kicks. Screams. Sobs. "You promised. You promised you would help. You promised."

He sets her down on the stairs as she cries. "I am, truly, sorry." Arlen cradles her hands in his own. "And we will do what we can. First, we will mend your hands, and then I will find a scout to parlay underground. Bring her to the herbarium when she's ready, Dorjan."

Charlotte crumples into herself, visibly shrinking smaller and smaller, a dying star. *Stay out of me. You're only going to see a flip-book soaked with tears. Stay out of me. Nothing but tears. Stay out.... Go deep, Charlie. Think. Look in me, Arlen—only pain and anger. Look on me. Only tears.*

Dorjan's green eye fills with pity, the blue eye curious. "You really think she still lives?"

Charlotte nods frantically, hyperventilating and hiccupping.

"Here, let me get you a drink. Just a moment." He's past

the basement door, he's—

GO!

Charlotte runs under the blue arch, back into the parlor, past the table and the sideboard, and through the narrow wooden door at the far end of the room. She slams it shut but it makes no sound. *Thanks, door. Bloody prints, damn, that leaves a trail. How do I lock you?*

Click. Without Charlotte's assistance.

The sconces above her flicker to life. Thunder from an approaching storm rattles the windows. Loads of latticed windows, all long and slender, lining a wall and extending from the floor up to the ceiling. Big beams overhead, everything varnished and shiny and complementing the…

The most beautiful piano in the world—clawed legs, glowing black finish. A cocked hat grand. A "How'd such a rare thing find its way into the middle of nowhere?" grand piano.

A soft G chord.

What, like a hello? "Don't you dare tell them I'm here," she whispers.

The piano stops.

Dorjan's and Arlen's voices carry from the reception hall. They heard, they know.

"Okay, House, you locked the door. Now, where can I hide?"

A door opens to Charlotte's right. Without thinking, she bolts through it and tumbles out onto the wrap-around portico, crashing on her cut hand. "Dammit, House!" she curses at the stone floor and her blood-smeared handprint, "I just got *in*. I can't be stuck outside."

Arlen's voice is muffled from the parlor, but Dorjan's voice reaches around the corner. He's outside.

Dammit!

Another door appears and noiselessly opens.

Wincing, Charlotte shakes her bloody hand and droplets fly onto the porch's steps and into the grass a few feet away. She slips through this new door and latches it shut. She curls up at the base of the door, listening for footsteps.

Charlotte finds herself in a room that's dirty, dark, and stale —a place left alone. Perfect. She pulls out the bandages Jenny packed for her and sets to work binding her cut hand. No more blood trails.

Two voices outside. "Charlotte?!"

Stay deep inside, Charlie. Block their mind reading. Focus on the darkness. Focus on pain. Hide the plan.

"These prints, Dorjan. She was here," Arlen says. "Somehow…"

"By heart's fire, if she ran back to that cursed tree—no. The trail ends too fast. Where the bloody deuce did she go? CHARLOTTE!" Dorjan, and really passionate too. "I won't fail Jenny again, Uncle. I don't care if the Artairs arrive. They should be here to see the fruits of their negligence. If you knew this poor human child as I did, you would aid—"

"Do you know how many of the commoners remain loyal to me? Three." Arlen's footsteps follow along a wall made of glass and iron. Really dirty glass: Charlotte can barely make out his form in all that dust and grime. *Weird that these windows —and everything in this room—are so filthy but the rest of this house is so over-the-top clean.*

"Miss Charlotte?" Arlen calls. "Any velidevour who does not cooperate with the Lady is banished, and you know that's as good as death. If we lose any more scouts, the supply of veli will trickle down to nothing, and then one by one, we die."

"If your precious Bloody Prince hadn't driven them all underground, you wouldn't be in this situation."

"Whom everyone says *you* put to sleep."

"I did NOT strike him down!" Dorjan cries as lightning flashes, outlining his silhouette on the grimy glass wall. "Yes, we argued, yes, we drew blood, and yes, I loathed his very existence. But I did not bear the deep, terrible hatred to strike him like a coward. CHARLOTTE!"

Rain erupts, hard and steady, drumming on the portico's slate roof—a barrage of white noise that makes it difficult for Charlotte to track their conversation. So she crawls away from the door and crouches next to the glass wall, where she can better hear the two men.

"I know. But the Lady and Cein command all the scouts to spread that story as far as their marks allow—Charlotte!"

The silhouette of Dorjan's head leans close to Arlen's on the grimy glass. "You do realize that this Smith Charlotte speaks of is Cein, don't you?" Their shadows hold still.

Charlotte's heart grows louder.

Let them help you, pleads the Voice

No! They know things they won't tell me.

"He's strong enough to change again, and perform magic besides. I can only imagine how much veli the Lady is hoarding if her favorites can venture so far from the Wall."

The Lady's favorites. Anna wasn't intended for Smith or for Jamie, but for this Lady. So there's every chance Anna's still with this Lady. There's still hope.

"But why lure this particular human into River Vine? I know the border child is likely more aware of them because she is the firstborn, but," Arlen's voice slows as he treads his logic with care, "if Charlotte's story is true, and Cein indeed used magic in front of her, then he would perceive her as a threat, more of a threat than the border child."

"There's more, Uncle. Did you see her wrist? Did you see a mark form?"

"It is difficult to see beneath the talisman."

"It didn't."

Pause. "Impossible."

"See for yourself when you can, but it's true. The mark never took. If it ever even was, then it's vanished completely."

Charlotte packs the dressings and feels under the chain wrapped around her right wrist. No scratch. The cut from the Wall did hurt for a long time during the walk through the woods, but now her skin isn't even irritated.

"But all humans are marked—"

"I know." Dorjan's shadow fades as he moves away. "So why not this one? Could the Wall's power be..."

"Gone..." Both voices fade, shadows whispering of ladies and veli and walls.

A flash of lightning reveals countless immovable forms furnishing the room. Charlotte strains her eyes, realizes that the glass wall contains bits of colored shards. A stained-glass wall. Shame about the dirt.

Flashes of lightning fight their way through the grime-covered glass, illuminating paintings, canvases, statues, paint jars, sheets of glass, and rods of iron—pieces of other lives she could touch and enter. Even the floor is littered, threads of gold and silver, like treading on the tail of a falling star.

That tail ends at a chair. High backed and constructed of dark wood, it faces a drafting table in the left corner of the room.

Then a flash of lightning glints off a flash of metal. A dagger, thrust hard and deep.

The chair is occupied. Legs, arms, and dark hair poke from it. And beneath it pools blood.

Fresh blood.

Bloody Prince

Charlotte approaches the chair and its occupant. *How did I not smell death so close to me?* Blood and glitter-stuff sparkle in the lightning: two colored, red and violet, like oil and water. *Aha! He's not human, he's one of those veli-de-somethings. Good riddance.*

Take the blade. The Voice in her heart sounds very sure.

But I have a knife already. From Jenny.

No use here.

Arlen and Dorjan responded to it. Or was that their way of being polite?

They want you to feel safe.

Dammit.

TAKE the dagger.

The hilt of the weapon isn't jeweled or rich—or however magical items should look. Unadorned steel, partially wrapped in leather and completely smeared in blood. It sticks from its victim's twisted back.

Charlotte's fingertips tingle as she wraps one finger at a time around the hilt. Her chest prickles and the sensation spreads like a shiver, warming her entire body.

Charlotte pulls.

The blade is bright, wide at the hilt but tapering very, very thin to the tip. Carving runs along the metal—feathers, but more delicate. Blood fills hair-thin lines forming veins along the blade. Like the dagger itself is alive, an extension of the body, an appendage she just severed and now holds. Droplets bead together and fall from the dagger's tip in tiny splashes of crimson stardust, draining the tiny veins clear. *Freaky!*

A thunder clap, and a sudden burst of lightning illuminates the blade. It glows like fire. Thud—the whole form slides onto the floor.

Nothing like a corpse to kill the magic of this room. Should probably call the police. And how's that gonna happen, Charlie? 'Hey, officer, come get me out of Fairyland.'

She stares down at the form. He looks like a recluse from the mountains: well over six feet, tight limbs, and facial hair that reaches to his chest. *A ZZ Top impersonator?* His hands are creased with dirt, his old-fashioned three-piece suit out of place in this strange wilderness.

He's also warm.

With a pulse.

"Okayokayokay, I, okay, gotta…" Charlotte had only performed CPR twice: on a CPR dummy, and then on her sister after pulling her out of the Missouri River. Everything about this guy screams grit and filth, and she's disgusted —but a life's a life. Charlotte opens his mouth, inhales before she can smell the breath of a bleeding man, and bends forward.

His body convulses. Charlotte manages to pull away just before crimson and violet drops sputter from his mouth.

"Careful, you'll hurt yourself. Lie still. Here," she tears off a piece of her shirt to wipe away the blood around his mouth. The stab went right through his chest: a single strike without any hesitation, no serrations or shallow marks around it. A strong strike. "Someone reeeeeally wanted you dead, huh? What the—?" Charlotte has to lean closer to see.

The bleeding's stopped.

The hell? I haven't even put pressure on yet. "Well, let's at least sterilize it. Thank goodness Jenny thought ahead." Charlotte soaks some gauze with rubbing alcohol from her satchel. "This may hurt a bit." Charlotte places the gauze on his chest.

His eyes open.

Blue gray, boundless, like the sky that hides North Dakota from the sun and soaks the plains around her grandmother's house with cold life.

But no, not cold, they… WOW.

He opens his mouth to speak, but Charlotte hushes him. "Save your strength. I have to find my sister, and then we're all getting out of here."

"Move away from him. Now." Arlen towers behind Charlotte. His voice is civil, but his diction sharpens to a command.

Dorjan stands in the light of a distant doorframe. "You, you, woke him. The Bloody Prince… you woke him."

"Dorjan!" Arlen turns around. "Show some respect."

Charlotte takes advantage, holds the dagger up and out, still warm as her own skin. "You do this?" Charlotte points its tip at Dorjan. "Or you?" At Arlen.

Sadness washes over Arlen's face, as if she's just destroyed something precious. A moment passes in silent breathing, then another. The sadness fades, and mischief returns one dark eye at a time. "I am not what you think. And it seems that the same can be said of you."

Huh?

Trust. NOW. The Voice in her heart flares up on each word.

Charlotte lowers the blade. No, Arlen's not the threat here, and neither's Dorjan. Dorjan could have ripped her to pieces, and Arlen could have poisoned her. And both bear a scent Charlotte long thought dead in the world: nobility. She slides

93

back so Arlen can kneel next to the Bloody Prince.

Arlen takes hold of the Bloody Prince's hand. "It is all right. You are among friends."

But the Bloody Prince isn't looking at Arlen: he's looking straight at Charlotte. She sees the strength, confusion, anger in those wow eyes. *STOP Charlie, don't be stupid.*

Dorjan stays put. The blue eye looks angry, the green relieved. "So… so. You know what this means, Uncle? My exile must be over. The Artairs can't exile me for killing someone who's clearly not dead."

Charlotte sets the blade down and cups the Bloody Prince's head in her hands. "You stay here. I have to get my sister back, then—" Wow Eyes clutches her wrist so tightly that her breath catches, his hand pressing her father's pendant hard into her skin. "You have to let go. Please."

Rasping. The Bloody Prince tries to speak, his fingers like talons on her wrist. So much strength for one who only began to breathe a few moments ago. Slowly, with his Dakota-sky eyes fixed on hers, he releases her.

Charlotte faces Arlen. "Look, whatever I did just now must be pretty major for you two to be acting like this. So you owe me. Show me these Pits, and you can take care of your own. Give me crap and I'm going to see just how sharp this slice of manslaughter is. Got it?" She picks the bloody blade up from the floor, waving it at the men. *Mean it, Charlie. Fill with blood and screams and pain. They can smell the violence on you.*

"Please don't make me say it again, Miss Charlotte. I am sorry, but the Lady, she works far too quickly. Now you must tell me: How did you do that?" Arlen points to the dagger in her hand, blood still dripping from its tip. "No one's dared pull it out. Ever."

"This isn't Arthur and Excalibur and all that shit."

94

Charlotte yanks herself free of the Bloody Prince and unsheathes Jenny's hunting knife with her free hand. She lunges for Dorjan and crosses the two blades at the base of his neck. He does not try to stop her, just stands there, very still, chin up, both eyes on Charlotte's. "You two are stalling. If I lose my family, so will you." The blades squeeze together ever so slightly.

Arlen begins to plead, but Dorjan lifts a hand. "Don't fight her. She's right. We owe her." His blue eye reminds Charlotte of a whiteout. "Just wish it wasn't over that half-dead louse…" And for a second, Charlotte spots the family tie between Arlen and Dorjan: the green eye has that same mischief dancing in its iris. "Be so kind as to remove those from my arteries, and we'll go to the Pits."

"No." Arlen's voice resounds over the thunderclap. "Not you." He rushes to Dorjan, placing a hand on his cheek and shoulder.

Charlotte can't help it—she turns away. The last time a grown-up really cared about her was too damned long ago.

"Dorjan, not when we can finally clear your name." Arlen turns to Charlotte and pauses. "I will take you, Miss Charlotte."

"What?!" Dorjan moves to intercept Arlen.

Too late. Arlen passes Dorjan and leads Charlotte back to the reception hall.

Dorjan spits the starts of several sentences, all with "no" and "can't," but Charlotte doesn't listen. *The old man knows how to find the Pits and where the Lady keeps people. And he radiates authority. Dorjan radiates strength and daring—cool'n'all, but not exactly authoritative.*

Dorjan pauses his spluttering and glares at her. "I am too authoritative."

Charlotte bites her tongue. Politeness has never been her thing, but today's been all about new experiences, so: "Please stop reading my thoughts."

"Then stop being so loud in there." Dorjan grasps Arlen's arm as his uncle stands before the door, his hand on the lock. "Please, Uncle. You're—you're not…"

Arlen gives a sad half smile. "Strong enough? There's nothing the Lady can't do to me that hasn't already been done, except hurt you. And by heart's fire, I will not let that happen. You must tend to—"

"I'm not lifting a finger for that Bloody Prince!"

"Stop calling him that, *now.*" Arlen sets to work on the lock. He has no key, but his fingers trace the lock as he murmurs words that Charlotte hears but doesn't understand. The air balloons around him with a static charge.

Bright color flashes outside the windows: orange.

Dorjan's scowl melts into a smile. "Ember's here! Brilliant, she can go instead of you, Uncle." He opens the front door for the small bird that zooms in and spirals downward, landing silently on the floor and shaking raindrops from her feathers.

Charlotte kneels, unsure whether to hold out a hand, a finger, or some birdseed. "Hi?"

With a stretch of wings, dust and feathers erupt and swell to a cloud of Anna's height. Now instead of a bird, Ember only looks bird-ish: a very delicate frame, large violet eyes surrounded by dark brown curls, some of which are tied back in orange scraps. Her whole body is clothed in orange, tunic and pants alike. On her wrist a tattoo, or maybe henna, that quivers and shimmers: a vine with leaves. When she steps forward slightly, it's apparent that she walks with a limp.

Dorjan huffs.

Of course, shape-shifting being a part of everyday life for Mr. D McPawPants.

Arlen ignores them all—still working on the lock, which is *way* stronger than it looks.

96

Ember gives Dorjan a curt nod and ignores Charlotte altogether. So much for polite hellos. "I followed Jamie and the humans approximately sixty miles, sir."

Arlen shakes his head but continues the murmurs. The lock begins to glow.

"At which time—"

Arlen continues to shake his head.

"—a human on the bus set about killing everyone—"

What the fuck! Charlotte grabs the bird-lady's orange shoulder and whips her around. Whips because *she is going to SEE me, dammit.* "What?!"

"—and proceeded to rip out the hearts for Jamie." Even now Ember barely raises an eyebrow Charlotte's way. Sneers a little, though.

Dorjan crowds in on them both. "Are you saying Jamie can imbibe outside the Wall?"

Charlotte's mouth falls open. "That's your question! Not about the people hacked to pieces, but if some fairy freak," she smacks Dorjan's chest with the back of her hand, "can eat *hearts?*" She blinks, imagines the gaudy dining room hosting the family out of *Texas Chainsaw Massacre*, dishing out seconds, laughing their freak heads off.

But it just doesn't jive with what she smells in the reception hall now: the nobility, the kindness. *How? HOW? Unless that lock isn't about the Pits, but a place to keep… people…* Charlotte quickly slams her book of thoughts shut. She can feel Dorjan's eyes trying to peer over her shoulder and into her mind. Must refocus. "Ember, right? Was the killer a big guy in an old coat with a mushy face, kinda like a pug, with tiny yellow eyes?"

Ember's curls bounce once as she seems to notice Charlotte properly for the first time. "You were not present." She lumbers toward Arlen, her left foot dragging on the floor at an unnatural angle. "How could she know that, sir?"

Arlen waves her off.

"I know a flippin' psycho when I see one," Charlotte says. Quick eye at Dorjan. "Usually."

"Hey!" Dorjan scrunches his face, insulted.

"You were eating bread and jam before. What, no human"—she shoves Dorjan toward the door—"hearts"—shoves again—"in the goddamn pantry?" She and Anna both were on that bus. They could have been there for Potential Homicidal Maniac's official drop of "Potential." Her kid sister might have been ripped open—but they took her, anyway. *You bastards, you—*

Her senses reel: there's no smell of bloodthirst, let alone violence, on anyone around her. But they talk about slaughtered lives like a trip to the grocery store. Her hands don't know whether to reach for help or snap wrists.

Dorjan grabs her hands, holds them in the space between his chest and hers. "We are not all like that." He casts his eyes at Arlen, whose veins pulse in his temples while sweat beads form on his hands cradling the lock. "We're not. Truly."

Charlotte swallows. The Voice takes that swallow, eases it down. *He is right. Think of Jenny.*

And Charlotte does. D could have ripped open the Blairs at any time, but instead he chases the squirrel and other freaks away to protect them. *Count your breaths.* One, two. She pulls away from Dorjan and swings one hand at the basement door. "If you're not all like that, then why's this door locked?"

"Because some doors are too old." Ember leans against the wall. The violet in her eyes pulses once. "Too dark."

Charlotte gives Ember the once-over. She couldn't be that much older, and with a limp, to boot. *Dorjan thinks I should go into a dark, padlocked place where bloodthirsty fairy freaks live—with her?*

"Mind your inner tongue," Ember says as she stiffens her back. "I'm stronger and older than I look."

Dorjan stands in the doorway, feet spread apart, hands

resting at his sides, eager to be away. His nose is reaching into the air, from one side of a breeze to the other. "I'm sorry, Charlotte, but I must leave you to Ember's care. If Jamie's successfully coerced one human to kill for him, he will employ more, and that slaughter on the bus will be nothing compared to the carnage I'm sure the Lady is eager to harvest. He'll be clumsy lugging an armful of hearts to the Pits—easy for me to hunt him down."

Charlotte joins Dorjan in the doorway to watch rain pound the portico steps.

The charge around Arlen has grown stronger, turning the air hot and difficult to breathe.

Ember asks, "Is there someone else inside Rose House?" But no one answers.

Charlotte won't look Dorjan in the eye. No, he doesn't get to see her fear. He's seen enough of her as it is. "You don't really have to go, do you?"

Dorjan opens his mouth, closes it and stares through the raindrops across the clearing to the distant pillars marking the Southern Road, the path to the Blair Farm. "I know Jenny's alive. I don't know if your sister still is. But," he adds before Charlotte can curse him, "you've already got something no one, and I mean no other velidevour, could possibly have."

Charlotte snorts. "What, an inedible heart?"

He ignores Charlotte's remark, and mischief flows from the green eye to the blue. "The blood dagger. What you pulled out of... you know who... is *extremely* powerful. I can't promise it will be loyal to you, but for now that is your bargaining chip for your sister and your one shot at getting out alive." He turns to leave.

"Hey." Charlotte bites her lip. It hurts watching the last connection with her world walk away from her... weird as it is, but still. "Be careful." She holds out her hand.

99

A corner of Dorjan's mouth lifts, just for a moment, before he takes her hand and squeezes it. "You as well, Charlotte. I am glad to have met you." His blue eye flashes lightning bright as he bolts into the rain on two feet. With a howl he arches forward, and black fire ripples along his body to create fur, tail, paws, head. Raindrops hiss and steam as flame crackles to the clearing's edge and out of sight.

"The lock is undone." Whatever magic Arlen's worked has drained his body brutally. New wrinkles line his face, and veins bulge on his hands. He pants fast, shallow breaths and swoons backward. Charlotte runs and catches him before his head can hit the floor.

"I'm sorry, sir." Charlotte gives him the title because, dammit, he deserves it. "I wish whatever you did wouldn't hurt you like that."

"Thank you, a moment, thank you, and I will escort you below." He manages to sit upright, but crooking his legs pains him too much.

"Just tell me how to get there and I'll go by myself. Anna's my responsibility. You've got a sick man up here."

Arlen wipes his brow. "I know. But this must be done. It must."

Ember, meanwhile, stands dumb at Arlen's side, eyes on the blood dagger thrust in Charlotte's belt. "They said it could not happen."

"Yeah, yeah, I pulled out Excalibur." Charlotte reaches for the blood dagger and places it inside the satchel. "I won't let you come with me, not in your condition, sir." She stares pointedly at Arlen, concern in her voice. "Dorjan's out there, and I'll be down there, and we'll put things right, okay? You and Ember stay here with the Blood"—Charlotte stops herself, rethinking the name as she quickly rebraids her hair—"the injured guy."

Ember's eyes grow wide. Obscenely wide. Bird-meets-anaconda wide. "He is awake? So he commanded Jamie to—"

"No, no, he's only been conscious a few minutes." Arlen's breathing slows to normal, but sweat continues to drip down his neck and temples, face ash gray, eyes hollow. "The Lady is the root of this, Ember, as always. And she must be as desperate as we are, if not more so."

Charlotte stands before the basement door. Smells seep through the lock and under the door that weren't there before: dust, damp, earth, ashes. Arlen's magic must have been really powerful to block even smells out.

If you have to lock it behind me, sir, you should. I will find another way out.

Charlotte wraps her fingers around the knob, and pulls.

A man stands before her, wearing a frayed gray tunic and pants, feet bare and scarred. His skin is rich like earth, his eyes and wrist like Ember's.

"About time you opened that door."

Charlotte hears Ember suck air through her teeth. "What are you doing here, Campion?"

Campion saunters past Charlotte and peers about as though he were house-hunting. "Ember, always a pleasure." He even bows. What manners. He also smiles. That grin chills the air so quickly that goose bumps ripple down Charlotte's neck and arms. "When this young lady didn't follow me down through the marble tree, I assumed the dog had lured her here instead."

Lightning strikes so close that the crack makes Charlotte

and Campion jump.

Ember doesn't wince once. "Three is enough, Campion. Children should not be touched."

Campion distorts his face and gasps in mock offense. "I'm afraid I disagree there. Wretch that I am, I've come to enjoy the taste of youth. Soooo. Gooooood." He licks his teeth.

Ember cannot pull Charlotte away in time. Or, she chooses not to. Either way: CRACK! Campion teeters, cradling his jaw as Charlotte shoves him into the wall, pinning him there with her forearm against his neck, her knee against his groin. "Where is my sister?"

A wheezing call, like a steam train whistle, momentarily brings everything to a freeze-frame as one, two, three, five fingers grip the wall like talons. The Bloody Prince shuffles into view, legs shaking.

"What are you doing, boy?" Arlen manages to walk over without stumbling and works to pry the talon fingers free.

More wheezing. The Bloody Prince is speaking, and Arlen moves closer to hear his words.

"I'm sorry, Miss Charlotte, but he commands you not to go down there."

"But—"

Arlen interrupts Charlotte to continue, "Ember, if you please. Now."

Ember hobbles to Arlen's side to help prop the Bloody Prince away from the wall. The wound on his chest is completely dry. He stretches his hands out toward Charlotte as though pleading for her to grasp them. She does not reach back toward him.

Campion observes everything as he coughs and pops his jaw back into place. "So let me see. You show up, and this delightful fellow awakens. I doubt Cein expected *that* to happen. You do not disappoint after all, Mistress Music. Care to see your sister?"

The Prince's inner clouds storm, their grayness thick and falling, crashing.

Arlen ushers the Bloody Prince to the stairs and supports him there. "Since when do you care about one meager human, Campion?"

Think meager think meager think meager. I'm just a pathetic, angry girl.

"Since that meager human broke three of my ribs on the borderland, and now," he shifts his square jaw this way and that, "has punched me hard enough to dislodge a tooth. Step down, old man." Campion spits glittery blood and the errant tooth right at Arlen's feet. "In the Pits your command is dust, and that's precisely where this young lady wishes to go."

The Bloody Prince coughs and staggers forward.

"She deserves an escort." Arlen's voice bites with every word.

"Fine. Send this princely fellow along with her." Campion kicks the Bloody Prince in the ribs so close to the wound that he crumples in on himself like burning paper.

Arlen grabs Campion's collar and lifts him, single-handed, up, overhead, down, SMACK. Weakness gone. Sweat glistens, fists harden. "Never. Do that. Again."

Charlotte turns and then hovers facing the doorway, her back warmed by the lamps and fires burning throughout Rose House. She touches her father's pendant, looks back on these... veli-people, all occupied with themselves.

NOW!

Not alone. The Voice in her heart tries in vain to pull her back.

Yes, alone.

Charlotte vaults down the steps and falls into cold darkness.

Audition

"Sweet C?"

Charlotte's head throbs.

"Sweet C!"

A lot.

She opens her eyes to happy sunshine and a paisley couch and maroon afghan. To walls bedecked with fabric art. To the smells of dark roast and chocolate chip scones.

Charlotte rolls into the couch and snuggles deeper. She's been waiting for a morning like this for years: no more Uncle Mattie leers, no more Grandma cackles.

Cackles?

Did she hear one just now? *Oh stop, Charlie, it's one of those dumb waking dream things. You've had plenty of nightmares before. Just finish waking up already.*

"There you are." Aunt Gail flurries in.

Aunt Gail never "walks": her body overflows with movement, and sometimes those movements want to go in different directions. Even though Aunt Gail comes into the living room, her left foot keeps tapping toward the door. Charlotte turns to watch her aunt plunk a steaming mug down on the coffee table and then bustle in the most roundabout way through the room, bumping the coffee table in the process. Coffee slurps over the mug onto the floor. "Napping's not like you. Feel okay, hon?"

"Yeah, I think so."

Aunt Gail sits on the couch next to Charlotte's feet, her shoulder-length gray hair styled with attitude. But Charlotte doesn't think too much of Aunt Gail's hair. She keeps checking her eyes, because... because something inside, some voice in her somewhere, says it's important. "Nerves, I guess."

"Let's see if you've got a fever. Anna!" she calls, "where's that thermometer?"

The holler's answered lickety-split quick as Anna skips into view with a thermometer. She's dressed nicely.

Nicely?

Bubble pop. Ballerina twirl. "Whatcha think? Thought I'd come to the audition and see what all the fuss is about." Tongue click.

Der hey, that's only been the source of Charlotte's obsession for at least six months. That's what hatched the whole plan of taking Anna, getting her to safety... but—but didn't something happen? "My audition." Even the words sound a bit lost to Charlotte, like she'd never conceived of such a plan.

"Well yes, your scholarship audition. Good golly Miss Molly, maybe we do need to call the university. Sure you're all right?" Aunt Gail presses her hands against Charlotte's cheeks and forehead. Soft and plump.

But she doesn't smell right, does she? That cautionary whisper refuses to shut up.

Of course Aunt Gail smells all right. She burns things all the time. Probably had to clean the ashes out of the fireplace.

What about Anna?

Dunno, she's not close enough to smell.

"Coming, Sweet C?" prods Aunt Gail. She and Anna stand in the doorway, waiting for Charlotte to join them.

Something hangs about Charlotte's shoulder that smells like rubbing alcohol. Pain shoots through her hand every time she tries to open and close it.

And where's the spilled coffee from a minute ago? Charlotte doesn't know. She doesn't want to know.

The ash smell grows stronger, but how can that be? She should be smelling old coffee grounds and hops, roses and woodsmoke—not death. She stares at the North Woods Monster mug on the coffee table. It has glowing purple eyes and pointed teeth, like—

STOP. Just a nightmare.

Aunt Gail's living room is precisely that: Aunt Gail's. All her favorite projects hang here. Mounds of yarn and half-crocheted whatnots stand stacked near the fireplace. Every piece of furniture a thrift store find, including the piano. Floor-to-ceiling bookshelves crammed with fantasies and mysteries. And in the corner, her go-bag, in case she gets called in to pilot the Flight for Life helicopter. It all looks perfect.

Looks deceive.

"Here now. Why not do a final run of your audition?" Aunt Gail dances her way over to the couch and sits. Anna does the same. The piano practically glows like some holy relic, waiting.

Bubble pop. "Penny for your thoughts." Anna pulls out a quarter, perches it between her fingers and begins its walk —clink, it drops to the floor. Picks it up again, starts to walk —clink. Anna hasn't had problems with that trick in years.

Anna smiles broadly.

Rather sloppy of them, don't you think?

Bubbles popping in the mind. The perfection over the rot. The teeth. The eyes.

Remember.

As Charlotte counts her steps toward the piano, she feels

106

a lightness touch her face and then tear away, again and again, like walking through a room full of cobwebs. Yet there isn't a single cobweb to be seen.

Leave.

Charlotte at last pinpoints that friend inside: it's coming from her heart, where Dad's pendant always touched. But then Anna took it, didn't she? But then Charlotte had to pull it from a tongue of black marble, didn't she? But then—

Charlotte brushes the cobwebs from her face and torso and senses a leather strap across her chest that she cannot see. A leather strap to a satchel from a girl on a farm where a raven and man with pointed teeth hunt and massacre people.

OH GOD, I remember, and now I'm inside their world. What have they done to mine?

Anna no longer chews her gum.

Aunt Gail's voice shoots through the air and speckles it all pretty like fireworks. "Sweet C? C'mon, we ain't got all day. Your audition starts soon. Lay it on us while you can."

Now seated, Charlotte rests her hands on the piano bench. "Just need to think a moment." She drags her left hand along her hip and leg, pushing the invisible satchel into her lap. "Always take a breath"—right hand on the flap—"to make sure" —opens it—"you don't start"—hand in—"too"—there it is— "fast."

Her hand finds the blood dagger and slices through the air.

The blood dagger slits a hole in the room itself.

No longer Aunt Gail's. No longer anywhere. The slit hisses as it widens, burning away the cozy living room to reveal…

Dark rock. Dry. Cold. A reek of death and ash. Light slithers along the ceiling in dim pulses, as though through tubes. The light's very soft, even colored with calming hues of lavender, violet, plum.

Ignore the light! the Voice slaps Charlotte from the inside.

Charlotte wriggles, realizes she's not even on a piano bench anymore. *This seat's rock too. And—tangling me?* Odd hair tangles around Charlotte's weaponless hand, stinging like bleach. She yanks herself free, holds her hand up to the hypno-light: whatever those hairs are, they still writhe on her hand, their ends in the air like they're sniffing.

"The hell?" She shakes her hand—they don't come off. The ends begin poking her skin. Pushing her skin.

They want in.

"Off. Now." She's got a dagger, and by God, she's going to use it, even if it's just slicing hairs—

But it doesn't slice the hairs. It burns them. Shrill smoke hisses and whips about her hand as the hairs burn off. No more bleach stinging. No stinging at all.

A new, soft stinging at her hip: the hairs on the rock where she sits. Charlotte rolls off the rock, lands on all fours. Beneath her hands run clusters of white roots, knotted and gnarled. They run up the walls to the ceiling (*Those roots can glow?!*) and over to the rock where she sat (*freakin' roots were drilling INto me?*). Now she sees the pulsing roots are taking their light *away* from her rock. They reveal the room to be a cramped little space, like some sort of landing. The pulsing roots lose their light beyond the doorway blocked by the fairy-freaks standing next to what was Aunt Gail's couch.

"Well." Fake–Aunt Gail's voice cracks and tumbles into a male register. "Well, that was a pretty trick."

Fake-Anna says nothing. She's evidently swallowed her gum too.

Charlotte repositions her fingers on the hilt. *Damn, your fear smells good.* "I'd be happy to show the Lady, after I get my sister back. The real one."

Fake-Anna pouts. Her lower lip turns to ash, then her whole self, like a dried-out sandcastle blows away in the wind. And out from the sand cloud hops a small mouse.

Fake–Aunt Gail gently picks it up, smiles kindly at the cute little mousey-wousey face, and throws it as hard as she can through the dark doorway. She turns to Charlotte, and her entire face transforms from kindly to vicious. "You know, that does feel pretty good. Think she'll break a few ribs too?"

Charlotte's head still pounds, and her hand still aches with the bandages all dusty and torn, but that's nothing new. Hell, she's fallen on burning cigarette butts and broken glass during fights. *This ain't shit*, she thinks as she tells her hand to open and close, *because dammit, I can and I WILL. Shift the legs, send the throb to the eyes to sharpen the senses. Dagger at the ready.* "Campion."

Fake–Aunt Gail shatters around him. That vicious grin doesn't change, though. "You know, I do believe I am starting to see why Cein took a shine to you."

But for all the menace in his words, Campion does not strike, doesn't even approach. "Where did that come from?" He gives the blood dagger a quick glance, but Charlotte can see his eyes are drawn to stare at it longer.

Deep down, under the anger and the fear, the Voice in Charlotte's heart proposes a reason: *He dares not approach you when you carry the blood dagger.*

Maybe Dorjan was onto something about this weapon being a bargaining chip, after all.

Charlotte rips the remains of her bandages off. Her palm stings when she tests her hold on the sheathed hunting knife, her sliced skin raw and angry, so she lets her left hand simply hover while adjusting her grip on the blood dagger. Charlotte

109

walks toward the doorway where Campion chucked the fairy-mouse. "This the way to the Lady? Too damn dark to see." She takes a few steps into the tunnel and leans against the wall. It wriggles.

The whole damn tunnel's overgrown with braids, twists, knots of white root. Lavender light, snowflake delicate, pulses away from Charlotte's feet and poofs out, just like a handful of fresh snow when you blow upon it. The pulses shrink, scatter, but all move in one direction: In. Down. The cold ash wafts out at Charlotte, wraps around her shoulders, and pulls her in. A giant mouth, breathing. Wanting.

"To the Lady? Depends." Campion perches upon the first of the floor roots, his toes wrapped around like hooks. "You going to behave with that thing?" pointing to the blood dagger.

Charlotte tenses. *Dad wouldn't have wasted ten seconds on a big mouth like you*, she thinks as a jab stings her temple. Her arm snaps up and out, driving the blood dagger into a root on the wall. Its tendril catches fire like a match, fast and hell-bright, before hissing out a couple of inches from Charlotte's head. *Damn, that was too close.* "Well, you can either take me to your leader like a good peon and find out, or you can watch me stab every single root in this tunnel and make Smokey Bear very, very sad."

Campion's teeth create a crescent moon that snatches hints of pulsing light. "Yes, I suppose I should. The Lady's just as eager to meet you as you are her. This way." He turns and walks on the balls of his feet, the roots never once flailing at him as he fades far too quickly into the borderless dark. The pulsing lavender light does not follow him, but remains around Charlotte. Waiting.

The necklace wrapped around Charlotte's wrist rattles like broken chainmail.

The Voice braces itself against Charlotte's sternum: *Be aware!*

Oh, Charlotte's not going to be stupid about these roots again. The blood dagger's warmth spreads from her palm to her feet and helps her focus. She's got to try and walk on those roots without bracing herself.

If the hair-sized roots can dig into skin lickety-split quick, there's no telling what one of the python-sized roots on the wall can do if she touches it for too long. She presses her weight onto one root, then another. Her breath catches at the groan, the crack, of roots buckling, but not giving way completely. She's sure it's just a few inches of roots cushioning her feet from the floor.... Unless this is no tunnel, but a bridge over a fathomless nothing.... *Stop it, Charlie. One, two. What would Dad do? Three, four. Know the score.*

Rot, age, old bones, twice-burned ashes—they choke the air like gasoline. What she feels is cold. Lots of cold.

All she can trust is what she sees, and what she sees right now is white, brittle wood beneath her, the lavender light pulsing more intensely now from her feet and spreading out and down the tunnel.

Occasional claw marks.

One bloody handprint that begins on one root and is dragged across seven more before vanishing. It's not a big handprint. There are little traces of purple in it too, almost like purple glitter.

Glitter. *Didn't Anna have purple glitter? NO. Five, six, get your freakin' act together, Charlie, and focus. Seven, eight, Dad, God, I wish you were here.*

"Charlie?" The voice is rich, deep, and kind.

And dead.

Charlotte's free hand wavers when a new breeze of gunpowder and chili wisps by. "D-dad?" *The power of this place can't summon the dead. Dad's buried in holy ground far from here.*

The lazing crescent moon returns, brighter than before.

Two violet stars glow in the darkness, sweetly bright, alive.

"He can also take you to your sister, if that is what you wish."

The lavender pulses of light beat faster and faster, racing to catch up with her heartbeat, she prays Campion cannot hear it from his perch among the last of the tunnel roots. His eyes are swirling, almost glowing, as the rest of him turns still, like the living tree-bones behind him.

"After all, this place is where dreams come true."

Charlotte slips backward but catches herself against the wall. One quick grab of a root. That's all. With curses. That's all.

But in that one moment, a light pulses in the roots that's different from the others: it's both lavender and golden, entwining like yin and yang as it glows through roots along the tunnel ceiling, down the other wall, into the floor, and then—darkness. Just like everything else past Campion.

Except for something new: A badge, shining like a star.

"Hey there, sweetheart. I've missed you."

"Dad!" Charlotte trips, twists one ankle, ignores it—*It's Dad! He's here for me, ME.* Her pendant tinkles so lightly against its chain, so hot in all this cold, but surely that has to be for Dad, for his soul here, ready to come out—

STOP! NOT REAL NOT REAL!

I will MAKE him real.

The Voice thrusts itself into her hand and cinches her fingers tight around the blood dagger. She doesn't wonder why the roots stop stinging her, or why Campion bows to let her by.

The tunnel of roots opens to a soundless darkness. Here, the roots once forming the walls and ceiling of the tunnel snake out to climb along walls that… Charlotte cannot see how high up they go. Cathedral high? Cavernous. There is a faint, faint pulse above her, and she can only assume it means the roots extend up to that ceiling too. The pulses seem to go in and out, in and out, like they weave through the dark rock walls.

Stinging.

She looks down at roots that are now anaconda thick, half a dozen tightly braided to form a narrow bridge. She cannot see beneath: a mist lingers there, damp and rotting like her grandmother's heart. And fine hairy rootlets reach up to pierce her sneakers.

Charlotte hisses a "Shit!" as she tries to slide backward, but there's too little room. She's got to move on. She cannot stand still, not when those little hairs glow just with the touch of her, sending new pulses of lavender light toward the badge. Her "Shit!" seems to spiral down into the mist and through it, leaving a star-shaped crack of darkness in its wake. Chatters leak upward to her, followed by a scratching, scratching, scratching.

"C'mon, Charlie."

All at once every smell of family smothers her: pumpkin cookies, sweat and cop car, berry body splash.

The lavender pulses flow into a white pillar behind the badge. No, not a pillar: the roots beneath Charlotte's feet join with it. The roots on the cathedral ceiling wind and twist down into it. A hundred thin trunks, just like that black tree, that tangled mess of nasty roots she saw with Dorjan.

This is a tree. Hanging from the ceiling. Upside down.

But that doesn't matter, not when she walks among the stinging hairs toward the badge, the new pulses that shape his form, peeling away from the pillar-trunk to reveal windblown ginger hair, eyes bright like Christmas trees.

NOT. REAL.

It's real if I want it to be, and I want it to be, because when I want him he is HERE, don't you see? I smell home, I am home.

LISTEN. And the Voice in her heart sends the prickles up her chest, up her neck, to her ears. Charlotte's ears fill with pressure, so much pressure she's going to scream until—

Bubble pop.

Shrieks and caws, tails and claws. Charlotte sees only the mist and her father, smells only home smells, yet hears only monsters skulking beneath her feet. The mist is spongy, damp, and so opaque Charlotte can't even see her sneakers.

"Charlie, sweetheart, I've missed you so much."

Retreat NOW. The Voice shakes her heart.

Shut up. He's right there. I can get him out, get Anna out, go and get Mom, and we'll all be happy. Stop RUINING it. She doesn't even mind the stinging. It's just her feet falling asleep, happens all the time. The pulses beneath her feet might as well be a runway, so lovely and lit and shining toward him, shining on *him*, and he's there, badge so bright—

The first shot strikes.

Blood dribbles out of a hole in her father's chest. But the smile never leaves his face.

"I love you so much, sweetheart."

Another shot, and he leans against the trunk. His mouth clicks open and closed as though his On switch is stuck.

"I love you s—"

And another.

"—o much, sweetheart."

And another.

"DA-AD!" Charlotte bolts into the line of fire. It makes no difference. *In the name of all that's holy, stop it STOP IT STOP IT!* But Campion remains behind her, laughing, fucking, laughing.

Blood flows freely from his sieve of a chest. The badge fades. The uniform decays.

The Voice in her heart sends the prickle down her arms.

Let go of that dagger and your sister will die.

"N-no…" At last close enough to touch, Charlotte confronts a face not really her dad's. The smile and eyes stare back, hollow like a doll's.

The pillar shivers, the doll dissipates. Its dusty remains slither down the white pillar and into the mist like thousands of baby snakes, home to Mama.

Sweat hides Charlotte's tears as she holds the blood dagger over her heart. "Anna! Where are you?"

"An-an-an Ha-ha!" Whispers and echoes mock her.

The mist sucks itself into the tree. Charlotte looks down. Nope, the floor of the cavern doesn't end just a few inches under her feet. That's got to be a three-story drop, easy —dotted by pairs of little violet lights. Eyes.

A thousand hairs peel off the trunk before Charlotte's face. They float freely, growing out to her, their tips close enough to tickle her nose.…

Like hell! Charlotte crab-crawls back and hunches forward in defense. *All right, you bastards. See me here, above you? I'm not scared. Look inside my head, and know I will drive this bloody dagger into every one of you until I get my sister back.*

But the hairs take her first.

They weave spider-fast over her weaponless hand and feet, tying her, trapping her, to the delight of the little lights below.

Like hell you'll bring me down.

Warmth floods the hand holding the blood dagger, and its engraved feathers glow as she throws all her weight into her arm and swings—

The root bridge shrieks as it chars and crumbles into ash.

And Charlotte falls.

The Lady

A root snags Charlotte's legs and tightens, bungee-jerking her body before she hits the floor. Jenny's satchel rips off her body and lands with a thump, a couple of feet below her face. The blood dagger never leaves her hand.

From her inverted position, Charlotte twists to get a better view of the cavern. In addition to the glowing and white tree with its labyrinthine tangle of roots, she sees staircases appear and disappear into the rock. Some connect entrances to tunnels, while a couple step down to the cavern floor.

Dark shapes hover in the holes and on the ground. The shapes move closer and become creatures, become people, become both at once: not enough fur or feathers, claws and teeth too big for the body, and also humanlike, with voices that can almost be understood, but not quite. Not quite human, these creatures are the Incomplete.

"I knew there was something off about you." Burly Smith hobbles into view. What's left of him, anyway. His limbs have widened and flattened, and claws have replaced several but not all of his fingers. Patches of fur grow through his Scenic Tours uniform. He pulls the greasy kerchief off his wrist to reveal a vine tattoo pulsing light. The face is half-badger, half-human, the teeth all animal.

What the hell has happened here? Why is everyone alive and decaying at the same time? "I know who you really are." Charlotte keeps her voice steady. "You're Cein." She points at Cein's belly with the tip of the dagger. "You left my shoes out. You wanted me to know you had Anna."

Cein laughs as he picks up Jenny's bag. "Told ya, sweetheart—I couldn't kill all of you by myself out there." He shreds it like a piece of junk mail. "Now here… I got plenty of help here."

"You need all these freaks just to take down little ol' me?" Charlotte tsk-tsks. "You know we humans have a word for someone like you. Coward." She watches Cein's stupid grin shrink and no longer cares that she's upside down. At least in this moment, she's triumphant. "So go on. Kill me. Coward."

Fur bristles through more of his uniform. Cein grinds his teeth. His claws are poised to strike.

"Enough," says a voice from the tree. A female voice, low and sweet, almost singing. "Who are you?"

Be aware! The Voice's cry from her heart rushes through her. The pendant catches and amplifies the light from the tree in its white petals.

"My name…" Charlotte slices the vine and flips to her feet, "is Charlotte." Brushing the ash off, she straightens her shoulders. "And you"—she aims the blood dagger's point where her father (*just a damn doll, Charlie, NOT your dad*) bled out against the trunk hanging in the air—"have my sister."

The chatter builds like a flood of cicadas among the roots.

Crack! The lowest branches split the trunk open, yet its brittle orange leaves refuse to fall. The white wood creaks and curves as it opens like a great flower, bends back, rejoins, and is made whole again.

The tree has become a throne, and on it sits the Lady.

Hell of an entrance.

117

She's draped in a silver dress that hangs limply around her shoulders. Her skin glows like the tree, her white-blond hair matchstick straight. She leans to the side and holds her chin in her hand. A long white finger traces her smile. "So. You are the outsider that intrigues my loyal adviser. Welcome." She rises. "I am Orna, Lady of the Pits, Ruler of the River Vine Velidevour."

Everyone bows—all except Cein, who beams with pride, and Charlotte, who doesn't give a fuck. Even the branches demonstrate their fealty, bending low to crown her body in orange gold and form a stairwell to the ground.

Charlotte tilts the blood dagger so the Lady can see it reflect light off its steel feathers. "I want my sister back."

Cein sidles up right next to Charlotte, close enough to slash her with his claws or at the very least disarm her. But he doesn't touch her. He just keeps ogling the blade. Reeking of roadkill, he heaves into her face, "Where'd you get that?"

The Lady's face furrows, her head swaying back and forth like a snake's. "My, what a pretty thing you've found. Let me see it, and I will show you what you seek."

One eager half-rat hisses, "Allow me, my lady!" and skulks toward Charlotte, its fingers of skin, fur, and exposed bone reaching for the blade.

Cein yanks him back by the neck. "You idiot! That's a blood dagger. Touch it and you're dead."

"All velidevour, take one step back. All humans, one step forward." Cein sweeps his arm with a flourish.

The half-rat obeys, because of course he would, with Cein and the Lady right there.

But Charlotte's far from obedient. "To hell with you and your stupid games, Burly Man." And not terribly bright at times.

His badger eye sparks like flint on stone. "Oh we aren't

playing a game, sweetheart, not yet. Because when I play," he leans in, and the saliva lining his warped jaw oozes out onto Charlotte's sneakers, "I play *dirty*."

Charlotte narrows her eyes, and says very carefully, "I bet you do."

Cein's grin stretches. This could be the start of the game already. "Now," he waves a claw, "go on up and say hello."

Roots snake along the ground and lasso her hips. Charlotte tries to sweep the dagger down to strike, but not fast enough: they wind around her arms and yank her up too quickly, too high. A fall now would kill her.

Being this close to the Lady compels even the Voice in Charlotte's heart to hide. The Lady's beauty is unnatural, ghost-like. Her eyes aren't violet like Cein's, nor are they full of feeling like Arlen's. These are nothing but orbs of darkness with no hope of light.

"Now, human, show me the dagger."

"Where's my sister?"

The Lady smiles. Her cheekbones lift, and it's almost a sweet face. But her smile slowly exposes black painted teeth, spanning from temple to temple, and she's a sitting night-mare. "In time. Now, *show me*."

One thin root raises Charlotte's arm like she's a puppet. Threadlike tendrils sprout and worm around her fingers. They want her to release the blood dagger.

Like. Hell.

The Voice inside Charlotte's heart bolsters her: *Your courage intimidates her. Do not falter now!*

The dagger does not fall.

The Lady's face, especially her smile, smooths to a mask as she eyes the dagger. "Curious," she says, her voice musical and honeyed. "I have not seen this weapon in many years. How did you get it?"

"Found it." *I sound like Anna with a designer shirt stuffed into her coat. Stare me down with your black holes all you want, Lady—I ain't saying shit until I see my sister.*

"She woke the Bloody Prince." Campion leaps several feet off the stone stair and lands softly next to Cein. "He is alive and healing as we speak."

The velidevour break into a hissing fit. Charlotte can smell their dead breath as they chatter under her feet.

The Lady clutches her dress and bites her lower lip. "If he is healing, then soon he will return."

Cein snarls at Campion. "Don't get her hopes up."

"I didn't say he asked for her," Campion says with a lot more volume than a peon should use. "Merely that he is awake. Perhaps if a human could succeed in doing what velidevour could not, then the power of his blood dagger is dead."

"Strange. I would not have expected that of his powers." The Lady pulls back the sleeve on her right arm to reveal a hand with a silver ring, its band a collection of delicate vines. A dozen silver leaves hold a stone: too opaque to be a gem, with deep purple pulsing inside it like a heart. "It is my turn now. Is this whom you seek?"

She waves her hand: rivulets of oil and lavender glow like black-light halos around the Lady's head, then ripple up, up, up to the ceiling, up to the thickest roots. They wriggle and penetrate much of the arboreal canopy, revealing spaces filled—filled with people.

Dangling like macabre Christmas ornaments.

Anna. Her chest flutters with shallow breaths. She has no wounds or bruises, but...

No. Oh God no.

Rootlets tap into her skin like veins and pulse with Anna's

life. With every heartbeat, a few more buds form upon the white tree's branches. With every heartbeat, a bud transforms into a leaf of hammered gold. With every heartbeat, Anna's skin sallows, her hair thins, and her bones grow more pronounced. She is smiling. She is dying.

And she is not alone.

Others hang by the roots. Pale, crumpled, perhaps dead. She knows them at once: Jackpot Sweenil. Studchin. Mumbles. All from her traveling group. She sat by them for hours one day, but the next? Gone from her memory and everyone else's, as if they had never existed at all.

And under them, even more hands, feet, arms, dry like corn husks. And GI Joe pajamas.

Charlotte yanks at her roots and launches herself up, but the roots hang her, spin her, make her a marionette for the Lady's amusement. "What are you doing to them?"

"As you humans breathe air and feed upon animals, we of the velidevour breathe desire and feed upon dreams," the Lady says as she stands behind Charlotte. "This was once a place filled with travelers seeking fulfillment to their fantasies, and we gave, gladly. The wells flowed together, and the water road made our world whole."

Charlotte looks back at her, the visions of trees like this all over the world, of kidnapped children, forgotten by everyone, buried alive. Her body pulses. Rage.

Yet the Voice inside her stays calm. *You cannot yet reach Anna on your own. You need the tree to free her, and for that you need this creature.*

Hide under the rage. I have something she wants, and she has something I want. She's got a funky mood ring with superpowers, and I've got a blade that can hack magic stuff. I am not afraid of her.

Orna waves her hand again, and Anna's cell phone appears out of nowhere. "Then, you humans evolved. You learned to harness power and knowledge with science. And so you began to fulfill your own wishes." A wave, and the phone's gone. "You found ways to satisfy even your darkest hungers. We, far more powerful than you could ever hope to be, had too little magic to retain one form and hunt among you. And without the hunt, we began to starve."

Chattering. Gnashing. Some groups huddle together to support the almost-dead, while others snarl over their anger and desperation. The groups soon meld together to form a ring of shadows beneath Charlotte and the tree. The stink of their desperation is all too familiar to Charlotte: the parking lots, the bets, the fists flying in her face.

"A princeborn family conquered this land and transformed it into a prison for their son. Then he was struck down," her hand gestures toward Charlotte and the dagger, "and I took his place. No princeborn family will come here. They dammed the water road. Our sacred white tree began to wither. So I," the oil eyes glisten, "gave it new life."

Charlotte follows the Lady's gaze to the tree. Its golden leaves begin to sparkle and fall. But they never reach the ground. The velidevour are waiting with hands outstretched for their manna. Some scrape and snap over it. Some simply shovel it into their mouths without thinking. A few share with those too weak to reach for themselves. Even Campion and Cein snatch fistfuls and eat like men starved for days. Within moments, the tree is completely bare.

The Lady surveys all this with lightless eyes and contented smile. She turns to Charlotte. "It lets one live in dreams, forever."

More roots slink into view among the bodies. They wrap around Anna's legs.

Don't you DARE cover her up. "You can't take kids. They, they don't get consequences, choices. They don't understand!"

"They understand enough. Want and need are the same

to them. And their dreams stretch beyond the simple covets. I often find they last far longer than the fully grown."

"You, BITCH!" Charlotte rapidly swivels her wrist, snapping the blood dagger through the branch binding her hand. With a quick downward slash, she frees her legs. As the tree bucks against her escape, Charlotte slingshots herself into the air and over the Lady's head, dragging the branches that still bind her. Unsuccessfully. New branches trap Charlotte's free hand and legs. Tied top and bottom, her belly exposed. One swipe of Cein's claws and out'll go her innards. Knows it too, the way his bloody grin grows across that split face of his.

"Do not think we hunt only children. We seek the elderly, the strong, the sick. We seek all." The Lady comes within a matchstick of Charlotte's face. "For all want something."

Charlotte swallows hard. "What I want is my sister."

"Is that so?" The Lady pulls back, amused. "Then who was this?" She points into the darkness.

The badge shines like a star. **"Charlie?"**

How dare you take the good and warp it into playthings. How dare you go into my head and make him evil, like you.

"Charlie, come to Daddy."

What, you think you can make me cry? Good luck. I know pain and I know death and I know you are scared shitless of what's in my hand, so, "Stop it."

The Lady laughs. "No, no. What you want—what you and your sister both want—is a life free of each other. You think the death of your father destroyed your chance to pursue your own dreams, so you forced your wishes upon your young, 'innocent' sister."

Sharp cold lacerates Charlotte's nerves, like an icicle stabbed into the book of her deepest desires. She hadn't even realized this most private diary had been thumbed through. "How do—"

"We all know, Miss Charlotte. Every velidevour, princeborn, and commoner alike, is a dream eater. We could all feel that want the moment you arrived on the borderland. But we never take all from Cein's traps. Only those who desire so much that they *ask* to be taken. In return for their wishes, they give us their lives."

As though by instinct Campion, Cein, and the other veli-devour begin to chant. Not one harmony, not one insane giggle. The words push themselves out and spread through the air like yeast in bread, pressing into Charlotte, around Charlotte, down upon Charlotte. The Voice in her heart struggles to keep her ribs from buckling....

"Wish for sleep
Sleep and dream
Dream your wish
Your life we'll keep."

The prickle in her chest migrates into Charlotte's ears. It feels like she's underwater, floating, discombobulated. The pressure... "Why don't you wish yourselves the hell out of here, then?!" she shouts, hoping she sounds louder outside than in her head. Charlotte's ears pop.

The chanting stops, but not the growls. Some in the back scrape their claws slowly across the stairs.

Oooo, I've hit a sore spot.

"What do you think these marks mean?" Campion points to his vine tattoo. "We didn't ask for this. We're all branded like cattle. Sure, we can move outside the Wall, but we can't eat out there or these damn marks choke us to death. The only way that we can be completely free is for the Wall to be destroyed."

The Lady's fingers trace the air around the blade that Charlotte still holds in the air above them. "Now, Campion, do

124

not give up hope. Perhaps we could all truly be free, Incomplete and Complete velidevour alike, if we had the power. That dagger, Charlotte, would give it to us." Another smile. "I could release your sister when you give it to me." Her adorned hand reaches out for Charlotte. The magic within the silver ring crackles.

Rock surrounds them. Starving, half-dead velidevour surround them. Life-sucking magic roots surround Anna, way out of reach. At least she isn't in pain.

Lies. That killer's not gonna let anyone go.

The Voice in her heart grips her soul and says with every ember of hope, every spark of strength: *You will not die yet.*

The bellows set such a fire coursing through Charlotte that she cannot help but smirk and say, "I think I'll keep it," as her hand tightens around the blood dagger.

Daggers and Monsters

The Lady's pretty face doesn't crinkle once. It doesn't have to. The mood ring pulses faster. Sparks dance in it and on it with fervor.

The branches binding Charlotte twist tighter, pulling and stretching her body. *Oh, THIS is when I'm going to die instead of two seconds ago. Torn in two, what a way to go.*

"I will get it, Lady Orna!" a half-rat breaks from the shadow ring and scurries up the branch stair before Cein can stop it. The Lady moves aside as the Incomplete jumps into the air and clutches the blood dagger with its enormous paw-hands: "Here you go-OOOHH—"

A contained explosion blinds them all as it engulfs the shrieking half-rat. The tree cries out as its branches burn.

The flames snap Charlotte's bonds and lick her hair, and then stop. They don't burn her—they don't *want* to burn her. The staircase collapses, and Charlotte falls with a fireball of roots and branches to the ground. The cold crack of the stone ground runs through her body like an aftershock, jiggering her vision, her teeth—and her hand on the dagger. For a second, Charlotte remains still, eyes darting to the dagger as it smolders amid the ashes by her side.

The ring of shadow melts back to the cavern's wall, leaving

behind questions half-spoken, half-growled.

"Be silent!" the Lady orders. "Where is it, where is it?!"

Campion peers through a hole in the branches and finds Charlotte. His head cocks to the side, curious. "My, my. You *are* full of pretty tricks," he says.

"She's under the tree? Get her!" Cein crams himself into the crawl space, breaking some branches while others wilt out of the way. His claws scrape the ground just a few feet away from Charlotte's head.

Charlotte rolls for the blood dagger and then slashes at Cein's face. He howls in pain as she army-crawls to the far side of the tree. "I'll rip your heart out myself!" Charlotte hears the saliva and blood gurgle in his mouth as he curses her.

"That is enough, Cein!" No longer a voice from a sweet lullaby, the Lady sings with pain and anger. She reeks of it. The tree reeks of it.

Every branch above Charlotte pulls away, and she remains on the ground, exposed. Yet no velidevour approach her. Oh, they sit in their holes or on the stairs. But none of those half-animal–half-person half-dead things puts one foot on the cavern floor. They're done chattering and growling too. Just silent, waiting, taking it all in. Their eyes may shine, but so do a deer's in headlights. These guys are spooked.

Cein spits words in a different tongue as he presses his kerchief over the sparkling gash across his right cheek.

The Lady stands but a few feet from Charlotte, skin aglow. Her ring sparks. "Now, for the last time, human: lay the dagger at my feet."

Charlotte allows herself one last look up at the cavern ceiling. Her sister's up there. Sammy Blair's up there. So many others are probably up there, stolen from their families' memories to keep the half-dead half-dead longer.

Charlotte focuses on her father's pendant. The silver leaves glow with their own light, and the white rose petals sway. And there's a warmth to its touch on her wrist, as warm as the blood dagger in her hand.

Arise.

She winces, because landing on rock *hurts*, but she stands up. Her fingers adjust their grip on the hilt. Now, Charlotte casts her eyes upon the Lady. Her voice reaches deep down to the Voice in her heart, and together they form these words: "You are killing my sister, and you will kill me. But I will not die to feed you. I will burn and burn you with me. Unleash what is in me and I will lay you *to waste*."

Silence.

Until Campion gives a wolf whistle. Because whoever heard a squirrel whistle?

The Lady backs away. With each step, the stone on her hand glows brighter. A single ear-splitting note emanates from the Lady and echoes back from the cavern walls, magnified. Wisps of light encircle her right arm. "Your fate is here then. *Granach!*"

Cein howls, "Finally!" and makes for a tunnel with all the other velidevour.

Campion whistles again as he skips off. "Hope you've got something up those raggedy-ass sleeves of yours."

The tree shakes.

Charlotte stands ready.

The tree blossoms like a bone flower.

She pulls out Jenny's knife and stands with both blades ready.

Oil pours out of the open tree, saturating the rock. It creeps toward Charlotte. Rock and oil meet, and a fine green mist from the tree settles onto the oil and swims through it, culminating into two pulsing points.

Two eyes.

From rock and black fluid, *IT* forms. Its head grazes the tree roots high above. Its claws are large enough to crush any human. A turtle's head and body, armored all around, but a neck like a snake's, and impossibly fast. Its eyes flare green, and its sharp teeth hide a tongue that clicks and clacks.

Charlotte runs one way—SNAP—another way—SNAP—no way around it—SNAP—no way to hide from it.

Cein laughs from his hole. Other velidevour shrink into their hiding places, eyes dimmed with fear. The Lady reclines on the lowest branches of the white tree between the granach's massive legs, amused.

Charlotte can't go on like this—SNAP—make a move or lose your head—SNAP—need to get ahead but—

Too slow. Claw-fingers grab her arm: Cein, from his hole, reaching out. "No back door this time, sweetheart."

Acidic green mist swirls around the granach's teeth as it grins, just a few feet from Charlotte's face. Cein has one of her arms, but her other is free. The blood dagger arm.

Burn it.

Charlotte lets loose a battle cry and lacerates air—no, more than the air. The blood dagger sparks a wing-shaped flame: the feathers etched in metal burst into feathers of flame, growing from hilt to tip and beyond, slashing the granach's face. It roars and falls back, crushing branches and wall. Cein pulls back into his hole to protect himself, shoving Charlotte toward the falling debris.

The Lady is no longer amused. "What... what is thisss?" she hisses like a giant snake. Her ring pulses bright enough to blind Charlotte—*I'm dead*—and the granach rears its head for another attack. But it's just what Charlotte needs: the granach smashes its head into the base of the tree rooted in the ceiling.

Earth and corpses fall with rain—rain!

Rain in Charlotte's hair, rain on her face. Mud and grass. Lightning in the air. Thunder is coming. Earth will give way to sky, and this ash will be washed away.

But the corpses are still falling. Live bodies are still falling.

Anna's legs dangle in the air. The tree that drains her is all that saves her from a lethal fall.

Aim true or she dies.

The Lady of the Pits does not move. Black and violet fire envelope her arm. She shrieks. A single, piercing note that booms to a crescendo.

Charlotte turns back and runs toward the granach's head, her dagger poised to strike, but a massive green pupil transfixes her with its fury. The head pulls back to snap, she thrashes, and the dagger slits the granach's neck. Oil bleeds out. It rears its head and ROARS.

The force of its roar knocks Charlotte off-balance and then—SLAM—its foot is upon her, claws out, pinning her to the rock. Its head bobs back and forth above her, pleased with its catch.

The hand holding the blood dagger is trapped next to her hip. But the one holding Jenny's knife is not.

She stabs the granach's paw deep and true, but the knife does not penetrate: oil flows around the knife and melts it, absorbs it. Seeps toward her now empty hand. The oil reaches the chain, her pendant—*I love you, Anna.*

AIM TRUE!

She opens her mouth and bites down on the black-green skin as hard as she can. Thick pain fills Charlotte's throat. Her vision shatters into green stars.

The granach whimpers and releases her.

The Lady's fire dissipates, bewildered.

The granach lunges at Charlotte with mouth wide open. But Charlotte has the blood dagger ready. Through the mouth and into the brain. Charlotte crouches between jaws weakening in death, the blood dagger burning through the granach with little help from Charlotte.

The granach moans as its life oozes away into the rock from whence it came. The whole creature melts, leaving nothing but a pair of tiny dull emeralds afloat in an oily black mess.

Darkness overwhelms Charlotte.

We are dying.

Yup.

"You think you've won?!" Orna curls her fingers around the ring and draws out an orb of white fire to throw at Anna.

The tree withers around her: Anna's falling, falling too fast. Charlotte senses the Voice in her heart quicken, commanding her limbs to move, her lungs to breathe. Racked with pain, she leaps into the air, catches Anna in her arms, and returns to the ground, gently, as if gravity no longer matters.

Her dreams are draining from her like blood.... the crimson stage, where applause ebbs and flows like water, where snow and coal keys beckon. Where she sits beside her old self, all anger and cocked eyebrows: *Well? What shall we play next?*

The velidevour peer out from the tunnels, silent. Rain dampens the dust, and a flash of lightning reflects in their motionless eyes. No one's trying to read Charlotte. No one dares.

Claws in her back: Cein jerks Anna away, crushes Charlotte to the ground, and hauls her up by the scruff of her neck to stare into his stupid goddamn black painted teeth. "I don't know what you are," he says, as fur busts through his shirt seams, "but you lost. No one here's gonna save you."

Aim true.

Charlotte brandishes the dagger in his face. "I know." She twists from Cein's grasp and throws the blade.

It flies like a phoenix and finds the center of the white tree.

Roar-cries—low, swollen, unearthly—shimmer through the rain.

Oil and lavender gurgle out of the wounded tree.

The Lady struggles with her ring to keep her precious tree together, cursing the day Charlotte was born.

But the bone flower wilts, and chunks of trunk drop to the floor. Limbs decay, roots rot black through the ceiling. More rock and rain. The entire ceiling starts to crumble.

"My beautiful tree"—the Lady's jaw slackens and stretches—"my precious creation." As she rises into the air, black fire flows over her legs—"YOU…"

She is going to eat me.

Cein yanks Charlotte out of the way, his other claw stretching out before him. "No, Orna! We can't risk losing you to this thing!"

He shakes Charlotte for emphasis. She can't feel her feet, and black oil is getting into her eyes.

"Enough of this." Campion steps over Anna as if she were dead. "Let them go."

"Commoner! You dare order the Lady of the Pits!" Cein drops Charlotte.

Ass.

"Not her—you!" Campion turns on Cein. "Look at what's happened. All of this is your fault. If YOU hadn't gotten greedy, she would never have come here. Give her back the child, and they'll leave. They won't remember, ergo, they won't come back."

Cein growls, but does not fight back.

Charlotte crawls away before Cein can stomp on her again.

"Yes. Yes, get them away from here." Cein turns to the

Lady, who's swaying back and forth as she watches a staggering Charlotte retrieve the dagger and hold it with ease. "Campion is right. We let them go, they'll forget us. Then you can rebuild with the power of the blood dagger, claim your rightful place among the princeborns."

Charlotte stumbles in the downpour and the darkness. Her hand secures the blood dagger in the scabbard where Jenny's hunting knife once hugged her thigh. Then her nose catches the faintest trace of berry, and she can almost see a bit of glitter: Anna. Charlotte's fingers find hair and follow it to a face. Find the nose, feel the exhale.

Anna still breathes. Twitches. She opens her eyes in time to see lightning strike the final remnants of the tree above them. "Where are we? Charlie? What's going on? Are you bleeding? Charlie!"

"Shh. We're getting out of here. Take my hand."

Anna acts like she's four again: she clings to Charlotte, and her gaze darts around just as it did when they walked past the rows of officers at their father's funeral. Anna trusted Charlotte then. Charlotte yearns to explain, but now's not the time.

Please let this all fade away from you, become nothing more than a nightmare you can shake off with morning.

The Lady cradles a piece of the tree to her breast. Dress soiled, hair coated in dust, she looks as bad as the other velidevour.

Good.

"Think yourself lucky, do you?" Orna's words echo around the sisters as they begin their climb up the long stairwell out of the cavern. "You are not. One way or another, I will make you pay for what you've done here."

Charlotte does not look back. "Bring it. And I'll humiliate you then too." *Cuz I'll be dead, you stupid bitch.*

Shrill. Strong. Piercing through the thunder: battle cries. Two huge pairs of wings swoop into the cavern.

Cein shouts something to the Lady like, "Not *now!*"

Wings of shadow, wings of light. *Oh, that's pretty.*

In all the screams and feathers, Charlotte doesn't notice her own feet leaving the ground, or the talons pinching her shoulders. Anna floats on the opposite side of the cavern. Shadowy wings above them, carrying them both away.

Marks for Two Sisters

Wings fly out of the Pits and into open evening air. The rain finished, clouds break before the sun in brilliant reds and oranges. It's so beautiful, Charlotte forgets she's still alive.

The wings descend and gently release the sisters onto cool wet grass. Familiar scents—D, Charlotte's bus funk. And jasmine: the jasmine smells wonderful. They are on the Southern Road, the way to the Blairs'. To safety.

"Come on." Charlotte doesn't have the strength to look up, let alone to say thank you. *Can't. Can't shut down till Anna's safe. See a little, smell a little, hear a little.* "This way." *I feel your hand, Anna, the life in it. Please forgive me.*

Voices come from behind. Orange wings flitter low, circling them.

"Miss Charlotte, you—you found her, and alive!" Arlen runs alongside a trail of oil drops.

Anna stares hard at him, her right arm twitching.

"So many miracles in one... day..." He sees where the oil drops come from: Charlotte's ears and back.

"Yeah. And we're leaving. Hope your prince is okay." She coughs black oil. *Dammit.*

"That's right, Charlie," inhale, "we're going to Aunt Gail's," inhale, "just like you said. A new life." Sob. "Starting over. It will be great, I know it will." Panic laugh.

Arlen approaches. "Miss Charlotte, please, you must let me—"

"You shut up and back off. *Now!*" Anna pulls Charlotte close, then grunts in pain.

What's wrong, Anna? Where are you hurting? We gotta keep moving, get outta this freak-show circus. And we're finally together. Finally the family we should have been from the start.

Arlen tries to talk, and maybe touch Charlotte, but Anna just yells at him again.

Most sounds come garbled to Charlotte now, like being underwater. And Charlotte really is. She's drowning from the inside out. "Promise me you'll stay with Aunt Gail."

Anna's words come out in chunks, worse than her bubble gum punctuation. "Don't. Not like that. You can't. Daddy's gone. Can't go. Just can't." Her right arm shakes.

The Wall glistens in the morning sun.

Ember stands in the middle of the road, hands out to stop them. Why?

"Just get away from us, whatever you are, just—just get, GET!" Anna screams and crumples to the ground, taking Charlotte with her.

Charlotte manages a "What's wrong?" before coughing more oil.

Arlen pushes up Anna's sleeve to reveal a vine of thorns growing around Anna's right arm and moving up toward her neck.

In harmony, from Anna's mouth and Charlotte's mind: *"What the fuck is that?"*

Arlen's eyes water as he attempts to clean the oil from Charlotte with a trembling hand. "It is the mark. What is claimed by this place must remain."

"Please, g-get rid of it—that m-mark thing… And this."

136

Charlotte unsheathes the blood dagger and tosses it with a soft thud, away from her. Rain drips from blades of grass onto the feathers of the blood dagger. Sun reflects upon the water and sets the dagger alight. "We j-just want to go."

"I'm afraid it is not enough. Your sister belongs here now. The closer you get to the Wall, the sooner she will die."

"No." Charlotte spits oil and anger. "No. She doesn't deserve to be here."

Arlen shakes his head. Tears age his face. "I haven't the power to relinquish what the land has claimed."

Charlotte hugs Anna close. Barely a bit of berry in her hair now. But the hair's still soft. And warm, not cold anymore. "M-me. Take me instead."

Arlen looks... skeptical? Excited? Charlotte's sight is fading dammit, she can't *see*. "You would take her place?"

Ember retreats into a shadow.

The shadow sheltering Ember belongs to the Bloody Prince. He towers over Charlotte. For a second, all the oil and gunk in her eyes ripples away. He looks so strong, like he never took a dagger in the back at all. Storms rumble in his eyes, unsure whether or not to rain. He bends forward and picks up the blood dagger: the blade glows, like embers in an old fire.

He and Arlen share a look, and Arlen says, "It can be done."

The oil returns, clouding her vision once more. But Charlotte can still smell Arlen. Still noble. Still sincere.

Charlotte holds out Anna's marked arm toward Arlen.

Anna struggles. "Don't. Stop it. Charlie, what the HELL. Charlie. He has a knife! CHARLIE! Don't FUCKING TOUCH ME."

Arlen grunts.

Sorry, sir, she doesn't understand. But let's just make sure YOU *do:* "You can't go near her ever again, do you hear me?" Her words come with oily, bloody saliva. "Ever. No matter where you velidevour are, you're going to leave her alone and make sure no one else touches her ever again."

Arlen's fingers squeeze Charlotte's hand in promise. "It is agreed. Ember, your assistance, please."

"I'll do my best, sir."

Anna's kicking ceases. Ember must be in human form.

"Th-Thank you. Both of you." Charlotte coughs again, for far too long.

Screaming: "Fuck you. Charlie FUCK. YOU. You can't make me. Go. I won't. Go. I won't. HE'S GONNA KILL ME! CHARLIE! CHARLIE! Char..."

Under all the screams, Charlotte catches lilting words. Arlen guides Charlotte's fingers past Ember's grip and down along Anna's arm: the thorned vine is gone. But something else is there. Not a vine. A wing. Anna's pulse runs wild beneath it.

"Charlie? What's he doing? Don't touch her! Let go! LET ME GO!" Grunts and kicks in the grass.

"Miss, I must ask you not to interrupt." Ember has her work cut out for her.

Then Arlen holds up Charlotte's wrist, moves the chain. A cold touch. Then warmth. Nausea. Burning, thin and fine, like hot wires. Hot wires around her wrist, up her arm, up her neck. *I'm drowning, choking—*

"It is done. Ember, you had best escort the child to the border family."

"I am not." Inhale. "Going." Inhale. "Anywhere without my." Inhale. "Sister."

Now, she's finally with me when I have to say goodbye. Charlotte's headshake is imperceptible. "I need to t-tell her goodbye."

Howling in the distance. Brush and brambles shake. Anna yanks Charlotte away from the howling, and then a damned cackle approaches from another direction. A raven. Jamie swoops in.

"Down!" a warning cry from Ember.

A sudden tug and release: Anna, and Ember?—*please be Ember who has her.*

Then something presses Charlotte to the ground and covers her with its body. The Bloody Prince.

Oil retreats from Charlotte's eyes again in time to see an orange body grappling with Anna, urging her away. She sighs with relief: *Ember, not Jamie.*

THWACK. Arlen smacks Jamie out of the air like the goddamn fly he is. To Ember he calls: "Protect the child!"

Howling. D leaps over the Wall, and with fangs pure and bright, he snags the raven by its leg and whips it toward a tree. The torn leg paints his mouth lavender and scarlet.

Feathers and beak become dust, and there lies Jamie with a fleshy stump, bus uniform in tatters, glasses shattered, eyes fixed on Arlen. "You. Sending your dog to steal from me." Eyes on the Bloody Prince, then Anna. Then back to Arlen. "Saving one for him, are you?"

D spits the leg against a tree trunk while Anna cowers behind Ember. And Ember winces at a real human's touch, but obeys Arlen's command to protect her. "Best move back, miss, to avoid the blood."

"Charlie, him!" Inhale, pointing at Jamie. "He took people." Inhale. "From our bus." Gasp.

Jamie bows on his only knee, but it sure as hell isn't to propose. "Silence, girl…. Sleep to dream…"

No, don't let him finish!

No one stops him.

No one has to.

White fire shaped like feathers envelopes Anna. Ember is shoved back by its force field.

Then it's gone. Blinks out. But its power remains, leaving the air charged: Anna's new mark doesn't allow the veli-devour to kill her—it protects her from them.

Jamie catches on, not that it matters. Because D moves in for the kill.

Anna catches nothing at all. "What the fuck was THAT? Charlie... They did—something. They did something. *Charlie!*"

I can hear you, but I can't see you, so take my hand, please take it. "You're okay, he can't hurt you now." *Words are hard with you so close, Bloody Prince. Stop looking at me with those... those damn eyes. I want to fly through them, but my sister needs me.* "Let me go, guy, or I swear I'll stab you myself. Get. Off. Me. Now."

But the Bloody Prince stays put, keeping her pinned to the ground as Jamie spits out a few teeth, eyes bulging at the one human still viable prey. His fingers rake up the ground as he starts to pull his body toward Charlotte, blood droplets as glittery as the dew on the feathers sprouting from his sores.

Arlen steps in front of Jamie. "Enough!" The word booms as loudly as thunder. "You and your comrades have perverted what we've held dear for far too long. Dorjan," he turns to his wolf nephew, "rid us of him."

D snarls with pleasure, and Jamie screams. Grass crumples under their bodies. Wolf jaws snap. Fists pound canine flesh, and Charlotte hears D bite and rip without hindrance.

"Ember, remove the child."

"Huh?" Inhale. "No. NO." Inhale. "You CAN'T. Charlie, tell them!"

"W-wait. Need—goodbye." No one listens to Charlotte. The Voice in her heart cries as Charlotte's trembling hand reaches up for her sister, feels, for a moment, feels Anna's fingertips, but too quickly gone. Because the Bloody Prince still holds her down.

"You can't take me. You can't. Charlie, don't you let them. Charlie, why are you letting them take me?! Charlie, don't let them, please! PLEASE! PLEASE, CHARLIE! I HATE YOU, CHARLIE, I FUCKING HATE YOU, CHARLIE!"

"Wait, I said!" A final burst from the bellows and Charlotte shoves the Bloody Prince aside.

But Ember and Anna are gone.

You must let her go.

"No..." Tunnel vision. She sees D break from his prey, leaving Jamie helpless, whimpering, cackles torn from him like the rest of his body, in tatters.

Human once again, Dorjan grabs Jamie by the neck and pins him against a tree. "You wonder, do you, why I do this. Why I hunt you and Campion, why I seek a duel with Cein. Know, then: I do this for Jennifer Blair, whose brother you unlawfully stole, an innocent, a borderland child. A *child!*" His fist breaks skin and muscle and bone. Blood splatters Dorjan and leaks from Jamie's mouth.

"Just... human... just... human..." he murmurs like a broken toy, hiccupping between words.

"A human worth far more than you or me," Dorjan says with a low voice that begins with a quiver and ends on a battle cry as his fist tears in and then slams out of Jamie's ribcage, heart in hand. The moment his last artery snaps, Jamie's eyes deteriorate into dull gems, onyx. Then mist. Another breath, and his entire body blows away in a cloud of violet embers.

Dorjan studies the black heart a moment before pitching it far into the trees. "Let me know if Cein and Campion get my message, will you?"

Arlen nods, although his focus remains on Charlotte, who sways as she stands in the middle of the grass road.

"You didn't... let me... goodbye." Her words taste foul,

everything smells foul. A hand touches her shoulder—*his* hand. "Don't you dare touch me, you bastard!" She slaps the Bloody Prince in the face. "I just wanted—" then bile overwhelms her throat, and she drops to her knees, gagging on oil, bile, and blood, stinking of decay.

When the darkness overcomes her vision, Charlotte knows it will not go away again. Only her hearing is left, and that too is failing.

"You and Ember. You must ensure the girl reaches family," Arlen says.

"What about Charlotte? Surely once she recovers, you can send her home." Dorjan's voice is barely above a whisper.

Steps on the ground, heavy and angry. Grunts and hisses in that strange tongue Charlotte can't quite place. A thud, then rolling in the grass.

"Must you two always resolve with fists?"

"He destroys everything he touches, Uncle. Look at our family!"

"*Dorjan!*" The name cuts like the blood dagger.

A bark of frustration. "Always, you choose him."

Charlotte listens to the grass rustle, to steps moving away: Dorjan is leaving. "She doesn't deserve this," his parting thrust.

"Then honor her by seeing her kin to safety," Arlen's arrêt brings their fencing to a halt.

"Masters," Ember's voice sounds small, almost chirp-like, "Jenny has found her. She's being brought into the house."

So she's safe. Jenny will help Anna get to Aunt Gail. She's safe. I did it, Dad, I kept her safe.

But the Voice won't let her rest. *Don't give up, Charlie, it's not over. There's still so much left to do.*

Can't imagine what.

Charlotte hears Arlen say, "Your turn now, Miss Charlotte."

Charlotte turns toward him in her world of numb and fog.

She forces her face to grin. "Lucky… me…"

Then black silence falls.

Charlotte's Unwanted Company

A breeze. Open windows, curtains swaying. Roses. Other flowers. Hay. Coffee. Paper. Anna?

Charlotte's eyelids flutter open. Sunlight. Lilacs spill out of a pitcher on a nightstand. One wall is lined with shelves —books, music books, flanked by doors. Dried flowers hang upside down from candleholders between each window. A few feet from the bed is a small table with an oil lamp. A pair of chairs frame either side.

A piano basks in the sunlight on the opposite side of the room.

The room looks and smells familiar. The piano and the doors connect in Charlotte's memory, but the rest is a scattered jigsaw puzzle with all the pieces blank-side up.

So Charlotte flips the pieces over, one by one: the bus. Crossing into Wisconsin. Breaking down in the middle of nowhere. Sleeping at a castle—another puzzle piece.... She smells hay now? *Oh, the mattress. O-kay.* Kind of a medieval-ish thing to do, but then Charlotte finds another puzzle piece, with a barn on it. Aha! A farm, she slept on a farm.

But then some pieces don't give Charlotte a clue. Lots of green color on one piece—trees, maybe. Another shows a mouth full of braces. Here's one with a big blue eye surrounded by

144

nothing. The last one's got two faded words: "stolen child."

"Anna?" *What the HELL did I do to myself on that bus? At least these pajamas are comfy. But since when did I ever own clean white anything?*

A dozen groans from beneath the mattress as she gets off the bed to open the door that's near the piano. "Excuse me? I was wonder—"

Thin white curtains frame long, slender windows that flood the room with sunlight. Cushioned armchairs face a fireplace, where a kettle whistles quietly. A small table, polished now, is surrounded by four chairs. A stained-glass arch of blue roses, a little mantel-top vase garden... Charlotte knows this room, and the reception hall beyond.

Rose House.

The Pits are real, the velidevour things like Campion the squirrel. Dorjan the wolf killing Jamie the raven. Arlen. The Bloody Prince. All of it. Real.

On her right wrist a vine of thorns and leaves is painted still and quiet. It looks like henna. But henna comes off in a couple of weeks. This will not. Ever.

Charlotte will never see Anna or any of her family again.

Her knees buckle. She slides down the doorframe, strands of her hair catching and breaking in the hinges.

I took her place to die. She was supposed to die, so I should have died. How, how was that not the sequence? Why the hell would they want me alive?

A soft chord: the piano strums good morning. Charlotte walks over and touches the keys with her fingers. Beautiful creation. For so, so long, this was just the sort of piano Charlotte dreamed of playing before the crowds—had life gone the way she intended.

Charlotte's fingertips caress the top board, those gorgeous

scrolls above the clawed legs, the keys themselves, so smooth. So full of songs, if she'd just sit to play.

Music, you are not worth my sister. Now here we are, stuck in this room together, probably to emphasize what an idiot I am. Why, why the FUCK of all things, does one FUCKING thing I love rob me of the other?

She kicks out one of the piano legs. The wood groans, pained, as the piano topples and crashes to the floor.

Charlotte buries herself in the bed. Pointy bits of straw poke her cheek through the rough linens, and the ropes that form the cot groan as she winds arms and legs together into one angry knot. *This has to be some stupid game, this nursing back to health. Just eat me already and get it over with.*

A door opens. Charlotte doesn't bother to peek out.

"Miss Charlotte, I heard you calling. Would you be interested in breakfast?" Arlen sounds far too cheerful. Or hungry. "You really should eat after what you went through. I must say…" Pause. Some plunked notes and a loud sigh. "I must say, we were all quite surprised that you survived at all."

Charlotte balls herself up. Even with the blanket over her head, she hides her face between her knees.

His hand moves over the quilt and settles just at her shoulder. "But then, you had no intention of outlasting the poison, did you?" Pause. "Well, if you would care for anything, please call." His weight leaves the bed.

End this, please. Now. I am so damn tired of purgatories.

No, the Voice says.

Shut up, you don't have a say in this.

From farther away: "I am sorry, child. Family: it is everything, isn't it?"

146

Charlotte will not answer, nor will she let him hear her struggle to hold back tears. *You said the land claimed Anna, and I've taken Anna's place. Please, sir, let your damn land claim me and be done.*

The door shuts. Charlotte gathers her hair, then braids, unbraids, and braids again. She rubs the mark on her wrist and wonders how fast it would do its work were she to climb the Wall.

The Voice in her heart scoffs. *Since when were you one to give up so easily?*

I'm not giving UP, I'm giving IN. There's a difference.

You have been whipped. Burned. Turned inside out. Did you surrender?

No...

Yet you surrender now.

Charlotte's head hurts like someone's pulling out her hair. *Oh, duh, that's me.*

She rubs her wrist. *So. This mark can kill me, huh. That blood dagger was supposed to kill me too, but it didn't. So maybe, just maybe, this mark can't kill me either. Who's to say? The only way to find out is to try—and make sure Anna is okay. So, no. No surrendering yet.*

That's better.

One last braid, and Charlotte tosses the covers aside.

"That's better."

"Hey!" Charlotte hugs her knees to her chest and stares across the room.

On a chair by the door sits the Bloody Prince, healed and clean shaven. His hair is cut so that it just covers his ears, curling, black with tiny flecks of silver. He has a smooth, clean face, like a young boy. Eyes quiet, just clouds rolling across the sky. *OH stop staring, Charlie.* He looks like he's on break from a Renaissance faire, what with jeans on and some stiff-looking white tunic. Two thick leather straps fasten to an iron ring just above his abdomen, and a third strap runs over his right shoulder. Bare feet. A tray of coffee balances on his lap.

"What happened to the piano?"

Charlotte glances down at the beautiful wreck. She's not going to let Lord of the Curls forget that he's the bastard who kept her from saying goodbye. "Got mad."

"I suppose a concert is out of the question, then." He sits on the bed just a couple of feet from Charlotte and pours the coffee. He notices Charlotte eying the blood dagger strapped to his back, but doesn't comment on it. "Even our kind needs a little help embracing a new day."

Charlotte accepts a mug and sips. It tastes like a campout at Pike Lake, where Aunt Gail would meet them and bring an old black coffee pot to heat over the fire at the crack of dawn.

She'll never know that kind of morning again.

The mug suddenly feels too heavy to lift. The coffee's steam blankets her thumbs with haze.

"You look sick. You're not pretending to be sick, are you?" he asks curtly.

"No, I just don't want any." Charlotte's determined not to share any more of her past with these velidevour than necessary. "So. Anna. She made it to my aunt's house? She's safe?"

"Who?"

Charlotte slams her mug down on the tray. Coffee slops over, filling the tray and splashing the bed linen. "My *sister*."

"Hey!" He whisks the tray off the bed, sets it on the table, and checks himself for stains. "I made that coffee myself. Do you have any idea how complicated coffee is after a century of sleep?"

Charlotte rolls her eyes and moves to the window facing the clearing. This guy's hopeless. "I want to talk to Dorjan."

His face scrunches up at all the dried bouquets—or at Dorjan's name. "Why?"

"I want his help with Jenny and the, whatcha call them, the border family."

"Dorjan? Help?" His quiet laugh has a sort of music to it that makes Charlotte want to join him, but not at Dorjan's expense. "Don't be so naïve. Dorjan's first and only priority is Dorjan. He's an animal."

"An animal that helped save my sister's life."

"Of course, because it was a means to his desired end." The clouds shift, and for a moment the Bloody Prince's face turns dark. Very dark. Like a you-can't-fool-me look.

"What the *hell* are you talking about?"

The clouds part. Bright, happy sunshine, probably bunnies and unicorns too. "Well, perhaps the acquisition of several human hearts provided him a fine compensation for his efforts."

Charlotte remembers Dorjan's words: "*We're not all like that.*" The earnestness of Dorjan's eyes, both of them, outshines Cein's teeth in Charlotte's mind. "He wouldn't eat those," she says, her spine and voice stiff.

"Ha! I've seen him do it. A savage practice. There are much more civilized methods."

"And what about you?" Charlotte stands and crosses the floor between them. "Let me guess: that dagger's just a fruit slicer."

He shuffles back a little, his eyes churning, filling, hiding. "Well—"

"Don't even. Don't even *try*."

Yet he does. "The purpose of the white tree is—"

"To suck people to death?" Charlotte holds up her hands and wiggles her fingers like some bogeyman, pressing him backward toward the door. "Stick all its little needle-y roots into you, stinging you freaking everywhere? I felt those things. They *hurt*. And they were *all over my sister*, Jenny's brother, other people's brothers and sisters. How the *fuck* is that civilized?" She tugs at her collar—to her left, covering her burns. "If that's what you have in mind for me, I'd rather have my heart cut out. Now." Shoulders back, legs apart in preparation for impact, for a punch, a stab, a... whatever he's planning when he stares at her clavicle like that. She can't read him and those eyes, filled with clouds, calm, beautiful, sad, like quiet rain on a spring day —*STOP IT, Charlie. Quit mooning around like some lovesick teenager.*

He finally breaks his gaze and attends to the coffee. There's a slight tremor to his hand as he lifts the carafe, pours. His forehead wrinkles and his full lips (*GAH!*) move, just barely, like he's checking his words. The pause draws out a scent, one that Charlotte can't place. Curiosity, maybe? No, that's like baby oranges.

When he looks up at her, there's a fresh smirk growing as he holds his cup, tremorless now. "I've already taken care that you'll never meet that fate."

Charlotte snorts. "But you were willing to do that to my sister easily enough." Scratches her hand, wrist—hang on. "Where's my necklace? The necklace, on my wrist, the—shit shit shit!"

The Bloody Prince watches Charlotte scuttle about the floor. "What are you doing?" He sets down his mug.

"My necklace. Did you see it?" she asks from under the bed. "Red pendant with, phith"—she spits out a bit of straw that fell into her mouth—"a white flower, silver leaves. The chain was broken, so I had it wrapped around my wrist."

"Mmm, it feels so good to move again." The Bloody Prince yawns and stretches. With a great thud, he falls onto the bed.

Straw dust rains down, and she sneezes twice before punching the mattress above her in recourse—sending down a fresh shower of dust and, of course, causing more sneezes.

"Well, if it's broken, then it's not really worth finding," he says. "Mmm, this morning is delightful. How about a sunbath on the roof?"

Charlotte shimmies out from under the bed, pulls up onto

150

her knees, and finds herself face to face with a guy observing his toes as they wiggle high over his head.

Oh, for crying out loud. "It was my father's." She emphasizes every word.

"Oh. Then it's an old thing too." He rolls upright, bounces off the bed, and begins to pluck the dried bouquets down one by one.

Imp.

"Old broken things, old broken life. New world, new life."

Are you shitting me? Broken life? No, Charlie, don't kick the other piano leg out. It's not the piano's fault it belongs to an ass. "My sister wasn't broken until you freaks got ahold of her."

Still he says nothing about Anna, instead futzing about with his pockets. Charlotte grows more and more tempted to slap the indifference off his smug face.

"Yes, well, such things happen. Aha!" He pulls out a necklace and holds it up for admiration. "What about this?"

Charlotte's admiration amounts to "Get that damn thing out of my face before it blinds me!" Charlotte blinks away the sun spots to see a pendant shaped like her father's, but made with tiny rubies and diamonds against a silver facing. "How did you know what it looked like?"

"I saw it on your wrist when you woke me up. Oh, and when you slapped me too. Impressively, might I add, considering the granach poison in your veins." He snatches the last bouquet from its place. "Hmm. Think this was marigold once." He tosses it onto the bed with the others.

"Did I have it when I came in here?"

"I suppose so." He opens a window and starts tossing the broken dried flowers into the rose bushes outside. "Why does it matter?"

Charlotte drops the necklace into the pile of dead flowers, where it tangles in the branches, then crosses her arms because that way, she can be on the high road, and not the low road, which involves shoving the Bloody Prince right through that window. "You're old. You were broken. Do you matter?"

He throws down the last of the broken stems and faces her. "Well of course I matter. *You* matter. But—"

"Why should I matter? I'm just a human, like those people on the bus Jamie had killed. I'm just another heart you can rip apart, or suck on, or whatever the hell it is you freaks do."

His body goes very, very still. "No, you're not."

"Then why am I still alive?"

He turns those wow eyes on her.

Dammit, he knows how I look at them. Don't be mean and aim them at me.

The Bloody Prince does look down. If not for his ass-antics, Charlotte would think his whole demeanor to be, well, bashful. "Because I wanted to meet you. You saved my life, after all. That is why you matter. Besides," he pulls the necklace out of the debris and holds it out to her, "you're not a thing. And the things you keep should be beautiful and pleasing, not old trash. So you can forget about your old thing and wear this. Without the bedclothes, I think."

Close your mouth, Charlie. Close it. There. Not, no, not even, no answer. No justifying that. No wonder somebody stabbed you in the back. "I thought the Lady said velidevour tap into minds and see dreams? See what we humans want?" She pushes his hand away and sits on the piano bench. The broken row of keys resounds with a death chord behind her. "Because *that's* not what I want. I want my father's necklace, not some obnoxious substitute."

The smugness melts. Even his shoulders droop as he looks down, then up and through his speckled curls. "She spoke with you?"

"She was so excited to hear you were awake. Couldn't shut up about you."

He picks up his mug, slowly traces its rim with his fingers. "Yes, well. She's an old acquaintance."

"She wants your dagger too."

"Of course she does. Who doesn't?"

"I don't."

A stalling sip.

Why are you staring at me like that? Not an imp, or an ass. Can't, quite, figure you out.

"She can never have it, though."

"Why not?"

"Anyone who is not me and tries to wield it, dies."

Charlotte circles the Bloody Prince and realizes how ready, eager even, she is to pull the blood dagger out of its sheath to show off its wing of fire. "But I didn't die."

He looks back over his shoulder with a smirk. "I know."

Oh, I get it. I'm a freaking science experiment. Goody for me.

The Bloody Prince is not standing by the windows, so that's where Charlotte goes. She gazes out and sees a garden with an overwhelming array of blooms. A perfect place for picnics, for a blanket and a book, for lying back and breathing it all in—

"Mmmm, I like that image. Keep it."

Now he's standing next to her, flipping her mental pages.

"Get outta my head!" Charlotte shoves him so hard he flips over one of the chairs.

Curse words in another tongue tumble out of his mouth as he rubs his elbow and staggers up. His steel-gray eyes forecast a storm. "You treat every man you know like this?"

"Yeah, actually, I do." *Glare all you want, Bloody Prince. I am not bluffing.* "I'm not a puzzle or a toy. This mark you tattooed on me," she whips her wrist at him, "says I'm supposed to be

Anna's substitute for the tree, so just patch me up and be done with it. That's what I signed up for, not your little mind games."

The storm darkens. Playfulness leaves him. "You forget, my lady, that I'm the one who allowed the girl to leave." He speaks with that vicious quiet calm Uncle Mattie liked best before inflicting new pain. "But if you'd rather she return…" He reaches into a pocket and pulls out Charlotte's smart phone.

Oh god, all the pain would be for nothing. "No!"

Charlotte lunges for it but loses her balance—her chest strikes hard against the floor at his feet. "Give that back, that's MINE," she hisses, feeling too damn keenly that here's this new thief in her life. At least Anna didn't steal from Charlotte—much.

The Bloody Prince dangles her phone over her head with a slappable grin of triumph.

"Humanity's love for science astounds me. Our kind could have never developed something like this—magic tends to make us impatient. And here I thought you could not possibly top the telegraph." He perches himself on the table, making sure she can see him scrolling through text and images. "Who in heart's fire refers to you as 'Sweet C'? Seems rather childish. 'Charlie,' however, quite fitting, considering your masculine behaviors, which, I must add—not at all becoming." One eye peers 'round the phone and down at her.

Charlotte looks up. Growls.

"Do not. Mock. My family." She plunks herself down by the open window on the opposite side of the room. *You like sneaking into my head? Let me write you a frickin' novel. You and me out in the school parking lot. Night, just that loud orange lamp over the door. My fists taped, I nail you first at the jaw to stun, then at the gut just for the pain and shove you down and kick—*

154

Taps on the screen stop. "Those thoughts are far too nasty for a lady like you."

"Unlike bleeding dad-dolls, sister-sucking trees, and—" she stops. Charlotte can't start on the thought that is her mother. That leads to Uncle Mattie, and more. "But I've never thought like a lady, cuz I ain't a lady. Never will be." The words come out quieter than the tappita-tappita-tappita of his feet on the floor.

The Bloody Prince is clearly too engrossed with Charlotte's phone, anyway. "This past century, humanity has gone above and beyond anything I have ever expected. Like these!" He shows her a picture of a fighter jet. "Do humans really trust a giant tube of metal to carry them through the clouds and across the oceans? Wouldn't a boat be safer?"

"What's the difference? A boat's just another massive piece of metal that could end up on the ocean floor with everyone dead, anyway."

Phone tucked back in his pocket, he walks over to a large steamer trunk at the edge of the bed.

"Now what?" Charlotte doesn't mean to utter the question aloud, but his answer—"Patience, MY lady"—tells her it's going to be a long rest of her life.

He opens the lid to reveal Charlotte's comfort-clothes: button-down shirts capable of hiding most of her skin, jeans, wrestling shoes, and sneakers. But on the side is folded something that Charlotte's not seen in years: her father's Milwaukee Police Department sweatshirt from academy days. She spent many winter nights bundled in that sweatshirt waiting for her father to come home. *How in brewing blazes did that show up here?* He chucks the baggy MPD sweatshirt with a grimace. "This does nothing for you. You need a dress." He closes the trunk, winks at Charlotte—*oh, please!*—and opens it again. "Here we go."

155

It looks like a short slip made for a little white dress.

"I do prefer something simple. It will match my other present for you perfectly."

The slip is the dress, its wisps a shimmery backdrop for the diamonds and rubies of the replica necklace he made her.

Good God, did all the past females in your life just swoon and beg to be treated like this? Okay, can't take the high road. Charlotte backs into the nightstand. Her hands yank the lilacs from the pitcher and strangle them as she counts her breaths, taking the high road, that stupid, stupid high road. "No, thank you."

"Why not? A lady should—"

"Stop calling me that."

"A *lady* should wear that which reveals her true self. Why hide all that incredible strength beneath such sloppy attire?" He holds the dress an inch from her body. "Do you require assistance?" He waggles his brows at her.

Charlotte pulls her best, sweetest smile—"No, thank you" —then slowly releases each finger, letting the strangled lilacs rain down onto the floor. And, while he looks blessedly confused, she takes the dress, along with the necklace, and drops them too.

"Look, I can't stop you from doing what you want, because you're all magical velidevour or whatever. I can't stop you from taking my stuff. I can't stop you from keeping me away from my family. But I don't have to put up with this shit." She kicks the pile under the bed. "Just rip out my heart and get it over with. It's what you freaks do to humans, right? Better idea: I'll just go to the Pits myself and be done with it, tell the real Lady that you said hi."

She makes it three steps.

"NO." The Bloody Prince presses her into the door. His fingers curl and grip like talons on a branch, and like an idiot, Charlotte's let him have both her arms. Droplets of sweat shine on his upper lip. His chest heaves, anger storms his eyes, but his smell is new: fear. "You will never, ever set foot in that place again." His face contorts, words pour out, out of control. "You belong here with the sun, and the rain, and the land, and me—with us, all of us. Not in the darkness. Is that understood?"

This closeness, too much… "Yes. Your Highness."

The Bloody Prince lets go, but the clouds continue to swirl like they don't know what to do with themselves. "Good." He bangs the trunk shut. "I couldn't care less what you cover yourself with. Do whatever you want." He leaves.

Charlotte lets out a quiet whistle. "What the Helen of Troy was THAT all about?"

Arlen's Humors

Charlotte listens as another door slams, then nothing.

Well, considering she never heard him come in, Charlotte reasons that the chances for privacy around here are next to nil. Might as well find a bathroom while he mopes elsewhere. So Charlotte heads for the door that opens to the parlor—

—and finds a bathroom instead.

Yup, total bathroom, all tiled in white with little red floral prints. Rather nice, actually. What became of the parlor? Charlotte doesn't bother to ask, but instead rushes through her cleanup before the bathroom decides to wander off elsewhere and dump her in, God forbid, Bloody Prince Bossy Imp's room.

Finished, she hovers over the trunk, wondering if it's just all stupid lingerie like *he* wanted, or if her favorites could be back, like *she* wants. With a quick glance out the windows and at the doors, she does an awkward wave of her hands over the trunk lid and whispers, "Can I have the other stuff back?" She cracks the lid open: MPD. *Hooyah!*

But they aren't her old things, not the *genuine* old articles, at least. Even though the MPD sweatshirt looks and feels perfect, it doesn't have the old sweat and the Old Spice scent she adores.

The Voice sounds exhausted, as if it could use a good sleeping in. *The house doesn't want to cheat you.*

Too warm for a sweatshirt, anyway. So Charlotte dresses in jeans and a thin green shirt dark enough and long enough to keep her skin covered. Sneakers laced and tied, Charlotte ventures for the nonparlor/bathroom door.

Now that she isn't running away or hiding from Rose House's strange occupants, the porch feels surprisingly normal. On her left, two half walls flank the door out to the patio. In front of her are the two thick wooden doors leading into the rest of Rose House.

Charlotte steps out and into the brilliance of the morning, her nose sifting through the garden fragrances that cling to the damp air. Then she remembers the dried bouquets. A moment's walk and she finds a pink rose bush littered with Bossy Imp's broken flowers.

Arlen appears around the corner carrying his basket of tools, his pants dripping wet and covered in earth. "Are you a gardener as well, Miss Charlotte?"

"What happened to you?"

"Oh," he looks down and coughs. "I'd just discovered some raspberry bushes for the first time in years and, erm, got rather excited in the watering process."

Charlotte chuckles in spite of herself. Despite all the monsters and horrors underground, Arlen walks and talks in a pleasant, somewhat-normal manner that makes the morning and the flowers, well, nice. "You know you can just call me Charlotte," she says as she plucks the last dead bud off the rose bushes and adds it to the pile at her feet. "I'm afraid there was an 'incident' in the music room. Where can I put these?"

"Oh, never mind them; I'll add them to my compost later. Come inside for some breakfast." He sets his basket down and ushers her through the yard. The walkway is quite narrow along the wings, but behind the center of the house, the portico swells into a great half-circle, complete with a wrought iron table and matching chairs. The garden continues along the back of the house, edging the outer perimeter of the half circle. And beyond the pristine garden, the wild forest resumes in full force.

"Do you keep this up all by yourself?"

Arlen nods proudly.

"Seriously, sir, this is awesome." Charlotte reaches out and cups a cluster of tiny white buds and breathes deep their sweet, spicy scent.

"I grew to love all bounties of the soil long ago. Every season gives me a fresh chance to create and nurture beauty to share with those I cherish." He takes out a pruning knife and cuts Charlotte's flowers and a few more for his basket. He pinches the stem of a lone peach rose between his thumb and forefinger and seems to lose himself in the maze of little petals. He slips into that other language again, but this time, it sounds like a poem, or even a song, its melody not unlike the morning birds welcoming the late summer's sunrise. After a few lines, Arlen catches himself and blushes. "Pardon, lost myself there."

Charlotte looks around at all the colors, all the life. The *life*, that is what touches her so deeply here. When she first crossed the Wall, the forest seemed so artificial with all its unnaturally heady fragrances. This garden—and even Rose House, in its way—feels... the first word coming to Charlotte's mind: Alive. Without darkness. "I can see why." She smiles, and means it.

Arlen gestures up and over Rose House. "We had some beautiful orchards in the Eastern Quarter once, but they

160

turned barren when the Wall was erected."

"But I thought velidevour eat hearts and—"

"We can enjoy any harvest or hunt as humans do, but such things cannot sustain us."

They walk on. Charlotte senses eyes boring into the back of her head. She peers past Arlen toward the row of long windows running along the west wing. "What's in there?"

"That would be Liam's studio."

"Who's Liam?"

Arlen's mouth hangs open a moment and he stammers, "Was he, was he not in your room this morning? He insisted on making the coffee himself, despite the fact that he had no idea how to grind the beans—"

"Oh, you mean Bossy Imp!" Charlotte clamps a hand over mouth. *Yeah, they can read your mind, but still, girl, manners!*

But on the other hand, not a total faux pas: Arlen bark-laughs like Dorjan, only with a touch of song to it, like Bossy Imp. "The *what?*"

"Sorry, I meant to say Bloody Prince."

"Yes!" Arlen pushes her past the last studio window. "The term isn't entirely accurate," he says as they come onto the patio. "More like a poor epithet used too often here in River Vine."

"So what would be more accurate?" Charlotte smells berries and maple syrup through a small window.

"Depends on Liam's mood. Ah, here we are." Arlen opens a wide glass door and bows her in.

The kitchen must be at least half of the central ground floor of Rose House. And Charlotte soon understands why: Arlen moves around the clean, modern space like a professional chef.

"You must love food as much as your flowers."

"I do, actually. And Liam used your phone to show me a few of the improvements humanity has made with appliances and I, well, couldn't resist updating things a bit."

"Wow. Jeez, that's quick. Abracadabra quick. Who'd you hire to do the installation?"

Arlen smiles. "Rose House is quite capable of completing its own renovations."

"The house is designing itself now, huh? Why am I even surprised?... But how nice of Bossy—er, Liam, to share my phone with everyone but me." Charlotte plucks a raspberry from a small basket near the door and pops it into her mouth before reaching for something else: "Ooo, is this a honey jar?" Smack! "Ow!"

Arlen points the wooden spoon at Charlotte's face like a knife. "Away from there. Those are not for you."

"Are they for Dorjan?"

Please say he's coming, he'd be the perfect source of information right about now.

But Arlen doesn't answer her question. "Do you wish me to speak with Liam about your phone?"

"No. No, thank you." A blue light's twinkle dances in the corner of her eye. "My battle. I'll... handle it." Charlotte follows Arlen past the patio entrance and through another set of glass doors, where—how to describe an olfactory symphony? Herbs and flowers Charlotte cannot identify lie all around her, even hanging from the beams above her. Their sweet harmony warms the Voice in her heart.

And then, this window of stained glass. It fills an exterior wall of the house: a cloudy sunset over the sea. Every shade possible of grays, pinks, blues, greens, purples, oranges—all there in shards and slivers of leaded glass. Charlotte's heart flutters like a bird unsure of the world outside its nest, but so badly wanting to touch it, to know it.

162

"I've always thought it one of his better pieces." Arlen lets his cut flowers tumble onto the long, narrow work table in the middle of the room. "Got the yarrow, need more colts-foot, should harvest some more archangel..." He wipes his hands absently against his trousers. "Frankly, I'm rather surprised he placed it in my herbarium." He returns to the kitchen to set a tray laden with oatmeal, maple syrup, and milk on the kitchen table.

"Hang on." Charlotte does a double take at the window, the kitchen, the window, the kitchen again. "There aren't two Liams, are there?"

Arlen chuckles and shakes his head. "I should hope not." He motions for Charlotte to have a seat and sets about inspecting his pots. "It has been so long since I've done any canning. It seems rather pointless when no one requires any human fare. But you've put the spark back in me." He smiles and shows her a large basket by the sink filled with strawberries and black currants. "From Devyn, a good friend and flyer. He always manages to bring me something special after Dorjan ransacks my stores. Hmmm, I may even bake some pies."

Charlotte hesitates, then tucks in. *Just in case I need the strength to... Oh, who am I kidding? I'm starving.* "I don't get it," she manages to say between mouthfuls.

Arlen finishes sifting through a drawer. "You don't get canning? Oh. No, you're not referring to this at all." He aims a small knife tip Charlotte's way, then lets it fall point-down onto the butcher block countertop. "No, I'm not trying to fatten you up. If we were to literally 'eat' you, it needn't be so barbaric as tearing hearts from rib cages. Although, yes, there are many who prefer consuming veli in blood, especially from the heart. We are," he pauses, searching for words, "predatory, by nature. Created not only *with* passion, but to feed *on* passion as well. And I'm sure you know how little stands between

163

need and want, even gluttony." He picks up a strainer, avoiding eye contact.

Liam's tongue-lashing of Dorjan echoes in Charlotte's mind, rippling around a shadow of Dorjan gnawing on apple bread, then on a heart, a pile of more hearts to go.... "What about Dorjan?"

Arlen doesn't look at her, but his grip tightens on the strainer. "What do you mean?"

"Liam said Dorjan eats that way."

Arlen sighs like a tired parent. "He would say that." Pause. "They've never liked each other. And it's worse in my presence. No, I'm not Liam's father—"

Charlotte stops chewing, allows a little smirk. *You're stalling, sir, but I'll roll with it.* "I didn't think so."

"Yes, erm, thank you. But I have taught them both. In different centuries, thank Aether's Fire."

Charlotte chews, swallows, loudly. Quick sniff of the air: no, no malice even now. "Do they—you—do you guys still—"

"I cannot answer for Liam or Dorjan." Arlen studies Charlotte's face for a long, quiet moment before he says, "We have all of us had our bloody days, Charlotte. For many it is easier to remain in them than to change. To change requires facing a past stained by screams." Pause. "It is not an easy trial."

Charlotte imagines D's jaws clamped onto Jamie's calf. "But now instead of killing humans, Dorjan's trying to kill another velidevour. Does that bother you?" When he doesn't answer right away, Charlotte adds, "My dad was a cop. I know that law and justice aren't always the same thing."

Arlen considers this. "Indeed. But here our laws are far more primitive. Besides," he says, looking away, "I know why he does it, and were I in his place, I would do the same."

Charlotte finishes her breakfast in silence. Through the open window comes a persistent loud hum... *A generator?*

164

Well, yeah, gotta keep that new built-in fridge powered somehow. Arlen glances her way every now and again as he prepares the fruit, jars, and pots.

"Look, I need a straight answer, and I don't think I'll get one from Bossy—I mean, from Liam."

Arlen's eyes dart over the doors and windows. "Yes?"

She brings her plate to the sink and faces Arlen across the counter. "I traded spots with my sister," *breathe, Charlie,* "so that instead of her life, you velidevour would take mine." *Good. Breathe again.* "Why wasn't I patched up to a tree? Liam said that's not happening."

Arlen washes a strawberry and offers it to her. "We have no plans of 'patching' you to anything," he says—no, decrees. Signs into law. The whole shebang, that's how final it sounds. "Despite what those underground may want," he continues. "And frankly, after what you did with the blood dagger, some commoners are afraid to touch you." His eyes twinkle with mischief again.

She can feel that he wants to peek into her mental book and see the memory for himself. *Know what? Go for it. See the fire like a wing cut the granach and everyone down. Totally epic.* "That tree had it coming."

"Not all white trees are bad, you know."

Charlotte scoffs.

"No, no, it's true. When left to their own devices, the white trees are beautiful and powerful portals for magic. How to explain..." he drums his fingers, scanning the counter for —teaching aids?

Charlotte leans back with arms folded. "Try me."

"Well, when we—do what we do, I'll say—it takes time. You may know that the body is made of four humors: blood, phlegm, black bile, and yellow bile."

Charlotte shakes her head. "That's what people used to

165

think. Science has shown—"

"Bah! Humans want tidy explanations to give themselves illusions of control."

"But they've got pictures and autopsies and—"

Bop! The wooden spoon's head, right on Charlotte's nose. "Care to go on?"

Charlotte shakes her head again, eyes crossed on Arlen's mighty spoon.

"Thank you. Now, where was I? Ah. The soul," he pokes her sternum, "is actually the fifth humor. It takes a liquid form—what we call dream waters, or veli—when it is purged from the body. Otherwise, it is never seen, touched, or smelled, mixing with the other humors to help keep balance inside a human. When the soul is intoxicated, traumatized, or in some other way overstimulated, the other humors are thrown out of balance, causing sickness and insanity and what have you."

Charlotte folds her hands and nods obediently, still skeptical. She isn't sure how all this jives with maps of the circulatory and nervous systems, but what the hell—she just doesn't want her nose bopped again. "Are bones still bones, or are those something else too?"

"Don't be cheeky." Arlen taps the counter with his trusty Spoon of Might. "Save that for Liam."

Charlotte snorts. "Yuh-huh."

"Now, humans are much like fruit trees. Tended and treated well, the euphoric desires of the soul overflow and seep out, as it were. Sometimes we drink the veli—its best potency is found in the heart itself. But mostly, certain plants, like the velifol—or white trees—feed from the overflow gathered by the water the great Aether has granted us—the wishing wells, harvesters of dreams, and the rivers like the Nile, where Magic breeds its ambition in humanity. The white trees and velifol plants used to thrive around such places, and cared for, a single human community can provide years' worth of sustenance, just as any tree in an orchard yields fruit year after year. Without the water road, Orna—you met her, ahem, underground—forced our white tree to root itself directly into humans, essentially 'chopping' the entire human orchard down. Yes, the humans she captured provided nourishment, but only for a very limited time. I'm amazed that your sister was still alive when you found her."

The fruit on the counter suddenly smells too much like the past, and home. "Anna thought 'need' and 'want' were one and the same. You should see her shoplifting record," Charlotte says, even though she closes her mental book to that and anything else. Anna isn't theirs anymore.

She isn't Charlotte's anymore either.

To see her just once, to make sure she's okay. To say goodbye properly. Before she completely forgets everything about me, her only sister...

She tunes back in to Arlen's explanation. "...what kept her alive. That, and you."

Charlotte rubs the back of her neck, eyes on the ground. "So what happens next? What will happen to the velidevour in the Pits?"

Arlen gathers up the last roll-away strawberries and returns them to the cutting board. "That is a matter for Liam to attend to."

"Why?"

"Because he's the master of River Vine."

"*Him?*"

Arlen raises an eyebrow at her incredulity. "And I wouldn't question him about it, if I were you," he warns, brandishing the fruit knife like a true warrior.

Charlotte throws her hands out to her sides. "What, he's gonna throw me into a dungeon or something?"

167

"Ha! He is rather used to getting his way," Arlen says, lopping off one green, leafy head after another and mounding them into a neat little pile near the edge of his cutting board.

"Yeah, I noticed that earlier." Charlotte glances into the reception hall. *Still moping, huh? Sure you don't want to saunter in here and demand that someone make you coffee in a bikini?*

"Well, I am going to ask you to be patient with him. He's very intrigued with you, you know."

"What kid isn't when there's a new toy around?"

"Hardly a toy or anything of the sort," Arlen says as he uses the blunt edge of his knife to slide the strawberries' leafy tops into a small ceramic compost bin. "He carried you back to the house and took care of you himself—I hardly got a moment to administer any medicine during the five days you slept. He even drew his own blood to feed your heart and fight the granach poison. And believe me, he barely had any left for himself."

Charlotte sneaks a black currant before setting the bowl next to Arlen's cutting board. "Because I pulled out the dagger?"

Arlen nods.

"But it's not like it was stuck. Anyone could have pulled it out. Like you."

Arlen cleans his hands and faces Charlotte directly. He bends low and listens: no sounds in the house. His dark-brown eyes reflect the sunshine and hide the mischief. A serious look, a cop look. He's been thinking this through, hard. "No, not like me. That's the point: no one could touch it. *Only the purest or darkest can break the heart's prison.* That is the spell on all blood daggers when they're turned on their bearers. A bearer cannot die by his own blade. Instead, he is doomed to sleep in a living decay."

Charlotte remembers the pool of blood, the lifelessness of Liam. But he wasn't actually lifeless at all. Someone had turned his body into a jail cell. *A prisoner in his own head for a hundred years. Damn, no wonder he's so caught up in himself.*

She throws a handful of strawberry leaves away. "'Purest or darkest.' So only two could save him. That makes me—"

"The purest, I believe. Oh yes," he nods away her disbelief. "You put all your dreams, desires, and very life aside for your sister. The purest of sacrifices: giving yourself to save one you love. That was why you could pull the dagger out of his body and not die. What happened afterward, however," his eyes twinkle more, "now *that* is a real mystery, one I cannot help but contemplate. So I hope you will pardon me if you catch my eyes on you for long, odd moments."

Charlotte snorts again and wishes, just for a second, that he could have been her uncle instead of her warden. "If your little curse thing's right, that means someone else could have saved him. Who's the darkest?"

Arlen raps the Spoon of Might against his own hand. "What could be darker than one who strikes someone through the heart from behind like a coward?"

"The murderer—well, attempted murderer." Charlotte pauses to sniff as a breeze plays with her hair. Fresh water: a river, or perhaps a lake. Not too far either. "Dorjan wouldn't have done that. If he wanted someone dead, he'd do it face to face, like with Jamie."

"I know that. And that you understand this after knowing him such a short time means a good deal. It's just a pity that so many others, those in power, are quick to punish him because he defies far lesser rules."

Before Charlotte has a chance to ask him what he means, a growing mass of limbs and hair jumps through the window and knocks Charlotte to the ground. "Hey!"

"Poppy!" Arlen gives the mass a sharp knock with his trusty spoon. "What have I told you about ambushing in the kitchen?"

"Arlen Arlen Arlen!" Doesn't faze the girl a smidgeon. She must be used to it. "Guess what, guess what? The orchards have *flowers!*"

The spoon falls with a clack from Arlen's hands, and Poppy continues. "The orchards are bloo—Ooo!... Who's this? Good morning!" She whips long brown hair into Charlotte's face and plunks her butt down on Charlotte's chest. "I'm Poppy. Humans shake hands when they say hello. Hello!"

Insane rogue brownie, OFF. Your feet are disgusting. Are Arlen and Dorjan the only ones who believe in shoes? "Charlotte. Hi." *GET OFF. Are you the one velidevour who doesn't do the mind reading? OFF!*

"Yum, strawberries!" The girl starts licking her own palms, then reaches for Charlotte's.

"Keep that tongue away from me, or I swear—"

Arlen hoists Poppy off one-handed. She half-stands, half-hangs there, still licking. "Poppy is one of our youngest scouts."

"I just started." She whispers like a kindergartener: as in, she doesn't whisper at all.

Another light tap of the spoon on Poppy's head and then Arlen sets her down. "Now what's this about the orchards? When did the flowers first appear?"

"Real flowers! Saw 'em and sniffed 'em!"

"Yes, yes, but *when?*"

"Um..." Poppy's face scrunches up. "Dunno. Not long? No one's gone that way for a while. Devyn flew over it last night and saw *buds*, he said."

Arlen backs away and contemplates his kitchen, the door, the garden. Antsy seems a good word.

"Sir?" *Note the polite address of respect and nonlicky behavior from one beleaguered Charlie.* "I could go look for you. Not like I have anything better to do." *For now.*

"N-no, thank you," Arlen says as he shuts the oven down. "Poppy, why don't you take Charlotte to the Western Quarter so you can explain the lake? All of River Vine is your home now, Charlotte. The house and grounds, all but the Pits are open to you. While you're gone, I'll move you to a new room upstairs, and return the music room to its original state... not to mention the piano." He raises his eyebrows on that last bit.

That was pretty shitty of you to do, Charlie. "Would you need me to help at all?" *I should. And this kid irks me.*

"Would you need *me* to help at all?" Poppy runs her tongue around and around her lips, for whatever reason kids do that, the little weirdo.

"No, and most definitely, no."

Charlotte palms a few more strawberries. *Well, she ain't a rabid squirrel, so there's that.* "Okay, then. Lead the way, Poppy."

Scouts

Poppy skips ahead of Charlotte as they walk out onto the patio and exit the Rose House grounds. From off to her left —west, by the looks of the sun—comes a breeze bearing the smells of jasmine, water, and mint.

"That's the Western Quarter. The lake's over there, and it's got… um… neighbors in it. The Eastern Quarter is thatta way. And that's where the river used to be."

"What happened to it?"

Poppy growls. It's not even remotely threatening, but Charlotte takes care not to laugh. "The *Wall* happened."

A genuine bit of anger there, then.

Poppy pulls back the branches of a white peony bush to reveal a narrow stone path into the woods. After few minutes' walk, Charlotte notices that sunlight has a hard time breaking through the leaf canopy above them, and the smells are now tinged with ash.

"I think I came through this chunk of the woods when I first arrived. That marble tree with the other door to the Pits: Is it around here?"

"South. You go and go on the path here and stick with the smell of the lake in your nose and the Pits will stay nice and far away." The path takes them past vibrant blue asters, purple and yellow cone flowers, lush green ferns, snow-white dogwood blossoms.

She keeps expecting to wake up from this, but all her senses know it's real. *Yeah, there's a hell beneath my feet, but… it's like I can breathe here, inside and out, for the first time.*

Voices echo from deep within the trees. Most blur by Charlotte in indistinguishable weaves and knots, but one voice, the highest voice, stands out.

"Something's wrong with Ember." Charlotte turns off the path.

"What are you doing?" Poppy hops back and forth along the path. "Ember's lots older than me and is buddy-buddy with Devyn, and no one gets on his bad side. You bug Ember, you bug Devyn."

"Can't be any worse than that demon turtle. Stay here if you want."

But Poppy sticks to Charlotte, clutching her arm as they venture into the sunless part of the Western Quarter. Leaves glisten from the last of the morning dew, and the glen traps the cool air. "Bad idea bad idea bad bad *bad*—"

Charlotte holds up her hand and Poppy's grip falls away. Ahead of them stand a gesticulating Ember and an apathetic Campion, his back against a tree.

"—and I've seen his plans, Campion." Ember's body glows like a tulip in sunshine. "He really wants to end the starvation."

"Don't get your hopes up."

Charlotte crouches behind a tree and watches, hoping for a clue as to why on earth these two would listen to each other. Nothing so far.

"—just words. That's all his sort can give."

Crack! "Yow!" Poppy and a thin tree branch crash past Charlotte's head and into full view of the other two. Poppy shakes molding leaves off, looking puzzled. "I fell down."

173

"You forgot to change," Ember and Campion say together for what sounds like the hundredth time.

There's a familiarity here. This used to be the norm: a camaraderie, I can feel it. So what the hell happened—the Lady?

Campion looks past Poppy to Charlotte. "Well hello, there."

"Uh, hi." Charlotte comes forward and helps Poppy to her feet. "Just out for—"

"Arlen said to show Charlotte around and that's what I'm doing and did you know we don't have to say 'human,' we can say 'Charlotte'? I can call her Charlotte." Hopping, she tugs on Charlotte's shirt as she talks and is about to start the loop all over again when Charlotte groans.

"Don't you ever take a breather? And you never even washed your hands from earlier! OFF!"

Ember limps over. "Campion said the blood dagger obeyed you, even flew for you." She pries Poppy's fingers open one at a time without looking down. "I wish I could have seen Cein's face."

"Full of pretty little tricks, I told you." Campion brushes debris off Poppy.

Charlotte squints at Campion, *Is this seriously the same Campion that laughed when that Dad-doll was shot to hell?*

Poppy gasps wildly and latches herself onto Campion's chest. "Oh Campion, you don't know! The orchards are blooming, real flowers and everything!"

He manages to cough a no.

"They have been dead my whole life," Ember says, hand on her lame leg. "To fly through those trees now, it was incredible."

A shriek, and a great wind from overhead wings. Charlotte searches the treetops and spots a gray owl as big as she is. Bigger. A familiar smell to him...

The flying shadow! He flew Anna out of the Pits.

Campion takes one look at the incoming owl and wrenches

himself free of Poppy. "I guess I'll have to see for myself."

"Devyn doesn't like him," Poppy tells Charlotte in another of her bellowing whispers.

Ember rolls her eyes. To Campion she says: "Please, just hear Devyn out. This affects all of us, above and below."

Campion pauses. Patches of light twitch on his clothes, like his whole body has an energy that requires willful curbing. No crazy swirling hues. No smell of fear or anger. Just one friend asking another friend to do something. The fact that he shrugs without a single wicked vibe when he says, "Sure," leads Charlotte finally to exhale the breath she's been holding since Poppy fell from the tree. "I'll hear the old man out. See what he makes of velidevour hobnobbing with the food chain."

Above, feathers fly into a whirlwind of air around a human form. They fall away to reveal a black man perching on the lowest branch of a gnarled oak tree, his hair as gray as his patchwork clothes.

"I knew you'd come," Ember says. "Campion says the Lady wishes to send the Incomplete to scout. Is this true?"

But Devyn does not answer as he leaps down. The ground shakes beneath him, and countless blades of grass bow *to* him in a circle. The land is old, he is old. Perhaps one respects the other.

"Oh, hi, Devyn!" Poppy bounds toward him, but stops when she hears him growl. Not exactly a sound Charlotte thought owls could make. *Well, learn something new. Guess a lesson has been learned about jumping on the owl-man.*

Campion nods to Devyn. "And have you met the master's latest acquisition?"

Huh? Oh. He means me.

Devyn's wild violet eyes widen and fix upon Charlotte.

Know what? Not scared. Not after demon-turtles and man-badgers

175

and abyss-eyed ladies. "My name is Charlotte." *You can even shake my hand. If you dare.*

Poppy grins and gives her a thumbs-up, as though Charlotte's haggling with a used-car salesman.

Devyn moves a little closer. Charlotte smells the authority wafting all about him, just like Arlen. Pretty strong too, so she says, "I'm guessing you've been in charge for a while."

Devyn's grimace fades. "Yes."

Poppy's jaw drops. "How'd you know he's the head of the scouts?"

"Yet *another* pretty trick." Campion's voice comes over Charlotte's shoulder like a little devil.

But Ember looks impatient with the lot of them. "A simple deduction. Arlen refers to Devyn with respect, and our submissive cues likely give away his rank. Am I correct?"

Oh, so I get to talk now? "Yeah."

"Fine. Now, the master's plan." Ember winces. Devyn lends her his arm, and she shifts off her lame leg. Poppy's right about one thing: Devyn's eyes change the moment Ember shows any sign of pain. They do indeed appear to be friends. "He has a complete process laid out, Campion. No veli or lives will be wasted."

"Would you listen to yourself?" No more tree-leaning. With every step Campion takes, another wrinkle sets around Devyn's mouth. "You're talking about the tyrant who struck you lame because you wouldn't find him a prettier one of these." Campion hoists Charlotte into their midst.

Hey, squirrel man, your grip hurts. I hope I did break your adorable little ribs.

"And now Arlen's kin speaks poison in his ear, which means we have NO hope of retaliation against the border man's rifle!"

Charlotte tries her damnedest, but she can't stop staring

176

at Ember's leg. Sure, she's personally witnessed Liam being an ass, but he actually crippled one of his own over essentially nothing?

Devyn speaks louder to silence Campion. "What happened to your family was a tragedy." He tones it down when Charlotte's eyes leave Ember. "But this is the risk we all take when we breed outside the border."

"The risk? The RISK?" Campion laughs.

Uh-oh.

"The border man was supposed to leave us alone. We're supposed to have a damned covenant. But he took my children and—" Campion's face breaks and cries and laughs all at once. "But *I'm* the fool. Tragedy always follows the fool, doesn't it, Ember?"

Charlotte cups a hand to her mouth. *The squirrel family Jenny found. Oh!*

Everyone remains quiet and still. Even Poppy. Maybe people tried to help Campion, back then when all that had happened—the babies, the rifle, the massacre. But it was all too late. Now, only a scented breeze dares to dry his tears. The rustle of leaves covers his sobs. And a faint sound, a moan, not from him but from within the green stillness.

"And now, there are too few scouts. My CHILDREN would have been fine scouts, good and loyal and I know there are too few healthy enough to hide among humans. But I don't care." The skin around Campion's eyes twitches as he cocks his head to the side, gaze on Ember unblinking. "I don't care anymore. I'm getting veli, and I'm getting it by blood. We all are Incomplete, Cein, all of us." He grinds his teeth, then smooths his face into a placid mask. "You are welcome to lead in the skies, Devyn, if you wish."

Devyn snarls. "Cein is no scout."

Charlette reaches out with her ears. Yes, in the distance,

it's definitely a moan of some kind. And the breeze carries pain with it.

"At least he is trying to preserve our race," Campion argues.

"Cein is a *disease* upon our race. If he has his way, we will all be starving, Incomplete, lacking the magic to transform fully, doomed to a life of blood and shadow. And then, then, my friend, the humans *will* find us, and they will slaughter us all."

Campion smiles.

What that must have looked like when he was normal and caring for his family. Oh life, you fucking SUCK.

"Let them try."

"Stop it, both of you. You're scaring Poppy." Ember abandons Devyn's arm to kneel next to Poppy, shivering in the tree shadows. "Yes, Campion, I remember you telling me tragedy follows the fool. What did I say to that?"

A pause. Then Campion mumbles.

"What was that?"

"Until the fool follows hope," he says again, his smile not quite so sadistic.

"You think I've forgotten the master's fire trials?" Ember's face is stern.

Silence. Campion doesn't even make a face. Whatever Liam had done in the past was deemed unspeakable. Charlotte hugs herself, her own fire trials locked far too deep inside herself for these velidevour to find.

"I am asking you, for the sake of who you were before the border man shot his rifle, to follow hope, not vengeance."

"You're asking me to believe the princeborn can build a tree."

"One that cannot be perverted by any means," Devyn adds. "There is no way to feed this population without velifol. It's our last chance."

Charlotte reels back. "Another tree?! Like hell! Arlen said—"

"See? This is what I'm talking about." Campion grabs Charlotte's arm and shoulder and twists. A little tighter and he's going to fracture a bone. "We're not meant to live together like this." He shoves Charlotte to the ground. "She's going to whine, and the master's going to do whatever his precious pet wants. At least the Lady puts our needs above all else."

On her knees, on the ground, Charlotte stares straight ahead at Ember, who stares straight back, Poppy still cradled in her arms. *We know our pain limits, you and I. They think they do, but they don't. That's why you walk on that leg and I walk at all.*

Ember's voice stays close to the ground, soft and quiet like the grass beneath them. "The master may have crippled me, but he's never killed one of us, nor has he driven any of us to death. I can't say the same about the Lady."

Campion's lips tighten. He says nothing.

The birds going after Jenny… Who knows how many veli-devour Mr. Blair's put down, and the Lady KNEW he'd put them down. Genocide of her own kind.

Talon fingers: Devyn pulls Charlotte free. "And that, Campion, is why we are in such dire straits now," he says. "Not because of the return of the master, but because of the Lady and Cein. They know our marks will kill us if we dare imbibe veli beyond the wall, yet they continued to send nearly every healthy winged scout to certain death. Why should humans cross the Wall of their own accord? If the Incomplete hunt freely in the human realm, humanity will brand us all monsters. River Vine will be destroyed. *No* veli-devour will survive."

Charlotte takes a quick, sly look at Poppy. The kid's still detangling twigs and leaves from her hair. *And that kid's a hunter. All these scout veli-things—they're not about the recon. They're about the hunt for veli. For people.*

179

The pain-smell rides on the next breeze, and the minute jerk of Campion's head tells Charlotte that he hears the moaning too. No acknowledgment, though. He just squints: first at Devyn, then at Charlotte. A single patch of light falls on his face like an ethereal mask. "Well, then. Guess we'll have to see if the master's plan is any good. Otherwise," he turns around, "off," he waves to Ember and Poppy, "we," dust and fur envelope him, "go." He scampers off, chattering all the way.

Charlotte opens her mouth to speak, but Devyn preempts her. "I thought you said he was getting better."

"He was so!" Poppy perks up and sticks her fists on her hips. "All nice and friendly, he even got my tail unstuck the other day."

Ember's eyes shut tight as she hoists herself to her knees. Charlotte moves forward to help, but Devyn pushes her aside and takes Ember's hands. Her eyes relax and open to him as he helps her stand. His hands remain clasped around hers as she mutters, "Every time Arlen's nephew returns—"

"Yeah, so, speaking of Arlen," Charlotte interrupts, "Arlen says you don't have to kill to get veli. So how's this new tree going to not kill people?"

"As long as it is rooted outside the Pits, blood will not be shed. Arlen has spoken about it with great hope," Devyn replies.

"Maybe I could—"

"No." Devyn swings the word at Charlotte, and it hits her like a sucker punch.

But it's Poppy who reacts: She shrinks, grows a tail. The tiny field mouse runs up Ember's leg and shirt, and down her arm into the safety of her cupped hands.

Devyn follows up with a one-two punch, addressing Charlotte, "You do not belong here. Campion is right about

180

one thing: the master's desire to keep you alive and untouched mocks the very purpose of our being."

Charlotte moves close enough to stare Devyn straight in the eyes. "Wanna go there? Fine, let's go there. You think I don't wish they had just left me to die? Go ahead, look in my head." She leans in, her nose practically touching his, and taps her temple. "Look inside my head and see that I bit your monster demon snapper freak and swallowed a ton of poison. I was all ready and set to die, but then your stupid master made me live again." She exhales. Inhales. Breaks away and walks backward, saying more to herself than to them, "I shouldn't be walking around with you, but I am, because I don't want anything else to happen to my sister."

Maybe Devyn cares. Maybe he notices the moaning has gotten louder, and the smell of pain has gotten stronger. Or maybe Poppy's squeaks annoy him. But Devyn turns his grimace off and plucks Poppy out of Ember's hand.

Ember speaks for them both. "All velidevour of River Vine know of your bargain. It is, difficult, for us to accept."

"Those damned House Feuds. Why couldn't princeborns leave us alone?" Devyn voice disintegrates into scraping growls.

"What the hell's a princeborn?"

The only answer Charlotte gets is a ROAR: loud, angry, and just so, so sad. Every tree about them shivers.

Devyn releases Poppy into the grass, and she scurries off toward the gardens near the house. "Pain is known to many here. For those who are young like little Poppy, it is all they know."

"That totally does not answer my question."

Another shadow flies over them, its piercing cry stinging Charlotte's ears. *Pain is right.*

"I must speak with Arlen before the master's solitude is

broken. Ember, take this one to the lake. The others from the Pits will not disturb her there." As Devyn kneels, his patches ruffle and turn to feathers. His eyes settle on Charlotte one more time—no grimace, but a hell of a lot of skepticism. She watches him shrink, his feet curling into talons, and when he turns, all traces of human likeness are gone. His wings knock her backward, and despite a wingspan the size of Charlotte, Devyn still maneuvers a stealthy flight between the trees and out of sight.

Skipping Stones

Charlotte's ears fill with the sound of Ember's foot dragging through the dirt. No more roars or moans. The smell of pain has faded too. Whatever was hurting must have moved farther off.

Not that Ember doesn't hurt. Charlotte watches Ember's fists open and close, and catches the tips and ends of words from another tongue. *You know, I didn't ask you to babysit me.*

"I have no intention of sitting on you, nor do I consider you an infant. Not completely, anyway."

STOP READING AND JUST TALK TO ME.

"Then use your voice."

"Sorry. I'm not used to speaking my mind out loud."

"Then I suggest you start before this conversation grows more awkward." Ember wavers when her good foot snags on a stone, but she steadies before Charlotte can help.

The wood gives way to a small green space, beyond which stretches a narrow beach that would bore any kid after ten minutes, and then, a lake. *Oh brother, what a lake—it has to be a mile across.* As far as Charlotte can see, much of the lakeshore is rimmed by firs and oaks. Not a ripple on that mirror surface, a facsimile sky lying at their feet, adorned with silvery herringbone clouds.

"Few velidevour come here, but on no account should you enter the water." Ember's curls bounce as she half-hops along to check the tree line. "The waterfolk do not take kindly to trespassers."

"Fish rarely do." Charlotte kicks a rock off one of the bordering plants.

"Don't touch that."

"Jeez, okay." Charlotte thumps down in the sand. She can't tell if Ember's peeved, annoyed, or what. All she knows is that Ember won't stop pacing, which has to be pretty damn hard with only one decent leg. "Look, I'm sorry for getting in Devyn's face back there, but—"

"You were honest. I respect that." Her eyes swirl at Charlotte, then at the skies. "My anger is not with you. The master spent days at your bedside when he *should* have returned to the Pits to dethrone the Lady and oust Cein."

Charlotte's fingers root into the sand. How deep is the ground between her and the Pits? Could she be mere inches from a tunnel now, where Cein awaits her with sharpened claws and a grin? Sitting suddenly doesn't feel all that comfortable. "I didn't ask for him to do that."

Ember's stare follows Charlotte no matter where she moves. "No, you didn't. What you can ask of him is to pay attention to his own kind. His plans have potential, but they mean nothing unless he *acts*. Devyn and Arlen are not strong enough to take on all those in the Pits. They cannot," she chokes and then pretends to have something caught in her throat, "they *should* not."

Charlotte shoves her hands in her pockets and stares out onto the lake. She doesn't want to deal with Liam, and he sure as hell doesn't look like someone keen to follow instructions. But if the good here are hurting, then Charlotte might be able to help. "You're right." She musters the guts to look

184

Ember in the eye. "I'll talk to him."

Ember gives a half smile you'd miss if you blink, but Charlotte doesn't blink. "Thank you." Then she nods toward the lake. "They shouldn't mind you, so long as you're respectful." Dust and feathers blow around her feet and up—"And keep to the paths"—and up, until the feathers and dust scatter from her tiny orange wings.

Alone in the beauty and the quiet, Charlotte picks a tree near the garden and leans against it. She closes her eyes and opens her nose. Water. Herbs. Flowers. Grass. Old bark. No creatures. No ashes. At last. Breathe out. In. Out.

Why save me? Mountain lions don't buddy up to rabbits. Arlen and Dorjan are nice enough, but Devyn and the others make it pretty clear that it sucks to be anywhere near me.

Wish Dorjan would show up. Can't do shit if Anna's not for sure okay.

Wish I knew why the hell Liam hung around comatose-me.

Wish Liam would give me my fucking phone back. If he can use it, so can I. Check in with Anna, and boom—done.

Charlotte opens her eyes to the green roof overhead. The trees here have to be at least three stories high, if not five. If she can climb one, maybe she can gauge the distance between Rose House and the Blair farm.

A shadow soars and circles over her: an eagle. It struggles in the air just above the trees as though caught in a net. Then its wings fold together as it plummets into the tree line just past the beach.

Charlotte rushes to its landing site, hoping to find another good guy like Devyn. A flyer could check on Anna so much more easily. She smells metal: Daggers? Arrows?

Never mind. "It's only you."

Liam spits leaves and untangles stems from his hair. "Whom were you expecting?"

'Whom'? Seriously? Figures he'd get his 'who-whom' right. Gah. "Someone *who* needed help."

"And I most certainly do." He flashes a smile and shows her his scratched arms. "The slightest graze of your lips would help immensely."

Charlotte snorts and marches through the sand for the opposite side of the beach. Not that it was far, but after a line like that, any distance is good distance.

The oaks on *her* side of the beach are perfect for climbing. The branches reach for the sky before arching low to the ground, like fountains transfixed and transformed. Emerald crowns every branch: a sure sign of strong footing all the way up. Charlotte double-knots her laces and picks the tallest tree by the shore.

Going up is always easy. Their old yard had a giant tree where Dad built them a tree house. He was going to add a rope, but Charlotte declared she'd never need to cheat her way up a tree. Nor does she have a need to cheat now. She climbs, eyes fixed on finding footholds, feeling her center, jamming each foot securely onto each hold. But what is that weird metal smell?

Charlotte peers down through the branches to see pieces of Liam standing below her, torn and dirty, and lackadaisical to boot. "What are you doing here, Liam?"

Liam shoves his hands in his pockets and curls his toes in the grass. He says matter-of-factly, "I am bored. I assume you are the same."

"Nope. I'm sightseeing."

"You should have asked! It would be my pleasure to give you an aerial tour. Shall I?"

"I don't. Think so," she says with extra enunciation, eyes

back to the branches ahead.

"Why not?"

"Well, for one thing, you'll just fly us into the trees."

"Nonsense."

Keep your promise to Ember. Get it done and over with, Charlie. Then he'll be gone and you can look around properly. "What about your special Lady friend in the Pits? Campion says she's going to let those half-and-half freaks out because they're all starving."

"You climb just as well as he does." Sidestepping Charlotte's question.

"You don't have to be a squirrel to climb a tree."

"How right you are."

Dammit, he's climbing too. So Charlotte climbs higher. The oak goes on. Thick branches grow thinner, although not thin enough to bend under her weight.

Charlotte spots Rose House in the clearing, the lake and its borders of forest, field, and sand. The trees, the fields, they go on, and on. But no Blair farm. No highway. No... normal. She really is in another world. *Oh, Jenny. Your brother didn't stand a chance.*

"I haven't done this in ages!" Liam's chest beats fast for his efforts, but he doesn't sound tired. His wow eyes shine like the sun on a cloud's edge.

STOP IT. You can't wow me. I've got thoughts to think and things to do.

It doesn't help that Liam grips Charlotte's branch and hoists himself up and onto her perch. Not bad for a guy who'd been stabbed and left half-dead for a century. "I've never met a human of good birth who could climb as you do."

"Then you've got some pretty boring human friends." Charlotte does her damnedest to study leaves instead of Liam's face.

Liam laughs, sort of. A lilt fades in and out, like Arlen's magic-speak, but something sharp deflates it. Something bitter. "Yes. That would be one way to describe them. At least society has finally approved of physical activity for the fairer sex."

Charlotte's eyes dart at him because she knows what's coming. "You call me a lady again and I swear, I will punch you out of this tree."

Liam purses his lips for just a moment to check himself. "But you're no servant, are you? You're an artist, a musician." He moves closer. Closer.

CLOSE ENOUGH.

"That is why I'm surprised you would endanger your hands. They already look a little worse for wear."

She glances down at them, all scratched and bloody from pushing her way through twigs and leaves. "I just play piano, is all." She rips one little leaf bit, then another. *Art. I just play it. I don't write it. Art. Whatever. Half-assed compliment.* "Arlen showed me that stained-glass sunset you made. Those statues and paintings in the studio—all yours too?"

"Of course." A breeze blows up from beneath them. Charlotte's loose hair drifts into her face as she inhales the garden, the lake… until the sweat and metal overpower them.

"My art displeases you?"

"What? No. You just smell." *Oh for crying out loud, Charlie, at least be civil to the guy who saved your life.* "Sorry, I'm, gah, that wasn't nice, I'm sorry."

But this time, Liam truly laughs. Without the sharp bitter pokes in the musical lilts, his unfettered laughter dances in its song. "Yes, I'm afraid I do. I always smell like a smithy after summoning ore from the earth. My apologies, I should not have approached you in this state." The sun races 'round the edges of Liam's inner clouds.

Charlotte smiles. "Bet the flight felt good. Before you crashed." Charlotte's ready for him to laugh again, even to laugh with him.

But his sunlight fades. Clouds gather, and dark ones too. Liam looks away. "Yes, it did."

Shit, Charlie, you've found a nerve. Get off it, he's being nice for once. "I saw that window you made in the herbarium. I've never seen anything that beautiful." *But don't give him too much or he'll turn his wow eyes on full blast.* "Honestly, what I saw in the studio while you were, you know, kinda dead, all of it—really good, bordering on fantastic."

"'Bordering,' eh?" The word amuses him, and an impish half smile plays on his face. The branch creaks as he shifts close enough to touch her. "It keeps the madness at bay. But you should not underestimate yourself."

"I don't write music."

"That is only half of it." He reveals the palms of his hands to her. Calloused. Scarred. Strong. "My hands give life to the canvas, to the clay, to the glass. Your hands give life to the music. If you don't play," Liam somehow remains balanced while sticking his hands in his pockets, "there is nothing, only mute dots and lines on a page. *That* is a gift."

Charlotte tears more leaf bits and watches them scatter like emerald snowflakes to the ground. *Dots and lines on a page… More words that are nice.* "Thanks." *But that's not a gift like turning a pile of glass shards into a scene so real you want to walk right in.* "Did you go to school?"

"Why? Is my inborn artistic talent not fantastic enough by your estimation? No, no, no." He waves the notion aside like a bothersome fly. "I assure you I am a natural in many, many ways. Allow me to escort you back to Rose House for a complete demonstration…. Where are you going?"

"Down." The nice thing about going down: she has to

focus on the branches, and not on whatever smug face he's got on right now. Maybe he isn't being dirty, but if he is, Charlotte has no wish whatsoever to encourage him.

Charlotte only gets a few branches down before Liam flips over and swings upside down by the crooks of his knees, his chin level with Charlotte's eyes. "You don't need school when you're gifted. Naturally."

"Yeah, well, gift or no gift, skills get old and blunt, like a blade." *Hint hint, Master Dagger.* "If you don't sharpen them, with practice." *Why am I breathing so funny? He's staring at my neck —he can't see anything. Gah, just get out of here.*

"Come now, Charlie, don't leave." His fingertips graze her hand.

"Don't call me Charlie." *That's for family. You are not my family. And don't you EVER touch me.* "I'm Charlotte to you."

"Charlie!" in a wheedling tone.

Sorry, Ember, I just can't. This guy's hopeless. He's a smart-ass who thinks he's better than everyone. And how the hell can he look at me like that and still be able to do such terrible things? What am I supposed to do? Condone mutilating people? Hell no.

Branches snap in her hands. Bark tears. Every foothold groans. Three splinters in one hand alone. On the last branch, she looks down to see clear ground. She lets go. "Shhhhit!" She lands on a large, knobby root. The splinters in Charlotte's hands are large and frayed—too risky to pull out by hand.

Liam lands feetfirst without a sound. "You should have let me help you."

"Yeah, thanks, Cat-Eagle-Man. Gaaaah, these are deep." Charlotte shakes her hands to dull the pain—or to distract her from Liam's half-gawk, half-furrowed look.

"Cat-Eagle—"

"Well, what did *you* do? Float down?" Charlotte sticks the

heel of her hand in her mouth to try to suck the splinter out. Nothing doing.

"I did nothing of the kind. Now give me your hand."

"Muh-uh." Charlotte moves backward, hand still in her mouth. *I know the Innocent Face. Anna used it all the time after getting caught with yet another stolen something or other.* She pops her hand out long enough to say, "That tree was fine when I climbed up. Admit it: you messed with the tree like you did the clothes back in the house."

Liam sulks and straightens his harness, his sword and blood dagger hilts poking above his shoulders.

"That's what I thought. Why don't you go to the Pits? Cein and the *Lay-dee* could use some serious messing up."

She turns her back on Liam and makes it two steps before his fingers tug and twist at her shirt collar. His breaths come fast, beat upon Charlotte's face with… fear? Anger? Both. "I am not finished."

But he's interrupted by a shrill squeak that morphs into a shrill string of words: "Charlotte, there you are! Well of course you know where you are, but I didn't know where you were, or are, or anyway, you're here, and I'm here in the same place! I've been away on—" Poppy blinks at Liam for a silent second like he's some sort of three-headed moose, then quickly drops to one knee. "Sorry, Great Princeborn, I did not mean to intrude." No hugs, no licks. No perkiness. Hell, she's not even looking at him.

Charlotte yanks herself free. "*You're* a princeborn? I thought everyone was talking about the Lady. She's the only one I've seen do any mastering around here."

RUDE. For the first time, the Voice in Charlotte's heart peals with anger.

I don't care. My hands hurt.

Liam's eyes darken. Not just night-dark, but tornado-dark. "Please state your business, Poppy."

"Just scout business, sir," she says, each word a small squeak.

"Under Devyn's orders, I presume."

"Yes, sir." Poppy holds her head up, although she remains kneeling. "And then I was returning to attend to Arlen's request that I escort Charlotte—"

"You will address her as Miss Charlotte, Poppy."

"She doesn't have to—" One look from Tornado Face shuts Charlotte's mouth. Fast.

"I said, Is that understood?"

Poppy's lip quivers. "Yes, sir. Escorting Miss Charlotte, sir."

"Consider Arlen's request of you fulfilled. Go and tell Devyn that I must meet with him. We need to discuss the tree and the state of affairs underground. That will be all, Poppy."

No need to tell her twice: Poppy vanishes back into the shrubs before Charlotte can take another breath.

"Why'd you have to be so hard on her? I don't care about some stupid—"

Liam faces Charlotte. Wind blows through his torn tunic and his hair, and Charlotte reels from the smell of his authority. *So serious. Like a cheesy romance cover without the cheese, a Harlen of Troy with his thousand ships—DON'T LAUGH, he's not in the mood.*

"I care. They are to treat you with respect, and you are to treat me with respect." The clouds spark with lightning. *Brilliant.*

Frightening too, my God—my heart's flying off without me.

"Never question my authority in front of the velidevour again. Is that clear?"

Heart's gone, and now so are my legs, but damned if I can't match you glare for glare, Pretty Boy. "Yes. master."

Time pauses. Another light wind, and all the fear and anger hovering about them is carried away from the lake and the flowers.

Rain drops on Charlotte's sneaker. Red rain. Red? No, it's blood dripping from her splinters. Her hand looks horrible. Feels it too. "I'm... I'm..."

Liam exhales and runs his hands over his face and hair as if to wipe the authority away. "I apologize. I should not have spoken to you as I would to a commoner, and I should not have turned the tree against you. Please, let me take care of your hands, Charlotte."

Charlotte's heart settles back into her ribcage. "One apology accepted." She watches her step over some young white roses to sit on the beach's edge. "I was, well, I was out of line." She speaks to the sand because saying sorry to a face is hard. "You're in charge. You don't need backtalk from an outsider in front of your own. That was wrong of me, and I'm sorry. Manners have never really been my thing." Charlotte sees his feet slide up next to hers. *Even his toes look strong... STOP IT.* When she risks a glance, the tornado face is gone.

"Clearly." Sunshine peaks through his inner clouds, and with a hint of a smile, he adds, "But then, nor are they mine." He reaches behind them to pluck a bluebell-like flower out of the soil, roots and all. Mischief creeps into his face as he holds it out to her. "Your hands, please?"

Charlotte squints up at him. "No funny business?"

He gasps at her, "An artist's hands are *never* a funny business."

Charlotte allows herself a quick smile and holds out her hands.

Liam cups the flower in one palm and guides Charlotte's hand to rest on top of it. His other hand closes around hers.

Liam's scars run thinly all over his hardened skin, but a gentleness hides there, and a warmth.

Petals wilt, roots shrivel, and then splinters flutter down. Liam opens his hands to reveal Charlotte's hand, fully healed. She balls her fists, flexes her keyboard fingers. "This is amazing, Liam. Really, thank you."

Liam's face brightens as he traces the lines where splinters once pierced Charlotte's skin. "Thank you. I have always been rather good at healing. Arlen taught me much when I was a child." His fingertips delicately trace their way up to where her sleeve hides her skin.

No. My scars. STOP. Charlotte crab-crawls backward and hunkers down into the darkest corner of her mind, away from the light that still shimmers around Liam's clouds. She must count her breaths, calm herself, try to make that freak-out less freaky. "What about Arlen? He's older than you, but you're his master too?"

Liam's still staring at the lines Charlotte drew with her feet and hands. "Y-yes? A technicality. He was my tutor first, before he vanished." His gaze moves to the lake and swims away as his hands rake into the garden. A burning stench fills the air, and any plant that touches Liam's fingers goes dry, curls, hisses, burns.

"Hey, Bigfoot," she chucks a small stone and gets a rib, "don't take it out on the plants."

Liam blinks, and only now acknowledges what he's done. "Oh! Oh. Sorry."

Charlotte curls her knees to her chin. It occurs to her that something may be locked up inside him, just like all the shadows that lurk inside her. He combs the sand with his toes.

Let's promise to not peep through each other's key holes. All right? And now this mental door is closed.

Liam laughs, a touch sad, but lilting, nonetheless. "My

apologies. I am not used to having company with such thoughts, spoken and not." His cheeks are still pink as he scrunches sand between his toes. "Tell me, how are you at skipping stones?"

Charlotte shrugs. Liam stands and crosses the beach to the lake's edge.

Well, bless the inventor of pockets because there is my phone, playing peek-a-boo by your cute butt—what is WRONG with me? You just go on ahead and look for stones while I stand up and move on over—

"Why is your hand there?" Liam glances over his shoulder at Charlotte's twitchy fingers hovering inches near his pants. He stiffens and moves away.

Dammit!

But he doesn't go far before he bends over. *And there's that butt again. Shut UP, Charlie!*

He straightens and turns to her. The sunlight in his eyes spreads across his face. "Come, I can show you how." He nestles a stone into the crook of his middle finger and whips. It skips six times before sinking. Ripples break the water's clouds wide open: pinks and oranges mix with the sky blues. "You won't learn if all you do is stare at the water." If he senses Charlotte's plan to steal back her phone, he's not showing it.

"Hmm? Sorry, I was just thinking about the water, how it looks like your window in the herbarium."

"Does it?" Liam hooks another stone and watches the colors break and blend. "I suppose it does a bit. Few sights compare with that particular shore." He offers a stone to her, flat and the color of a storm cloud.

Dammit, now I'm seeing storm clouds everywhere. "No, thanks. I'm a better spectator."

"I saved your life, you know," he says with a smirk. "The least you can do is skip a stone for me."

Excuses fill Charlotte's head, some snarkier than others, yet she closes the distance between them. What could come of one little stone?

"Here." He opens her hand and guides her fingers to cradle the stone just as he did. "Don't grip too tightly or it will go nowhere. And your arm…" He positions himself behind her so that his entire torso touches her back. His heart beats like eagle wings, and for a moment her own heart beats back, flushing her ears and face. "Needs to be like a whip, not a hook. But don't let go too early or you'll hurt someone. Like me."

They move as one for a few practice swings: one, two, three, breathe. One, two, release. It skips twice and then sinks. Liam groans.

"Hey, I did it! I've never gotten one, ever!" Charlotte pulls away to grab another stone. Three skips! A sound, bubbly and odd and silly, rises up from her gut and escapes her mouth. Charlotte is laughing.

She ducks around Liam for more stones. "At the same time now." A stone for Liam, and an unforced smile from Charlotte. Although they stand a few feet apart, their limbs sway as though bound together. Ripples collide and spread, blues exploding to white and pink. Pink lands on purple. Oranges slide through them all.

Charlotte draws in the quiet air and releases it. In, out again. Bismarck had no room to breathe. It made her hurt. It made her hurt others, the way Liam hurt Ember.

So Liam's done cruel, terrible things. So has she. For once, Charlotte decides to tape her inner judge's mouth shut. They're both struggling to breathe. Breathe now. No need for the past. No need for the future. Just a stone, a shore, and a friend.

I like that.

As her stone comes down for its third skip, a fluid form

of greens and blues snatches it midair and vanishes beneath the water. "Hey, what was that?"

Liam narrows his eyes and aims. "Mermaids. Waterfolk." He flings the stone at the first stray ripple. The water hiccups.

So *that's* the waterfolk that Ember spoke of. Silly Charlotte, thinking the lake would be normal.

Charlotte slides her shoes off one at a time, then her socks.

Liam smiles broadly. "And what other clothing may we discard?"

Charlotte snorts. "I want to meet the waterfolk."

"You *what?!*"

"Now, don't you go making my shoes vanish," Charlotte says as she rolls up her pant legs and walks into the water. The water is October cold on an August day.

"You're mad!" Liam lunges forward, but halts at the water's edge with Charlotte just a few inches past his reach. "Get out of there!"

"Why? I'm what, a whole whopping foot in the water?"

"Wha—der—mermaids! Waterfolk do not tolerate trespassers, they'll do something!"

Since when is Bossy Imp-Master Dagger-Bigfoot such a wuss?

"The water's not even to my knees, Liam. What are they going to do? Tickle my toes?" And she kicks up a good splash of water at him. "This stuff's not acid, you know. It's just cold."

"I know what it is!" he snaps back. "Now, I order you to get *out* of there," he says with a puffed-up chest.

Full of hot air, Charlotte's sure. But she smells his fear, and can't bring herself to laugh. "Fine." She stomp-splashes back to shore. "Happy now?"

"Yes." His whole body sighs like Charlotte just disarmed a bomb with seconds to spare. Charlotte rubs herself dry with her sleeves and puts on her shoes, wondering how an eagle who soared into the Pits to save her life can be so scared of a little water. "Would it be too much to ask that you listen to sense next time? The waterfolk are not afraid of spearing feet. Ask Arlen, and he'll tell you."

"Guess swimming's out, then."

"Well, if that's what you wanted, let's have our own pool. Or perhaps a hot tub? I'm interested to see how one feels —your phone's moving-photographs intrigue me. It will be private, I promise you," he says, eyes dancing to match the skip in his backward step.

But Charlotte lingers. The distance grows between them. "No, thanks. I'm fine. Think I'll go up the tree again. You have fun."

But Liam ignores her, his gaze fixed ahead and up. "The roof will best suit our purpose. Away from most eyes, and in the sun. Your skin could use it."

"What?" Charlotte's mouth hangs open. She shoves her hand in her pockets, legs planted in the ground. "No, it doesn't."

"Of course it does. Those disfigurements, those scars, look terrible." Liam shudders, but doesn't turn around. "Were you in a fire? Because your arm and chest are fairly—"

"I know how they are." *FUCK, should have known. I woke up in clean clothes, so at some point I didn't have any clothes on. So Liam saw... everything.*

"Where you are going? Charlotte, wait! What did I say?"

Charlotte half-runs, half-jogs through the woods. She crunches as many branches as possible to disguise her sobs. She pays no attention to the direction her feet take her, as long as she stays beneath the trees and out of view of any aerial tours.

She just had to let her guard down. He saw all her scars and thought she was in an accident—and feels sorry for her. *It's all just pity. Because who would want to hang around a beat-up piece of nothing?*

You are not nothing.

What I am is done. I'm going to the Wall. I want to know about Anna. If the mark does its job—then whatever. Done with it all.

No, you're not. Shame and anger flood Charlotte's head, but the Voice in her heart remains warm and sure. *Now, be on your guard. Others are near.*

Animal. Pain. Ash. Different smells, different directions.

Survival trumps all. She will not die before she knows Anna is okay.

Charlotte slows her pace just enough to use the ferns to quiet her footfalls. Deep moaning from her right: the one in pain, the one they all ignore.

Something stings Charlotte's wrist. But it's no bee: the vine of her mark is thickening. Her skin flares where thorn points twitch.

Which way was she running, again?

Just ahead lies the glade without light. In that glade squats the marble tree. No wonder she smells ash.

No more emotional running off for you, Charlie. Now just slink on through here and pray no one's—

Chattering. Campion as his squirrel-self perches on a branch just above her head.

"What, you get locked out?" says Charlotte in lieu of greeting, immediately shifting her feet for fight or flight.

Fur bursts into dust as the body transforms. "The Pits are a terrible place to contemplate one's thoughts, and you've given me much to contemplate." His grin would put certain comic book villains to shame. "A strange bit of luck, finding you here. Lost?"

"No."

"Mmmmmmhmm."

Not my best fibbing effort.

"In gratitude for shaking things up around here, allow me to escort you to the Southern Road. Then from that point on, I shall eagerly seek the opportunity to break your ribs and liberate that throbbing little bit of red-blue muscle. Fair?"

Charlotte hands quiver at her sides—*oh, for a dagger, a bow and arrow. Hell, even a slingshot.* "Let's backtrack the route you used when Dorjan brought me over."

"Odd request," Campion says with a shrug, "but I can accommodate you. Or can I? Let's see if you can tell."

Charlotte walks with Campion away from the marble tree and what feels like east, south—yes, a bit of both. The forest takes on that phony green stillness she experienced when she first came here, but the perfume-y-stench isn't quite so pronounced. The ground's a little different too, with some flowers budding here and there. And there! She snags a whiff of canine. Old, but there. And bus funk. *Damn, I must have really stunk that morning.*

"We-e-e-ell?" Campion draws the word up high and down low. Charlotte's too slow to realize he's been watching her face all along. "You've caught it: we are on the same path. What pretty little trick told you this time?"

Charlotte glares at his cocky face, but the sun's light behind a tree line distracts her. "I smell my bus funk."

Campion laughs. Pity, if not for the mania, it'd be a great contagious laugh, the kind that tickles you without trying. "Yes, you did reek. But then Cein does love to amplify the oil and the grime. It excites the residents below."

Sunlight at last! The warmth feels wonderful on Charlotte's hair. She begins the trek south and bites her cheek to distract herself from the thorns climbing up her arm.

"A-hem? North is the other way."

"I want to talk to Jenny."

"Do you now?" Campion trots alongside Charlotte, head bent in mock-thought. "Wonder why… You don't care about her welfare, or you would have seen her to safety before coming here."

The NERVE? Of course I care, but I didn't have much time—

"You don't care about her brother: you haven't mentioned him at all despite knowing we brought him here."

He's DEAD. I can't—

"In fact the only human being you think of at all is completely out of Jenny's reach. Pointless, really, to be here, and alive…" His voice trails off and beckons Charlotte to follow him into its hopelessness.

Charlotte slows. *Can't do anything.* Stops. *Can't do anything.*

The pain-filled cry erupts in the woods.

The Voice in her heart slaps her from the inside out: *WAKE UP.*

Thorns pierce Charlotte's shoulder.

I WILL get to the Wall. I WILL talk to Jenny.

Campion's eyes unleash new swirls, but Charlotte shakes off the magic and walks on. "So why do you want to speak with Jenny?" he calls. When Charlotte does not answer, he adds, "Jenny's father will not allow her to leave their home for the duration of the day, not after her trying to protect Arlen's precious nephew and his pack."

Charlotte refuses to speak aloud, but deep down inside she swears she *will* get over the Wall to see Jenny somehow, even if her right arm no longer works.

The green stillness pulls back like a theater curtain. Ladies and gentlemen: The Wall.

Thorns scratch Charlotte's collarbone. She blinks back

the pain as best she can.

"Tell me…" Campion leans against a tree midway between her and the Wall. "How do you know your sister is safe?"

The question strikes deep like a knifepoint. "That's why I need to talk to Jenny."

Campion looks up, but not at her. "You forget, missy, that you've been erased from the world. The girl's forgotten you."

"She never forgot her brother, Sammy, after you erased him."

"I'm not talking about Jenny."

Bastard. Charlotte's fists clench tight, tighter. "Fuck you." The words drop to the ground as she walks past him, eyes fixed on the Wall. Thorns hasten their upward creep, now almost at Charlotte's neck.

Campion spits on her heels. "I forgot to mention earlier: I have an offer from the Lady Orna."

Still no moss or vines on this side of the Wall, but something is caught between the stones. It dangles, a string of pearly dewdrops, and a dash of crimson…

"The Lady agrees that our world will have peace again only once you're gone. I'm here to tell you she can help you escape River Vine and return you to your sister. That is what you want, isn't it?"

Charlotte unleashes a wicked, maniacal laugh that would scare tears out of a child. "Says the guy who promised to rip my heart out."

"Quiet, the princeborn will hear you!"

"You all want me dead? HERE I AM!"

"I said *quiet!*" Campion shoves Charlotte to the ground. "The princeborn will never let you leave, and she knows that if she kills you, then he'll in turn kill her. That's the last thing she wants! We may be many things, but above all, we are survivors."

Thorns wind around Charlotte's neck like a choker. Somehow she staggers forward, crawling, and claws at her neck. One's got a point just above her larynx, but she's going to keep right on talking, just to annoy Campion. "So what am I, a third wheel?" she rasps.

"If you mean a distraction, then yes. All she wants is you gone. And she's figured out a way to do it."

He speaks truth and lies, whispers the Voice.

Well, duh. Now Charlotte's right leg is being poked and scratched beneath her trousers. She pauses to breathe, but it's damn hard, like breathing smoke. "Go on."

Campion points behind them in the direction of Rose House. "The blood dagger. You can hold it and not die. If you bring it to the Lady, she can recite the spell that will remove your mark."

"Yeah. And then cut my heart out." In a crevice between two stones in the Wall, white petals shine within a daub of crimson. She has to move closer, to touch it—she must, even if she has to drag herself with one working limb. "I'll take my chances with the Wall."

Campion bounces backward, whistling and chuckling like all's so pretty and delightful. There's no doubt in Charlotte's mind that he's unlocked the rest of his crazy. "Enjoy your last piece of home, because they'll never let you go. And if the stories about Master Liam are true, they'll never let your sister go either."

How FUCKING dare you.

Then she hears his chatter fade to nothing, and the smell of ash dissipates quickly. She realizes that Campion has left her to the mercy of the Wall.

Charlotte continues to crawl, forcing thorns into her knee and wrist, deeper than mere ink could ever penetrate, and she doesn't care. A thorn stabs her behind the ear, and she doesn't care. Because she's just feet away, inches away. She reaches out and grazes it with her fingertips: a red pendant with white flower and silver leaves. A broken chain. Her father's. Her family's. Hers.

Can't get up again. Thorns on leg... stomach. Her vision blackens, and she buckles in pain. The thorns must be inside her head, piercing behind her eyes. "JENNY!"

"There you are!" Liam's voice swoops in. "You shouldn't wander off like that, especially in the Western Quarter. Someone from the Pits could try to take you. And you make yourself pretty obvious, screaming like that. And who's this Jenny you... were screaming..." His footfalls slide to a standstill.

I am gone. She is a ball of flesh wrapped in thorns, pierced by curses. She cannot move, speak, hear, smell. *Help me, Liam, please.*

Strength and fear and will—oh what a will!—grip Charlotte by the arm and pull her away, as if the Wall is hell-bent on consuming her.

Thorns shrink back from Charlotte's mouth and eyes. Charlotte gasps for air. Liam drags her a few more feet from the Wall and collapses alongside her. "*Mac an donais*, woman, what were you thinking?!" Each word comes with a heavy gasp.

Charlotte still feels the vine around her neck, but it no longer chokes her so much as scrapes her, leaving pain as it retreats. Gut and leg now thorn-free, she rolls to face Liam. The smell of sweaty fear matches the tremor in his hands and voice. "I had to, get something." The necklace sparkles in the grass between them.

Liam sits up and wipes the sweat off with his sleeve.

"You do realize you nearly *died* for a broken trinket."

"Back off." Charlotte's hand rips the necklace from the ground before the grass can steal it. "Go on, lord it over me that you saved my life twice. La-di-bloody-da."

Something is wrong. The Voice in her heart pokes her gently.

Liam's not just being an ass. Even as he continues to upbraid her, visible pain writhes around his neck. Maybe on his body too, just like her. *But how could he be just like me?*

Moaning. The animal in pain. Charlotte hears it from somewhere far off, maybe the lake again. She crouches, crawls, and eventually works herself up to a walk. Thorns continue to shrivel from her neck and collarbone.

She tries to gauge where the moans are coming from and doesn't notice Liam, who apparently is still scolding. Or yelling. Take your pick.

"—and for the last time, stop *doing* that!" Liam jerks her sleeve so hard it tears off. "Do not walk away from me when I'm talking to you."

No thought. Instinct. Charlotte kicks his knee. Hard. Her force and his force and their anger and their exhaustion topple them both. "I oughta take that dagger of yours and rip *your* goddamn shirt to—"

Both stare at the thorns on Charlotte's arm. They're not merely painted on her skin: they're hard and coarse, almost three dimensional. Tiny points of blood dot her arm.

This mark shit really did almost kill me.

Liam stares too, equal parts fascination, disgust, and fear. He opens his mouth to talk, but all he does—all either of them does—is breathe. It takes some willpower to do that without thinking about thorns stabbing lungs.

A sound of great wings and a sudden whirl of leaves approach them from up the road. "My master wishes to see me?" Devyn drags every word through the dirt. The sunlight on his ragged appearance does him no favors. "Although I would rather we not meet so near the border," he says as he offers Charlotte a hand.

Normally Charlotte shoves aside that kind of chivalry, but in this case, she knows Devyn's favor is not to be taken lightly. "It's all right, Devyn. I'm done here. I told him about the Lady, although I don't know if he cares." Her body's still pretty shaky, partly because of the mark, and partly because her plan was an epic failure. No way can she get near the Wall like that again. No Wall, no Jenny. No Jenny, no info on Anna. That means a go-between, but whom to trust? Dorjan, maybe, if she can find him. Or her phone. *Yeah, like Liam's ever going to let me have it.*

Liam stands and looks at them both. Then, with eyes resting on Devyn: "What do you want me to say? No, I don't see Orna's designs as a threat. Let her writhe about. The commoners will hear me and know I have the true vision of prosperity for us all."

"Perhaps it would be prudent for the master to remember that the commoners are starving *now*, and have been for days. Their patience grows short." Devyn speaks through gritted teeth.

Charlotte understands now why Ember holds Devyn in such high regard: not just his no-nonsense approach, but his tirelessness and dedication. He truly cares about his own. Someone has to. Charlotte gives Liam a final, hard look. "You need to take care of your own before it gets worse. Please. Now, if you'll excuse me… *master.*"

Liam's gaze does not break from the Lady Charlotte until she is completely out of sight. When the pain in his own body becomes too great, he pounds his fist into the nearest tree, obliterating its trunk into dust, and flies with Devyn across the clearing and into the Eastern Quarter. *So much risk, and for what? Broken trinkets and old memories.* Liam grunts in disgust. *The past cares for nothing—it gives nothing. Why in heart's fire does she cling to it so? She'll learn. I'll show her, and she'll learn.*

Charlotte follows the grass road all the way back to Rose House, ignoring the two enormous birds soaring overhead, veering off into the opposite wood.

A New Cord

Charlotte stomps into the music room without saying a word to anyone and closes the curtains.

The piano looks fixed, but cornered, like a scared animal. It even strums a high minor chord so Charlotte knows it. "Yeah, I don't blame you. I really am sorry for, you know, kicking you and stuff." Charlotte lays the necklace along the music stand and rests her hands gently on the keyboard lid. "All I could think of was my baby sister, that if I hadn't put my music first, these things would've never hurt her."

The piano strums a soft scale from the necklace down to Charlotte's hands.

Guess we're okay now. Good.

For hours, Charlotte remains in the music room playing —well, banging—the piano. Her fingers run through the song of the sea, past her mother and the 5:15, to the rock through the rain, and back to the sea. *Quadrophenia*. Once her music of choice to drown out her sister's bitching, again, and again, and again. Now to drown out this new world. Leave her to her music. Wasn't that what she always wanted?

A knock. Sconces flicker electrically to life.

"Charlotte?" The door cracks open, and in pokes a mug

of hot cocoa with a strange rattling noise. Despite everything she's felt earlier in the day, it's hard to be mad at the one who has yet to lie, yet to be rude, and yet to approach without something for her stomach.

"Come in, Arlen."

He closes the door behind him and tosses his rattling box of matches onto the table. "Rose House has done away with tapers everywhere, I see." He kneels next to Charlotte, slumped on the floor by the piano bench, necklace in hand.

"Keeps falling off." Her face is salty and wet.

"Liam said you found it by the Wall." Arlen sets the mug down and checks her mark, neck, and face. His hands linger on her cheeks so she cannot look away. "I hope you don't plan on getting that close again." Every word rings strong, sad, and grave.

"No, sir, I learned my lesson." *Not that I'll admit it out loud in front of Liam.*

One hand moves from Charlotte's cheeks to the top of her head and rubs her hair just above the ear.

Did you just pet me like a dog?

"Oh, heart's f—oh, I am sorry." Arlen shrinks back so red in the ears you'd think he'd been boxed.

But Charlotte smiles and shrugs off her tears. Sometimes the odd gestures are perfect.

"I doubt he understands its significance to you," Arlen says, offering a handkerchief while his eyes study the petals that glisten with Charlotte's tears.

Charlotte feels the broken link. "He tried to make a copy—" She pauses to honk her nose and attempts to clean up.

"Yes, I know. There is no replacing a memento of love." Arlen holds out his hand. "May I see it? Perhaps I can help."

Charlotte clutches the necklace and plunks the snotty handkerchief into his hand instead.

Arlen purses his lips, gingerly stuffs the used handkerchief into his pocket, and tries again. "I won't leave the room with it, I promise you."

Charlotte takes a steadying breath. "It's the chain." Her voice cracks as she places it in his hand.

"Yes, I thought as much." His fingers trace the flowers and the metal, pausing. "A," he traces the flowers, "unique," traces its shape, "piece." His face hardens with thought. Smooth-hard.

Seriously, where are his wrinkles?

But then Arlen's eyes crinkle and twinkle above his smile. "I see why your family cherishes it." With great care, he slides the pendant off the chain. "I could make you a new chain, if you want. Until then, would this suffice?" He pulls a thin leather cord from his pocket, threads it through the pendant, and holds it out for her approval.

Charlotte ties it around her neck and rests the pendant near her heart, right where it's supposed to be. The words "thank you" feel so small and stupid, but she mouths them anyway. What she would have given for someone like Arlen in her life even five years ago. *You, sir, are One Who Makes a Difference. You make the horrible less so. I think Dad would have liked you.* "I didn't find it without help...." She drinks the cocoa and tells him all about her encounter with Campion. "And he said…" She swallows hard.

Twinkle's gone again. "What?"

"Campion said that it's because of Liam, with him being the Bloody Prince and all, that Anna's still here." She waits for his response. *Please, sir, please do not lie to me.*

Arlen closes his eyes and growls. Not the typical "argh, I'm angry" that puny human beings make. When Arlen growls, the floorboards shake. The lights in the sconces blink, and when he stands up, all the shadows in the room concentrate

210

around him. For that second, he looks like a bear ready for a face-off. "Cretin." The bear-shadow fades, but Arlen's eyes remain dark as he turns away and sighs. "I will say this much to you. There is a deep, deep vein of cruelty in Liam's blood-line." Arlen's voice retains the menace of the beast. "Very deep."

Charlotte watches the last cocoa drops swirl in the bottom of her mug. "Campion said Liam punished Ember because she didn't find girls pretty enough to hand over for…" *You're eighteen, Charlie. So act like an adult.* "…stuff." *Or not.*

"For 'art's sake,' was his typical excuse, whatever that entailed." Arlen moves from window to window as if to check the locks. *It's always easier to mess about with little things when the big things hurt too much.* "We have had so little for so long. It has been difficult under the Lady Orna, but she is no worse now than Liam during his angry days. There was a time he demanded scouts bring only young females so Liam could imbibe veli as they modeled for him. Those scouts who did not acquiesce to his whims were beaten or burned. Ember was the last to undergo the fire trials." Arlen checks the piano's leg, apparently impressed with his own repair work. "Devyn and I made sure of that."

He really did it. Liam really maimed Ember, and maybe others, for something so dick centered and stupid. Why can't I see this in him? I see the worst in everyone—my best talent. So how come I can't see it this time?

"And that is all I will say. He should be the one to speak on behalf of his own past."

"Can you prove it?" Charlotte stumbles forward with her dried snot, torn clothes, and leafy hair to keep Arlen from leaving.

"Prove…?"

"That Anna's safe. You've got to have proof, right? That she's with Aunt Gail?" *Please don't let me drift, sir. Please.*

Arlen shakes his head as he slowly moves Charlotte away from the door. "Ember only witnessed your sister with the border family. Perhaps Dorjan can tell you if she made it, but even then, none of this is tangible proof."

Charlotte swears under her breath, but knows that Arlen's right. Dorjan's word is worth something, yes, but Charlotte wants something she can see, like a video or photo. If she can't see Anna, then she wants to hear her voice on the phone. Even if she talks to Jenny, would her word be enough? "What about, I don't know, an enchanted mirror or something?"

Arlen scrunches his face. "What in heart's fire—this isn't a fairy tale, child. Magic has laws just like humanity. Very rarely does it thrive in a thing without life. It takes a living soul to contain Magic, and no one's about to put that into a looking glass. Now, let me show you to your new quarters."

Sunset: pink light enters through the windows of Rose House and makes itself at home on the floor. It's only Charlotte and Arlen in here, yet the house feels so full of life, humming just beyond Charlotte's hearing whenever she touches the walls, the bannister, the furnishings.... Perhaps it's the art that gives the house that hum: so many frames of all sizes depicting landscapes, seascapes, cloudscapes.

"Liam did this too?" She pauses at a large oil painting of a lightning storm over a deep mountain valley. Her nose almost smudges the canvas as she studies the delicate threads of light weaving in and out of the clouds. "He's like you in a garden, Arlen."

The mischief grows bright in Arlen's face as he leads her up the stairs. "I'm not sure whom you compliment more in that comparison."

Neither do I, frankly, but one thing's certain: you two have a knack for beautiful.

Again, with the flushing red ears. This time, with a bashful smile.

The second floor envelops Charlotte in cozy comfort. Warm red carpet covers a spacious hall at the top of the stair and continues down the center of the corridor into the east wing on Charlotte's right. The west wing, abutting the staircase to her left, is almost entirely walled off, with the exception of a single door south of the staircase. Gold-threaded flowers set in brilliant red paper dress all the walls from floor to ceiling and glitter with light reflected from the sconces.

Yet none of this compares to the exquisite doors Charlotte finds a few feet directly in front of her. Glass shards and copper ribbons paint towering clouds of steel blues and grays. And even without sunlight streaming through, Charlotte feels dawn's promise at its center, as morning hues of cream, pink, peach, and orange suffuse the steely clouds, emitting such warmth that she's sure if she were to open those doors, she'd find morning on the balcony outside.

"All our quarters are on this floor. I live in the back half of the east wing," Arlen says, pointing to the right, where two doors flank either side of a corridor that splits the east wing into north and south halves.

"You can also reach the top floor of the library, the third floor, through there," pointing to the far end of the corridor in the east wing.

"A library! Brilliant." Books made her isolated life in North Dakota bearable.

"Oh, we have everything. Well, maybe not much from the last century or so, but it's still a good collection."

"I should read the classics, anyway." Charlotte says, her voice still a little lost in the clouds. She walks away from the top of the stairs, letting the bannister guide her around to one window facing out into the clearing, framed by doors on either side. "What about this room?" she asks with her right hand on a doorknob.

"That leads into Liam's quarters. He's got the whole west wing to himself. I'm not sure why, and Liam's never bothered to explain." Arlen's fingers graze the wall between the staircase and the balcony. "I was certain he had a door here earlier."

"Maybe he expanded his studio, and his bedroom?"

"Hmm... That room to your left is yours. Go ahead. Please enter."

Room? This is so not a room: it's an apartment. And Charlotte momentarily forgets to breathe.

The door opens to a spacious, light-filled suite. A vanity, a small table with a chair, is positioned near wide picture windows to her right, overlooking the clearing. A king-sized bed with a cedar chest at its foot to her left. Directly in front of her, on the far wall, a partition provides access to the rest of her living suite: a second room extending at a slight angle into the east wing. Set in the far wall of this second room —*oh, wow, an actual* sitting *room!*—Charlotte spies an old stone fireplace that looks like it was lifted from Aunt Gail's living room.

The bizarre color scheme throughout the entire suite reminds Charlotte of Aunt Gail's eccentric tastes in quilting and fabric art. But that isn't the only reason the apartment is flooded with color. Charlotte pauses to admire the partition dividing the suite: a glorious stained-glass work of art. A meadow, a riot of flowers. A single glass shard for every petal.

"How… where…" Charlotte shuffles openmouthed from one end of the apartment to the other.

Pressed flowers on the walls, just like Mom. Girly clothes in the closet, just like Anna. Books on the shelves, just like Dad. Afghans thrown everywhere, just like Aunt Gail. Every piece is a piece of her home, here, in this place. "Did you do this?"

Arlen coughs when Charlotte glances back at him. "I confess that I did peek into your mind, just a little, to see what comforts you would enjoy. It's been centuries since I've done anything like this for a girl. I think you can guess where Liam inserted his peace offering." He taps the stained-glass partition as he walks by. "Although it's strange what Rose House did on its own without my guidance." He pauses for a moment, lost in the embers that flicker faintly in the hearth.

Surreal. I like it, sir, don't get me wrong. To have tangible, good things from my family reminds me I had a family. They weren't just a dream. But now… now, that's all they can be. A dream. And that bloody hurts. Still. "It's perfect, all of it. Thank you." When Arlen doesn't answer, she adds: "What's wrong?"

"Hmm? Nothing. My apologies. I'll leave you to get settled." Arlen inspects her quarters one more time as he crosses to the door. "I can speak to Liam regarding the return of your telephone, if you'd like."

The phone. A shot at real proof. These velidevour people would never be able to impersonate Anna properly. She needs that phone. *Ask nicely, right? Easy as that.* Charlotte lets the sarcasm ooze off that last thought before asking, "What if, well—could *you* take a message to Jenny, the border kid?"

"Me? I do not know the family. I am sorry."

"But you—"

"I said no." His smell changes into something harsh, strong, and bitter. "I cannot reach them, not like Dorjan. I am just too old for that sort of thing. If he returns to Rose House, I will tell him about your request." His voice dries, and his face falls.

You can't regret getting old, sir. It's not as if you built the Wall. "So what's the best bait to get his attention—meat or pastries?"

Arlen chuckles quietly. "Both, of course: steak and kidney pie." And he bids her good night.

Too Many Inner Storms

Left alone, Charlotte pops off her shoes and scrunches her toes into one of the many thick shag rugs strewn about her quarters. Grains of sand slide from her feet to the fuzzy strings. *Kinda shoulda cleaned up before dragging the beach in with me.*

A door by the closet unlatches. Charlotte stares, fists ready, and tiptoes over. She kicks the door—nothing. Slowly reaches for a light switch—and finds the bathroom. The same one that appeared next to the music room earlier that morning.

"O-kay. Please don't do that again, House." *Still. A shower would be nice. Wash the day's crap off. Shirt's half-missing, anyway.* Charlotte begins to undress, then startles when she hears the doorknob to her quarters turning. "Hang on!"

"Charlotte?" Liam gets the door open a crack.

Thwack! Charlotte's shoe smacks it back. "OW!"

"Just because you're master here doesn't mean you can waltz in whenever you want!" She dives into the closet behind her and feels around in the darkness, slipping into the first shirt she grabs. When Charlotte pokes her head out of the closet, she sees Liam leaning against the partition, rubbing his nose.

"A simple Do Not Disturb sign would have sufficed."

"Like you'd listen."

"Well, we'll never know now, will we?" He slides each panel

to inspect the shards, tracing the copper lines with his index finger.

No thorns on your neck—good. Imp smile back too, I see.

"Well?" Charlotte perches herself on the armrest of the couch by the fireplace and buries her feet deep between the cushions.

Liam takes it all in, inspecting her quarters: the quilts, the books, even the clothes in the closet. "Why did you run away at the lake?" he asks, his head buried in sweaters. "We were just starting to enjoy ourselves."

"The idea of jumping into a hot tub with you is not what I call fun."

"Aha! Now, here is a style befitting you." Liam pulls out a strapless cream lace dress. "Worn for a performance, I imagine. Surely nothing less than an aristocratic audience could produce such a change to your appearance."

"Outta there," Charlotte commands as she slides off the couch's armrest and squirms into its cushions. "It's all stuff my sister filched to make me girly. I have to, you know, fix it."

"Pity. I was hoping to see at least one dress on you before the century ends."

"Yuh-huh. Give me my phone back and I'll tell Anna you dig her style."

Liam shrugs with a melodramatic ignorance. "I have no idea what you're talking about. I did have a telephone once, but then someone in this room plotted to steal it, so now it's hidden."

Crap. Knew I was too obvious about it. "I'll wear the dress." *Shit shit SHIT! How'd that come out?*

Liam turns off the imp and steps up to the couch. He leans against the edge of the couch and props both arms on top of the backrest so he can loom over the still squirming Charlotte like a mythical mix of cougar and... eagle, she supposes.

You're gonna fall off there and onto me any second. NOT okay with that. I'm not. Seriously. Turn those wow eyes off now, because damn, they're all I see.

"You'd do that for me?"

What the hell am I agreeing to?

Then the couch tips backward. His limbs tangle with hers, her face in his chest, just as when he'd held her down while Ember took Anna away.

Damn. Damn those arms and damn the rest of you. You kept me from saying goodbye. You kept me from Anna. You kept me from comforting her, from protecting her. That was my job as her big sister, and I FAILED, and God it hurts like Uncle Mattie's belt. "Off."

Liam pulls away a little, puzzled. He has maintained his manners. He has maintained his humor. And now he is maintaining the close contact he thought she preferred. Yet the Lady Charlotte's mind darkens with anger, and the countless candles hidden in the forests of her eyes are being snuffed out by him somehow. *Control, must control the situation. Gain control, gain the girl.* "You'll still wear the dress?"

Guys and their one-track minds. "I want my phone back."

Liam rises to his feet, but keeps Charlotte's hips pinned between his heels. "And you have to model for me."

Ember limps across Charlotte's mind, and her jawline hardens. *Because that always turns out just swell for the model, doesn't it?* Her hands slowly travel up the backs of Liam's calves.

Liam's breath seizes in his throat as he glows in triumph. Her long fingers spread across his muscle, and he wonders what quick work his dagger could make of her wretched denim trousers, torn as they already are. She reaches the backs of his knees, and such a playful expression dances on her face that, by heart's fire, he's gained the girl!

Then Charlotte jerks herself through Liam's legs with such a force that he nearly tumbles over. Finally clear of his looming body, she somersaults into a ready stance behind

219

him. And before he can utter a syllable, she kicks the dress into the closet, slams the door shut, and bounds over to the fireplace.

Liam scoffs and goes to the closet—because he saw plenty of pretty things to wear her down with—and twists the knob. And finds it locked. He tries it again. He *wills* it to open. No, still locked.

"The exit's this way, genius." Charlotte crosses the room and grasps the doorknob to show Liam the way out.

Liam, eyes scrunched shut and therefore blind to her pantomime, repeatedly taps his head against the closet door. Confusion doesn't even begin to describe this scene for him. "But you're the one who proposed wearing the dress in the first place."

"That was before I read your pants." Charlotte stands, arms crossed, to the side of the open door. "Not as cool as reading minds, but it's enough. Or should I ask what's going on in there right now?"

Liam opens his eyes: the bed stands between him and Charlotte. One good jerk, and she'd be on it. *Gain control, gain the girl.* Liam's gut churns, as it so often did with that vision and its execution over the centuries. But this time, his gut churns too much, and the vision sickens him. To see the Lady Charlotte stand in such a way, knowing him to *think* in such a way, sickens him all the more.

"Good n-night?" His voice cracks a little. "But the moon's barely touched the clouds."

"Kinda been a long day." Arms still crossed, a long and steady look at his eyes.

"I could show you what I have in mind. Not often do I reveal my plan to the subject, but as you are a fellow artist…" his voice trails off as he grins at the sound of his compliment. "I think I want to do something with clay." His hands glide over an invisible mount, waiting to suit his desires. "A bit of strength, a touch of beauty—"

"Oh, I get it. I can be one of those young models you suck the life from as you work."

Silence. The stench of discomfort fills the room. Liam retreats as if Charlotte's words are slime encroaching into his artsy-fartsy space. "That was another time. I was different then." He stands, shoulders drooped, refusing to face her.

The Voice reaches for Charlotte's fists, still curled tightly under her armpits. *His stature has changed, inside and out. Is there malice?*

Charlotte stares at the ceiling, trying to ignore the question, waiting to hear a breath, a snarl—any cue she learned in high school from boys stupid enough to deem her a target. But the foul smell of cruelty never creeps into her nostrils. Shame? Yes. Oh, that funk's everywhere. *Damn well better be. An ass with his slinky lingerie this morning, and an ass just now with that dumb dress.* "Let me be clear," she takes a page from Arlen's playbook and speaks with the slowest, sharpest diction possible. "I don't care which 'you' you are. Pull that shit again, and I'm sticking that dagger where the sun don't shine."

Liam considers this. Shrugs. And nods. "Fair enough."

Charlotte leans against the open door and closes her eyes, both hands behind her back, clutching the doorknobs for balance. She taps the back of her head against the edge of the door to the rhythm of "5:15"—*out of my brain is right*—and says, "Now. Can we just agree we both were asses and move on?"

He exhales and looks at her with relief. Then his eyes slide down to her neck. "I prefer the necklace I made for you."

Charlotte snorts despite herself, one hand reaching for her pendant. "Don't you go making this one disappear so you can pull that monstrosity out again."

"Monstrosity? I'll have you know..." his voice fades. His

eyes don't leave her chest.

Charlotte rolls her eyes—*please, I'm not nippling out*—then looks down at where he's looking. Her shirt is a thin beige, bordering on transparent. Crap.

"Do those still hurt?" Liam asks without a trace of imp or master. "I could fetch some lavender and comfrey from the garden, try a working on them. His eyes are heavy with gray.

Dammit, this shirt. Now my scars look like spots on a cow! Thank God I've still got my bra on. Charlotte bolts for the closet, emitting a stream of "shit shit SHIT," as she rips the closet door open and hides. "No!" she finally hollers, and the big MPD sweatshirt mercifully falls at her feet. "I mean, no, they don't. Hurt, that is. They're nothing, really." She emerges to see Liam standing next to the closet door, puzzling over the doorknob.

He sees her sweatshirt. "Speaking of monstrosities..."

"Oh, shut it." She brushes by Liam to plunk herself down on the couch, upright once again. "How was your meeting with Devyn?"

"Concise yet productive, as always." He moves with measured steps around the couch and stands near the mantel, hands folded behind him.

"He doesn't seem to like you very much."

Liam gives a strained half smile, eyes on the ground. "Indeed he does not. Fortunately for me, he and Arlen get on very well. A few genuinely like Arlen, while the rest humor him. But they all despise me."

"Wow. That pretty much sums up school for me right there."

With more measured steps but without requesting permission, Liam sits next to Charlotte and says, "You put too much store by them, you know." He gasps a bit. "Scars, they can be like the past: neither leaves us, not really. But neither should they define who we—who *you* are, in the

222

present, or the future."

Charlotte's gaze slowly shifts from the hearth to Liam. The flames reflect in his clouds like a campfire reflects in its own smoke.

We. Your locked door keeps back something pretty bad. Your cruel streak, maybe. Well, I won't disturb it. I like you a lot better this way.

Liam slides closer—only a little, he promises himself —and pinches a small fold of the MPD garment between his fingers. Charlotte tenses but does not speak. "I could show you what I mean if you'd, well, model for me. Without loss of veli. And without this monstrosity. Please." The word "please" comes with an effort.

Charlotte bites her lower lip. The clouds inside Liam's eyes look hopeful, promising, like the first rain after a drought. He's trying. She knows he's trying. But talking about her scars means unlocking the door inside, and she cannot, she will not, unlock that door. "No, thanks." She tries to pull away, but he does not release her.

She wants to snark at him. But Charlotte forces all that aside with a few calming breaths. Maybe she just needs to meet him halfway. *So, change of topic.* "Can I see that glass building on the roof? It's a green house, isn't it?"

"Of sorts." Liam gets up and walks through her quarters to the open door.

Liam steps aside. "Females first. Or is it safe to say 'ladies' again?"

Charlotte tries to hide her smile as she walks through.

Back in the foyer, Liam guides Charlotte to the wall closing off the west wing from the rest of the second floor. The light from the sconces catches in the copper ribbons of the doors to the porch outside, causing Charlotte to pause, chin up, shoulders back. She's sure she feels… atmosphere, something, tickle her neck—but it's just stained glass and not real, or is it?

"A-hem." Liam leans Joe Cool–style against the scarlet wall.

Charlotte shakes the cold, tight air off her face. *Must be a draft through the door.* "Sorry, just, lost myself in the clouds for a second."

Liam's eyes flash lightning quick from Charlotte to the window and back. "And what did you see, beyond the clouds?"

"Huh?"

"Never mind." His chest heaves with a large exhale. "Now, mind you, this is just for tonight. For the first time in centuries, Devyn and I agree on one point: you should not visit the third floor on your own. I do not want any commoners to catch or harm you accidentally."

Charlotte rests her back on the wall next to him. "So long as they don't touch my artist hands, right?" She wiggles ten fingers in front of his face.

"Nice to know the rest is up for claiming." He swipes at her fingers playfully before tapping a knuckle lightly along the golden lines in the wallpaper. "Ready?"

Leaning her full weight against the wall, Charlotte opens her arms expectantly, waiting for Liam to go down the stairs, the corridor—to lead her somewhere.

But he simply stays put and taps the wall three more times. "Are you certain?" he asks, adding an eyebrow-waggle for good measure.

"Li—OOH!" The wall behind Charlotte opens, and Liam grabs her by the shoulders to keep her from tumbling backward.

Liam's curls bounce playfully as he continues to hold her but at a decorous arm's length. "I did ask if you were ready."

"I was ready for stairs, but not," she regains her balance

and slaps his hands away, "for abracadabra bullshit behind my back."

Liam hops past her and perches toes-first on the ledge of a stair. "These are stairs. You can't expect Rose House to roll out a grand staircase as easily as a hallway carpet, now can you?"

Charlotte recalls the floating bathroom. *Okay, so that was a bit smaller than a grand staircase. Guess it's a good thing the plumbing's magic too.* "N-no?"

Liam rolls his eyes at her and jaunts up the dark stairs three at a time, the denim of his pants hugging very ripped thighs—*stop staring, Charlie!*—not to mention a perfectly carved ass. *GAH!*

Charlotte bonks her head against the wall of the stairwell as a result of her gawking, and follows, watching the calloused, muddy soles of his bare feet as they move up the steps. Which is easy to do because she's crawling more than she's walking. Because stairs this narrow don't seem to be made for human feet. *Come to think, yeah, they probably aren't.* Not to mention how they rise up, then dip down, now dip *more* down to the right, now rise to the left. *We better meet a faun by a lamppost pretty soon, or I'm calling foul on you, House.*

At last Liam's feet pause on a tiny landing before a thin, rectangular line of light. He opens a door and ushers Charlotte into an extremely narrow hall lined with doors stretching out before her like a cramped hospital.

Rose House's third floor.

"Step to the center," Liam whispers, "and quickly."

Lights flicker on and off as they pass. No plush red carpets here. White. Sterile. Too damn eerie. Peculiar metal strips snake in and out of the doors, running along the floor near the walls like so many unspooled ribbons. Charlotte feels the hum of life vibrating through the strips and does her best to avoid stepping on them. Only a foot-wide path in the center of the hallway is clear of strips. *Step on a strip, break your grandma's hip. Hmm. Maybe I should start stomping on these.*

Out of the cramped hall, they enter a large chamber, surely as big as the reception hall downstairs. Into this central chamber, the east and west wings converge. Charlotte checks behind her—the corridor had sliced through the middle of the east wing, and it looks like another corridor does the same through the west. The metal strips continue to ribbon throughout their floors too. The strips flow together along the central chamber's white wood floor, like roots beneath Charlotte's bare feet. They thicken and meet at the base of a large bundle of metal strips that twist and turn around each other to create a pillar that looks like it poured out of a Dalí painting, or…

"Your tree." Charlotte keeps her distance. Beautiful and terrifying, it glows like a forged thunderstorm. "So it works like the white tree in the Pits?"

"As long as the commoners do their work, yes, it should. The roots enter those rooms," indicating the doors that line the corridors, "but they never so much as touch the human." Liam pauses in his study of the trunk to look at her. "I hope that is acceptable."

Charlotte can't stop staring openmouthed at the silvery branches that reach up and out, through a hole as big as a SWAT vehicle in the central chamber's ceiling, and then still higher up, fanning out into a shimmering canopy in the glass house above. Then Liam's words sink in. "You want my input. What I think, it really matters to you?"

"Of course it does." As though it were foolish to think otherwise.

"You really did all this?"

"Yes. If the vision in my head is clear and complete, then

226

the rest follows seamlessly." Liam points to small indents in the trunk, what appear to be footholds laddering in an upward spiral to the glass house above. He offers Charlotte his hand. "It helped that I had quite the concert to keep me energized."

"You heard—oh, that was such a messy job." Charlotte's cheeks burn. All that chaos just to pound out the anger. What she played, how could that possibly be compared to creating those windows or this tree?

Liam's proffered hand does not waver. No wow eyes, no imp. Just a hand. "What? I enjoyed it. I didn't think a piano could sound like the sea." And now a crooked smile.

Charlotte gives him her hand, thin from diet, fights, and practice. His thumb closes over her long fingers and draws them toward his shoulder, as though this tree is a dance floor and a waltz is beginning. Step, step, up. Step, step, up. 'Round and 'round until they are standing on the top of the trunk. There, Charlotte sees eight tiny sets of stairs continuing up along the eight major branches. She'd have to be a tightrope walker to maneuver those.

The glass house, wide and high, completely encases the branches. The branches thin toward the edges of the tree's corona and eventually meld with the frame of the glass house, where shelves of narrow troughs are fastened to every wall.

Liam shows Charlotte one branch for a closer look. "The veli, or dream waters, flow through the roots from the rooms, move up the trunk and through these branches, and trickle into these troughs to grow velifol, the dream leaves. Few eat or drink the veli—what is the term?—'straight.' Too potent, you see. So most will imbibe a derivative of the leaves."

"Like tea," Charlotte says, Arlen's tin collection in mind.

"Precisely. I prefer it in tea as well." Liam reaches into a trough. "But events shouldn't have progressed to this point. I should have cared for the white tree—not let Orna drag it down to the Pits. Should have paid attention to how Arlen lived… placing his own needs last. He tried to teach me that for years. But when I returned home it…never really stuck." Liam tips his hand, and the dirt rains back into the trough. Storms blacken his whole face, and the stench of anger swells in the air, but only for a moment. "He deserved better. They all did, didn't they?" The question hangs in the branches between them.

Charlotte folds her arms. Pent-up shame swallows Liam like folded wings. "You can't hold yourself responsible for the Lady's actions."

"Ha!" He stares at his reflection in the glass.

Shame. Misery.

He needs you, the Voice pleads.

Bully for him. What about me?

After all the running and fighting, it's strange that Charlotte needs the Voice in her heart to spur her here, when it's just a guy and a girl on silvery branches in the night. But she does. Even with the bellows warming her, moving her, her hands tremble as she reaches out to clean the dirt off his hand. "Just look at it, Liam. This tree. You did this, and it's brilliant. Ember and the others were pretty skeptical, but you've shown them you care." Her hand squeezes his. "You're making things right. That counts for a lot."

To give him space, Charlotte tiptoes along one branch to reach a glass door set in the west wall of the glass house. She opens it and steps out onto a roof made of long, flat slabs of stone. Tall, curved battlements stand at attention every few feet along the ledge.

The waning moon does not have to reach far from the treetops to hide behind the thick clouds overhead. A night breeze stirs her hair, and she breathes in the soothing floral and herbal notes drifting up from Arlen's gardens below. Charlotte walks to one of the many crenels in the battlements, places her hands on the stones on either side of her, and peers out. Everything seems a green stillness now, but deceptively so, like a blanket thrown over a child. Something's moving under the green covers, ready to pop out at any second.

The air brings a faint smell of shame: Liam follows her out onto the rooftop and comes to a standstill behind her, silent. The smells of shame and of roses do not mix well.

"Arlen says people accuse Dorjan of doing it—of stabbing you, I mean. But I don't believe it." *Brilliant, Charlie. Charming, upbeat topic choice.*

A pause. "You don't want to believe it, or do you have a specific reason for not believing it—proof of sorts that he didn't do it?"

"Arlen trusts him, a lot. And Arlen doesn't seem the type to give his trust out, you know, willy-nilly."

Another pause. "I don't like him, but I don't think it possible of him either. Whoever did it didn't have a smell or sound. Likely a cursed lover or something." He smiles at his own drama.

"But I thought anyone who isn't the owner of the blood dagger dies when they hold it." Charlotte shudders as the half-rat's screams echo in her head. Even Cein wouldn't touch the blood dagger. But the Lady did ask for it....

"Yes, everyone except you." A sidelong look.

What am I smelling? It's not bad, but it's not, not what I'm used to. "Y-yeah, Arlen told me about the curse. The 'purest of hearts' and stuff."

"Mmmhmm."

A couple beads of sweat trickle down Charlotte's spine, and she inhales the scent of roses, mint, and lake water from an incoming breeze. She hopes this is enough to cool her down because she doesn't dare take off her sweatshirt. "What is the difference between the velidevour, the 'commoners,' and the 'princeborns'?"

Liam's face smooths and sets like a statue. "Princeborns are the aristocracy of the velidevour. We are, I shall say, different, in power and in breeding."

"'Breeding'?" *What the hell am I asking? Danger, danger, Charlie Aegir!*

"Legend has it that the original sixteen kingborns were the offspring of earth and Aether, Source of all Magic." Liam seats himself in the crenel before Charlotte, nearly blocking her entire view of the clearing. "You saw the raven turn to dust, just as humans and animals eventually do when they die. We are creatures of the earth, one and all."

Charlotte rubs her calves one at a time with the back of her foot. *You started this conversation, Charlie, now finish it.* "So for kids and all that—"

"Commoners can mate with nonhuman animals, producing more velidevour. But offspring of human and any velidevour, commoner and princeborn alike, rarely survive because they quickly gorge themselves on the human mother's soul and die of gluttony before birth. Princeborns cannot have litters like the commoners. The embers in a heart's fire cannot be so carelessly spread about, or the fire will be lost entirely. Our magic, our kind, it is… precious." A fleeting darkness flickers across his face. "Or so I'm told. Which, then, makes it fortunate that for us, physical intimacy is one thing, and procreation quite another, especially with the magic required to ignite a new heart's fire. The two acts can be quite mutually exclusive, don't you see?" The imp grin spreads from mouth to eyes—hell, even his hair's got a little extra bounce. "I can relocate us to more comfortable quarters and—"

"And finish that line with *anything* having to do with a demonstration, and I'm shoving you off the roof. And don't you go all pouty on me, because I know you've got wings, Fly Boy."

"I wasn't!" Liam says, although he's none too pleased that her logic cut him off so quickly. "I just think it best to remove ourselves before any commoners lurking about see you, that is all."

"Yuh-huh." Charlotte crosses her arms and glares at him skeptically. But between his boyish sulk and the sweet night air, she finds herself rolling her eyes and laughing to herself. Whatever cruel streak Liam has must be pretty weak compared to the gentle warmth of the Liam who taught her to skip a stone. "Honestly, Liam, you're hopeless."

Liam laughs too, albeit softly. "I've been called far worse."

Charlotte strolls to the next crenel in the battlements. She searches the clearing around Rose House for the space where the cursed white tree had been. A hole remains, and it's covered with a dome of metal and glass. *Should be concrete instead. They deserve to be buried in their own darkness, Cein and the Lady.* She looks up at the clouds, the fragment of moon, and sighs. "Why couldn't there be stars tonight?"

"Stars are boring."

Odd pronouncement.

Liam jumps up onto the battlements and begins hop-walking over Charlotte, who's still seated in a crenel, back and forth, and back and forth. No easy feat, but then he is part bird. "With clouds, you never know what will happen. Rain, lightning, snow. Or perhaps nothing at all. Infinitely more interesting for their unpredictable nature than bright, steadfast stars." He pauses to look squarely at her.

"I like the stars. I like finding the constellations." Trips to

231

the woods. Campfires late into the night, and even after the fires had gone out, she'd watched the smoke curling in the air as her father pointed to the stars that guided him at sea. Charlotte wouldn't have minded the Navy, not at all. Music's great. But it feels open, out there, on the sea.... Life is open there, wide open. But she couldn't leave Anna behind. Not there.

Not that I've done better. She's still out there, without me. I was supposed to teach her the stars. I was supposed to teach her about the monsters.

Liam almost knocks Charlotte over on his leap down. "The sea is far more pleasant. Think on that."

I will think about my family whenever the hell I want, Bossy Imp. Without a running commentary from you. "I saw your paintings of the sea. No stars. Not a twinkle. Why not? Night skies too difficult for the natural genius?"

"No." Liam puffs up his chest as clouds swirl in his eyes. "I just don't care for them. Every human artist does the stars at some point. Your precious sister can walk into any gallery and stare at the stars all she wants. So she doesn't need you. There. Problem solved."

"Bastard!" Charlotte shoves Liam hard, his words echoing over and over: "*She doesn't need you.*"

How DARE YOU!

"*She doesn't need you.*" Yet Charlotte cannot unhear what he said.

You DON'T know her.

"*She doesn't need you. She doesn't need you, need you, need you....*" On and on it goes, reverberating off her temples, driving tears from her eyes.

And you DON'T KNOW ME, so FUCK YOU. Charlotte's heart lurches, sinks, twists.

Calm down. The Voice in her heart spreads from Charlotte's chest and paints her insides with quiet. *Where does the anger lie?*

She grabs her father's pendant and counts her breaths. *One, two, oh who am I kidding? Three, four, I'm far more pissed at myself than at this guy. Five, six, what does he see? An ugly chick who's pissed, hurt, and scared shitless of being forgotten. Seven, eight.* "D-don't talk about Anna that way. Please." *Nine, ten, let's try again.* "My dad taught me about the stars. Did your parents teach you how to paint?"

No approach. No movement at all. Stunned, like a bird that's flown into the wall of the glass house. "They gave only one lesson, over and over."

The sudden reek of anger and shame flood the air so quickly that Charlotte holds her breath to keep from gagging. Liam looks up, and Charlotte sees lights delicately swirl in his eyes. No. Not lights. Tears.

Liam swallows, then resumes: "Power is everything. That was *the* lesson." Half laughs, half smiles, half looks away.

Charlotte swallows too. That half-living look on his face, that half-dead curve in his back: that was her school self, right there. Barely surviving on what had already been destroyed inside her. Everyone else thought she was just being a bitch. Idiots.

Charlotte approaches until her feet intercept the line of his downcast eyes.

A pause. "Your feet must be cold."

Charlotte shrugs. "Thought bare feet was the look around here." She offers her hand.

His warm hand enfolds hers. His heat travels quickly up her arm to her chest, neck, cheeks. "Blasted shoes always pinch so," his voice low, warm.

Charlotte snorts, and smells that new, different something overriding the shame and anger like rain that cleanses the air of old rot. He pulls himself up to her, his wow eyes ON and—

A mournful roar from the lake region. It builds and builds and builds, shaking the treetops in waves.

"What is that, anyway?" Charlotte points in the direction of the sound, somewhere near the lake. "Everyone's so hands-off and hushed up about it. But it's hurt, isn't it? It needs help." She catches the same scent of pain from earlier that day. Sadness too—no, harsher than that. Grief.

Talon-like fingers close over her shoulder: No gentle warmth this time. "It must be left alone." Liam's voice is emphatic. A decree.

"*It* is in pain." She shrugs off his hands.

"*It* is none of our affair."

Charlotte rounds on him: "*You* were none of my affair, and now here we are. But God forbid you get your own hands dirty, so I'll talk to Arlen. He's not afraid of helping lost causes."

But Liam cuts her off from reentering the glass house with his awesome slab of a chest, the same authority that revealed itself when Poppy spoke out of turn to him before. Yet his speckled curls look so limp, and his face creases with fear and worry. "I know it's a trap."

"So that thing has to suffer in a trap so you don't get your hands dirty?"

Charlotte can hear the Voice in her heart tisking at her words. *A bit thick.*

Well, he's being an ass. Doing right is almost always a dirty, painful business. High time he learns that.

Silence. A darkness spills like sludgy water from Liam's feet across the rooftop. A power fills his face, so hot it hurts to look upon, yet his voice shocks with its cold: "Indeed, doing right is often a painful business. So what great wrong were you righting that called for your body as a sacrifice?"

"SHUT UP!" Charlotte launches herself at Liam and

234

sends them both crashing through the glass house and down, smacking into the silver tree's branches as they fall. Snap, clang, crack, Rice Krispies, and THUD.

Charlotte rolls away, leaving a glittery trail of crushed glass and blood, and lifts her head to find Liam bent nastily across the tree's base. *God, I broke his back! No, please, just, this fucking anger and WHY did you FUCKING have to say that?!*

He coughs. Blinks. Sees her.

Can't let him see through me. RUN! Charlotte catapults up and into a run with barely a breath in her. She has to find a way out, away. *Please, House, I need your help!*

The first door on the left unlocks. Through it, then lock it. Charlotte spins around to find herself inside an empty white room.

"Charlotte!" Liam's coughs grow louder.

"I'm sorry, Liam, but I'm done," Charlotte calls out with a sob into the emptiness. "I have to go away. Please, House, let me go away."

A hole opens at her feet. She falls through it just as the door bursts into a cloud of splinters.

Pastry Massacre #1

Freefall, then SPLAT. The crash is loud, sploshy, sweet, horrific.

Charlotte sniffs at her crimson hands: raspberry pie. Licks a couple of fingers: really, really good pie. Assesses where she's landed: on a kitchen counter and in a sticky mess. The entire countertop and nearby wall are coated. Crust now cakes the ceiling where the trap door was a moment ago. Arlen, still bent over an open oven door with white mitts, pie in hand, gawks for a moment, then says, "Well... I hope you don't mind apple instead."

"N-no-oh..." The word is lost as Charlotte grunts in pain. She forces herself to sit, even though her hip joint is screaming. But as she pushes herself upright, she slips, falls, and thumps onto the kitchen floor.

Arlen throws the pie in the oven and examines her. "Don't worry, nothing's broken. I can make you some tea to deal with the pain."

"No time. Liam—"

On cue, he slides down the handrail from the second floor and lands with a soft grunt. He moves with uneven steps into the kitchen, eyes storming.

Arlen stands in front of Charlotte, blocking Liam's view as he wipes his hands. "Her hip bone's bruised. She requires

236

healing, or at least a respite from whatever it was you're—"

"Serves her right," Liam scowls. "Nearly broke me on the tree upstairs over nothing." He cocks his head, ready for a backlash.

"She didn't mean to." Arlen turns the kettle on, calmly, as if there's no pastry massacre underfoot and on the cupboards.

"Did too," Charlotte mumbles through her hair. No sense denying it.

"See?!"

"But she did not nearly break you over nothing. Hold all the contempt you like, but I know you, Liam." Arlen places one hand on Charlotte's back and holds out the other. "And I know Charlotte does not react without reason." Charlotte attempts to pull her feet in and center her balance, but between the pain and pie filling, she only gets a few inches off the ground before slopping back down. "Yes, you're right. Best stay there, and I'll bring the healer to you."

One fall is embarrassing. Two, humiliating. *I'm going to curl up and be the ugliest raspberry muffin in the world.*

"She's the most ungrateful, defiant—"

"*Master* Liam," Arlen eyes him while selecting from the great collection of drying plants hanging in the herbarium, "had you minded your manners, I highly doubt Miss Charlotte would be in this state in my kitchen, and my kitchen in this state."

Slip-slop. Charlotte watches a chunk of pie fly past her face and go splat on the cupboard. *Did Liam just kick a pie?*

"I did. I was very polite, and decent, and then, THEN, she had to propose—"

Hey, I'VE got a slice in this too. "Something's hurt in the woods. I've heard it ever since I got here. Why doesn't anyone help it, why's it so impossible? It can't be *that* impossible."

Liam crouches over her. Such a musk of anger, and fear,

237

again. Nauseating. And cold: his body carries the cool night air in with him. His breath breaks through her curtain of hair. "I did not save your life only for you to throw it away."

Charlotte refuses to breathe until Liam finally pulls back —rolls back? No, he's *slipping* back, off the balls of his feet and, slop!, ass-first into the mess with a nasty thud against the cupboard. She parts her hair curtain to peek out and sees Liam, body a red-purple-y mess, raspberry-stained curls over eyes.

He looks ridiculous. So does she.

Charlotte can't help herself. She lets out a snort and says, "All we're missing is the ice cream." And laughs.

A harmony falls in cadence with her laughter, but deeper, rich and beautiful: Liam.

Not a peep from Arlen, though. When he approaches —with a most careful tread—bearing Charlotte's tea, he is double faced. Oh, the smile on his face is genuine, especially when Charlotte tells Liam he "missed a spot" and flings a gooey shrapnel at the last bit of white on his tunic, but his eyes tell another tale. The mischievous sparkle Charlotte's grown to like so much is drowning in grief.

"This will help the pain. As for what you hear, it's best you keep away. Please."

Charlotte nods and waits for Liam's I-told-you-so triumph, but he doesn't give it. That's because Arlen has braced himself, glaring fiercely, against the counter. Liam's no better, head in his hand and staring at Arlen's clean palm outstretched to him. They're both seething, and that silent anger sizzles all the pie goo like eggs on summer's asphalt.

Charlotte doesn't understand. She wants to, and yet what did she just fight with Liam about? No, no more questions or interrogations. Charlotte gulps the tea down, and feels more than warmth in her stomach: a weird tickle walks over her bones, then springs off the tips of her toes. The pain is gone.

One hand at a time, Charlotte slowly slides herself up the cupboard until she stands next to Arlen. She smiles in thanks. Looks down at Liam, still stuck in himself. She takes a deep breath. "I'm sorry."

A few curls move as he lifts his face.

"I'm sorry I shoved, it's just," Charlotte chokes, wondering how she can explain, but the truth just tumbles out before she can stop it. "I'm so used to no one giving a damn. No family, no friends. Nobody." She swallows, then adds, "Not to mention my thoughts being, you know. Mine."

Arlen squeezes Charlotte's shoulder. The sadness and happiness in his face mix, transmuted into a look of warmth and hope.

This velidevour cares about me. Me.

"You've every right to your inner privacy," says Arlen. "Don't you agree, Liam?" And he reaches out again.

"I really am sorry, Liam." Charlotte feels her concern pass to and through Arlen, as though they're a life chain on cracking ice. "You hit these nerves in me. Really, really raw nerves. I can't just beat on you for doing that. You deserve a warning shot first, but I didn't give one. I'm sorry."

Arlen coughs. Pointedly.

Liam gets the hint and uncovers his face. "Good. Glad that's settled."

A pause. Another cough.

Liam watches himself squish goo between his toes. Swallows. And with a softer voice, says, "And I apologize for not respecting what—who—matters to you. That was wrong, and I am sorry."

Charlotte narrows her eyes. She knows a half-assed apology when she hears one.

You are not the only one new to repentance, the Voice says with a gentle nudge on her ribs. *Give him time.*

I'll be here until I die. That long enough?

"Well, now that you two have mended," Arlen motions toward the door, "I'm going to need you out and away so I can—"

"Don't even try, sir. We made the mess, so we'll take care of it. Riiight?" Charlotte gives her smile freely, her own inner imp drawling on that last word.

Liam scratches the back of his neck. "Erm, I'm afraid my skills are lacking—"

"Bah. Time to learn." Charlotte dives into the drawers by the sink to fish out several washcloths and towels, tossing them to Liam. "Here, you can do the easy part and wash down the counter. I'll mop the floor." She finds a bucket from the cabinet under the counter—sure enough, everyone keeps one there—and fills it with soapy water, then sets it on the floor. "Where's the mop?" she asks Arlen as she reworks her hair into a loose, sticky braid.

Arlen's so gobsmacked at the sight of Liam quietly washing the counter that it takes him a moment to remember. "In the closet on the other side of the refrigerator. Yes, over there."

For the next half hour, Charlotte and Liam clean while Arlen chats—not about whatever was in pain outside, but about baking. Pie-crust ingredients, folding methods, how pie filling reacts to this or that. When he reaches what he calls the "lard versus butter debate," Charlotte has to bite the inside of her lip to keep from sighing. She glances over to Liam, only to find he's silently miming Arlen's speech using his washcloth for a pie: "Only lard allows you to roll a pie crust thinly, like so...."

Charlotte stifles her laugh. Poorly.

Arlen pauses his lecture. "Something amuses you?"

"Oh, you know, just picturing Dorjan's reaction if he knew about all these pies."

"Ha! No, best not tell him. The poor boy would probably cry."

Tap tap tapping on the window, small and frantic. Their three heads turn to see Ember hovering by the window, chirping with urgency.

Arlen steps out to meet her.

The air about Liam hums. Charlotte senses the authority rippling up his skin. She quickly wipes the last bit of crust off the hanging pans. "What's going on?"

Liam hushes her and moves closer to the patio door. "Trouble." He refills a bowl with soapy water, then holds the bowl over his head, and tips. The hum about him amplifies like a microphone's feedback, and the water clings to every inch of curl, clothing, skin, the lot. When the magic goes silent, the water runs off Liam to the floor. No more goo on this guy. Even the blood dagger strapped to his back glistens beneath the lamps.

Only there goes the floor again. "Hey."

"Wait." Liam whips a towel onto the floor. Another hum sounds: within seconds, every drop of water soaks into it.

"Why didn't you do that before? We could have been done ages ago."

"Because," he purrs at her, curls framing a boyish smile, "we would have been done ages ago."

Charlotte does not know what to say.

Arlen returns to the kitchen with a furrowed face. "You cannot put it off any longer. You must hold court before

241

Cein leads the Incomplete out into the world. Use Rose House, if necessary."

Lightning flashes in Liam's steady gaze. "Yes, I suppose Orna can't be put off any longer." His gait toward the basement steps is so calm, too bloody calm for Charlotte's liking as she follows in his wake. They pause in front of the basement door.

"There's got to be something I can do," she says to Liam's back, to Arlen's face. "I can't go all abracadabra like you guys do, but I've taken down half my school's wrestling team." Which, as she says it, sounds rather piddly compared to Cein and the rest.

"Worthy victories, I'm sure," Arlen says as he wraps an arm around Charlotte's shoulders. "But this is Liam's battle now."

Charlotte's heart and gut trade places. "Please, let me do something."

Liam opens the door. Glances over his shoulder at Charlotte. Winks. "Wish me luck." He shuts the door.

"Be careful!" she hollers. She has no idea if he heard.

Part 2

Can you see the real me, can you?
—Pete Townshend

Old Flame

A little orange bird watches closely from the banister.

"I think it'd be best if you return to the kitchen with me, Charlotte. You ought to have some supper."

"I'm really not hungry." A deep, deep cold creeps into Charlotte's bones, as though the Pits themselves can seep into her with all their death, hisses, teeth, magic ladies dressed in lingerie. Charlotte huddles next to Arlen, shivering.

"You must keep your strength, especially if something is to happen."

Charlotte gives him a wry look. "Can you sound *any* more ominous?" Still, she accompanies him back to the kitchen and sits on a stool by the counter.

"I must say, I do like these modern conveniences. Indoor plumbing is so agreeable, and refrigeration opens up so many possibilities." A burner going and a small pot on the stove, Arlen pulls a large container from the refrigerator and scoops out some stew.

"Can I ask you something?"

"Of course."

"The Lady and Liam. They a thing a long time?"

"'A thing.' Oh! Well. Depends whether you define a century as 'a long time,' I suppose." The scent of mushrooms, peppers, and tomatoes permeates the room. "And you saw Orna. She is very beautiful."

Yeah, 'cept for those black painted teeth. Charlotte blows a bit of hair out of her face and holds up her head, heavy with visions of the Pits… and yes, of those two. "I saw. So what, she pull a *Fatal Attraction* and boil Liam's pet?"

Arlen looks at her quizzically as he searches a cupboard for some dishware. "What do you mean?"

Charlotte crooks an eyebrow at him. "The break up."

"Ah." Arlen stifles a chuckle. "Liam's conquests tended to be human women, who, I'm sure you've surmised, usually don't have the strength to obsess over a man after a hundred years. But then, Orna is no human." He sets a bowl of simmering goodness before Charlotte.

Can't even think of the last time I had honest-to-god vegetable stew this delicious. Try not to glop all over the place, Charlie, you're not a wolf. At least I know Arlen's used to lousy manners. "Who *is* she, anyway? She's not like you, but she's so different from Cein and them."

Arlen pours himself some hot water for tea. "Orna slithered out of the depths of the Pits centuries ago. Her lineage has always been a puzzle to me. One thing is certain: she craves power, and Liam comes from a very powerful house." He unlocks a small, battered tin and measures a pinch of what looks like fresh lavender petals. "The heir of a princeborn family, Liam could rule an entire region, perhaps even the entire race, if the princeborn families were to ever end the House Feuds."

Charlotte watches the petals spark and dissipate in the water. "Is that velifol?"

Arlen smiles in response.

Charlotte teethes the spoon, thinking.

No wonder the commoners hate Liam. The Lady's the one with the plans to feed them, but Liam had to go off and make her an ex. If he couldn't be bothered to give a shit, then they went to the one that did. Even awake he still did't do bubkes about anything, because he was too busy with his latest distraction. Me.

No wonder she wants me out of here. Maybe she's the one Arlen called the 'darkest of hearts.' Maybe she can hold the dagger and not go up in flames. Maybe Campion was telling the truth. Maybe the Lady can use Liam's dagger to get this mark off…. What am I—NUTS?! She's a fucking liar and a serial killer. Shit, Charlie, THINK.

Charlotte doesn't see Arlen close his eyes, nod, and softly release his breath, not wanting to trespass on her thoughts: she's studying the mark on her wrist, holding it close to her face. It looks like henna, yet not. An ornate birthmark would be more accurate.

Moments pass, then: "About these tattoos. I've seen the vine-and-leaf combo on commoners like Campion and Poppy. Does mine have thorns because I'm human? And what about princeborns… and you?"

Arlen chokes on his tea. "Why do you ask that?"

"Because I saw—"

The front door bursts open to Campion, more ragged than ever. "That damned nephew of yours had better cease his hunt, old man," he kicks the door shut, "or Cein's going to take that precious border girl out from under the protection of his bloody muzzle."

Charlotte flies out of the kitchen and past the stairs. "Don't you fucking DARE." She balls her fists, ready to swing the moment she gets a chance.

Yet Campion goes right on standing there, amused. "This pet requires discipline," he addresses Arlen over her shoulder. "I'm sure I've got a gag somewhere, if you need it."

"Be silent," Arlen snaps.

Charlotte sidesteps to make way for Arlen, hoping he'll body slam Campion as he did before. Arlen's glare promises

247

as much: even Campion's face turns serious, although that could be from Ember landing on his shoulder, chirping into his ear, or from the growl that moves up and down Arlen's throat.

"You know I cannot stop Dorjan, just as I cannot stop what happens outside the Wall."

"Impotence is no excuse."

The growl magnifies.

Arlen lunges at Campion. But Campion's ready for him, and the two snap light and time as their bodies clash. Hands locked in hands, Campion's mad grin, Arlen's mad grimace, Rose House itself feels ready to crack beneath the pressure of their magic.

Ember's feathers explode, as she re-forms in human shape. Her arms loop around Campion's neck and she hangs upon his neck, an orange albatross he can't cut loose.

Charlotte jumps into the fray too, thinking as loudly as she can: *Don't listen to him, sir! You're like the Clint Eastwood of velidevour, and only an idiot would talk to Clint that way.* "Look, you want a cage match, Campion? Outside. Right now. You and me," Charlotte calls him out.

Campion studies Charlotte with sly eyes as he holds his hands up, promising Ember, "All right, I'll say my piece from the Lady Orna and go. Deal?" Ember waits for a nod from Arlen before she mumbles an agreement.

"Is Liam down there with her now?" Charlotte asks.

The question breaks Campion off the fight completely. "Really. He of all things is your first concern?" Campion smirks as he helps Ember slide down his back onto her good foot. "I'm sure he'll be fine once he and the Lady… reignite their passions. But that's not the message. We down below hear the new tree is completed. The Lady Orna wants it in the Pits."

Arlen crosses his arms. "No."

"It won't be the same underground. The new tree depends upon Rose House. Come hunt with us tonight, and then you'll see for yourself when we return." Ember's words, so simple and direct, take the smugness out of Campion's shoulders.

Charlotte steals a glance at Arlen. He almost looks anorexic. He needs velifol more than anyone, but he often gives his meager share to feed others. He deserves better, so much better. *But how? Another bus of sisters and brothers? The white trees can't have always needed humans before, or Arlen couldn't have left his "bloody days" behind.* "The tree's supposed to help everyone that lives here," Charlotte says with a wave toward Arlen. "You know the Lady will just make it sick and wrong like she did the first one."

Campion laughs. "A human defending a tree. Oh, this is rich. Cein would love this." He doesn't let Ember's chastising eyes stop him now. "Speaking of which, the offer still stands." He points to Charlotte's mark. "You stay here, and you'll just be devoured like any other human. The princeborns can't protect you forever."

"Master Liam made it clear that the young lady is to be treated as his equal, nothing less." Arlen takes hold of Charlotte's arm and pulls her behind him. "Now, if you still have half your wits, you'll attend court below and hear him out."

"Me? Sorry, no. I'm off to hunt and be hunted." To Charlotte, Campion says, "The offer still stands. A far better deal than your sister received, believe me." He vaults to the open front door, transforming midleap, then scampering off.

"Bastard!" Charlotte charges after him, even though the purple fur vanishes in the night. She must catch him, get answers, prove he's lying to her, if he's lying to her.

But Arlen snags her just outside the door. His arms lock around her torso, but still she kicks up a storm, screaming, "Fuck you, let GO. I need to find Anna. Gotta follow Campion.

Arlen, let go NOW!"

Ember steps in her way, hands outstretched to catch or block. "You must calm yourself, Miss Charlotte."

Charlotte growls and snaps "Piss off, Em—" Her snap's cut short. Because her eyes see… baby blues, long red hair. Anna. Even with a price tag half-sticking out of her shirt. Anna. It's her sister, real as real can be. Charlotte stumbles forward, wanting so badly to whisk her up, so afraid this is just another bubble ready to pop at the slightest contact.

"Poor taste, Ember," Arlen says sharply. He reeks of authority and sadness.

The Anna face furrows, confused. Anna moves her head, looks down upon herself. "Oh, I am sorry. I didn't intend—" Anna disintegrates into a pile of ashes and feathers on the ground.

Charlotte crumples to the ground with them. *She was here. For a stupid, torturous moment. I fucking hate this place.* Charlotte hugs her folded legs and stares into the depths of River Vine. The cloud bank gives way to a glittering ribbon of the Milky Way. A raw breeze twists about, chilling the stars, causing them to grow and shrink.

Arlen kneels next to her, bending low to find her face. "Charlotte, you cannot venture out there. If you go—"

"I die," she says softly. "Got it."

"We must trust Dorjan—"

"Who I can't go find either, or I die."

"Well, y—"

"Isn't anyone else sick of death?"

Patience, the Voice in her heart attempts to soothe her.

But it's a vain attempt: *Fat lot of good you've been tonight.*

Arlen's hand rests on Charlotte's head. "Yes. Which is why I think it's best you come in, where it's safe." He rubs the hair above her ear until she looks at him.

Ember stands behind Arlen, jerking her head in the direction of the woods. To the marble tree, to where Campion went, and where she's not supposed to go. To the Pits.

Holy SHIT I forgot, with Anna. Liam's in the Pits!... Got to calm down. Wait until Arlen leaves.

Charlotte blinks herself back to the portico. "Think I'll just sit here for a bit. I'll be good."

"I'll keep an eye on her, sir."

Don't look at her Charlie, don't make it weird.

"Oh. Well, thank you, Ember." Arlen squints at Ember, then rests his hand on Charlotte's shoulder, squeezing it. And a look of concern ripples down from his eyes to a smile that carries a hint of mischief. "Best not to dawdle then." He quietly shuts the front door and, with a wink, walks away into the dark toward his garden.

Court

"So what's going on, do you know? Can you know? Can you, I dunno, link minds with another commoner down in the Pits and—"

"Stop," Ember barks.

Charlotte freezes, eyes searching the clearing for some enemy, some scent of an enemy, SOMEthing.

"Not your feet, your mouth," Ember says with an audible huff.

Why you little—fine, whatever.

They pass the eagle markers at the entrance to the Southern Road. Charlotte walks on the balls of her feet, just in case Campion bounds out and they need to get on the defensive. Yet there are no chatters, no mad grins.

As they progress southward, the scent of bitter tension heightens through the woods, and a painful moaning rides the high air and circles them: a duet of tears. It could be a tortured velidevour, one that Campion's got under his claws maybe, something that can't fly over the Wall and die by Mr. Blair's rifle. "Who's Campion got out there?"

Ember only shrugs, and diverts from the road into the green stillness. Together they move in silence, avoid tripping over errant tree roots. Charlotte almost tramples a small flowering

252

bush except for Ember's warning chirp. *Beats a chatterbox mouse, that's for sure.*

Ashen air webs the lower branches. Ember holds her hand up: just ahead of them, amid the dark, brooding solidity of trees in the night, there is a space, a hole of such blackness that no light can escape. A tree-shaped space.

They've arrived.

Charlotte leans in. She almost sneezes as one of Ember's curls tickles her nose. "Seriously, what about Campion?"

"He may find us, he may not." Ember states matter-of-factly, and then ventures cautiously, "Why? I thought you were fearless."

Please. You're just kissing up after that Anna thing, and flattery's not going to work on me. So. "Just sick of walking into situations blind."

Ember stumbles a half step but quickly recovers. "This staircase," she gestures to the hole, "leads down to a tunnel which connects to the atrium. All tunnels lead to the atrium, and that is where Master Liam and the others will be. And we should be able to reach the atrium via this route, unde-tected." She nods and leads on.

Charlotte follows, unable to suppress a shudder as once again she feels its cold bleakness. "Could work, so long as no one smells us." Her half joke falls flat.

Ember's fingers glide over the trunk. "The Incomplete lack proper senses. And they will not care when they smell me."

"What about me?"

A gust of air. An even greater darkness spills before them: Ember's found the latch in the bark that Campion the squirrel pressed when Charlotte first showed up so long ago. "Let us hope you remain invisible." The black mouth swallows her orange body whole.

"Thanks a lot," Charlotte mumbles. She hesitates just inside the black maw. A hissing breeze, almost like an inhale, sucks her inside. She half-stumbles down a couple of steps and finds herself level with Ember, whose swirling eyes are all that's visible in the darkness. Damp settles on the stones in a cold slime.

Charlotte flips the pages of her mental book back to the last time she visited the Pits. The way Arlen spoke, there must be dozens of tunnels, splitting off the main tunnels, many intersecting and interconnecting. An underground maze. Easy to get lost, yes, but hopefully easy to avoid detection too.

Charlotte uses her nose to guide her steps, following closely in the wake of Ember's bird scent. More scents reach her: the smell of damp and death. Of anger.

"The water road is completely dry!" Burly Man Cein's words ricochet past them.

Ember approaches the tunnel's end without hesitation, Charlotte a few steps behind her. But something blocks a large part of the opening, perhaps a little wall, or an old cave-in. No. This mound has eyes, or holes for eyes. Lipless smiles, or toothy grins. And dried husks for bodies. Skeletal fingers from a disembodied hand beckon motionless to Charlotte, as if to say, "You'll be in this pile soon."

Jenny's brother Samuel is in there. Everyone in that grisly pile had loves, hopes, ideas—a place in the world now sewn shut and forgotten.

Hisses and grumblings well up behind the mound.

"There is nothing left for us but what we take from the lands beyond the Wall." Cein receives a wave of assent, even a few cheers.

If Charlotte wants to see what's going on, then she must get nearer. But she hesitates to trespass on the hallowed mound.

These are forms simply waiting to be ash. Focus on the living.

Says the Voice toolin' around in MY body. But you're right —gotta focus, Charlie. Just a pile of bodies, empty husks. Just kneel. There. Bend forward a little, level out with the mound. Is that a chin stud? Gah, don't look, don't THINK about who's next to you, just hold the hell still. Charlotte crouches alongside Ember, hidden by bodies and bones, and together they look out onto the atrium below.

"First his family dams the water road." Cein paces on the far side of the atrium.

The floor before Cein sways and slithers. From her overhead position, Charlotte sees a bunch of Incomplete crawling near tunnel entrances, murmuring in animal-speak, but a few are completely humanish, like the guy and girl in ragged harlequin costume, accompanied by Poppy, hopping in circles around them. An old man with white hair winging over pointed ears sulks next to Devyn against the far wall. A stone's throw from Devyn's feet are steps leading up to a platform.

"That was not done at my behest." Liam stands with the Lady at the top of the platform. The remains of the throne and the white tree lie in scraps strewn about their feet. "And the well on the borderland is intact, I'm told," Liam continues with his hands on his hips, exercising his privilege to express his annoyance.

"Is that a joke? You know the curse of *your* family ties us to River Vine. *They* cut our white tree off from the current. All that well's good for is a meager handful of velifol now and then." The glow in Cein's eyes, the painted smile—all of it too damn dazzling for Charlotte's liking. He seems to reflect the Lady's radiance, with the silvery draping of her dress barely covering her vitals.

And the Lady, Charlotte realizes, is reflecting light too, for above the platform hangs a static waterfall. Countless

255

lines tumble out of a wide, gaping mouth set into the wall high above the platform. On every line are strung glittering glass droplets. They all turn slowly, this way and that, giving light and taking it. Charlotte watches as one turns, like a tiny disco ball, and it flashes in her eye—

"Charlie, I'm right here!" Bubble pop. "Come on down!" Bubble pop bubble pop.

Liam's gaze flicks up. "WERE THE POWER WITH ME—"

Ember shoves Charlotte into the tunnel wall. Bubbles of light pop before Charlotte's dazed eyes. "What are you doing?" she hisses, her curls bopping Charlotte in the face as she whips back and forth between Charlotte's face and the mound of bodies. "You tried to walk right over the pile and past the tunnel opening. That's a fifty-foot drop down to the atrium floor. Thank heart's fire that the master saw you and shouted, or the Lady might have seen."

And thanks to me, the distraction, those Incomplete could have ganged up on Liam and torn him apart.

Ignore the dead river, the Voice inside her heart braces itself, steadfast. *It cannot harm you as long as you keep your distance.*

"Gaaaah," Charlotte half-grumbles, half-spits to herself as she shakes her head once, twice, thrice of the bubbles and baby blues. "Freakin' magicadabra crap. I'm fine now. Seriously." She scramble-crawls back to her hiding place. No curious glances their way.

"Were the power with me," Liam begins again, no longer hollering, "I would give you all my blessing, and set you free from River Vine. But none of you can hide as you are in the world beyond the Wall, and I cannot release you."

"You are a traitor, Liam Artair." The Lady holds her chin high, as if she's the homecoming queen ready to flick her hair at the homecoming king for stranding her on the dance floor.

"I fail to see how my imprisonment betrays you." Liam has yet to draw his weapon, but a heat glows in him, just beneath his skin, that Charlotte's certain would burn to the touch. His eyes wield no storms now: they're like twin suns, bright and searing, to eclipse the Lady's darkness. "*I* was the one betrayed, and whoever did it will be punished."

The atrium echoes his promise, and the weight of the echo forces the Incomplete into silence.

"And I am here now. And while I would *love* to run my blade through the poisoned heart of my betrayer, you," he pauses as he takes a few steps down the platform toward Devyn, "are more important. You." He turns to look at a tunnel overflowing with huddled Incomplete. "And you. All of you." He gestures toward Poppy and the harlequins.

"Ooooh, he picked me me me! This is great!" She gets a dozen claps and four hops in before Liam's commanding stare puts an end to that. "Go team," she squeaks.

But to everyone's surprise, Liam agrees. "Exactly. If we work together under my plan, no one need starve again."

"Your plan?" The Lady's laugh crackles beneath the glass droplets. "Dearest princeborn, we both know you care nothing for the ways of the throne." She draws closer to him, her fingers caressing his sleeves. "I did all the work so you could play. You always trusted me to do what was best for our people." Her face comes within a breath of Liam's. He remains still. "You can trust me still."

A solar flare erupts upon the platform, surely to melt the atrium and any magic within it. Liam: his arm on fire, flames long and licking, his hand around the Lady's throat. He lifts her off the ground, her thrashing and cursing to no avail. Even when her sharpened fingers lash his face, he does not, will not, flinch. "I told you before: you and I are no more. You will never be lady of my house, and you will never again

257

grace my bed." He drops her, just another bit of old scrap on the pile of dead tree limbs.

Growling, fierce, enraged. Cein poises to launch from the base of the steps.

Liam remains where he is, dagger sheathed, between the Lady and Cein. "She may have helped you survive these many years, but what kind of survival has it been?"

"At least we live," growls Cein through bared teeth.

Liam scoffs and approaches the hissing Incomplete grouping themselves around Cein, who is still crouching, still waiting for an opportunity to strike. "Perhaps, but look at you. How much veli do you require to transform, Cein?" Liam bats a lone tuft of red hair on Cein's mostly bald head. "You cannot possibly hunt enough in this region to satisfy your hunger."

Cein growls but has no response as he hobbles up the platform toward the Lady.

Liam opens his arms wide to encompass the Incomplete surrounding him. "Let me help you build a better future, where the well runs deep and the water road flows freely again."

The Lady laughs, and the Incomplete hiss and spit.

"Go on" A new voice interjects.

Incomplete heads turn in unison like a beat box marching band.

Devyn just stands there with arms crossed. His authoritative demeanor silences the entire gathering. Even Cein, snarling aside, refrains from backtalk.

Charlotte can't help herself—she steals a quick glance at Ember. She's beaming.

Liam, for the teensiest split second, smirks. "My plan will take some time, and all the veli we can gather, but with a new stratagem and a fresh access to the border, we will have humans coming to us voluntarily. They desire a haven where they can seek what their society deplores. We simply give them what they want, and we can be assured of our prosperity."

"And you know this how?" the Lady asks as Cein helps her to her feet.

Liam pulls out Charlotte's phone.

Guess I should have searched his pants more. Jeez, Charlie, can you focus for two seconds?

"I learned by utilizing humanity's single power over us: their technology. I hear you've had many tools like this come your way over the past century, Orna. Had you not been so eager to destroy them, you wouldn't be so ignorant now."

Animal-speak floods the cavern. Silver Hair tugs on Devyn's shoulder to speak. Various claws and fingers point at the phone and at the Lady. Poppy says something that sounds a lot like "Cancan dances are ruder!" which everyone ignores, because it's Poppy.

Charlotte nudges Ember, whispering, "How old is the Lady, anyway? Or are you all immortal or something?"

"The Lady? I am not certain—possibly a few centuries. It's not just time that ages us. Use of our powers ages us too. On meager rations the weak don't last long. The strong can hold out for possibly a few centuries. Velidevour can live hundreds of years, even millennia, but starve for too long and you lose your ability to change. Incomplete are as any mangled beast in the wild—doomed." Ember sucks air through her teeth, then adds, "Unless one mates. That weakens and ages all velidevour. I am strong because I have yet to mate. Like Devyn, I refuse to bear children in prison."

River Vine. Prison. A beautiful, seemingly endless prison. But Charlotte has only been awake in River Vine for a couple of days. "So how old is Liam, then?"

"Arlen once said the princeborn came when the human world was in turmoil, and all those in Europe flocked

259

together to strike where human civilization was born."

Okay, hang on. How would someone inhuman describe human history? Birth of human civilization. Arlen knows Greek and Roman medical terminology—he must have been talking about the Middle East. Add Jerusalem, when thousands of Europeans tried to take it over. "Liam was born during the Crusades." Holy wars. Death, persecution. A world suffering from constant ass-grabs for power. No wonder his family's known for wickedness. The real wonder is that he isn't still ruled by it.

Devyn raises one hand, and the animal-speak simmers down in moments. He lowers his hand toward Cein, *allowing* him to speak.

Cein sneers, but doesn't let Devyn's one-uppery stop him. "Decades under the living decay have wrecked your senses, *master*. How do you expect to accomplish all this without sustenance? You keep the last human for yourself. The Lady would never steal from us!"

"No, I would not." The Lady glides forward, her throat red and pulsing, devouring Liam with her eyes. "You paint us a pretty picture, beloved, but nothing more. Our treaty with the border family has provided us with barely enough veli to sustain our bodies but not enough to increase our numbers."

"Is that not your own fault?" Liam counters.

Cein balks at the remark, but the Incomplete around Devyn grow quiet and uneasy. It doesn't help that Devyn nods slowly in agreement as Liam presses on. "Do you deny that you stole a boy from the border family?"

The Lady's face breaks into yet another dazzling painted smile, almost like she's going to laugh. Funny how not a single Incomplete does the same. Poppy even shivers and squeaks, "Campion did it! I told him, bad, it was a bad bad BAD idea, but he did it! I said he should grpmh fthilfyfg—"

One harlequin covers Poppy's mouth while the other sits on her.

The collective gaze of the velidevour, Incomplete and Complete alike, shifts away from little Poppy toward the platform. The air reeks of accusation.

Liam raises a single eyebrow Cein's way.

Cein draws his burly self up into a knot of vicious muscle. "Do you know how many of our kind have died at their hands?"

"They are the border family. Covenants between velidevour and neighboring humans have always, *always* decreed the border family *untouchable* to velidevour magic. It is no fault of theirs that you banished so many commoners out of River Vine for supposed treasons, ensuring they die by their own marks or the border man's hands."

The air thickens with anger, and the cries of the Incomplete drown out anything else Cein wanted to say.

The Lady's entire body glows like the full moon in all its splendor as she raises her voice above the din. "There is power here that can save us!" She steps closer to Liam as she speaks. "We need only gather enough humans and stray velidevour into River Vine for their veli."

"*Strays?*" The white-haired man yowls like a cat as he stiffens up to speak. "Oh, it's well enough for you to kill mere commoner velidevour like *us* for *your* freedom. And what if there *are* no strays? Will you drain us dry like all the pitiful humans up there?"

Charlotte and Ember duck before heads turn toward their hiding place.

"If Artair drives his blood dagger into the Wall, I can channel the veli to flood the crack and break the Wall." A low hum radiates from the stone ring on Orna's finger and fills the atrium. All the commoners, even the yowling old man, fall silent to the subtle song.

Charlotte's fingertips itch. They itch. She holds up one

hand, her fingers are yarn, and undone—she's undone—being pulled apart, veins unknotting and all, she's undone—

"You know she will come to me of her own accord. She is desperate for her family and will do anything to reunite with them."

—being pulled apart, veins and all, apart and across, across the space to the ring, the ring, the song of the ring and call of the ring and undone, she's undone, she's all stitches and skeins and coming undone to the song, the song—

OW! Charlotte blinks and sees Ember's eyes blaze bright against her pale, grim face. She's pinned Charlotte against what has to be the sharpest rock on the tunnel wall.

Heart and mind connect first. The Voice within unleashes a battle cry: *Defy the Lady!*

Charlotte holds up her whole hand not made of any god damn yarn, and squeezes it into a fist. *Hell, yes. I ain't no stitched thing to snip. My guts and glory are MINE.*

"She is not loyal to you. She sees you as nothing but an immature, selfish boy who forces her to follow his whims."

You bitch! Charlotte grinds her teeth as her body swells with insult and fury. And shame. Because the Lady is right about what Charlotte thought about Liam, in the beginning. *But I know there's more to you than that, Liam. I can feel from your blank stillness that your grays are swirling, uncertain whether to storm or weep. Don't listen to her, Liam. Listen to me: you are more than that.*

The Lady holds out her bone-white hand, glowing like some angler fish's lure. "Let her death mark a new and lustrous beginning for River Vine. For us."

Cein grins over the Lady's shoulder.

Charlotte shivers at the sight. *Like he's the devil sitting on her left shoulder after he's eaten the angel sitting on her right. I swear I see its feathers in his teeth.*

"You speak as if you care about us. Then let the Incomplete out of River Vine. Let them hunt, and heal. Everyone's welcome to tag along, even ol' beaky there," Cein challenges Liam, with a nod toward Devyn.

Ember's face remains blank but eager. Her body curves to crouch closer to the opening as she searches Devyn for a sign, any sign of what to do, but he gives none in their direction.

Liam closes his eyes to the Lady's glow, Cein's painted teeth, the lot. "We cannot survive as the stuff of nightmares." He shakes his head, speaking in a low voice that nevertheless resonates through every crevice of rock in the underground. "We will rise, and rise strong, through *life*, Orna, not death."

"And how many of you wish to wait for this 'rise,' when you can have it here and now?" The Lady opens her arms to the commoners, and many of the Incomplete approach, drooling, their half-human, half-animal jaws full of cockeyed teeth. They easily outnumber Devyn and Liam eight to one.

"We are leaving River Vine tonight, with or without your golden claw of approval, *master*." Cein gives his Burly Man smile.

Ember's mouth flutters as she says something about seconds, about veli, about hearts, and Charlotte can't listen to the rest because she does not understand why Liam's *still* not getting out of there. Most are now encircling him, while the rest are cornering Devyn at the atrium wall. Silver Hair takes one look at Devyn, and Devyn tilts toward an exit.

But Cein's voice cuts him off. "Who says you're dismissed?"

The Lady's ring begins its song. "All commoners shall follow Cein tonight. Death to all traitors!" She throws up a fistful of pebbles. The pebbles scatter midair and grow, grow, grow, flying to plug one tunnel entrance after another, locking some in, keeping others out. Charlotte and Ember sit back on their haunches, as a boulder comes whistling toward the mouth of their tunnel—

"Enough of this!" A shaft of wood from the white tree explodes, drilling a hole through the rock now plugging their tunnel and embedding itself somewhere deep in the tunnel wall. When Charlotte dares open her eyes again, she sees Liam, still on the platform with arm outstretched from the throw, chest heaving. "You've forced enough pain upon these commoners, Orna. Tell them to back down, or they will die."

The harlequins drag Poppy over to Silver Hair. "Go get'em, take that, and that, and rrrrruf, and a grooooowl, and a—" She maintains an incessant blow-by-blow commentary, but no one's listening to Scrappy Doo.

Charlotte notices that there is a group that doesn't want to fight, and they're taking whatever hiding place they can find against the wall, while the droolers—still too damn many —remain in place. Frozen. They do not cringe. They do not retreat.

Liam looks to Devyn.

Devyn releases such a howl-screech that it knocks one Incomplete into a groveling mess. He strikes one with his elbow, then bends low, kicks another. He somersaults into the air and bursts into a cloud of dust and feathers and flies, dives, talons sharp, raking a third Incomplete's neck.

The Incomplete mobilize, launching themselves, with claws and teeth and cries.

Liam throws his dagger in an arc. He punches an Incomplete, then leaps into the air behind his blade. It spins into his hand and bursts into flame. His eagle cry magnifies the fire-dagger's song as it slashes open the faces, chests, and flailing limbs of the Incomplete.

Three Incomplete jump over the fray to ambush Liam, but he kicks one and grabs another off his back, flinging him to the ground. When a third lands on his shoulders, Devyn flies to Liam's aid, sending the Incomplete tumbling to the ground. A swirl of dust and Devyn has hands to strike and snap the Incomplete's rotting arm.

"We've got to get down there," Charlotte says as she searches the walls for a foothold—hell, she's ready to jump anyway, she can take them, as she did before with the blood dagger.... The one that Liam is using.

"The master can't risk losing you, so *you* are not going anywhere." Ember shoves Charlotte into the tunnel wall—again. "Stay. Here. Understood?" She doesn't wait for an answer, but jumps from the tunnel's mouth, her body morphing into a bird so small, yet she flicks and scrapes an Incomplete's ear before it can bite Devyn's leg.

"Protect the loyal!" Liam's command sizzles in the wavy air about him.

Ember changes once more above the huddled velidevour, so tiny, but her human fist and elbow strike with a force that fells an Incomplete in a single sweeping blow, spine broken.

No one notices that Cein is changing, hair and muzzle growing, more badger than Burly Man, with teeth the size of Charlotte's arm. Patches of humanlike flesh still exposed, still some red balding scalp, with still humanish eyes atop a badger jaw. The human leg crooks to fit under the body, the half-person ass barely covered by a tail. The teeth, the snarl—Cein calls the living Incomplete to circle Liam, while, with a kiss from the Lady, he rounds on Devyn.

Panic bleeds down Ember's face.

Devyn hunches back and leaps through his own dust to emerge changed, his shadow wings unfurled like his screams into the air, eyes locked upon Cein who rises up onto his badger-human legs, mouth open.

The Lady's ring sings, and the Incomplete change, their bones splintering, binding with scraps of the white tree and transforming into living, moving bodies of thorns. One snares

Liam's leg. One mutates between him and Devyn. Another attacks Liam's exposed back.

DON'T YOU DARE DIE ON ME, LIAM.

In another part of the melee, a flash of orange feathers rips through the air faster than Devyn, faster than ring-magic, and stabs Cein in the eye with a well-aimed beak. Cein's giant muzzle shrieks, violet and blood streaming down his cockeyed jaw. His claws flail, nicking Ember's tail.

Devyn wrenches Cein's badger-arm behind his back while Ember flies back to the loyal contingent where she transforms, human body surging with defiance.

Liam beheads one thorny Incomplete, hacks the leg off another. But their thorns keep growing, slowly smothering them and vying with the tears that course down their grotesque faces.

Liam looks upon them, flaming dagger pointed downward. He looks up at the Lady through his bloody, starry curls, the master of sky and strength.

"Don't, don't just stand there—KILL THE TRAITOR," commands the Lady.

The two thorn-infused Incomplete move pathetically, teeth grinding so much their jaws crack. Snicker-snack. Cein's pain-filled breaths echo through the atrium as he too tries and fails to obey the Lady.

Devyn transforms and stands with Ember at the head of the loyal contingent, eyes alert and fists at the ready.

Only the Lady and Liam still stand upon the platform. Across the atrium floor, splintered bones and thorns hiss dying magic. Blood glitters and steams off Liam's body. War looks beautiful on him. Flames lick the blood within the engraved feathers on the dagger, which he points at the Lady. "Take that stone ring off your hand, or I will use this to take it myself."

"You wouldn't dare." She laughs, then crouches. Her fingers stretch and harden into fang-like claws, complete with black venom dripping from every point. A louder song reverberates from the stone, so loud, so strong, an opera soprano belting in their ears—

A final wing of light, brighter and hotter than before. Liam's battle cry is *angry*, vicious. The fire-feathers are as long as the dagger itself. And the eagle cry overpowers the opera diva....

Feathers burn away and only haze remains. The Lady cowers on the ground, singed, jaw clenched against rage and tears. She does not fight as Liam approaches her and touches the stone on her ring. The metal leaves anchoring it in place shrivel as if the stone wants to go with Liam.

He returns to the center of the atrium, and in a single spin creates a ring of fire to burn open every blocked tunnel. Sheathes his dagger. Looks upon those left alive. Speaks. "Orna may have kept you alive, but she forced you to live an existence of fear and pain. Too many have suffered because of her." Liam's voice almost softens. "It is time to leave this life of death and shadows in the past."

Do you mean me? You do, don't you—oh enough, Charlie. Shut it.

"My parents left behind a safe-store of velifol for my use. I will have Arlen bring it here and ration it out among you. Then, once the scouts return with their prey, we will renew the velifol garden."

Poppy's head starts bouncing out of the small crowd. "We're getting super-duper velifol? That's AMAZING. Do you think it's a different color? Will I get neato powers? Will we—vhrmth grmpth thylflufl." Harlequin hands muffle her head and mouth. Liam takes one last look at Orna, who has yet to rise, still staring intently at him. Cein lies on his side near her, one arm broken, tongue quivering on the stone between those painted teeth like a hunted animal too stubborn to die.

So many dead, in ashes all around him. Liam shudders: he used to create with destruction, unleashing the glorious colors of violence upon his canvas, to paint such pictures of death that the world could not possibly forget. All gray dust, in the end. Muted. Coarse. Worthless.

Enough, by heart's fire, enough. "It is time to think of the future of River Vine, and all that we can make of it, as long as we must remain here together, in this place. I am going to do whatever I must. I hope you will do the same."

A burst of feathers and fire, and Liam transforms, circling them once and then flying out through one of the many tunnels.

Raw Senses

Up and out, move up and out. Out of the Pits. Charlotte follows the perfume-y, heady scent of the green stillness she knows lies somewhere above. Slime slickens the tunnel wall beneath her skimming hand, and the stench of battle wanes with each step she takes: she's going the right way.

At last her eyes find a dim lightness ahead, and she hastens toward it and up the stairs and out of the black marble tree, emerging to find a patch of asters and new grass at her feet. She inhales the clean night air and shudders as tension slowly releases its grip on lungs, heart, nerves, and muscles.

A flutter softly lands near her. "This is not a place to laze about."

"'Laze about'? I just got—never mind. How'd you get here from that other tunnel?"

"All tunnels open and close to each other, if you know where to look."

"Sounds like a damned labyrinth."

"Damned is right." Ember's limp is more pronounced as they take the grass road toward Rose House.

Charlotte tries to bite her tongue, but her tongue bites back. "Wouldn't flying be easier?"

"Devyn will lead the scouts' hunt after rations are dispersed.

I shall save my wings for then. I'm still," Ember cracks her neck, "a touch sore."

"Sore? I'm amazed you didn't break a wing, let alone your neck. You're the tiniest kickass warrior I've ever seen."

It might only be a trick of the moonlight, but it looks like Ember's smiling.

River Vine itself feels more at ease. Grass and trees sway gently in the wandering night breeze. The two pause to gaze up at the stars.

They're so brilliant, Dad, so alive.... Dammit. Anna. I wish to God I could know in my bones and heart and all my humors where you are.

"Your sister is not here." Ember says it like it's a fact beyond reproach.

Charlotte sighs through her nose. She doesn't want to start something after the battle Ember went through in the Pits, and yet—her tongue overrides her will, again. "Campion said otherwise."

Ember doesn't flinch, doesn't shrug, doesn't blink. She just keeps looking at the stars as if she's waiting for another wave of trouble to come. "Campion says a lot of things."

"But it's like I can *see* otherwise."

"Of course you can. Fear is easy for our magic to manipulate."

"Could *you* be any colder with that statement, woman? Jeez."

Ember holds her hand to her mouth and breathes. "My breath isn't cold."

Now Charlotte bites her tongue, keeps it bitten, but allows herself an eye roll. Then stops. "Where is it?"

"Where is what?"

"Pegasus. The constellation. It's all screwed up. Those are —those are WAY too big to be stars. And are those planets over there? Hey, where are you going?" Charlotte has to run to catch up with Ember, her pace stronger and steadier than Charlotte could ever pull off after beating up a gaggle of baddies.

"Velidevour should not linger under naked skies lest they become a target of the starfolk."

"Star*what*? Like aliens?"

Ember shakes her head curtly, eyes fixed on Rose House.

The inhuman wail of the forest rumbles out of the trees and over the clearing. "Something's gotta be hurt. Can't we help it?"

"Only if you wish to meet *them* in the process." She waves a hand at the sky behind her. "Once is enough for me."

They cross the remaining grass in silence, Charlotte's eyes darting between the grass road in front of her and the stars and planets above her. They move slowly, like an airplane across the expanse. Could those be airplanes, and the velidevour don't know it?

Back at Rose House, Charlotte pauses on the front portico and turns for one last look at the Western Quarter, where the wails and roars hide. Ember continues through the kitchen and out the back where Devyn waits.

Aggression and distress, Liam and Arlen, their smells mixing with the echoes of argument, knock Charlotte off-balance. She falls against the door as it closes and steadies herself. Through the arches and pots and cupboards and glass, Devyn's eyes meet Charlotte's. He nods to his right, and shakes his head. He might mean, "Leave those two alone." Or, on the flip side, "This is hopeless. Just break those two UP already."

But where are those two, Liam and Arlen? The emotions mix with another smell: paper, old paper.

Charlotte tiptoes across the gilded dining room (*jeez, I breathe in here I'll break something*) and kneels next to an ornate door with a golden keyhole. She sees snippets of shelves, Liam's back, Arlen's hand, throwing his argument into the space between them.

"—no way can I justify turning over all the preserved velifol to that depraved mob below us. To the few honest scouts, fine, but not to Cein or any commoner willing to see you die." Arlen's voice is sharp and forceful.

"It's not your decision to make. I'm not hoarding for the slim chance that my family would show up. They're never coming back."

"And why not? They must be told sometime, or they will punish all of River Vine for insubordination."

"They couldn't care less. If they really cared about me, they wouldn't have left me in that living decay for a hundred years. So, NO, no one is to inform them. Is that understood?"

Arlen steps more clearly into view, hands curled into fists at his sides. A purse of the lips, a nod, then: "As you wish, Liam. But at least consider your own health. You've hardly touched a drop since your recovery!"

"I'm not hungry."

A pause from one corner, then Arlen continues: "You are different."

A pause from the other corner, then: "Would you rather I wasn't?"

Arlen capitulates and heaves a long sigh. "I am not saying that."

"Perhaps this would all be easier were my dagger still lodged in my heart."

"I am—" Arlen does not finish.

Liam is no longer listening. His angry footsteps take him out of sight.

The herbarium and kitchen and OH SHIT! Charlotte slides across the dining room table Dukes of Hazzard style and flees across the reception hall into the parlor. *House, I need to hide somewhere not obvious, please!* But only the door to the music room lies ahead, so she grabs it, yanks it open—*Oh, my trusty bathroom, what a blessed sight you are. Amazing as ever, sweet House.*

Charlotte locks the door as she blinks in the brightness —and at the unexpected and welcome change to her bathroom. In place of the shower stands a large tub with sweet-smelling sachets hanging from the faucet.

Charlotte looks down at her clothes, sticky and sour and now covered with grit and grass (*PLEASE tell me that's grit and grass and not bone and hair*) from the Pits. Her legs are sick of standing, sitting, and pretty much all the other-ing they've been doing today.

Bath it is. And if Liam barges in? The closet's got plenty of shoes.

Upstairs.

Dammit! Charlotte takes a deep breath to ready herself for the run to get a fresh change of clothes (and shoes)… only to see her quarters, all afghaned and cozy. *Hope this means the music room's back where it belongs.* Charlotte digs out the heaviest pair of hiking boots she's ever seen, perches them next to the tub, and turns on the faucet.

Steam cleanses Charlotte's lungs as she strips and immerses herself. She opens the sachet of lilac petals and sprinkles them on the water. Some float languidly on the water's surface, while others tickle her legs, abdomen, chest. Her fingers set a few petals dancing through the water as she clears them from her pendant, her only piece of home. She closes her eyes and thinks.

Ember has no reason to lie about Anna. Campion has every good reason to lie. Liam would lie if he felt like it, but hopefully by now he knows better. Arlen dodges things he doesn't want to talk about, so not a liar, but an omitter.... Someone around here has got to be worth the trust.... There is Dorjan. He's strong, and can move over the Wall with ease—but he's not going to leave Jenny at risk....

A knock. "I see no Do Not Disturb sign, but I'm not risking another assault by footwear."

"What do you want?"

"Can I at least speak with you?"

"I can hear you just fine."

"I feel foolish talking through a door."

"Then don't talk now."

She hears Liam mutter something about a prude.

Hmmph. Just because you saw me in the buff when I was unconscious doesn't mean you have an ogle-pass, especially during hygienic procedures. "Tell you what—you blindfold yourself with a real, honest-to-goodness blinder of a fold, and you can come in."

"Fine." Liam enters, singed and bloody.

And beauti—STOP IT.

A drooping pinkish flower, roots and all, is tucked into his dagger's brace. A large black sash covers his eyes. "Is this acceptable?"

"Yes."

Liam feels his way to the sink and leans against it. "May I please sit?"

"On the toilet, if you want. Lid's down."

Liam's mouth curls with distaste. "I would rather not heal atop a cesspool, thank you." He reaches out, finds the bathroom doorway, and sits with a grunt, legs bent upward and arms wrapped around his knees. His bare toes tap imperceptible rhythms on the tile floor. "I like the tub. You should have said something earlier—I could have made it big enough for two."

"One more line like that and you're out."

"You would deny an injured man the chance to cleanse his wounds?"

Liam lifts the remains of his shirt. A tried and true stomach —*don't you DARE swoon, Charlie*—lacerated and burn blistered. Charlotte winces at the deep gash along his ribs bordered with what looks like black powder. Like wood ash. He sits there, flirting with Charlotte of all people, when anyone else would be moaning for a nurse.

Charlotte can't help it: she smiles. And lobs a soaked washcloth right at his knees.

"Hey!" Liam starts in his seat and knocks his head against the doorway—as if he does not have enough injury upon his person. A return volley seems vital to show her he is not a creature of weakness, nor a trifle to mock with her laughter.

Her laughter. She laughs with youth, mischief, light, song, all at once. "If you need more water to do the magic cleanup you did after the pies, let me know," she says.

Very well, then, my lady. "Excellent." Liam removes the flower from his brace, and adroitly molds the flower, root and all, into the gash across his abdomen. His face, his hands, all remain steady as flower touches muscle and bone. "Thank heart's fire for knitbone." He arranges the washcloth over the wound and begins a soft, lilting spell.

Charlotte blinks slowly: even her eyelids are weary from the day. And the lullaby of water and word makes the steam a blanket around them both, tucking them in, hushing them into a sweet doze. Water threads through all his cuts, down and up and over Liam's skin, yet the washcloth remains soaking wet.

Where's the rest of the water coming from? she wonders through the haze. With one arm covering herself, Charlotte grips the tub and discovers a single, steady stream that flows up and over the lip, down a claw, and along the floor to Liam. "You little sneak."

"You offered."

Although Charlotte sighs with melodramatic exasperation as she adds more water, and even grumbles about magic not knowing how sinks work, Liam hears the truth of her feelings. He listens to her body move in the water with a soft, simple grace, not at all like her battle stance from the morning. He recalls seeing past her armor plates, her hard angles and smoldering temper, when they were skipping stones, and knows the grace she carefully guards inside her. Now he is but at arm's reach. And his astute perceptions can reach very far, indeed.

Charlotte watches the cobwebs of water overrunning Liam turn black or red as they clean and heal. But one area remains untouched: the dark marks on his right forearm. *Marks on his right arm, like me, and he had thorns around his neck by the Wall, like me.* "I'd like to ask you something personal." Her words lumber in the damp air, uncertain how they'll be met. "Honestly, you don't have to answer if you don't want to."

Liam sits very still. "I will answer."

"Does River Vine have the same hold on you prince-borns as it does on humans and other velidevour? Can you *not* get over the Wall either? The reason I'm asking," she continues, seeing his face scrunch, "is because you were *definitely* in pain when you got close to the Wall this morning. Just like me. Because of this mark," she holds up her wrist. "And it looks like you have your own set of marks there," pointing to his right arm.

Liam rubs the mark on his forearm for a few quiet

moments. "Only healthy velidevour should go over, such as the scouts. It is not easy, traveling, acquiring, and returning on a dwindling heart's fire."

"So when you're fully recovered from, well, being stabbed and bleeding all those years, you'll be able to leave?"

"Maybe." He doesn't explain. His face announces the matter closed.

"Okay. Thank you for being honest about it." *Not that you are, not really, but I'm not pressing. Promise. I asked you for privacy before, so it's only fair I give you some too. Focus on washing up.*

Slop. The washcloth dangles from the sink's edge, a pendulum of dirty water droplets plop to the floor with every swing. Liam slides within arm's reach of the tub, clean and dry now. The smooth set of his mouth, the hard set of his body: serious thoughts must be brewing in his mind. "My turn."

No blindfold covers that kind of penetration. Charlotte scrambles out of the tub with the sudden urge to cover herself, to hide from blinded eyes that still see too damn much.

"How did you get to the kitchen from the third floor?"

"I... don't know." The towel's wide enough to cover breasts and groin, but not the burns. "I thought hard about needing a way out, and then, suddenly, there was a way out. That's all there was to it." *Please stop looking at me like that. You sure that blindfold's on tight? Gah, Charlie, just get into some pajamas and change the subject already!* She skitters to the closet and selects a pair.

"Is everything okay in the Pits?" she asks as her head pops out of her pajamas. Then something dark and soft flutters to Charlotte's feet: the sash.

"I don't think I have to tell you what you saw." Liam crosses the room to the fireplace, where he moves one hand in a clockwise circle above the hearth. The logs ignite, and the room turns soft and warm amid soft crackles.

"Yeah, well things got pretty grim down there. So how come you're not taking any velifol?"

"I like it when you worry about me." He smiles like a sad imp. "But honestly, I'm fine."

Charlotte grabs the sash with her toes and tosses it toward the couch. Liam bends stiffly to pick it up and wind it around his fist. Wind. Unwind. Wind. Charlotte sits before the mirror and starts combing her petaled hair. Stroke. Petal. Stroke. How easy it is to distract with little things when the big things feel far, far too big to talk about.

No, no more of that. "It's pretty noble, you sharing your rations with all the velidevour here. Why didn't Arlen want to?"

"Because the survivors of the Pits have only seen results with Orna, and not with me at the helm. He is certain they will attempt a coup because Orna promises survival, has delivered on that promise in the past, and survival, no matter how miserable, is often preferable to uncertainty."

"Dunno. That kind of survival seems pretty pathetic when there's a shiny new tree upstairs ready to work its magic."

"Untested."

"But you're working on that too, aren't you? Ember said something about the scouts going out... t-to hunt."

"Did she?" Liam meanders over and smacks the wall beneath her windows. Its whole face creaks and stretches, and the three windows combine into one fat three-paned bay window. A three-sided bench covered with large, soft cushions pops out of the floor like a kernel of popcorn. "Ah, much better." He yawns, plops down, and pats the seat next to him.

Charlotte bites the inside of her cheek. It seems more appropriate than rolling her eyes, especially when talking about her people—their prey. "Will you use a bus too?" *I'm not even sure I want to hear the answer, so I'm just going to stare at myself in this mirror, and I HATE staring at myself, and get the rest of these petal-knots out of my hair.*

Liam leans forward to study her fingers as she separates strands, drops petal-knots into the wastebasket. "No. But initially, I confess, you could say there will be similarities. But only at the outset, I promise." He reaches into his pocket and pulls out the lavender stone that once adorned the Lady Orna's finger. "I know I make little sense right now, but please, for the time being, trust me?"

Not a demand, a ploy, or a decree. Just a simple request.

Were you not asking for one worthy of your trust? The Voice in Charlotte's heart has a sly edge now.

Don't you go turning my own words against me. But yes, I'll try. For Anna's sake—because there's a chance you'll help me find out what's happened to her, find out if she's safe—I'll trust you, Liam. I'll try.

Liam holds the stone up in the lamplight: its color swirls and alters. "Now this explains a good deal about Orna's ability to pervert the white tree. Matriarchs and patriarchs alike bear stones such as this to mark their power as heads of princeborn families."

"So does that mean Orna is a princeborn like you?"

"Not as far as I know." Charlotte smells a hint of bitter-citrus puzzlement, and dares to look at Liam through the mirror. The clouds in his eyes have grown thick from concentrating on the stone. "She just showed up in the Pits' labyrinth one day, saw I was lonely and... I just never bothered to ask. The water road did flow past the Wall, once upon a time."

"Like the Blair well. The border family, I mean."

He nods. "I always assumed her to be a traveler waylaid by, erm, me."

Charlotte snorts. "Nice one."

Liam's laugh comes in spite of himself: a short burst of music escapes before he can pull it back. "The real question is this: how could she have possibly come across a stone ring? Every stone is considered a vital weapon, a source of incredible power."

"More powerful than your blood dagger?"

"Depends on the bearer," Liam says with a crooked smile, but then he pulls that back too. "What I do know is that a stone's loss would not be taken lightly. Its owner either is dead or is himself broken." He tucks it away in his pocket. "But that investigation can wait until the velifol garden is growing strong again."

Charlotte sets the comb down. The comb's teeth hold her gaze a moment, their straight, uniformed row like the seats on a bus, a bus full of Sweenils and Studchins and Annas... "More innocent lives?"

"I would not trap innocent people."

"Not even models?"

Liam turns away. Puzzlement dissipates in shame. "Not anymore."

Cryin' out loud, Charlie, give the guy a chance. He was just beaten to shit trying to keep the real monsters from killing people. Get up, go over to the popcorn couch next to him, and show him you're willing to hear him out. So Charlotte does.

And Liam takes it all in: her attentive face, the flickering lights set deeply in emerald eyes. The damp strands of dark gold framing a thin but heart-shaped face. Her folded hands resting on folded legs. His words halt in his mouth, unsure of their order, fearful of being misunderstood. "We will only bring those lethal to the innocent. You know how easily their kind hide in society."

"My sister was hardly innocent, but she..." Charlotte rubs her face hard with her sleeves. *Who cares if Liam sees, because I NEED him to see that she matters, she can't NOT matter.*

Liam reins in his sneer and buries it beneath his hand. He

allows himself a moment to lean against the sofa and glare with such intensity out the window that the very glass begins to warp. *That selfish wench never ceases to douse the lights in the Lady Charlotte's eyes. Her memory is tiresome, and does nothing but bring pain, yet the Lady Charlotte insists on loving the one least deserving of her attentions.*

A crowd of shadows trickles into the clearing. Liam quickly fixes the glass and motions Charlotte to come closer. "It begins. Look."

Charlotte's hands travel to her hair and begin the braid-unbraid rhythm. She spots Ember's color, Devyn's cowl. There's a flibbertigibbet of a shadow that could be Poppy. There are those harlequins, and the silver hair, and perhaps Campion there, at the end. The rest must be prey.

HUMAN. They are human, on their way to Liam's tree with its silver needle roots—

"No." Liam's wrist grazes her temple as he reaches up to tuck a loose strand of hair into her braid. His heartbeat thunders there, just for a moment, before his hand slides down her braid and down her arm to find her fingers. "The tree will not touch them. Not at all."

Her heartbeat races to catch up with his. Hands still wound together, she asks, "Promise?"

One corner of Liam's mouth turns upward. Charlotte mirrors it.

"Promise."

Faces close. His breath tickles her cheek.

I'd have never let Anna get this far with a boy. Not that Anna had bothered much with dates, preferring the excitement of fooling security. Anna loved a thrill, she—

Liam coughs, hard and loud, and frees himself. Even when the cough subsides, his face is all lines, throat tight as if to hack up bile.

But his smell tells Charlotte more than anything: hot vinegar. Jealousy. Over what she can't determine, nor does she have time to think about it, for the shadows are entering Rose House, herded like cows, single-file to the butcher's kill floor. "Are any of those people going home?"

Liam swallows back the words he yearns to say regarding the sister. *The Lady Charlotte now fixes all her attention upon the prey and all their worthless ties to the world. She knows none of these people, yet she cares for their welfare. The right words must be said, or she will spurn me. Then she'll demand that selfish waif again.* "I instructed the scouts to seek only those who've taken a life and escaped justice. Now they will have their reckoning, as painless as a blessing, and the world will be free at last of their stain."

Charlotte gnaws her lower lip. Oh, she can remember her father throwing the newspaper down upon reading about technicalities, mistrials, hung juries. "What about her?" She peers down at one small, hunched-over form shuffling along-side Devyn. "No way she's a killer."

The right words. Find her ear—don't touch it with your lips, fool, she'll strike you! Just close enough to let her hear only, the right, words. "A defenseless woman in appearance, but her heart shares many stories: of a shelter for those without homes. Of coin flowing from the magistrate to care for those homeless, whom she then poisons with slow, steady patience, day after day, meal after meal. Society cares little about one less vagabond. Or seven."

Her fingers continue to braid, her eyes upon the woman.

"I mean to draw humanity's monsters here, to give us their veli as they sate their black passions. I will alter the Wall's mark, leaving them free to go home. When their black passions arise, they will come back, and in so doing, spare humanity from the consequences of those passions." *Yes, your fingers slow as you hear my words, see as I see.* "They'll feel compelled to come back."

282

Charlotte watches the small old woman, guided by Devyn, disappear through the front door beneath them. Ember enters next, leading a man with raging mullet. "Damn, I was hoping she'd bring Homicidal Maniac from the bus."

Liam releases a long exhale. "Yes, she was keen to find him. Let us hope the next hunt is more fruitful."

Charlotte shudders. "So long as she takes Dorjan with her. Homicidal Maniac could snap Ember's wings off with two fingers."

A humongous man strokes Poppy's neck and shoulders as she leads him along. Charlotte's fingers pick up speed, and then some. "You'd throw your kind to those monsters?"

"How did you know what he is?"

"It's not difficult."

Odd that the Lady Charlotte can detect the man's perverted taste from behind this glass, yet she is not so keen to mark the old woman's crimes. Her mind darkens as the sea under a clouded sky. She shivers, and not from cold.

Liam draws himself ever closer, determined to soothe her. "Velidevour aren't harmed by a prey's desires, never fear. Imagine if we could get people like him out of society, away from the children."

Liam senses her breath becoming shallow and closes his hands around hers, reveling at the touch of her skin, warm and cold like fire and winter's night. "I have never met someone so willing to risk her life in the darkest places for my safety." *Heart's fire, the rhythm inside her beats like a pack of horsemen on the hunt. Why does she refuse to look upon me?*

"Safety nothin'. Just nosy, that's all."

"Concerned for my welfare, then." Liam manages to guide Charlotte's hands away from her hair, but where to put them —his chest?

The last of the shadows are marching into the house:

283

Campion leads a woman—no, a girl. Red hair. Baby blues.

It isn't real, the Voice in her heart says sternly.

But Charlotte's so damn sure that it's Anna, HER Anna. "Who's the human kid?" She shakes off his hands and presses her own against the glass, straining for a better look.

"What?" Liam only glances at the empty landscape. "No human children were taken. I gave strict instructions, and believe me, Devyn would ensure those instructions were followed."

I thought you were ready to trust, the Voice in Charlotte's heart flicks a rib like one would flick an ear.

She winces, thinks, *But since when does Campion listen to Devyn or anyone else?*

There has to be a logical explanation.

Says the thing inside me that never talked until I was next to a wall that surrounds a magic land with shapeshifting dream-eating pit dwellers beneath a room-moving house. Yeah. Logic. That's the name of the game around here.

Charlotte turns her focus away from the Voice and realizes Liam hasn't moved beside her.

Liam realizes Charlotte's thoughts have been far from him for some time. "Did I say something out of place?"

"I…"

"And you have yet to say anything about what I've told you, shown you."

"I think I should just go to bed. Please." Charlotte stands, nearly knocking Liam off the window seat in her rush to get away.

He opens his mouth to argue time again, but changes his mind. *What is that word Dorjan used about the Pits once? Flummoxed. Yes. This lady has me flummoxed. I HATE being flummoxed. And there she goes, under the bedclothes, braiding. I have been well mannered. Restrained. I have done nothing to displease. This silence is going to press itself upon her until she is compelled to open her mouth, or I will cast a spell on her myself. Patience!* "Well, what do you think? Is it not a humane solution? A 'win-win' as your people call it?"

"It's hard to say. I'm not for using people up like batteries, but… you're just talking about the bad guys who got away, right? Like molesters?"

Heart's fire, she speaks! "They're not hard to seek out, especially when they're sleeping." Liam's voice surrounds Charlotte, and she balls herself into one corner of the bed. "The more forbidden, the deeper the desire. And certain desires have certain scents, like child lovers, who reek of spoiled apples." *Allow me to hold your hands once—damnation, don't cross your arms! Deep breath. Compliment the lady. Sweet words, sweet movements.* "You have very pretty hair, you know. There's no need to tie it back."

Charlotte refuses to meet his eye, annoyed. *He goes from ridding society of sickos to giving me hairstyling tips, seriously?!* "I like it out of my face."

Fine. I shall stretch myself out on this bed. If you won't look upon my face, perhaps you would prefer to look elsewhere. "I have a number of nice attributes myself."

She snorts.

"Well?"

Still bound into a knot, she only unburies herself long enough to say, "Your eyes."

"As heavenly as the sky?"

Silence.

Evenings with one's lady should not be so tedious, should they? Time to come to it. "Perhaps you haven't noticed, but we shall be together here for what I imagine will be a very long time." Liam raises himself up on one arm and dares—yes, he dares —to touch her calloused foot. It appears a visit to the herbarium will be in order tomorrow. He shall make a paste to

285

soften her, head to toe. "We've enjoyed each other's company for most of the day. Why not continue?"

"Love is really that casual to you." Charlotte shocks herself with the words spat from her mouth. Her eyes grow wide, frightened.

Her mind reels in darkness: he cannot reach in, cannot understand what she wants. Why can't he see her?

Liam stands motionless, does not hinder Charlotte's escape from the bed to the hearth. *That word: love. Just a sort of want, isn't it? Need and compassion mixed together. But with friendship too, so there's that. And desire, and sacrifice.* "Of course it's not casual, it's…" *That word. It's not just a prey's want. It's… It requires more thought than this. It is certainly not a word to spit like an insult.*

Liam scrunches his toes in the carpet. Gets up. Reaches the door in silence.

"I don't think your eyes are beautiful."

He stops and turns.

"I picked your eyes because they're honest. The feelings they show, they're raw, open…" She reknots.

Liam opens his mouth to speak—no. Nothing will unravel her. And so he leaves Charlotte to her solitary hearth and shuts the door quietly behind him.

Driving Back Nightmares

Charlotte dreams again of a concert hall, but this time no piano, no spotlights, no calls for encore. The stage smolders beneath her feet. The curtains rain ash.

Anna sits in the front row, beaming with pride for nothing. Aunt Gail next to her, tears just beginning to streak thinly down the laugh lines at the corners of her eyes. Her father, nothing but a life-sized porcelain doll with a smile painted on his face, a badge of shiny plastic.

And then an usher comes forward, followed by Cein, Campion, Devyn, and Ember. He lets them all in, the veli-devour smacking their lips.

Charlotte tries to scream, but instead vomits black oil. It pools at her feet and transforms into a white sapling. Its roots slither toward the front row, toward her family. She has to stop it, but can't. It keeps her apart from them and holds them down. Cein's teeth grow, grow, grow. Charlotte looks stage right: Dorjan sits robed in crimson jelly on a throne of steak and kidney pies. Stage left: Poppy waves a massive foam Facebook thumbs-up.

Then Liam's fire-wings soar overhead and burn the theater, the velidevour, her family, all to dust.

A river fills the heavens, velifol overruns the floor, and a mournful wail pierces the air: Arlen, crying....

Don't let me drown! Liam, SAVE ME!

Her eyes fly open. Gasping, perspiring.

Light flickers in the sconces on either side of the foyer. Thick carpet muffles Charlotte's feet as she tiptoes through the stained-glass doors to the narrow balcony outside. The cold, smoky air reminds her: autumn's coming. This autumn was supposed to mark a new school, new home, new life. Charlotte sighs as she cups her chin in her hands, elbows braced on the cold iron balustrade, eyes cast downward.

Dim rectangles of light float up to her from the kitchen below. Someone else is awake.

Down the stairs. Past the kitchen, past Arlen, who is pouring himself something to drink.

The moon provides just enough light to create ghosts out of curtains. But the smell of inked melodies and flowers calms Charlotte's nerves. The moonlight glows on the ivory keys. A breeze slips into the room behind her, causing the sheet music to rustle, whispering a soft nocturne, a sweet adagio.

I need a break, from Liam, from everything that's happened, didn't happen, is happening. To think.

Charlotte settles herself on the bench. The piano strums a faint hello as Charlotte walks her fingertips once around her pendant. Then, with steady hands hovering just above the keys, Charlotte rests her eyes on the sheet leaning against the music rack. Beethoven, Piano Sonata No. 14 in C Minor, the "Moonlight Sonata." She knows this one by heart. Quiet, full of measured climbs and falls. A chance to watch the string vibrations shake the moonlight. To breathe in the lake, the garden. To think about the people here. To think about how Anna surely isn't among them.

Trust them. The Voice inside her heart hums with the music.

But I saw her.

Did you?

Dammit, I don't KNOW. I can't go look, not now, not when Liam's probably up there.

You promised not to go up there.

DAMMIT, I know.

Charlotte's hands lift from the final chord.

Applause. One of the sconces lights to reveal Arlen, sitting in a chair by the door. "I apologize, child, but I could not help but come and listen. Clearly music is not just an ambition for you, but a passion…. What is troubling you?" His shoes squeak as he walks over, a trail of wet footprints behind him. Watering the garden must be one serious business around here. Arlen sits next to her, and waits.

Do I need to talk about it? Ugh. Can't you just, I don't know, flip through the last few pages, and see for yourself?

A little upturn in the corner of Arlen's mouth, a little extra sparkle of mischief in his eyes. "No."

No point in mincing words. "He didn't like the fact I didn't want to do with him what all the other women of his life want to do with him."

Arlen exhales through his nose and turns away. "I thought as much."

"It's all right." And oddly enough, it is. How many centuries has Liam just gotten what he wanted? And now he's trying, actually trying, to change. The evening's been so overwhelming with uncertainty and blood and hope. Forgiveness can have its place in there too.

Charlotte wanders among the harmonies of "Love, Reign O'er Me" and waits for the music's rain to wash the last hard feelings away. "Guess I was supposed to be like everyone else."

"Well, I'm glad you're not. That's exactly the sort of

289

behavior that brought him here in the first place. His mother had many plans for him, but they were disrupted by his antics."

Charlotte breaks the chord. "Begging your pardon, sir, but your kind doesn't seem the type to have much of a family life."

Arlen's bitter chuckle sends a shiver up Charlotte's spine. "No, not really. I could certainly tell you some stories about my childhood." Shadow battles moonlight for space around Arlen's countenance.

Charlotte does not dare ask about Arlen's childhood, but cannot help but think of a young Liam—child-Liam, to be precise. Not a hundred years old, but ten. "Why doesn't he want his parents here? Wouldn't they want to see their son?"

A line travels from the corner of Arlen's eye to his hair. It could be a wrinkle or a tear—it's impossible to determine in this light. And when Arlen faces Charlotte with such a strange mix of despair, rage, and pride, she cannot even liken the scent to anything known before. "I'm sure you've seen it among humans: some become wonderful, able parents and some, well, don't. Unfortunately, all princeborns must marry and bear children, whether they're fit for the task or not."

"And Liam's family?"

Shadow overtakes moonlight. A reverse halo frames his body. "Certainly not." He coughs. Shadow shatters. Light fills his face, and he is Arlen, Wielder of The Mighty Spoon, once more. "I suppose I should make sure he's all right."

Charlotte brings the fallboard down gently over keys. "I should get to bed, anyway." The two walk upstairs and part in the foyer.

Alone and in bed, Charlotte stares at the ceiling. She wonders what the velidevour are doing with the people upstairs. With the one that might be Anna.

Not real.

We don't know that, not for sure.

You really think Liam and Arlen would deceive you in such a way? The Voice in her heart drips with skepticism.

I don't know. Arlen's got a darkness in him. Liam's is epic, apparently. But they've both got a warmth to them too. Arlen cares. And Liam... he can care. Maybe I can too. After I know who's upstairs.

Velifol Blooms Under Glass

Paper. Woodsmoke. Yarn.

Charlotte blinks and hides from the sunshine. Deep under the covers, deep in thought.

Don't. The Voice in her heart tries to redirect her from carrying out a plan that's quickly working its way from her head to down her feet.

Shut up, you're not in my brain, you're in my heart. And if you give a shit about my sister, you're going to let me make sure she's not up there on the third floor.

Foolishness.

Shut it.

This promises to end in failure.

Charlotte gets cleaned, gets clothed, and gets out.

There is only one access. No one in the foyer. Charlotte doesn't smell or hear anyone downstairs either. No one in the kitchen, herbarium, portico—no Arlen. Maybe they're all upstairs.

You know someone will see you the moment you set foot on the third floor.

Charlotte ignores the Voice like some ignore their conscience and slips out to the back patio to scrutinize those windows, that rooftop, the brilliant tips of the glass house on top. She *must* find a way up there. She can climb, maybe, if she finds a gutter or something....

Creaking, crying metal. A slim iron... vine? is growing out of the ground. Wide, flat leaves are folding out from either side: a ladder.

Well, that's convenient.

Foolishness! The Voice sounds alarmed.

Shut UP, no one asked you. Charlotte pats the ladder leaves —cold, hard, firm—and climbs, swift as a squirrel, to the rooftop battlements. She peeks through the crenels. The coast is clear. There is also no place to hide.

She treads lightly on the balls of her feet to the glass house. The branches of the tree glisten as that violet liquid, the veli, streams up from the roots in the third floor, up the trunk, up the branches, and down into the soil troughs. Charlotte moves closer. Such teeny tiny shoots just peeking up, glowing and transparent, so beautiful—

BRAZEN foolishness.

For the last time, SHUT IT. Liam showed me how to climb this tree... and that was at night. Now I've got all the sunlight in the world, but I can't spot the damned steps in any of the branches. So Charlotte climbs onto the nearest branch and slowly clambers down to stand at the top of the trunk. She studies the trunk for where the veli does not travel, and steps accordingly. After a few long, breathless minutes, her feet reach the third floor.

No sunlight in the corridors. The entire third floor is blanketed in a thick darkness with only small circles of light: the windows to the rooms.

No smell of Anna here in the center. Closer to the east wing? No, no smell. West? Hmm. There's a faint touch of her shampoo, maybe, not yet gone.

Charlotte moves on her toes to peer through the windows.

Not that there is much to see. Every room contains its own sort of fog, and a bed on which a human lies. The velidevour are everywhere—one on the bed stroking the human's face, one straddling the human. One ginger-haired girl even stands on the corner of the bed forming weird shapes in the fog that look like... bats or cheese platters, Charlotte can't decide. No human stirs. And nobody is young—some middle aged, but mostly older. No one her age, or Anna's.

I told you.

But I saw Campion last night, with her.

A wave of lake air and forest earth assails Charlotte's nostrils. A screech attacks her ears.

RUN.

Charlotte trips on her own damn feet and rolls into the central room.

A gust of wings blasts at her back. Talons catch a few locks of hair, but don't keep. The great owl circles round, the tips of his wing feathers grazing the floor. Charlotte runs for the tree, toes barely touching the trunk as she lunges, lunges, almost to the branches and glass house—*SHIT, CAN'T BREATHE.*

Talons tighten around Charlotte's throat and lift her up through a hidden door in the glass house's roof. Then they dive down, crashably close, and Charlotte's dropped with a nasty thud onto the stone roof. One breath later and the talons are on her again, only now they are fingers, Devyn's fingers, gnarled yet strong. He grips her by the neck, growling in the tongue Charlotte's heard Ember and Campion use between themselves. He shakes her hard, like he expects an answer, then curses to himself. "But you know no Mawdre. Let me say again: You would ruin everything for your own greed."

"Not. Greed. Anna... saw..."

Devyn narrows his eyes and pulls her close. "No, you *need*

to save. You could not save your father, so you need to save everyone, save even those who do not want to be saved. You, will, ruin us."

FUCK you Devyn I just want my sister back. Let me go. I'll SHOW YOU. Please someone help me.

A battlement cracks.

Please, House please. I know you listen to me, please!

The battlement begins to give, but then a blur of curls and storm eyes and an arm, a strong arm, enfolds Charlotte while the other one rips Devyn away.

Liam turns to the Lady Charlotte, who gasps for breath. The marks on her neck are swollen and ugly. "Charlotte? Are you all right?" He sets her gently upon the ground. She winces at his touch. Nothing, not the prey, not the velifol, not Orna, none of them—none of them matter, not when the Lady Charlotte recoils from him. He rises, and looks down upon the villain. "How *dare* you."

Devyn pulls himself up, his breath broken. "This human will never let us live in peace. She could destroy what little good you have done. Now will you listen?"

"She is *mine*." Liam's dagger shines in the sun. Veins spark beneath his skin. Feathers form.

You must stop this. The Voice in Charlotte's heart spurs her to act.

Charlotte tries to grab Liam's leg, but he's too far. "Liam, don't, it's my fault, it is!"

A new smell of water and animal: Arlen, through the door and into the thick of it before Charlotte can blink. "What in heart's fire is going on?" He stands between Liam and Devyn with fists clenched. "Devyn is loyal to you, *you*, Liam!"

The feathers burn away, but the hurricanes in Liam's eyes do not break. "You call this loyalty?" He points with his dagger to Charlotte's neck, then to Devyn's face. "How can I possibly trust him?"

"I told you, Arlen," Devyn wipes his grit-encrusted face and brushes by Charlotte without a glance. "Humans aren't meant to live here as we do. She's poison."

Liam leaps, lands on Devyn's chest, dagger in air, ancient words flying from his mouth like the froth of a rabid dog. Arlen thrusts himself in their midst again and again to pull them apart, speaking one tongue, no two.

Charlotte's voice suddenly grinds out, "Campion has my sister!"

And all action halts: Arlen's forearm freezes under Liam's neck, and Liam's dagger stalls in midair above Deyvn, whose hands still grip Arlen's and Liam's arms.

"That's why I came up here. I saw everyone come back with their prey last night, and I saw, I thought, no, I SAW, Campion with Anna, and I need to know. I need to know so bad." Charlotte opens her mental book to that moment, littering its inner pages and her body with tears, but she doesn't care, as long as they look, see, understand. "Just when I think I can trust someone here, someone else tells me something that screws it all up. And I'm sick of it. I want to see the human Campion brought in. *Now.*"

Devyn breaks from the tangle first. He slides out from under Liam and Arlen, neither of whom look at her. "You leave your mind too open." No pants-wetting glare from Devyn this time, but a sympathetic look, which, considering the past few minutes, cannot be easy to give. "You leave your mind too open. Shut it, or kill us with your fear." He faces the other two and says: "Yes, I am still with you. But remember what I said, old friend." Devyn kneels as the dust and feathers swirl from his ankles. His wings burst through the cloud, and he rises, sending his magic into the morning breeze. He dives through the door in the glass-house roof, out of sight.

"Charlotte," Arlen says quietly, "Campion never returned. He is still hiding from Dorjan."

"But…"

Liam collapses into one of the crenels in the battlements. The dagger falls with an insulted clang on the ground between his feet. He cradles his head in his hands.

"Are you still in pain?" Arlen asks.

Will you please heed my warning next time? Even the Voice in her heart sounds sad. They all sound so damn sorry for Charlotte, when she's the one who bungled matters in the first place.

"Your neck, Charlotte." Arlen makes it sound like her neck matters.

But it doesn't, it really doesn't, because I did something that could have been so terrible and stupid and no matter what, it's all my fault. "I'm so sorry. I don't want to ruin everything. I've already lost one home. I don't want to lose this one too."

That really came out of my mouth. River Vine equals home. I never called Grandma's home. Ever. But this place, in a matter of days: home. All it needs is Anna, and it'd be—oh GOD, I'm so messed up.

Softness grazes Charlotte's cheekbones: Arlen, wiping her face with a handkerchief. "I must return to matters below. I expect you can keep yourself out of trouble for now."

Charlotte does her best to nod. Arlen closes Charlotte's fingers 'round the handkerchief and walks with ease down the branches. His kindness churns her gut, and then the thought of Liam attacking Devyn, stabbing Arlen by accident…

Liam has yet to move.

She goes to him now, with slow, small steps, still clutching Arlen's hanky. Charlotte feels a timid warmth from the eyes hiding behind those speckled curls as she picks up the blood dagger he dropped and wipes it on her jeans. The hilt's leather is smooth and warm, like a glove warmed by the hearth.

Comforting. Safe.

"Strange, watching someone touch that piece." Liam rakes his fingers through his hair to reveal his face. "That used to result in a lot of screaming and death, you know."

"It still does," Charlotte attempts a half smile, "I can tell you that."

"You really feel no pain, holding it in your hand?"

She shakes her head. "No. It's…" *I want to say it's as raw and honest as the clouds in your eyes, but how can a dagger feel honest?* "It's warm. Like holding another hand. Now, let's put this away." She tucks the dagger into its sheath on Liam's back, and uses Arlen's handkerchief to wipe away a streak of dirt beneath Liam's eyes. *Let's put it all away, all the mistrust and fear. Can we, please?*

"This vision of Campion and your sister. This is why you turned cold last night?"

Charlotte moves to the battlement that cracked when Devyn choked her. The stone now stands strong and still. The crack continues to thin, like the stone is healing itself. Liam does not seem to notice. "Yeah."

Liam sighs and heaves himself up. "Then Devyn is right. Your mind's too open about the wrong things."

"What do you mean?"

"Any velidevour here knows about your sister, your dead father, your love of music, and your protection of the border-land child." His eyes rest on her arm.

She stays where she is. Every muscle in her grows taut and hard, as if the door inside her needs bracing to keep his shadow out. *Don't, Liam, please, all the fear and mistrust comes from there. Do. Not. Enter.*

He doesn't. "How did you even reach the roof? I had the stairwell hidden."

Relieved to have his scrutiny focus elsewhere, Charlotte

brings him to the far edge of the west wing and points down at her vine ladder. The leaves shrivel at Liam's touch, but regrow with Charlotte's.

"It responds to you." Liam faces her as if she can explain in vivid scientific detail the root of, well, the root.

All Charlotte can say is, "I asked for my own way up. Obviously, you're not me." She pockets Arlen's handkerchief and climbs nimbly down. As soon as her feet hit ground, the iron vine shrinks back into the earth. The portico stones settle, and all is as before.

"Meet me in the library," he calls down.

She waves, and goes inside.

The Apparition Wins

Well. That was a LOVELY way to start the morning. Nice work, Charlie. Nearly got a good guy killed by another good guy. Played right into Campion's little mind-fuck. Like you didn't know he's full of that shit. You see one flash of red hair, and you go nutzoid. You never lost it like this when the wrestling captain and his cronies tried to prank you and corner you for a beatdown. Idiot.

The Voice blocks Charlotte's pummeling thoughts before they kick her heart yet again. *Now you know. Liam's tree works as promised.* The Voice settles the churning acid in Charlotte's gut. *It's the dregs of humanity, the criminals, that the velidevour will be feeding on, no longer the innocent. It is now up to you to heed Devyn's words: stop broadcasting your vulnerabilities to your enemies.*

Charlotte nods to herself as she grips her pendant tight. *Gotta control my own mind against these mind-controlling fuckers. But I still need my phone back. Because I'll never be okay unless I know for sure. I need to make Liam understand.*

The library by far is the shabbiest, messiest room in Rose House. The shelves that span its two floors are stuffed with papers, folders, broken books, books upside down, books stacked every which way, books hanging halfway out.

Some lounge chairs sit in front of a massive stone fireplace occupying an entire wall. Large, ornate tables line a wall of windows, and a desk is shoved next to an iron spiral staircase leading to the second-floor balcony, which wraps around the perimeter of the room. On each step of the spiral staircase are stacks of ledgers, the oldest dating back to 1798.

Charlotte breathes in the old furniture and older paper as she walks along the shelves, searching for English titles. Not easy, actually—lots of Latin, Greek, what looks like Arabic. Shouldn't there be Gaelic here? Charlotte pauses in front of the most lopsided shelves of the bunch and wonders if she should empty the thing and fix the shelves as a sort of apology for the morning. *Hey, I nearly got Devyn killed, but I'm moderately capable at home improvements, see?*

More books on the floor, fallen from the lopsided shelf. Well, these she can at least tidy, and maybe see if there's at least one English title in the bunch.

And there, at the bottom of the pile: *Twenty Thousand Leagues Under the Sea.*

Oh... oh, Dad. Those campfire nights, my feet on the Nautilus and my head in the stars, my hand on the... on the... huh. A loose board. A purposefully loose board. Tiny little hiding place, this, and—well bust, my, buttons. My phone! My phone, my phone! I've GOT IT! "Thank you soooo much, House. Let's get this sucker turned on—"

"How did you find that?!" Liam vaults over the iron banister and yanks the phone from her grasp before planting himself on the floor. Anger ripples out from his face right down to his toes.

Charlotte throws gestures across the mess behind her. "I, I thought I could clean this up, just, fix one little thing, you know, and, and there was this book," says the girl pointing to GOBS of books, "and a floor board was loose, and there it was, and..." Charlotte can see by Liam's hanging mouth she might as well stop. She grips her pendant, counts her breaths, waits for a word, any word, rebuke or thanks, just, *something*.

Liam's mouth closes.

Well, that's a start.

His fists unclench. His shoulders droop. Even his toes relax against the floor. But his expression remains tired and sad as he backs off to perch on the desk. He plunks the phone down and begins to speed-read through one of the many ledgers.

Charlotte eyes the exit. Sure, she could leave. Hide with the piano again, or under the fake-aunt quilts in her room. Or, she could be braver than that. *Suck it up, Charlie.* She approaches with arms wrapped about herself, lest she touch another forbidden thing. "Can I help?"

Liam pauses mid-page-turn. Continues. "Doubtful."

Charlotte's neck hairs bristle, but she shoves the snark back down. "Even if it's in another language, I could try to find the right numbers or symbols." She allows herself a small corner of desk to sit on. "Liam."

His hand rests there upon the page, frozen by his own name.

"Liam, please. I want to help you."

He swallows back something big and nasty, and in that moment resets himself: his toes twitch, his fingers tremble, and his chest inhales. "Arlen kept," he blows away the stubborn curls from his eyes and tucks away the rest, "Arlen has kept records of every velidevour and human presence at River Vine. But neither of us can find a record for the year 1910."

"Was that the year you came here?"

"No. That was year I was stabbed. I was here long, long before that." Bitterness permeates the air around him.

Charlotte shifts a little closer, careful not to touch the phone, let alone look at it.

"I was dumped inside these walls about the time the

Europeans began making themselves at home on this continent, but could I actually be kept near them? No. Nowhere near any colony of familiar humans. Here. In the middle of a woodland culture I never had the chance to learn or understand in order to rule a group of velidevour who just happened to be staying at River Vine at the time." He chucks the ledger at the shelves. Something snaps, causing a shelf to tip and send its contents down the side, breaking the next shelf, and so on for a few more snap'n'crashes.

Guess that explains all the lopsidedness.

"The only good thing about being stuck in that horrifying chair was that I at least slept the last century away instead of dealing with," he waves at the world around him, "all of this."

Charlotte remembers her first day awake here after her rescue mission to the Pits and how she'd dealt with "all of this." She barely made it into the afternoon before shutting herself away from River Vine, determined to hide behind a wall of music. But that had been her choice. Being here had been her choice, even if made under duress. Liam never chose this place, never wished to be cursed with his own weapon. "These velidevour are lucky to have you. Not before, when you were an ass" —Liam smirks at that—"but now? You're using your talents to lead and guide them, to help them, and they know it."

The air changes. The bitterness evaporates, giving way to something newish. Something Liam's given off before: when a light crimson heightens his cheekbones.

"I take direction too." He winks.

Charlotte starts with a snort that quickly gives way to a laugh. *What. An. Imp.* "Not with that mouth full of sass, you don't." So easy to laugh when this Liam sits next to her, the one with a ready smile and wit, the one who taught her to skip a stone.

303

Liam observes as the laugh softens the Lady Charlotte's face and brighten the lights in her eyes. Her hand hovers between her leg and his. *She must, of course, reach for me. Then I will hold her, and she will know. She laughs with me now, seems so at ease, she must know already. But, but: if she does not, she will turn cold again. But no. I will not allow another cold night. So business first, then.* "I need to know that you will not go back up there," he says firmly. "Growing velifol is an extremely delicate process. If you interfere again, I'd… I'd have to do something."

Charlotte hugs herself. Liam recalls the knot in which Charlotte had tied herself the previous night because of her, the kin that's anathema to him. Even a vision of Dorjan would be preferable to this apparition of the sister who unscrupulously intrudes each time they begin to make progress.

"Anna's really not up there? That was really just Campion getting inside my head? She just looked so real."

Liam shakes his head. *Witness my manners: I am decent even as my inner hand shakes to cut that sickness out of you.* "You have to trust me."

"I do trust you." She unfolds, and rests one hand, palm up, upon his thigh.

She knows, she reached for me, ME, and I will draw her fingers to my lips and I will—

"Now I need you to trust me."

Mac an donais, this apparition will not LEAVE. "I thought you said this was your home."

"It is."

Yet the Lady Charlotte shivers as her mind floods with memories of sweet little girls and their sweet little family. Too sweet. Your skin grows sticky with the past. I know snare's bait when I see it, woman. Your plump, ripe berries of happiness can rot in the grass, for all I care. "Your mind and body speak otherwise."

"I can't help that. Anna's my little sister. I've been taking care of her almost her whole life."

"You just said you trust me."

"I do, Liam, I trust you with my life." She turns her hand. Liam silently curses all trousers. But she must feel his supple thigh underneath, for she blushes. Deeply. "But if I can't…" The words trail away as she looks down.

Of course, that is where she wants this conversation to lead. Of course, back to *her* and the infernal device. The apparition beams, triumphant.

"If I can't hear her tell me she's okay, I'll go crazy. Please, Liam. Please." Charlotte struggles to catch Liam's eyes, but he's always looking past her, or through her, or somewhere else not her face. Whatever he sees alters him, inside and out. Jealousy wafts from him, and it's all Charlotte can do not to pinch her nose shut.

Liam snatches the phone and pockets it. "How nice that you worry for your precious sister," he says, words stumbling over themselves. "How nice you give her all sorts of thoughts and attention, when all she did was give you grief. I can see why love does not come easily to you, if all it brings you is pain."

"W-w-what the… what? I… What the FUCK are you talking about, Liam? She's my SISTER. The only real family I've got. You know I love her—why are you like this? Why?" Her voice is a hoarse whisper as pain coats her throat.

"I cannot give you back your phone because the second you hear her voice, you'll want to see her, and if you can't see her, you'll 'go crazy.'" He shoves himself off the desk, storms to the shelves, ready to tear them all down. He shuts his eyes to the apparition, to Charlotte. He sees nothing but one choice. *Cut out the sickness.*

He flies back to her side and jerks her marked wrist into the air between their faces. "What do you think this mark

305

means?" His bitterness bleeds into his voice.

Charlotte's voice shrinks. "I-I have to stay here."

"Yes, you have to stay here, because *you do not exist elsewhere.*" He flings her arm down. "No family, no sister, knows you beyond the Wall. You live in no one's memory. You are less than a ghost." He glares at the space next to Charlotte with such an evil eye that the metal staircase begins to warp. *Damn you, girl, damn the protection I gave you, damn the life you leech from the Lady Charlotte still.* "*This* world is where you live. Breathe." And he breathes deep as though to show her, "Feel." But the apparition does not leave her side. The Lady Charlotte wilts before him, the sickness too far spread.

Charlotte cannot move. She doesn't know how, not when her mind buckles and shivers. *Jenny must remember me. I know I'm in Anna somewhere. I can make Aunt Gail remember, I'm not forgotten, I'm not gone, I can't be gone, what else is there to me but blood and bone and memory?*

Just like that, the storm subsides. The metal staircase returns to normal. Liam deflates, retreats. His eyes sparkle as though wet. "Enjoy the sweet company of your ghosts." One curt nod, and gone.

Twenty Thousand Leagues Under the Sea still rests on her lap. One tear, two, splash upon its cover. Charlotte wipes them away with Arlen's handkerchief. She stands up, ignores the book's loud thump on the floor. Ignores the tears still shining on her face. She has to get out. Go somewhere. Anywhere.

Dead River

The wind blows her south, but Charlotte fights against it because she needs to fight SOMEthing.

I screwed up on the roof, and I screwed up with Liam. But I'm not wrong, dammit, I know I'm not. My family. My heart.

She leans in when the gusts yank her braid, punch her shoulders. Still, north she goes, even as the air tunnels through her ears and presses so hard inside that her eardrums pop. Charlotte's taken enough hits to the head to know how impaired her balance becomes when her only functional senses lie in the soles of her feet: she can't see or hear and isn't entirely sure whether she's going forward, backward, or sideways.

Of course, it doesn't help that she hasn't the least idea where she's going, or where she even is. She didn't get this far with Dorjan after first crossing the Wall. The grass road feels like the one to the Blairs', but it smells less of the woods. The oaks and maples are few and far between here, giving way to new trees, smaller trees, sweet living snowfall of fragile petals from their fragrant blooms....

August is not a time for spring blossoms, and yet here they are in an abundance Charlotte's never seen before. White, pink, orange petals dance and fly around her. Vines bearing grapes crisscross among the trees. Berry bushes embrace tree trunks.

Sunny patches of ground sprout pepper and tomato vines. This whole place feels alive, awake, and eager. Charlotte kneels to stroke some baby spinach leaves and watch the plants grow, as if they've gorged on magic plant food.

Branches rustle. Rustle again. Rustle to the point where Charlotte wonders if a family of fat possums is rooting around, trying to take a nap.

Nope. Just Poppy popping into the scene again. This time climbing in an embarrassing fashion to snatch a small peach from a low branch. SNAP.

Crackle, pop. Do I run over there, run for help, or, oh, never mind.

Poppy blinks a bit as she props herself up by Charlotte's feet. "I fell down."

Dang pesky little thing keeps turning up, just, whenever. "Forget to change again?"

"NO. Well, no, I don't think so, maybe I did, but come on, hands this big can hold a peach waaaaaaaaaay better than teeny eeny weeny mousey hands can, and I didn't want to drop the peach because then it could explode and I would never get another peach forEVER, so I had to—"

"I get it."

"—and I almost never get to come here because the She-Bear does these circles and always comes from the lake to—"

"Wait, wait, wait." Charlotte leans against the peach tree. She can feel the warmth flowing up and down beneath its bark. A peach bursts from a blossom and falls—Charlotte catches it without looking. She holds it over Poppy's gawking face. "What's the She-Bear?"

"Nasty thing. Nasty. Scary." Poppy crawls on all fours and lowers her voice. "It sounds all sad and stuff—"

"Like in pain?" *Of course, those roars, moans, cries—*

"—but then you go near it, and it'll *chomp!*" Poppy moves too fast for Charlotte to react. She grabs the peach with her teeth and shakes it, spraying everything in a three-foot radius with juice.

"Dagnabit, Poppy!" *So much for clean pants today.* "So. What, now? There's this crazy bear just patrolling River Vine like some guard dog? Arlen never said anything." *Not to mention Mr. Dog Dude himself.*

"Almost took Campion's tail once," Poppy goes on, licking her hands, way too pleased with herself. "Almost took the princeborn's head. It hated Jamie so much, made him sick. Course he's dead now."

Charlotte's memory of the feathery, pus-pocked git has not waned. "Yeah, sad, not really. So what do you veli-de-commoner people do about the She-Bear?"

"Leave'er alone. That's what Devyn says to do. And he's righty right—right cuz I still have my tail!" A few slurps suck the last bit of pulp off the pit, and she rolls it between a couple of trees and out of sight somehow.

Charlotte follows the path of the peach pit on the ground, curious how something can vanish on a flat landscape. Her chest prickles, but Charlotte wants to keep walking, past the apple and plum trees. She wants to keep walking to find the pit. She wants to keep walking because she needs to keep walking. Down a gentle slope and to an old riverbed, a dry riverbed, a bed for sleeping, warm, inviting, with smells of chili and gunpowder and berry shampoo and family who remember her and need her.

Back away.

But the riverbed, it smells like, like home. It's where I belong.

Back away NOW.

Charlotte feels little tugs on her arm, hears a little voice chirping "dead river." *Leave me alone. I'm going to bed.*

Forgotten magic knows no kindness. Keep. BACK.

A great shadow swoops overhead and lands in a whirlwind

309

of feathers. Devyn rises from the little storm cloud, eyes stern.

Charlotte wants to say: *Leave me alone. I'm going to bed.* But the thought doesn't reach her tongue, and she keeps walking toward the riverbed.

Devyn's mouth forms words that don't reach her ears, and then his hand pulls back and slaps Charlotte full force, sending her to the ground.

"DAMMIT, that hurt!" Charlotte winces, touching her red cheek.

Poppy frantically wipes sticky dirt off her hands and face as she says, "I *told* her that's the river that came from the big river and used to go under the white tree, but she didn't *listen* and—"

"Of course she didn't." Devyn kneels, leans over Charlotte.

Poppy pouts. "Stupid river-killing Wall."

Devyn looks at Poppy with a sidelong glance that strikes Charlotte as funny, and when he says, "Stupid indeed," she almost, almost, busts a gut. But then her brain starts ringing again, and she remembers: *Oh yeah, I HURT.*

"The water's gone but the old currents still run beneath the dust, withered into cords that snare any living thing that touches them. They are not a power to be trifled with."

"Noticed." *No tears, you big baby, it's not like you lost any teeth. Consider this Devyn's getting even for your shit this morning. Get up. Brush it off.*

Devyn turns to Poppy and stares her into stillness. "You are needed on the third floor."

"Should I take Miss Charlotte back? I can take her back. I can make sure she doesn't get lost, I know all the little paths 'round the orchards and…"

Devyn's glare is lacerating, so much so that Poppy loses her voice, points in random directions, and manages to squeak a "Going" before a prompt gone.

Brain now dully humming, sure of her feet and hands

and humors, Charlotte does a quick study of the riverbed. A single row of stones borders both shorelines. Nothing touches the dirt—not a stray leaf, branch, or petal. Even the peach pit is gone somehow. The river's not very wide either. Charlotte imagines the length of an old police car would just about span it. "Lemme guess: 'big river' equals Mississippi? Boats catch some sort of magic current, divert to here." A simple, effective trap. And since the Mississippi has always been a highly trafficked river, it's no wonder River Vine prospered before the Wall. "This used to be a part of the water road, didn't it?"

"Who told you about a magic current?"

In the back of Charlotte's mind come spurs, making her want, need, to walk onto the riverbed. But Charlotte knows what these spurs are now, and she clutches her father's pendant to buck the spurs off. "No one. I just figured the wishing well at the Blair farm, your old white tree here, and, I mean, you call it a water road. Plenty of humans see the Mississippi as a water road without the magic hoo-ha."

Devyn's face settles into a formation that almost, *almost*, could be taken for a smile.

Charlotte curls one corner of her mouth in return. *Let's trade smirks, you and me, Master Owl Warrior.*

But the moment is already gone, and Devyn's face darkens again. "Once upon a time, humanity depended on magic: prayed for it, bargained with it, feared it. So magic flowed as freely as Nature's seasons. Veli currents moved in rivers. Velifol and white trees bloomed along their banks. The power of human dreams connected wishing wells to their legendary rivers, and velidevour found they could travel the water road to any place these dreams thrived. Only the bloodthirsty hunted humans. Why kill when we had but to drink of the rivers, to pick the velifol, to pluck the white tree's leaves? But now..." He shakes his head. "Because of the Wall, I do not know. Perhaps ours is the only community of velidevour. Perhaps the velidevour scurry and fly in every human city. I've not been far enough from River Vine to know."

"Mmhmm." Charlotte's attention is only half-present, senses still too curious not to reach out, however timidly, just in case there's something to catch...

"This is not a place to grow lost in thought, especially for a human."

"Heh. Yeah, I learned that lesson. I was just thinking about the Mississippi. Human history in general. How there's a hell of a lot more to the world, its gears"—she shapes cogs and wheels in the air with her finger—"how it all works, it's more than people really want to think about."

This time Devyn is the one who almost-laughs. "It is better for our kind if they don't."

"Charlie." A whisper in the breeze.

Charlotte's senses hit the throttle: eyes wide, ears wider, nose widest. *I heard that, I know I freakin' heard that. Where, where, WHERE?*

"Miss Charlotte?"

Devyn's use of her name brings her back. He has never addressed her by name before now.

Shit, he knows something's up. Close the mental book, batten down the hatches, go down deep, Charlie. "Yeah?"

"Not that I like saying this in front her, but Poppy is correct: you should keep out of the orchards. River Vine has always seen your kind as prey, nothing more. The princeborn may not always be able to save you, and forgotten magic knows no kindness."

I told you so. The Voice in her heart struggles to rein in Charlotte's senses.

Charlotte nods. "I just need a minute."

"Charlie."

312

Trapped

Charlotte watches Devyn fly south toward Rose House. She still clutches the pendant to ensure any thoughts in her head are officially hers.

The "Charlie" whisper could have been the dead river.

I told you, forgotten magic knows no kindness.

But can dead rivers mimic smells? The berry body splash and the bus funk. That's new. That's not like the Pits.

Too convenient. Too easy to believe.

For all the flower petals taking their turn in the dance above and around Charlotte's head, not one lands upon the riverbed. Withered leaves never blow across the stones lining the sides of the riverbed to touch its soil.

Charlotte counts her breaths to help steady her heartbeat as she advances toward the riverbed.

The Voice in her heart drags her back like a leashed animal.

Forgotten magic and fear overpower you far too easily.

No, they don't. See? This is me, walking away.

"Ch-Charlie!"

"Anna." Charlotte whispers the name, and her body breathes, hopes. Anna is no ghost.

Neither is Charlotte. She is action personified, albeit rash, impulsive, unheeding. She flies alongside the dead river, careful not to overstep, but she must fly on the hope that the bus funk and the baby blues—that maybe, just maybe, they're past that mouth, that dead river's mouth, where the stones rim the depression in the ground like rotting teeth. Past the mouth, where the orchards give way to the elms. Past the thin layer of elms, where Charlotte finds herself in a clearing.

"H-help!"

Charlotte slides to a halt, into a crouch, fingertips just touching the soil to steady herself. Eyes fix upon grass blades and branches. Her nostrils and ears twitch to a peculiar muffling. A chomping. A chewing.

"Charlie..." So faint, helpless, dying.

More chomping. A muffled "Ur dfmth thyfltft." From the Eastern Woods, the forest on the other side of the road to the Blair farm.

Charlotte bolts toward the Eastern Woods, snapping branches. Twigs and leaves slit her face, but she continues to run, ready and raring to crack open any jaw that dares hurt her sister.

A dark form huddles over something among the bushes just ahead.

Charlotte leaps and screams, "Let her go!" The dark form has no time to turn its wretched face before Charlotte lands upon its back, sending them both rolling through the grass and into a tree.

No baby blues in sight. No red hair, no bus funk.

No pleasantries from Dorjan either. There he stands, covered with massacred pie. Charlotte's got a fair amount of the crime scene on her pants and shirt too.

Jeez, Charlie, can't you get through one day without being covered in this stuff?

"What..." Dorjan shakes out his hands and starts again,

"What...?" Spits hair out of his face, and *really* starts again, "What, was, that?!"

Charlotte strains her senses again for the whispers and bus funk. Nothing.

Dorjan's blue eye flares with impatience, his green eye with concern.

Hey, don't mind me. I just thought you were eating my sister. My bad.

"Sorry." One sticky chunk glops down the trunk. Dorjan stares on, because even for Charlotte, that's about the weakest sorry that's ever been sorry'd in the history of sorries. "So where in the flippin' doo-dah-day have you been?"

"I, O Slayer of the Delectable, have been thatta way." And off Dorjan marches. Thatta way, skirting the clearing to reach the Southern Road. Charlotte manages to keep pace with his trot. "This was *supposed* to be a brief respite from sentinel duty. If Campion isn't on the borderland, another Orna follower is." He turns from the road, passing by familiar ferns and blue asters—they're on their way to the lake. "Damned maddening is what it is."

Charlotte's mind rewinds to the weird silver squirrel, the kid shivering behind those glasses.... "You should recruit some help. Like Ember. She helped you get Anna over..." Charlotte's words go hard and sticky, sour to the tongue.

"Yes!" Dorjan's hands shoot out before him, flicking pastry filling. "If Liam marks Jenny like he did your sister, no veli-devour would be able to touch her! Brilliant!"

"Even other princeborns?"

"Of course. Well, except Liam. He made the mark, he can unmake it, I suppose."

"Did he unmake Anna's?"

"Can't imagine how, with her driven to Appleton by the Blairs while you were recovering." Dorjan stops walking. "That," he points to Charlotte, "doesn't have something to do with this," he draws invisible circles around himself. "Does it?"

"I said I was sorry." *Stupid dead river and stupid me for stupidly listening to it.* "Aren't you worried the She-Bear's gonna smell your sweet berry-fied self"—she waves a hand vaguely around him—"and barrel over here for lunchtime?"

Pause. "Nope."

Charlotte follows Dorjan into the shallow depths of the lake to wash up. "That's all you've got? 'Nope'?"

"When you've got more than 'sorry,' I've got more than 'nope.'"

Scrubbing suddenly seems way more important than hearing more than 'nope.'

Why will you not trust him? The Voice pleads.

I heard. Smelled. I... I don't know. I just wanna scrub all that forgotten magic out of and off of me somehow.

"Hey, knock knock knock." Dorjan raps Charlotte's head three times before her glare tempts him to ding-dong ditch. "You're not going to explain why you clobbered me, are you?"

Charlotte falls rear-first into the shoreline's damp sand and holds her head up. No voice calling her name. And of course, Anna's smell is gone—it's not on Dorjan, not anywhere. Just Dorjan's overpowering dog funk. "Mistaken identity." Pause. Too damned hard to look him in the eye. "Sorry."

Dorjan kneels in the water. His fingers swirl the grains of sand, the circular current turning the water murky and the grains invisible. "This place is made to confuse a human's sense of reality. It's no different than Mr. Blair sitting in a duck blind with his duck call and decoys floating in the pond nearby." His blue eye reflects the flames under—under!—the water, flames that lick his fingers, shrinking them. "Ignore the decoys and the calls. Okay?" Worry lingers in his green eye as his face burns, chars, shrinks, stretches into a muzzle, pointed ears, blackened body, alert tail—and there is D again,

316

Jenny's favorite, her trusted friend.

Must be nice, having a trusted friend. "Yeah, okay."

Dorjan the wolf takes a few steps forward, mouth open, closed.

"I said okay."

He shakes his wet fur vigorously, inches from Charlotte's face, and his wet nose nudges hers.

"I said OKAY, OKAY!"

His tongue lolls (*har har, Fuzzy Britches*) as he backs out of the lake and runs into the woods, to the south, to be sure.

What I wouldn't give for just one soul I could trust. Charlotte picks up a stone. Plop. Tries another. Plop. "What am I doing wrong, Liam?" she asks aloud, unsure if she exists even to him anymore. What can she be when she's less than a ghost?

The pain-filled roar gives little answer. Mourn-full, hurt-full. So full of the feelings Charlotte knows too damn well. Those are the feelings that drive one to a parking lot to unleash on the fools who don't know any better. Nearly killing the one heart that matters. *Oh Anna, you were so brave, and I was such a fool.*

A shadow skims the lake's surface: an eagle, lifting himself higher and higher above the water, and higher still, past the tree line, then crumpling as though shot. It swoops just over Charlotte's head and skids to a sand-cloud stop on the beach. Feathers burn away, and Liam coughs himself into a sitting position, cradling one hand close to his chest. "Looking for that blasted telephone again? Or no. You're trying to contact the border family from the treetops. Well don't let me interrupt." He refuses Charlotte's hand, turns away from her eyes, which darken at the sight he cannot hide: curled black thorns digging into his hand, fingers, wrist. *Never let a lady see you weak, boy.* He stands, shakes the hand as though a curse is but stray leaves to be knocked free in the air. He pretends the thorns do not take their time in retreat, a few trailing threads of blood as they return to slumber upon his arm.

"What are you doing here?"

"You said my name."

Charlotte looks up from his thin blue tunic with some reluctance. "You've got good hearing."

"Merely one of my many lovely assets," he says, strutting away, voice tinged with bitterness. "Not that you care."

"For cryin' out loud..." Her words fade into a grumble as she balls up a wad of mud and fast-pitches it at Liam's back.

"Ow!"

"Oh, I'm sorry, I figured by your flying that you must *like* to get hurt. Don't act like I didn't see those thorns on you. I bet they could've killed you, for what, flying too high? Is there some kind of invisible ceiling up there for you? Something like that Wall back at the Blairs'?"

Liam's smell is answer enough: bitter, rotting anger.

"Fine. Far be it from me to judge whatever 'pleasure in pain' kinky shit you and the Lady got into in the Pits." Charlotte's stomach lurches with the words, the vision of those words... and she scratches her scalp vigorously as though to scrape the vision out. *You just had to go there again. You just keep doing this to yourself, Charlie.*

Liam stiffens. "I will have you know, Miss Charlotte, that I do not fly for the, as you said, 'kinky shit.'" His mouth fills with gloriously poetic words to wipe away whatever crude nonsense is going on in the Lady Charlotte's head, but there is no time to share them. Her face contorts as though she's sick —but she is not sick. She is laughing. Such a song to it, her laughter.

"Okay, please, Liam, promise me you just, jeez, don't talk like me ever again. That was horrible."

318

His poetry turns dumb upon his tongue. "I fly because for a few precious moments, I feel free. I feel that if I can just... press myself closer to the heavens, the lightning itself could snap this... damn... bond." The words are as the pits of grapes: irritating to spit out and embarrassing to spit in front of another, and a lady, no less.

Charlotte's hand struggles, unsure of whether to pull back or to find his shoulder and pull him closer. She's loathed self-pity ever since her mother had begun buying antidepressants from Uncle Mattie in order to forget about the two little girls desperate for her love. Charlotte hated feeling sorry for herself and her nightmare of a life in Bismarck. Now Liam, always so proud, so incorrigibly proud, says he's more than happy to fly despite his lethal mark. "So I have to accept my new life here inside the Wall without a struggle, but you get to kill yourself trying to escape over and over again?"

Storms brew in his eyes and on his face.

Give him space to think. The Voice in her heart nudges her away, just a little, leading her to a single round stone. Charlotte kicks it right up to Liam's big toe.

He picks it up, tosses it—it sinks with a merciless plop. "You have no idea how much I miss it, the flying. What it's like to live in the clouds for days on end. To be free of orders, of family obligations. Just me and the sun and a desert of clouds. Just me and the lightning in a concert of thunder. You have no idea."

Actually, yeah, I do. But Charlotte slams that thought shut before life in Bismarck blackens everything as it always does. Her bitterness is thick enough to choke on.

Liam finds his legs foolishly difficult to move, his lips more so. "Why did you call my name?"

Silence laps the sands.

Mac an donais, *those memories again draw tears to her eyes, eyelashes*

319

alight with diamonds in the sun, and yet within, not a single candle burns against the darkness.

At last Charlotte limply gestures at the water. "Couldn't skip a stone."

Liam's clouds break: no longer stiff, he kneels quietly in the sand and assembles a pile of smooth, flat stones from the earth.

But something whimpers. Something young. Like a child.

A girl. My sister. My hurt sister. Anna.

Charlotte walks into the water, unable to see far with the tree line.

"What in heart's fire are you doing?!" Liam lunges, yet remains on shore. "The lake is filled with traps. I told you the waterfolk are extremely territorial."

Ya big baby, you'd think I was standing in acid. "Liam, I'm fine. The water's barely up to my knees. See?" She lifts each leg out of the water to prove it. "I'm not melting."

"Get out of there! You'll die!" *The Lady has the audacity to smirk at a time like this?!*

"Five years of swimming lessons at least taught me how to not drown in a foot of water. Now, you comin'?"

Liam shifts his weight from one foot to the other. "So… you can move through the water without a boat?"

His anxiety stuns Charlotte all over again. "Liam, can you even swim?"

"Birds don't swim."

"Explain ducks."

"I am not a duck."

"Then it's a good thing I'll be around for the next sixty years or so. Your first lesson: get in the damn water." She wades to the water's edge, clasps Liam's hand firmly in her own, and guides him in, his hand gripping hers in an iron vise. After watching Liam face the Lady and the Incomplete in the Pits without a twitch of fear, Charlotte finds she cannot stop rolling her eyes at his childish, whiney panic.

"It's so cold. What was that? I think something grabbed me. Don't step there!"

Charlotte can't hold the exasperation back any longer. "Oh, would you just stop?!" Finally, they round past the tree line. "The water's perfectly clear here. You can see every little thing in the sand. Not a stone to stub a toe in sight."

"What are we even doing here?" Liam splutters as an inlet just starts coming into view. Water splashes, and a whimper begins anew. "Devyn's right. You have to stop saving whatever poor wretch you find."

"Saved you, didn't I?" Charlotte turns on him with eyes as cold as the lake. "What makes *you* better than everyone else?"

Both now see the inlet, and there, in the water, is a bear cub, struggling, pulling, yanking, only able to raise two of its paws above water. It squeals for help.

Charlotte tries to look into the water to see what's holding the cub down. At a glance, it appears to be seaweed. Oil gathers in droplets around black leaves. "Looks like it's caught in something. It's a lot smaller than I thought, with all the roars and growls and stuff, but—"

"This place... I know this place...." Liam grips her shoulder hard as his eyes dart about. "We must leave at once," he murmurs quickly into her ear.

"After the cub's free. Can I borrow your blood dagger?"

Damnable stubborn savior of all! "I tell you, I almost died near here, right in those trees. Back up with me now."

"Then no one else should almost-die here." Charlotte digs her heels in the sand and shoves Liam with one hand while grabbing the blood dagger with the other. "I'm not letting that cub drown."

"Charlotte, wait!"

321

The water is *cold*—the cold that numbs blood and bone marrow. But that cub is screaming, crying, so like a little kid that Charlotte cannot, will not, leave it trapped like this. The water reaches Charlotte's chest by the time she stands within arm's length of the cub. It stops screaming and studies her, eyes full of fear. It continues paddling in place, soaked to the bone and shivering.

"Hang on, little one. You're going to be okay." Charlotte keeps the dagger under the water in case its sight would scare the cub. "I'll cut you loose."

"Charlotte, get away, NOW!"

The forest shakes with a ROAR: ancient, powerful, and very, very angry.

Silence.

The cub growls and barks like a dog trying to get its master's attention. Like it's talking.

Leaves rattle, lake water ripples away from the shore. Charlotte and Liam, too far apart to see each other whisper the exact same words: "Oh no."

Trees bend like withered cornstalks, and they see THE bear, the She-Bear, massive as a tank, with every claw a dagger. It stands upon on its hind legs and BELLOWS.

Liam rips through water and throws Charlotte, dagger and all, behind him just as the She-Bear crashes into the water, jaws open to swallow Liam whole—

Liam grips the beast at the teeth, his veins full of light and terror as he holds the She-Bear's maw wide. *You will not shut it on the Lady Charlotte this day. If I do but one right thing in my wretched life, it is to keep. Her. Alive.*

Liam's body slides backward in the sand, his teeth grinding down a scream.

The cub cries and splashes wildly.

Charlotte crawls and stumbles in the water. *LIAM! Oh God,*

what do I do, worse than the granach and Anna and my fault, always—

No.

Charlotte gasps, shakes, grips the blood dagger.

No one need die today.

"Not today!" Charlotte echoes the Voice in her heart and dives into the water. She swim-flies past the cub to the She-Bear's leg, and strikes muscle.

The She-Bear arches back, dropping Liam like a wet leaf, and roars loud enough to send Charlotte reeling through the water, loud enough to shake the sand on the lake's floor.

"Get out of here, Charlotte!" Liam staggers up, swivels around: he cannot see her—there!

Charlotte throws herself into the water yet again, this time going for the cub. The She-Bear sees, smells, knows, then falls onto four legs. It will shred her—

"Here!" Liam falls, jumps, and yanks on its lower jaw. A paw slams down upon him, but he grips it, and then grips the second that threatens to crush him. "I will die before you know her blood, I swear it." And he digs his heels into the sand. He sees into its vicious eyes, tastes the rage steaming from its breath. Here, he will destroy the beast and die a watery, glorious death.

The seaweed tightens itself around the cub as Charlotte swims closer. The cub struggles upward for air, but it is too late: the seaweed is dragging it down, down, and even more seaweed wraps around the cub's legs, intent on drowning it.

Charlotte plunges forward, wraps her arm around the cub's body—

No one need die today.

Strike! In a single, fluid sweep, Charlotte slashes with a thin blade of fire, defying the water and charring the black seaweed into cloudy ash. Charlotte grabs the cub by the scruff and launches them both to the surface. It flails wildly, scratching

323

her all over. *Who cares about scratches when—LIAM!*

"Hey!" Charlotte shakes the cub by its scruff. "Tell your mom to leave him alone," pointing her chin toward Liam and the mauling She-Bear.

The cub kicks all four feet like an infant and lets out—a laugh?

The She-Bear stops snarling. It releases Liam in order to rear up on its hind legs, as big as any elm along the shore. Liam collapses into the water—a bloody, gagging mess.

Hold on, Liam, please.

The She-Bear walks, almost like a person, toward Charlotte, eyes darting between the dagger and her face.

"I'm not going to hurt your baby," Charlotte says, her voice shivering. "Just leave him alone."

The She-Bear growls.

"Here. So you know." Charlotte throws the dagger over to Liam, who seizes it and vanishes beneath the surface. Charlotte wades close enough to the shore to set the cub upon the sand.

The She-Bear growls again, but softly, and falls forward to be level with Charlotte's face. Its injured leg is nearest Liam, who shoots out of the water, gasping, dagger high—

She is not your enemy! cries the Voice inside her heart.

"Liam, don't!" Charlotte holds up her hands to stop him in time.

The She-Bear snorts once, twice, cautiously sniffing the air around Charlotte.

Liam's mouth falls open as the She-Bear shakes itself vigorously from nose to tail, unleashing a dozen water balloons' worth of spray on all sides. With a decisive harrumph, she ambles to shore, where the cub is rolling in the grass, still laughing. A gentle nuzzle along its baby's body, and the two stroll out of sight, the little one's laughter trailing behind them.

Liam staggers forward and then disappears under water

again in the vicinity of where the cub was entangled. "Liam, what are you doing?" Charlotte hollers into the water, but he stays under, pulling at something.

She dives under to find Liam desperately grappling with long vines of black seaweed. Tugging, combing, prying fronds apart. Then one vine wraps around his arm, trying to drag him down to the lake floor. Another vine sprouts from the main and sneaks toward the blood dagger, just inches away from a sinkhole. Charlotte lunges for the dagger, grasping it before the seaweed can reach it, and slashes Liam free of the black vines.

The two shoot to the surface, sputtering and gasping for air.

It isn't until reaching the shore that either can speak, Charlotte first. "What were you doing down there?" She looks at Liam, threaded with blood, steaming, hacked up as though he walked through all his stained-glass windows.

But Liam won't look at her. He pounds on to the sand, kicks the last of the skipping stones, almost sobs, and at last says: "I tried to retrieve it."

"Retrieve what?"

He looks to her neck.

Her father's pendant is gone, a few faint scratch marks from the cub in its place. "It fell into the water, and the cursed weed got a hold of it. I tried—"

Charlotte's strong embrace silences him. She continues holding him, and he doesn't even notice Charlotte replacing the blood dagger into its sheath on his back.

"You could have drowned," she says into his curls.

"But your necklace—"

"—is just a thing. It's not," she holds him tighter, "not this."

Liam brings his hands to her back and rests his head upon her shoulder.

No, a thing is not this at all.

Charlotte feels Liam's chest compress with a heavy sigh, his breath tickling the wet hair on her neck. Now she has nothing, not one true untainted possession from outside the Wall. But now, she does have friends, real friends, and she helped a mother reunite with her child. It almost makes the separation from Anna worth the pain.

Liam releases her so suddenly that Charlotte teeters off balance. Then he bows to pick a stone and whips it as he stalks away from her. Two skips, then plunk.

Charlotte enters the awkward silence. "I'm sorry I took your weapon again. I just didn't know what else to do."

No skips. Plunk. "Must—" *Not wench, not brat, not selfish, be civil, civility marks the man, boy*—"Must she *always* be on your mind?"

Charlotte bites her lip, furrows her brow. *After all that almost-dying in the water, he's still pissed about Anna? I almost get him killed: he's like, no biggie. But when I think about family: then he's like, how DARE you? What the—? Arlen said Liam's parents weren't fit to be parents. Maybe Liam just doesn't get what makes family worth thinking about at all.*

Charlotte draws a breath, picks a stone, takes a shot. Plunk. "I almost lost Anna to a river once. It was right after Dad's funeral, when we moved out west." Plunk. "We were at this memorial or something, and Mom was… she was throwing Dad's stuff into the river. And Anna tried to get his badge back." The bear cub's flailing legs had been so like little Anna's, just with fur. Charlotte lets the tear fall, past and present blurring together in her vision. "If the current had gotten her, and with all the winter ice floes, I'd have lost her then." Plunk. At least their mother was still aware then, still thankful when Charlotte managed to get air into Anna's lungs.

She hugged them both, still enjoyed their touch. But that was before they had reached their grandmother's.

Liam watches the Lady Charlotte's posture. For all her grace, she struggles with fluidity in motion. Her ghost trips her, holds her back. If he cannot cut the sickness out, then he will drown it with his own strength and feeling. He will not be defeated by some damned apparition.

It starts here: to move his body behind hers, to brace her with his strength when she needs it most. Like now. The curve of her spine down his stomach, her hair flowing down his chest. To keep and guard that warmth and light in one's arms? "The problem with you is that you are too stiff. Relax." They sway together, and when the stone they both hold flies away, it makes four skips before vanishing into the lake. "So how was it?"

Charlotte blinks. "How was what?"

"My first swimming lesson." His smile, so close and open, melts all the shivers memory carries in its mist.

Laughing with him feels even better, feeling the rumble of his chest against her back, sending tremors down her spine. "Well, normally the fight to the death comes after you learn how to dive, so I guess you're doing pretty well. Gotta get your arms flying in the water instead of flailing."

"I suppose we can't do that in a hot tub."

Charlotte snorts. She doesn't say she's thankful to see Imp Liam return after all the masochistic flying, but does say, "N-no, though I think a warm fire and some tea would be good."

"I think my idea would be a lot more fun."

"Next time we fight a bear, it's a date." She starts for Rose House, uncertain her legs are there after all that adrenaline and... feeling.

"Can I hold you to that?"

Warrior Queen

The library's fireplace breathes its heat. Cocooned in thick blankets, Charlotte feels the frost and burn of December memories: ice skating on Pike Lake, hunting down the perfect Christmas tree. Uncle Mattie finding out that Charlotte had asked someone about custody of minors and then pouncing on her, dragging her and her supper out to the backyard in below-zero cold to spit in her bowl and shove her face into it, bellowing with rage, "*Bitches eat on the ground with the rest of the dogs.*" Uncle Mattie pressing so hard on Charlotte's neck to keep her prone, her face in the bowl, suffocating, her nose and mouth stuffed with cold Hamburger Helper. Her hands and knees grinding so painfully on the sharp gravel, sleet, and ice that her lesions, abrasions, and dark bruises got the attention of the school counselors... who were all chummy with Uncle Mattie. Everyone was chummy with Uncle Mattie, the fucking... fuck.

Steady yourself. The Voice gently pokes her inner fire and adds new kindling. *That nightmare has no reach here unless you give it.*

"But what in heart's fire were you *doing* in the lake?" Arlen calls from the kitchen. "You look like Dorjan's pack challenged you to a wrestling match. Or was it the waterfolk? Please tell me you didn't annoy the waterfolk."

"No, not today, just a swimming lesson," Liam calls from down the hall. "The first of many." He slips into the space between Charlotte and the ghosts, draws her attention to him with his sly smile. "Right?"

Charlotte smirks. "Maybe." She whisper-mouths: "Aren't you going to tell him about the She-Bear?"

Liam briskly shakes his head, saying in a low voice, "And receive yet another lecture on respecting the territory of others? I think not."

Arlen arrives with a tray of tea, and the smells of citrus and cinnamon rising from Charlotte's cup help her to thaw.

Yet Liam declines the cup Arlen offers. "You drink it," he says, refusing to even look at it.

"But surely you must have *some*—"

"No, thank you. I don't need it. I'll... have what she's having," he gestures with a great wave of the blanket.

Arlen leaves—although not without a long, exasperated sigh.

Charlotte holds her steaming cup and inhales the kindness steeped within. "Didn't take you for such a picky eater."

"I will have you know that I am master of my own domain," Liam says with blanketed bow, "and that includes whatever I bring to my lips."

Oh God in heaven, what a cheesy grin. "Never a missed opportunity with you, is there?"

"Nope."

"Here," Arlen announces his presence and practically drops the mug into Liam's blanketed hands. "You don't like oranges or cinnamon, remember? And that's what she's having. So rather than make a third trip, I used ginger and honey with the peaches instead. Now, I'm going back to the velifol garden, *Master* Liam." His melodramatic bow gives Charlotte the giggles, and when Liam mutters something about "always forget honey-comb," Arlen calls out from the hallway, "Then grow some limbs and make it yourself!" Charlotte almost snorts tea all over the floor.

Liam drinks it anyway. "How are your legs?"

"Un-numbed. Your hands?" Charlotte winces when she checks them yet again, gashed and inflamed as though Liam had spent hours tying knots with barbed wire.

"They'll heal." Liam savors Charlotte's thumb gently stroking what little skin is left upon his hand. The dull throb beneath the gashes disappears wherever her skin touches his.

"You turned down the velifol tea, didn't you? I bet it would help you heal faster."

"Certain injuries caused by magic require stronger cures." *Your lips, for a start.*

But Charlotte's mind is busy cataloging the plants in the herbarium. "I'm sure Arlen's got more of that knitbone, or whatever you used last time. I can look, if you'd like."

Liam shrugs the thought away before she can let go. "You forget: pain is nothing new to me."

Charlotte's eyes dart down. No, she hasn't forgotten, but she'd rather not go through that door again. She tries a little imp herself: "Why, because you're invincible?"

Liam laughs midsip and splatters his blanket with tea. "Ha! No. No, I am not. Besides, that was no ordinary bear." He sets his cup down to whisk Charlotte's hands together inside his own. He speaks in dramatic, hushed tones: "I wouldn't say this around the others, but you saved my life, you know. I think a reward is due." *Is this not what the old tales tell, of the hero who rescues, of the rescued who rewards?*

Charlotte's deadpan stare says otherwise. "Honestly, Liam. So what was it?"

"Not sure." Liam strips himself of his blanket. Beneath his dagger's brace, the shirt has come all but undone, still clinging damp, defining every muscle as he adds more wood to the fire.

Charlotte brings the mug to her face before Liam can catch her ogling.

"That She-Bear, as you call it, has been here as long as I have. Few velidevour will even whisper its name, especially Arlen, although I do not understand why he of all those who live here would be so reticent to talk about it." He curls up by the hearth and holds his hands over the flames. Charlotte crawls forward to watch Liam's sigh bend the flames this way and that. "Such anger and hate in those teeth and claws... Those are very powerful feelings, Charlotte, especially inside a being of magic."

The lights dim in Charlotte's eyes, and Liam immediately recognizes it: hidden deep, in the farthest recess of the longest reach, is a door inside her. An old woman cackles and curses while a young girl cries. A woman spits insults, and a man laughs to the crack of leather—

"Those feelings can do some serious damage in humans too," Charlotte says, lips barely moving.

Liam nods, unsure what to say. Of one thing he is certain: no mere ghost hides behind that door.

A log falls in the fire. He begins the ancient lilting words of his healing spell, calling the flames to lick magic's anger from his flesh. "Gaelic," he says before Charlotte can ask. "We learn the spells in the language of our childhood. I grew up in Ireland, the land of my father."

The lights return, brighter than ever. Charlotte's eyes widen with curiosity, her tongue tangles in its questions. *Oh oh oh! Which county? Were there sheep? I hear Ireland's got a ton of sheep. GAH, that's stupid. What about family, like cousins'n'stuff? School? Friends?* So many questions, yet Charlotte hesitates to ask a single one. Arlen said Liam's parents were not fit for family life. *God knows I ain't sayin' shit about Bismarck. No double standards, Charlie, that's not fair.* Charlotte watches Liam play with the fire:

his fingers call the flames to dance, collapse, burst forth like waves against a rocky shore.

Then Liam's words return to her. "Why did you think the cub was a trap set for you?"

Liam's face stiffens. He pulls his hands away from the hearth. The fire extinguishes itself to embers. "My mother said so." Thunder rumbles through his inner skies.

"Maybe it really was a trap for velidevour, not humans, and your folks didn't want you getting caught."

Liam's voice blazes low and hot. "It was a trap, but not for us. The cub was imprisoned. I felt that cursed vine. It would have drowned the cub if the She-Bear or anyone else had attempted a rescue. It is no wonder such a powerful beast never bothered to destroy the bonds. No," bitterness coats every word, "that was just a sick trick on mother and child. Who knows what they did to make my parents spite them so. And of course I dared not spoil their fun, so what's one more lie, one more... in the sick, twisted games they play." He spits his own bitterness into the hearth. Flames erupt so quickly that Charlotte slides backward, fearing another burn. "Sorry. It's difficult to control things when my emotions get the best of me." *Damn his "my son" and "this is for the family." Damn his smile and laughter. Damn it all to the cold embers of death.*

Charlotte connects the dots: if Liam's family had never come to visit him, then that meant the cub got stuck in the lake roughly the same time Liam was left in River Vine. "How long have you been here?"

"Three centuries. Give or take a decade." Shame drapes his shoulders, thicker than any blanket. Liam looks more wounded now than after fighting the She-Bear.

"For three *centuries*?! Who would do such a thing? It was just a baby, a baby," she whispers.

Open yourself. The Voice in her heart coaxes.

But—

You can do it.

Charlotte repositions herself so that her back is pressed along Liam's side. To feel his touch without facing the penetrating storms in his eyes eases her mind, and she finds she can riffle through a few memories without the risk of tears. "My dad used to tell me of some of the things he'd see when he got domestic calls. How parents would tape their kids to the walls so they could go partying. One kid's tortured and molested while another's spoiled like a princess. Kids barely old enough for school left in charge of infants and nothing but garbage on the floor to eat." She chokes. "He was a cop in Milwaukee. Was Milwaukee around before you, erm, got stuck here?"

Liam shrugs. *Family again. Of course, that is what I want to discuss ad nauseam. More family matters.* "Humanity's not changed much, then."

Charlotte absently strokes the scratched skin where her pendant once hung. Liam closes his eyes and listens to Charlotte's inner rhythm, his inner wings beating in pace. "I'd tell myself every day that Dad might not come home because he had to save someone, and you know, even when I was really little, I was okay with that. But at the end of a shift the day after Thanksgiving… he's on his way home, sees a car weaving around, pulls it over. Some girl, high off her head, freaks and grabs her junkie boyfriend's gun and shoots him through the window. And that's it: end of story." She shoves her sleeves into her face.

"He was a very brave man." *What else can I say? At least she is not thinking about the selfish whelp.*

"No one braver." Charlotte smiles, wiping her nose with her sleeve. "Back when I was—I had to be around six, because Anna was just a toddler—there was this guy abducting kids from parks. He'd have this dog with a broken leg, showing it off to kids, and then say to them that the dog couldn't jump into the van all by itself and they should help him."

Liam listens with a furrowed face. It sounds too old, too familiar: no different in spirit from the actions sometimes taken by another house for quick veli. "This ruse worked?"

"Four times. Almost five. I was on the monkey bars, and Anna was in a sandbox...."

Liam escapes his darkness and finds Charlotte's memory full of sunlight and bright-colored structures, with bright-colored ladders, curious squares that frame a tower, strange tunnels children climb to reach the tops of open half pipes for a quick slide down. A cherub with curly red pigtails teethes on a small rock. In a troupe of young ones, a girl emerges, lithe as wheat in wind, skin radiant with summer, hair long and free. Young Charlotte, queen of the tower.

"And here this skinny but nice-looking guy comes along with a big dog that's got one of its legs in a cast. Well, of course we all went over to pet it and feed it crackers and whatever was in our pockets."

Liam takes it all in. The scene is too pleasant, too sweet. The memory itself sticks to the soles of his feet.

"Then this guy starts asking if any of us will help him get the dog back to his car because he's really tired. And there we all are, all eager and shit, trying to grab at this dog like we're guppies and he's got bread on a hook."

She is right, they do: all hopping and moving in one little cluster wherever his hand beckons them.

"He gets us to the van, and now he's asking if someone could get into the car and help him put the dog in its cage. Only this cage, it takes up the whole back of the van."

Liam sees a horseless carriage of metal: no windows. Too few doors. He sees the cage, and that little stalk of wheat stiffens with realization. The memory sours and melts: the colorful structures drip into pools, like wet globs of paint on a palette. Sunlight narrows to a single point upon the cherub.

"This cage is big enough for a kid. And then Anna starts saying 'Me! Me! Me!' And this guy smiles with the creepiest..." Charlotte pauses for breath.

But the memory carries on whether she intends it or not. The fiend grins as he reaches down for the eager cherub, already so selfish, and the queen of the tower, already so selfless, bursts from the crowd and screams, "STRANGER!" Not Liam's battle cry of choice, but it surely frightens the other guppies into silence.

"I kicked him *so* hard, and I punched him right in the crotch."

The fiend abandons his dog and bolts with a peculiar hobbled gait. Liam kneels nearby, not to watch the fiend, but to let the rest of the memory fade among the adults running to their children, abandoning their books and benches and drinks. He does not care to see the woman who whisks up the cherub and hugs Charlotte from behind. He refuses to look upon the uniformed man whose arms embrace all three. Too sweet, too bloody sweet with those damn ghosts. He wants one last moment with the little warrior queen, triumph glowing within and without. This is the Charlotte who now leans against him, still fighting the monsters.

"The police caught the guy when he tried pulling the same stunt a month later. I got my own police cadet badge, even. It was just shiny plastic, but Dad, he pinned it on me himself—"

Colors spool from the memory palette, and what was once the tower and tunnels turns into a large room of uniforms talking, moving, blurring together. But one man, lights brimming in his eyes, just like Charlotte's, takes his time to pin a silvery something to Charlotte's shirt.

"'Don't you ever stop fighting, Charlie,' he told me. And I didn't. Even when Mom took us." Charlotte stops talking.

Liam opens his eyes: he is back in Rose House. A breeze sneaks through the library's open window to play with a ledger's pages. His shoulder quivers. Charlotte is shivering next to him.

"You learned much from your father." He does his best to sound sincere.

Charlotte looks up, resting her head on Liam's shoulder. The ceiling has no advice as to whether she should change the subject. "Eh, from Mom too. Just not—not always good things." *No, not going there. Keep it shut, that whole damn house of dead things shut.* Her fingers splay out on the floor by her hips, rooting herself in this present before another memory carries her off.

If Liam reaches down right now, he will have her hand. From this, he could turn to face her, hold her, have her.

And yet something inside does not wish all this. It's hatching, and insists on coming out regardless of the bile surrounding it. "My father addressed me all of three times my entire childhood: the day I was born…"

CRACK. Charlotte flinches at the bullet sound of the crackling log, eyes focused on the sparks.

"The day he left me in Arlen's care…"

Embers billow with a storm's energy, the golden threads of fire like lightning jumping through the heavens.

"And the day he came to see whether or not I had grown enough to suit his company. He saw raising a son as a chore, preferring me only as a man. So when he decided the time had come for me to enter manhood…"

Whatever logs remain shred into a mound of splinters.

Charlotte isn't sure what to say. "Maybe someone should

have sunk *him* in a lake." She shifts to see the curls hang limply around Liam's face. The gray in his eyes grows dark, thick: the sorts of clouds that bring rain down in sheets, blinding you, burying you—

"Ha!" Liam studies Charlotte's face so intently her cheeks flush. "No, this isn't enough. Come, I'll show you."

30

One Window's Memory

Liam leads Charlotte into the herbarium and faces the stained-glass sunset, the glass sea sparkling in the sun like true water. Charlotte murmurs, "I really love this piece," but Liam shushes her and holds out his hand. "Physical contact will be required if we are both to enter."

Charlotte raises an eyebrow but consents. "You've done this before?"

"Myself? Yes. With someone else?" He carefully looks away before mouthing a small, "No."

A shock, like Liam has dragged his feet on carpet for ten minutes before touching her. But the shock changes all of Charlotte's perceptions. The iron frame thins into nothing. Shards grow, grow to overtake them, surround their feet, heads, eyes.

Liam grips her tightly: "Hold... hold..."

Where's the floor, what am I feeling, did I just step into painted glass? Whoa, just call me Alice.

They fall deeper into the window. The very glass moves with the tides. She smells the water, hears the waves, sees them ripple. The clouds move in over the sun. Gulls cry out.

Then shards shatter all around them, yet do not cut. Charlotte loses Liam's hand as she plummets through open air, nothing but sun and water and stray clouds beneath her, falling to her certain death—

And soft, brown feathers swoop from below to above her: talons take hold of her shoulders, their sharp points digging into her skin just enough to hold her without drawing blood. Here inside his memory, Liam flies as high as he wishes, and here inside his memory, he can touch the stratosphere, not mere treetops.

The talons release her a few feet above ground in a thick patch of tall grass crowning a large sand dune. As she lifts her head, Charlotte hears the soft crash of waves behind her and smells a world of life in front of her, teeming with plants impossible to count: orange, purple, yellow, pink, white blossoms, large and small, short and tall, bloom as though Liam's glass had transformed into living petals of sunlight. A sandy path borders the flowerbed and leads left to a small batch of vines where gourds, tomatoes, and peppers are still young and green. Behind the blooms and produce stands a stocky wall roughly four feet high. Were Charlotte to hop over it, she'd land in a field of wheat, its seed heads burning little tongues of flame in the setting sun. The rock wall continues on, patching together various squares of wheat, corn, and pasture for the goats and sheep on the gently sloping hillside.

But Charlotte wisely keeps to the sandy path, which takes her away from the shore, along the flowers, the vegetables, and goes on another few dozen feet to a cottage constructed of the same white rocks as the wall. With its quaint thatched roof, windows, and door, it looks less imposing than the wall. A domed rock structure the size of a garden shed stands behind the cottage. Beyond the cottage grounds, the grass grows tall and coarse along endless sand dunes. This house, this place, stands completely and utterly alone in its world, with nothing but the plants and the ocean, the winds and the sky for company.

339

Liam cries out one last time as he soars over the ever-changing colors of the sea, then finally swoops over the shore and lands lightly and gracefully at Charlotte's side before the flower garden. His feathers burn away to reveal the silver flecks of his hair glowing with dusk light. He breathes deeply and whoops at the sun. "If ever our kind could love a land, *this*"—Liam opens his arm to embrace land, sea, and sky— "is Cairine. At least, that's what Arlen called it. Mother said it was foolish to grow attached to land because it can so easily be taken from you."

"So, that cottage over there—that's Arlen's home, where he tutored you?" As if on cue, smoke starts puffing out of the chimney. Bees meander around the cottage and hop along the blooms. Charlotte cups one flower and holds it as close as she dares to watch the bee's dance for nectar. "This place is *gorgeous*, Liam. I love it already, and I'm only in your memory of it."

Liam sits in the tall grass with Charlotte and digs his fingers deep, finding the old earth.

"Do you know every single one of those flowers?" Her eyes follow the trail to the cottage garden.

"Learning their names was easy. Applying them properly took a long time."

"How long did you live here?"

"Ten years."

"How often did you go home?"

"Never."

Charlotte releases bee and blossom with a "Why?" upon her lips, but Liam distracts her by pointing to the cottage: its front door has opened. "All true art connects to our inner selves. I used my vision of this place for the window itself, but the real memory is about to begin. Watch the cottage. But stay here—never interact with the past."

They watch a small procession: first, a little boy, face round and dimpled, dark curly hair constantly over his eyes. His long-sleeved tunic is of deep, royal purple, a golden eagle stitched upon its chest. A leather belt, with a short wooden sword sheathed through it, reveals the child's wiry frame. The boy is crying.

Charlotte glances worriedly at Liam, who motions her to turn around, to continue watching.

Patting the boy along is a woman, her long, slender body as graceful as a flower in the breeze, bending to comfort the boy while deep in discussion with whoever is behind her. Hair concealed by a white veil, hands adorned with exquisite gold, she is attired in a long purple dress with flared sleeves that extend from elbow to knee. She too has an eagle embroidered on a girdle around her waist. Yet all this perfect elegance does not strike Charlotte as much as the woman's eyes. They are intelligent —fiercely intelligent. Charlotte wonders why this woman isn't a jungle cat instead of an eagle.

Next comes Arlen, although it takes Charlotte a moment to recognize him without the salt-and-pepper hair and beard. He is a little shorter than the woman. His worn blue tunic, leather vest, and trousers reveal a strong body and a powerful face: a force to reckon with.

After him comes another man in fur-trimmed attire. He too is shorter than the woman, but broad shouldered, with proportionately bulky legs and arms. Flaxen hair cut short, a flat, large face, eyes almost too big for the head. The mouth plays around, almost on the verge of leaving the face altogether. He looks like he could be a Santa Clause or a serial killer, depending on his mood.

These two with Arlen—these are Liam's parents. I can just tell the father's an asshole, and he hasn't even done anything yet. But Charlotte keeps this to herself. It seems rude to interrupt a thought one is physically in.

"You won't hear much talking," Liam whispers. "When we got here, I was instructed to play by the shore as they spoke inside. Then they called me in, Arlen looked me over, and nodded, agreeing to what I guess was taking me on. We're about to see my parents leave me behind."

"But why—"

Liam shushes her.

The crying little boy breaks free of his mother, runs to the garden, and begins kicking at the flowers. "I won't stay, I won't! I'll fly away, I'll fly away and you will never see me again and then you'll be sorry!" A confetti of petals and shredded leaves floats around him.

Poor kid, oh, I just want to give you a big, long hug.

"Liam!" his father bellows. Liam stops immediately and approaches, shivering. The man kneels, but refrains from touching him. No comfort from that quarter. "I expect any son of mine to do what he is told. Are you my son?"

"Yes, Father."

"Then you will stay with Arlen until I find you ready for the family's duties. And no tears. That is not our way," he adds when little Liam begins crying again. "Arlen has much to teach you that will benefit your future as well as the future of our house. Is that not so, Treasa?"

Liam's mother stands apart from the men as if she's studying them and not her son. When little Liam looks up at her with watery eyes, she stoops to his level and holds him close. "Oh, my brave little eaglet, it is just a while, just a short while. You will be home before you know it."

"Such coddling, Treasa." Liam's father gives her a dirty look. "You are a true princeborn, boy. Start acting like one. Do as Arlen instructs, and you, along with our house, will be all the better for it."

"But must we do this now, Bearnard?" Treasa asks, fingers

342

gently raking through Liam's curls. "He is but five. Even the humans wait until a child is seven—"

"I will not have our son compared to those inferior creatures!" Bearnard snaps.

"But she speaks the truth, Bearnard," Arlen says. "To cut his days of innocence short will do the little one no great favor."

At this Bearnard's face twitches, and his eyes grow glassy with a wickedness that would happily drown a cub for fun. "What is it, Arlen? Plans of your own, eh?" The two men begin speaking in rushed, angered tones, the words lost....

Treasa pulls Liam away from the cottage and closer to the shore, just a few feet away from Charlotte.

"Father hates me," little Liam whimpers.

"No, he does not hate you," Treasa coos. "He only wants so badly for you to grow quickly and become a man, a man just like him."

"I will grow up as fast as I can! I will be just like him! Just please, please don't send me away!"

"Oh, my eaglet, we will never be far." She guides his watery eyes to the setting sun. "The sun and moon will always pass from me to you. If you listen carefully, you will hear my messages of love every day." She cleans his pudgy cheeks of tears. "The grown world is just too dangerous, and your father and I need to move fast and far to hold our alliances against the wicked houses. When the world is safe again, we will return for you, I promise." She embraces little Liam deeply, lovingly, then stands facing the cottage.

Charlotte chokes. Her mother has not hugged her or Anna in years.

Someone begins to sing a deep, resonating note, yet no one's mouth is open. Bearnard raises his hand, adorned with a single large ring. Charlotte gasps. *Oh, weird, it's the ring making the song. Just like Orna's ring in the Pits!* A higher voice joins in harmony when Treasa raises her hand. Arlen, too, raises his hand, revealing a single large ring, although his lips remain sealed and Charlotte doesn't hear a note coming from him. In a flash of fire, both parents are gone, leaving the child Liam and Arlen alone.

Charlotte turns toward the present Liam. His eyes have not moved from where his mother stood.

Arlen approaches the little boy and sits on a patch of soft grass. Both stare out to sea. Neither looks at the other. "This is a difficult day. A difficult day for us both." A pause. "When I get sad or angry, and there is little I can do, I take some stones like this and—" he picks up a flat, rounded pebble and sets it skipping away on the flat, foamy waters between waves "—toss my bad feelings to the water. It empties my heart. Then I fill it with better things, like sweet earth, beautiful flowers, and good company." He hands little Liam a stone.

Still shaking and hiccupping from all his sobbing, he closes his tiny fingers around it, scrunches his tiny face at it, and, with his tiny fist, chucks it. Plop. Right into a wave. "I didn't do it right," he whines.

"No matter. We can practice after a nice cup of velifol tea. Would you like some honey? I keep a small hive behind the cottage."

"May I play with the bees?"

"Bees do not care much for play, I'm afraid...."

The conversation, the people, the beach, all fade and flatten. A screeching sound of metal bending, and Charlotte finds herself standing before the window, Liam at her side. His hand trembles inside hers. She grasps his arm and turns him away from the window's memory. "You okay?"

But Liam's gaze will not break away from the memory preserved in glass. "Fine. Just, fine. Don't tell anyone, please? Going in there, I can... fly higher. Escape, be free, however briefly."

"Okay." Charlotte swallows all her questions and says the one thing safe to say: "Your mom was sure worried about you."

Liam bites his lip, then says, "She feared I would run away, so she told me what I wanted to hear. She never came. Just sent messengers to check on my progress, too busy with her precious politics, all her plans and promises intended for me when I was deemed ready."

Come here, boy. *Listen to your mother. Like this,* boy.

Liam drops her hand. His inner clouds retreat as he steps backward to the herbarium's door. "Must check on matters. Excuse me." He bows curtly and leaves.

Super Poppy's New Cape

"No, I beg *your*—oh." Arlen trips into view, knocked off-balance by Liam as he strides out of the herbarium. The velifol blooms droop in Arlen's arms and lose their last glow.

Charlotte leans against the work bench, thoughts still trapped within that glass sunset, all the anger hidden beneath its tranquil hues, as Arlen spreads some of the flowers upon the bench for drying.

"Excuse me," he says, but receives nothing. He tries to catch her eyes, and fails. Finally, Arlen dumps the rest of his load on a bench and grabs Charlotte by the shoulders to move her.

Shit, I'm caught! Charlotte slams her head forward before blinking herself into the present. Conk! Two heads collide and rebound like oversized croquet balls. Wrong time, wrong place, wrong head to smack, if those half syllables of another tongue are any indication. "Sorry." *Great mantra, Charlie. Just. Great.*

After a few grunts and jaw-shifts, Arlen finally rights himself and asks, rubbing a forehead reddened by Charlotte's own noggin, "I didn't receive this," he points to his head, "because of him," he points to Liam's hasty exit, "did I?"

"No, sorry, just—" Charlotte pauses, eying the velifol before

346

moving closer to the stained-glass window, where she really doesn't want to be, but her curiosity is overwhelming. "Liam told me about, about living with you, here." She braces herself lest the window pull her back in. "And also a little about his parents."

"Ah." Arlen dusts his hands of dirt, of memory, or of both. "Ah," he says again, his fingers drumming off-beat upon the table between them.

Please, sir, I'll take a scrap, a petal, anything you can tell me.

"For centuries, the princeborn houses have been locked in a feud—do not ask me why. Even I haven't been able to find the catalyst. Treasa and Bearnard Artair do much to push this feud ever onward, always one step ahead of the other side. Liam's birth, while wanted, also complicated matters."

That Serial Killer Santa wanted a kid? "Liam said they travel a lot."

"Yes." The drumming intensifies. Arlen's shadow forms despite the sunlight flooding the room.

Sir, please don't growl, don't go all dark on me.

"Among other things." Crack! A wedge of table breaks off in Arlen's hand.

"Are you——?"

Arlen pulls himself back into the light as his Gaelic murmurs heal the broken table.

"His father looked, I mean, sounded, like a nutjob, but his mom seemed... kinda nice?"

Arlen snorts. "Treasa is many things, but believe me, she is not nice. Nor is she motherly. She is a manipulator to the highest degree. Nothing gets past her, and nothing outwits her. Liam is her son, yes, but he is also a piece on her chessboard." His eyes fall upon the metal denoting Liam's horizon. "We all are." A brief cough, then, "I must see to... matters. If you'll excuse——"

Hey, that's what Liam said. "Making sure no one bothers the She-Bear?"

Arlen halts, pales, flushes. He stares at the window like a grandma at mass, eyes glittery with magic and tears, and then growls, yes, growls at Charlotte as she holds her breath to the anger-stench that could wilt roses. "Do not approach them. They are dangerous and out of your powers. Is that understood?" He storms out, leaving the velifol scattered willy-nilly on the work bench.

The hell was that about? For a guy who's lived for centuries on top of cave-dwelling psychos, he has one weird She-Bear taboo.

Someone walks in front of the window, tall and dark. Dorjan, perhaps, although he is not alone: he's got someone under his arm, someone smaller, with hair flying about her face, who whimpers—

"Ch-Charlie!"

Oh God, no, no. "Anna?" Charlotte tears out, nearly cracking the door's wooden frame as she yanks it open to the terrace, where she stops. Her lungs draw air in, out, in. She smells: yes. Berries. And canine.

Dorjan is guarding Jenny at the farm. You know that. The Voice in her heart sounds so sure, but how can it be so sure all the time? It can't see Anna.

"Charlie."

There, for a split second: baby blues behind the flowers.

Charlotte sprints, trips on an errant gardening basket, stumbles into the woods: nothing. But a new smell laces the air, charred and old.

"I've always enjoyed the taste of a pickpocket's heart."
FUCK you. NO.

She tracks the scent with a hunter's haunched gait, ever-ready to sprint or duck into hiding.

"Especially in a pretty pie."

Who the hell's out there? Who the hell are you, messing with me, messing with my sister?

The smell encases everything in a gray haze. It feels like it should be that warm, crisp taste of burning leaves, but it's not leaves burning, not quite....

Charlotte stops. There's no grass beneath her feet. No sunlight. Cold and dark, dirt and ash.

Well, fuck-a-doodle-doo, I'm back here. Again. The last place I should be right now.

Yes, the black marble tree stands before her, tall, fat, its black center hollow gaping open. A bonfire burns just outside its mouth. A foot sticks out of the flames like a flag stiffly unfurled. Hands twist and contort in their dance with the flames. Faces shrivel and liquefy in the orange-violet heat. And the sulfurous, calcified stench of burning hair overwhelms her senses.

Don't throw up. Don't breathe more dead people. Is that red hair?

"Little tails, little tails, where could you be? Could mummy have you hidden—" Campion breaks through the haze and shadow, carrying a corpse on either shoulder. He dumps them like dirty blankets. "—in the old oak tree?" He surveys the fire, kicks a leg back into place. "If you're hungry for hot dogs, I can see if there's a finger or two left downstairs. Or are you perhaps looking for someone else? Let me guess.... Red hair?" He combs his fingers across his scalp. Out spills long red hair. "Big baby-blue eyes?" He taps either temple. His violet eyes flash blue.

Charlotte's breath locks against her larynx. She hates how her body trembles, but it takes all her willpower just to spit the words "Fuck you."

Campion shakes the Anna hair and eyes to dust as he leans

349

in. Charlotte sees white, yellow, black hairs stuck to Campion's shoulder. And a tooth. Or two. "Naughty, naughty."

A torso rolls, upsetting the flames and sending up a fresh volley of sparks and tongues. Charlotte jumps. *Too damn many hollow, staring eyes. Can't see a bit of blue anywhere.*

She is not there, the Voice in Charlotte's heart says urgently. *But someone will be.*

Huh?

"It's Suuuuper Poppy!" Poppy leaps from the black hollow of the marble tree with a colorful cape. "Da da da DAAAA!" She holds its straps around her neck and twirls. "Like my new acesser-… accesso-… like it?"

The "cape" is a boy's body in G.I. Joe pajamas. Sammy Blair, Jenny's brother.

Charlotte closes her mouth. Hell, she closes her whole damn brain while Campion nods in approval. "I like it! Although we should break the arms more to tie it properly. I could always see if we've another small one below, maybe in another color."

Charlotte's whole body stings like every inch of skin fell asleep and is only now waking up. Her nerves crave blood, oxygen, understanding, some god-damn sense from of this world.

Poppy pouts and spins so her back is to Charlotte. "But I like the colors on this one."

"You're not breaking a damn thing." Charlotte hoists up the body from Poppy's shoulders, so small, so light, just a little guy, like all the other little guys on a playground watched by the monsters.

"Oh, hi, Miss Charlotte!" Poppy spins back around. "It's cleaning day downstairs, cuz boy, was it ever a mess! Especially after you and the granach went all—" she holds Sammy's hands and mashes them together with "rawr rawr!" sounds.

"Knock. That. OFF."

Poppy's mouth shrinks, her eyes grow wide. "But he's dead."

Never before has Charlotte wanted to slap someone so much.

"Piss off, Punky Brewster." She faces Campion with the body, warmth pulsing through her to counter the cold husk in her arms. "So this is it? Manhandle them, toy with them, hack them to pieces, and then just burn'em like a pile of garbage?"

Campion picks up bodies by the necks and tosses them in. "Well, yes. They're dead."

"These are people. They deserve some sign of *respect*."

Campion picks up a hand that rolled off the pile and tosses it on top. "Oh, and I'm sure you bestow the same honor on all the apple cores and chicken bones of meals past."

"Those are—"

"—not the same? Just dumb plants? Stupid animals?" Campion moves in close, his lavender eyes sparking with baby blue. "Eeeeexactly." The swirls brighten, seem to whisper—

"Anna in Rose House
Silver roots in every limb
Liam holds her for himself
In a hidden space
She dies
Mere feet away from you
Too ignorant to care."

No. No no no.

His eyes deceive you! The Voice in Charlotte's heart slaps her.

She blinks, shakes her head, does her damnedest to NOT look at Campion's teeth, sharp and bright in the haze. "Not this one. This kid is no chicken bone." Charlotte breathes deep

351

through her mouth. What little's left of poor Sammy's hair flutters against her chin. "Please."

Campion's smile broadens as he leans back and says, "Hey, hey! Manners! But is this," he tilts Sammy's head, and Charlotte can swear his baby teeth are rattling within his withered mouth, "the one you're *really* looking for?"

A burst of birdsong and feathers: Ember flies through the sparks and lands to transform next to Charlotte. "I saw smoke and thought something might be wrong."

"Ember! It's cleaning day! Wanna cook some fingers?" Poppy hops up and down, pointing to the bonfire.

Campion sucks his thumb and pulls it out with a light pop.

Ember's lips squirm. "N-no. Miss Charlotte, perhaps you should go back to Rose House before..." the question fades when she sees the body in Charlotte's arms. "Are you, are you helping them?"

"No." Charlotte walks away from Poppy's "I'll get the fingers!" and Campion's "Ta ta for now!" and vomits on the ashes. Then she straightens, picks up her burden, and starts for the Southern Road.

Ember's voice is close behind. "What is this?"

Sunlight heats her skin and deeper. Sammy really does look like a thing, a person-husk, a frail mummy with a withered smile. She doesn't know whether to cry or to puke again. "You don't recognize him? It's Jenny's brother. From the farm."

Ember takes a step back. "Yes, I can see that, but what is this that you're doing? You can't just... lob his body over the Wall for his family to find." Ember waves from Sammy to the road's end, where the Wall awaits. "Besides, this land keeps what it claims. The Wall won't allow otherwise."

"I know that!" But in truth Charlotte wanted to do that very thing: get Sammy home. It was such a good idea, until Ember actually said it aloud. What good will a pile of dust do Jenny, or Sammy? Did she just save the boy from burning only to have him explode in midair? Because that's respectful.

"I'm taking him as far as I can." Before Ember can open her mouth, Charlotte adds in dismissal, "I'm fine. Go, do whatever you were doing." And southward she walks, alone with her burden, the mark on her wrist starting to itch.

Sweat trickles beneath her arms and down her back in the sun's heat. Such sunshine is meant for a day of swimming, of beaches, of returning stolen swimsuits to the shop. Not a day to carry a child's corpse home. *Red hair? No, it's a boy. But one blink and it's a girl, I'd swear. Red hair, baby blues open and dead.*

The itchy tingle on her wrist grows, slow and sure, up Charlotte's arm.

As the smell of apples, pears, peaches, mint, and so much else rides the southerly breeze to tickle Charlotte's nose, she can't help but wonder if Sammy knew such sweetness before the Lady sewed him into her nightmare underground. Were his dreams brought to life, or was Campion's terrifying face the last thing he knew?

Pain's tendrils start to block other questions. The Wall is but a stone's throw away.

Charlotte steps into a copse of trees, just a short distance from the Wall—her arm throbs in time with her heartbeat, but she will not bury Sammy where the velidevour can dig up his grave and play dress-up with him. She arrives at a quiet spot with blue asters and wild oak trees. Any closer to the Wall, and she'd be unable to bury him.

Bury him with…? Oh, for chrissake, Charlie, you don't even have a shovel! She rests Sammy's body atop the asters and then leans against a tree, slowly hitting the back of her head against its trunk. *Stupid, stupid, stupid.*

"You might need this." A shovel falls softly next to her: Arlen, his long black coat flapping in the breeze.

32

Burying Samuel Blair

"How did you—"

"Ember."

"Ember's one fast flyer." Charlotte picks up the shovel. *As light as Sammy. Horrible comparison.*

"She is swift indeed. And, I must confess, I was looking for you—to apologize for my boorishness this morning."

"No big deal." Because it isn't, not when Sammy keeps changing into Anna each time she shifts her gaze. She has to get him into the ground, safe from fires and manic velidevour. She finds the center of the flower bed and begins to dig, carefully setting aside the blue asters for later.

After several minutes of quietly watching her and listening to the mournful sighing of the leafy canopy, Arlen says, "This burial is not something you have to do, you know."

Charlotte does not stop. If she stops digging, the pain in her arm magnifies tenfold. "Yeah, I do, I have to. You meet Jenny, you'll know I have to."

Canine overpowers the scent of soil and asters. D leaps down from the Wall, cocks his head, and transforms. "What in heart's fire are you two doing here?" Dorjan's person-self looks even thinner, if that's possible.

Then he sees Sammy. His face pales to an eerie glow in

the glen's shadow as his whole form droops like a hanged man.

"Oh." With staggered step, Dorjan kneels by the body, fingertips but a petal away. "Oh, little one." His lip quivers. His voice is hoarse. "This should not have been your fate."

Arlen's hand rests upon his shoulder. "You were not here, Dorjan. What could you have done?"

Dorjan spit-growls. "'You were not here.' Bloody story of my life. I'm never where I should be."

The pain slithers around Charlotte's shoulder and chokes the joint. Charlotte drops the shovel, her grip nonexistent. "Hey." She holds out her good hand, bridging the space between her and Dorjan. "You're here now."

Dorjan's brow furrows. When he notices the dropped shovel, a touch of color returns, and he says, "Yes. Yes, I am." He sets his jaw and looks a moment at Charlotte's efforts so far, a slight depression in the earth, and nudges her gently. He steps into the grave, transforms, and sends a steady stream of dirt into the air. Charlotte steps back to avoid flying soil.

Charlotte flexes her good side. "Wouldn't happen to have a knife or something in those pockets, would you?"

"Just my pruning knife." He holds it out with shaking hand. "Why?"

Charlotte selects the tree nearest Sammy's grave, and carves:

HERE LIES SAMUEL BLAIR
BELOVED BROTHER AND SON
NEVER FORGOTTEN

Arlen sighs as he kneels at Sammy's feet, eyes lost in Charlotte's words. "Such a caring heart. Were I in your sister's place, my brother would not have come for me." His face breaks for a moment under such a wave of sadness and anger that Charlotte thinks him ready to cry. A long silence passes.

Dorjan's face peers up from the hole, his blue eye wet

356

with sorrow, his green eye steely with determination. "It's ready." He climbs out, and the three of them gather asters, scattering them to line the floor of the grave.

Dorjan climbs in one last time. "Didn't think flowers grew this far from Rose House anymore. It's... it's nice."

Charlotte nods a little. The mark wants her collarbone now. "Yeah." She positions herself at Sammy's head, while Arlen moves to Sammy's legs. Despite badly shaking arms, Charlotte and Arlen lift Sammy and lower him to Dorjan, who rests him gently upon the bed of asters. Charlotte sprinkles a few petals upon him, then Dorjan fills the grave.

Arlen watches with wet eyes. "I cannot deny my place in his fate. I should have been more watchful."

The thorns start their journey across her chest, but Charlotte remains at Arlen's side. "There's a big difference between being more watchful and being outnumbered." She even nudges him.

He winces, but still manages a small smile.

"Charlie!"

Charlotte's ears recoil, then reach, reach as far as they possibly can past Arlen, Dorjan, grave and all. *Stay totally still, dig deep, show nothing, say nothing.*

"Charlie, Charlie, Charlie!"

Her name echoes in sneaky whispers among the leaves. If Arlen hears, he does not show it. "Are you all right?" he asks her.

"Charlie, they have me, please, Charlie!"

"Ugh, her eyes are frightening." Dorjan stands next to Arlen now, the burial finished.

Charlotte ignores their stares—not hard when thorns pierce skin and threaten to turn her lungs into swiss cheese. But she will finish this, dammit. She plucks a final sprig of aster to lay upon the loose soil. A final moment's silence out of respect.

Please, Anna tell me where you are. I'm listening for a sign, any sign.

"There she goes again, Uncle. Like a rabbit in a fox's maw."

Charlotte bites her lip and snaps back, "And what about you?"

"What about me?"

Arlen gives Dorjan a sidelong look. "You do look terrible."

"Well, I don't see the point of resting if I'm just going to be attacked by that one." Dorjan's sharp chin juts at Charlotte.

"I said I was sorry," she says through gritted teeth as thorns hunt for a vein in her neck. She walks away from the stares, away from the Wall, away from death that will—*please, for the love of god*—just stay dead.

"Charlie."

I'm coming! I'll find you. Charlotte's ears want to go east. Or north. Or somewhere, she doesn't know, because she hears more footfalls behind her and really, really doesn't want to get into rabbits and maws again. If only her nose could catch a scent. At least the thorns creep away from her neck and chest, allowing her lungs to take in all the air she can.

Dorjan and Arlen quickly flank her, shift her, and the three return to the Southern Road for Rose House.

"You will promise not to come this way alone again, won't you?" Arlen breathes deeply as though he'd just been running. "The mark nearly took you. Again."

"I know." *Calm down, Charlie, just get them off your back so you can go into search and hunt mode.*

Foolishness. The Voice in her heart always uses that word with such bloody confidence.

"And stop wandering off by yourself," Dorjan says.

"I KNOW."

"All this solitude's turning you edgy."

Charlotte glares at Dorjan and tests her marked arm. Still too many thorns to try a quick back punch, dammit.

"Edgy?" Arlen looks confused.

For crying out loud, sir, don't encourage him.

"Another word for 'nervous,' Uncle."

"I do hope this 'edginess' is not because of Liam," Arlen says as he rests a hand on one of the stone eagles marking the Southern Road's end at the clearing surrounding Rose House.

Charlotte keeps right on going. "It's not."

"Here, Charlie."

She freezes a dozen steps away from the others. Charlotte doesn't see how her head darts, how her nose holds high in the air to sniff, how her fingers all twitch to catch the very feel of scent.

But Arlen and Dorjan see. Arlen holds a finger to his lips. Dorjan remains quiet, his blue eye curious, his green eye fearful.

Arlen's boots move silently through the grass toward Charlotte. "What is it, child?"

"Nothing." She tosses the word out like scrap of food to a stray. She's got to listen harder, smell harder, look harder. She gave her whole self to save Anna once, and now she's got to do it again.

Fingertips touch the back of her head.

Charlotte spins, fist flying—

Only to slam against a living wall: Arlen's flat hand is as hard as his eyes.

"What in heart's fire was *that?*" Dorjan jumps, taken aback by the unexpected collision of flesh.

Arlen's fingers clamp down. "That is what I'd like to know." He pulls Charlotte's fist down to her hips before letting go. "This wouldn't happen to have anything to do with the roof incident, would it?"

Charlotte swallows air, swears the hint of berry splash now trickles down her throat. "I said I was sorry."

"Why, what happened?" Dorjan asks.

"She thought Campion had escorted Anna to the veli chambers."

"That ass of a vermin," Dorjan cracks his neck and says with too much damn emphasis, "He is messing with you, Charlotte."

"I know."

"Did you honestly think I was *eating your sister* when you jumped me?"

"I said I was sorry!"

Arlen's dark eyes turn into some sort of antilight, piercing Charlotte, searching her. His coat whips about his legs, folding him into a darkness, dark as the Pits.

I see. I know, I know you've got her. I know you're all in on it. You god-awful fucking fairy freaks, I know she's here, and I can't let you know that I know. But I'll prove it just like before. 'Trust' and 'believe' my ass.

"Charlie, come back!"

I won't be long, I promise.

The Voice in Charlotte's heart kicks against her ribs as though locked in. *Foolishness!*

Fuck you, I know, I KNOW she's here.

"Uncle, she's the doing the rabbit thing *again*."

"I said I was sorry, all right?!" Charlotte shrinks from Arlen's reach and stares them both down with wild eyes. "I. Am. SORRY. I'm sorry I thought you had Anna, I'm sorry I head-butted you, I'm just a little spent after fighting giant bears and watching psychos treat corpses like costumes."

"Wait, what?" Dorjan's mouth hangs open.

Arlen looks like he was gut-punched twice. "You didn't, you couldn't... have killed them—?" His legs buckle, his color drains—Dorjan catches him before he can pass out.

Now it's Charlotte who finds herself confused as the two

360

speak in half Gaelic, half… French? Arlen pulls a small silver flask from his coat pocket and takes a quick swig, then hands it to Dorjan.

Dorjan opens it, sniffs it. "Pure veli." He takes a long swallow, and gags. "Right. Fine. This ends today if I have to drag Campion out of the Pits myself. And *you*," Dorjan pokes Charlotte hard in the chest, "whatever it is you smell or hear or see, it's not what you think it is. Stop. Listening." Then to Arlen: "Will you—"

"I'll be fine," Arlen says, taking one more swig for himself, hands shaking uncontrollably. "Go. See. It must be done." He numbly watches Dorjan run, leap with a flare of dust and fire to become D, lost to the forest shadows.

Charlotte's eyes also follow Dorjan. *All that darkness, I should have known, too much darkness. Can't trust the darkness. Don't trust the darkness.*

"CHARLOTTE!"

Charlotte blinks, and realizes that Arlen's face is an inch from her own. He inhales, exhales, stirring up the smells of past days in the garden, the sounds of laughter and banter and music in Rose House. "Something's poisoned you against us. But it will not have you. I cannot lose any more family to this, not again, not…" Arlen's head bows.

Family. I'm… I'm family?

The Voice in Charlotte's heart struggles against the lock. *Trust! Believe!*

Charlotte swallows air again. No berry splash. She looks over Arlen's head at the tree line. No tiny baby blues. And sunshine bathes the clearing.

Fully awake, she brushes the loose hair away from her eyes and sees a man aged by worry and fear. Could this be the same Arlen who body-slammed Campion? His hair's whiter, and more lines streak his face. The little flask glittering between them looks too heavy for him to hold.

"This. Please, get Master Liam to drink this by whatever means." He wraps her hands around it and pulls her to the porch's edge. "I have to go… to see. For myself." He turns, stiffens with a thought, then turns back. "Go inside, remain there, and on no account leave before Dorjan or I return." His brisk walk transforms into a run as he vanishes in the direction of the lake.

Anna's Plea

Charlotte shuts the front door behind her. Legs weak, she closes her eyes and leans against the door, its dark, smooth surface cool against her forehead.

The Voice in her heart reaches out to her, still locked in. *Don't give in, Charlie*, it pleads. *Don't fail your dad; don't be like your mom. Don't give in to the nightmares from the dark.*

Too much darkness, all bleeding together. She exhales slowly as she opens her eyes and stares at Arlen's flask in her hand. *Weird: this flask is cold, and come to mention it, really damn heavy for such a tiny thing.*

Rrrrrrrrrrrip!

Charlotte starts. *The parlor's empty. Glitzy dining room vacant. Library out of earshot. No one's in the kitchen.*

Another rrrrrrrrrip splashes into the air and ripples above Charlotte's head. She scurries up the steps to find a new door, ajar, at the top of the stairs. The old cedarwood doorjamb is gouged in several places, like someone kept nicking it for not gauging its size properly. Blue, silver, gold, red—paint smears of a dozen hues and widths mark the half-open door. Such a door can only lead to one place: Liam's studio. *Upstairs now? Not downstairs? Criminy, House, stop jig-sawing it up like you're some puzzle box!*

Charlotte enters. Half-completed panes of stained glass line the wall immediately to her right, and old paint speckles the grout beneath her feet. Five half-sculpted torsos squat beside heads of clay on a wooden workbench to her left, accompanied by two other clay sculptures, both fully formed: one of a disembodied hand grasping for something invisible and unattainable, and one of a vicious face with slit eyes staring down on a defiant girl. Canvases are everywhere—some ripped up, littering the brick floor, trampled and broken. Every canvas is covered with portraits of women from across the centuries, all with alluring looks in their eyes, all with fingers poised to caress a face, all depicting languorous bodies reclining in the grass, in sheets, in the water. All beautiful. All wrecked.

"Liam? What are you doing?!" Charlotte half-hops over the canvases, breathing through her mouth all the while to deal with the overpowering mix of paint fumes and frustration. In the far corner across the room, Liam hunches over another canvas, rips it in two, and chucks it—

—right into Charlotte. "OW!"

"*Mac an donais,* I'm sorry!" He obliterates another canvas against the wall next to him as he rushes to her side, cupping her cheeks in his hands. "Are you all right? Can you still see?"

He holds her so close his exhale brushes her lips. "Oh-kay." The syllables barely hold together. She weaves her fingers with his and coughs her lungs out of swoon mode. "Why are you ripping up your paintings?" She pulls his hand down and surveys the wreckage. "They're all portraits of, ah, beautiful women." *Oh, please don't tell me there are nude studies in here too.*

"I'm looking for someone." He resumes flipping through canvases stacked against the wall.

"How about some tea?" Charlotte fingers the flask behind her back. "I see you've got a kettle by the kiln."

Liam glances down at Charlotte's other hand, the one holding the flask, and smirks. *So Arlen sends the honey with the medicine. I know your tricks, Teacher.* "Tell Arlen no tea for me, thank you."

Charlotte fidgets. "He's, um, out." Her eyes flick toward the door opposite Liam's canvases. It's the same door Charlotte used when she first arrived at Rose House and hid from Arlen and Dorjan. *Am I back on the first floor again? How the heck do you make rooms, and people, move so easily, House?*

Liam resumes ransacking his canvases. Yet Charlotte cannot bring herself to leave. For all of his talk of her and her music, this is worse than her kicking the piano. He's destroying years of work. Just to find one person.

"It's okay to ask for help, you know." She approaches him, reaches for his hand, so rough from his destruction, and tugs. "I'm pretty good with faces."

Liam stands very, very still. "I'm looking for a girl."

"Oh." Charlotte scans the ripped canvases, the other piles near Liam: "Kind of a lot of, erm, that. Can you be more specific?"

Silence.

Liam holds a portrait of a girl as young as Anna, hair long, red, and vibrant against the pale skin of her chest, her curves casting just a hint of shadow. Lying on the edge of a pool, grass tickling her skin—he had even painted the goosebumps from what could have been a cool spring breeze. The ripples in the water carry shards of her, along with reflections of a clouded sky across the bottom half of the painting.

As young as Anna. She looks like Anna.

For a second, the water within the painting seems to ebb and flow. The air is fresh with spring grass. The red hair blows across the girl's face. She blinks, she purses her lips, she speaks—

"Charlie, he's gonna kill me!"

365

Liam rips the canvas.

"Char—"

"NO!" Charlotte snatches the halves from Liam's hands and shoves them back together. Nothing but stale paint fumes and silence. *You were, in, this? No. That, I know that this, no, you could not be in here, no. The eyes are wrong, not baby blue, just... blue. They are wrong. Aren't they?*

"Charlotte?" This time, the voice calling her is low, deep, and male.

Charlotte blinks. She's pressing her face against the top half of the portrait.

Liam leans close, with wow eyes enveloping, wrapping protectively around Charlotte and keeping out whatever hissing lingers in her ears. His arms reach out to do what his eyes are already doing.

But Charlotte jerks away, steadies herself, and then shoves Arlen's flask into Liam's chest, forcing him to retreat to arm's length. "Please have some, Liam. Okay? Even starving artists have to eat sometime."

Liam allows a rueful smile. "Only because you used your manners."

Charlotte snorts, and watches him unscrew the cap. Vibrant wisps of lavender whirl about the rim as Liam brings the flask to his lips and downs the lot. His body shudders for a moment as though he's just swallowed vinegar. Then Liam throws the flask with its dregs onto the torn portrait of the redhead. Both burst into clouds of glittering dust. His shoulders lift, free of an old yoke at last.

"Charlie, he's gonna kill—"

Liam watches as the Lady Charlotte grows rigid, frightful, with eyes wild as a forest fire. "Come, I need some fresh air." *Perhaps that will cleanse this wretched poison out of us both.* He holds the door open, and Charlotte walks through in a daze.

"Charlie, please."

Hang in there, Anna. I'll find you soon.

Along the path south to the lake, woods grow sick and strange. Branches press Liam and Charlotte together. Fruits ripen too quickly and rot upon their stems. The flowers are far too pungent, churning the bile in Liam's belly. Yet Charlotte sees little, smells less.

A bough breaks. Someone hisses. A jaw snaps. Liam's hand reaches for the hilt behind his head.

Talons sweep by Liam's shoulder and carry Charlotte up, away—

Charlotte blinks and realizes she's not on the ground, she's not with Liam, she's been run through in the shoulder —she screams.

Devyn's piercing owl screech stuns her to silence. He maneuvers her in and out and above the trees. Charlotte whips her limbs up to avoid striking a branch.

Violet eyes, there, watching from the ground, but Devyn moves too fast for her to see who bears them. They fly just above the tree line in a straight course toward the lake. A few stones lie scattered, the memory of their flat smoothness still lingering on her fingers and distracting her from the talons digging into her shoulders. Moments later, Devyn sets her down on the sand as Liam bursts upon the beach, dagger in hand.

"What is the meaning of this?" Liam cries as Charlotte curls up in pain at his feet. Blood soaks through the tattered sleeve. *He dares, he dares to take what's mine. I will snap his talons one by one.* His eyes storm. "That is the second injury you've given her this day."

Devyn transforms in a crouching position on the sand.

He averts his face, staring at the lake water, his voice almost silent: "Ember has heard talk from the Pits, Princeborn. Dangerous talk."

"In what way dangerous?" Liam rips a sleeve of his tunic and ties it as tightly as he can around Charlotte's arm. *Oh, but for some knitbone, some fireweed, anything. Why do her cheeks redden so?*

"Unrest, Princeborn. Some were prepared to snatch her," pointing to Charlotte, "from your very care. That is why I acted." Devyn eyes the dagger, then the woods. "Cein is very determined to return River Vine's rule to his mistress."

"And Orna?"

"The Lady is nowhere to be seen."

Charlotte fits herself against Liam, the heat of him spilling into her. The Voice in her heart drinks in the heat and kicks at its lock again. *Trust. NOW.*

"What should we do?" she asks.

"Stay out of the Western Quarter. Fly to Rose House, or better yet, fly across the lake, north to the Wild Grasses. As far from Orna's reach as your marks allow."

"And what should we do at nightfall, exactly?" Liam shakes his head. "Under a naked sky, we'll be dead by morning."

Charlotte peers past the men, searching the brush for eyes. No velidevour. No baby blues. Yet leaves rustle. Something breathes in there. Something hungers in there. "If they want us so damn bad, why aren't they just coming out? We're cornered right here, by the lake."

"No velidevour trusts the water," Devyn says as dust and feathers swirl up his legs. "Princeborn, for Arlen's sake, do not linger here. As for you, girl, beware your own senses." The gray owl vanishes above the tree tops.

"Charlie, don't leave me!"

Charlotte struggles to stand facing the forest while Liam

sheathes his dagger, moves to the edge of the water, and looks down. *So many women gave themselves to that face. They submitted to every bloody whim that formed behind that face. That face once thought every portrait a trophy to display and mock.* Liam picks up a rock, studies it. Chucks it at his reflection.

Charlotte hears whimpering. A muffled scream. She wills her legs to run, but the Voice in her heart freezes her limbs. *DECEIT.*

FUCK you, let me GO. Charlotte tears at her own chest as if to rip the Voice out. She half-sobs, half-breathes, "And what of *your* Anna?"

Liam moves with measured steps to stand between Charlotte and the trees. He sees her legs shake, the forest blaze in her eyes.

"Your painting... that last redhead you shredded looked a lot like my sister. You know. Anna."

The apparition floats gleefully behind Charlotte, teeth white, predatory. Liam yearns to stone it to a new death. "Her name was Antonia." The very name stings his tongue. "She lived in Saint Petersburg. She was beautiful, intelligent, but completely submissive—my mother introduced us. I should have known such a girl would be my father's type."

He brushes Charlotte's shoulder as he whips a stone into the water. That glancing touch empowers the Voice in Charlotte's heart to scream, *Listen to him!*

Charlotte picks up a stone.

"Charlie, I need you! Strike him and save me!"

That... doesn't sound right.... She wouldn't say that.... Would she?

Charlotte blinks, and finds she's holding the stone out to Liam, who takes it for another throw. "But your dad was still married, wasn't he?"

"That only matters to preserve the line. My parents have an agreement. Their marriage was a political alliance, an alliance based on power and position, so each just turns a blind eye when the other seeks, shall we say, a different pleasure elsewhere." Something swims far out in the water: the mer-folk water people everyone blathers about. Liam hurls another stone and strikes at the creature in the distant water. It dives in an angry ripple. "I took after my father. Overtook him too. We competed over magic, over lovers. Mother never seemed to care before Antonia." Clam-sized eyes appear—Liam grabs a fist full of rocks, aims—*Like this,* boy; *come here,* boy; *for the family,* boy—and Charlotte smacks the lot out of his hand.

"Hey, don't take it out on the mermaids."

"Charlie, don't let him hurt me too!"

He won't, I swear. Charlotte grabs a stone. It swells in her hand to the size of her fist. But she is unaware. She does not pause to question this.

Liam, however, stares at her hand, at the stone in her hand, his reverie broken.

"If you and your father 'competed' all the time," Charlotte's words plop like pebbles in water, "how is it out of a bazillion years of livin', it only takes one girl, one human girl out of all those other girls, for your parents to go berserk?"

A little voice slithers behind her earlobe and curls down, wet and sweet: **"Oh yes, Charlie, that's good. Deceit: he's full of deceit. You can silence him now. One good hit with this rock and he's down. That's all you need. And you'll be free. You can save Anna."**

WHO ARE YOU?! The Voice runs through Charlotte's body to her hand, forcing her to drop the rock with a sickening thud in the sand. She swipes at her ear. Something like black-and-white bird feces falls into the sand. A few droppings remain on Charlotte's fingertips.

The Voice begs Charlotte to clean her hand in the lake—

Purge it, NOW!—but Charlotte is still too filled with visions and rage. She flicks the droppings into the air, doesn't see them fall. Doesn't see them regroup.

"Do not. Lie. Liam."

Liam moves from the water, eyes never leaving Charlotte. *The waterfolk must have hexed the stone she holds, because no commoner is near enough to exert such a strong control over her mind.* "My father had his eyes set on Antonia, but she looked my way." Hypervigilant, he endeavors to walk backward, toward the path to Rose House. With Charlotte indoors, the spell *will* be broken. "It all came together so neatly: Mother and Father away, leaving only me in the house. The girl coming to the manor with payment for some promise from Mother, I don't know. I didn't care. I simply took as she gave. Father found out, of course, from Mother. *She* always finds out."

Red flashes behind a tree. Baby blues barely peer over the trunk. **"Charlie, run away with me."**

I will, if I can just get to you.

And another wet, sweet line tickles her ankle, leg, ribs, neck, back to her ear, under her hair, invisible to anyone but the Voice.

"Yes, you can reach her. But you must strike now in his confusion, so he will never hurt little Anna again. Then you can join her, and save her."

A little jab, no different from a mosquito's, pierces Charlotte's skin.

Skull.

Mind.

"Strike now." It insists.

The Voice runs inside Charlotte and finds darkness bleeding from the outside in. The darkness snakes through Charlotte's mind, a forked tongue tasting for fears, swallowing memories of her sister whole. Charlotte cannot smell its stink of hatred.

371

"Strike." It demands.

Charlotte's vision begins to cloud.

The Voice blocks Charlotte's heart from the sibilant barrage and clings to that which this darkness cannot mute: *Liam. Look at him, alone and in pain, just like you. You cannot leave him. You cannot leave him in his sorrow, Charlie, look at him. HIM.*

Charlotte buckles forward, retching into the air. Liam slides through the sand to catch her lest she fall. And then he catches sight of black worms, small but quick and agile, half a dozen gliding through the sand and canyoneering up her trouser legs.

"Charlotte, Lady Orna's curse is upon you. We must dispel it." He grabs the waist of her jeans—

"Evade! He will force himself on you and on your sister!"

And he misses: Charlotte swings her leg and kicks Liam's guts as hard as she can. "HA! Bet you say that to all the girls, Lover Boy."

He grunts, rolls in the sand, out of Charlotte's reach, but he does not draw his blood dagger. Liam can't even form a fist as Charlotte's face contorts, the worms now appearing out of her shirt and crawling up her neck. "Charlotte, please, let me help!"

"I didn't *ask*"—kicks at him again—"for your goddamn *help*"—kick—"not for me, but for my *sister*."

"Yes, Charlie, you begged him to save Anna, your only family, and yet he spurned you. He deceived you. He is NOT your friend. Strike him again. Again. Again!" A hiss inside her ear, battering at her heart, her mind.

The Voice under siege in Charlotte's heart cries out, *Look at him! He's not defending himself. LOOK!*

The worms slide around Charlotte's ears and temples.

They ring her head like a crown.

Liam's inner wings cannot beat fast enough to vanquish his fear. *The worms too close to burn off her, too damn close, can't run the risk! I must get her to Arlen, to Rose House—to listen. What can I give her to make her listen?* Liam jerks up his sleeve. A vine of thorns is tattooed on his forearm nearly to his shoulder, the ink black like a disease. "Charlotte, look here. Here!" Her eyes have gone vacant, but still Liam risks another blow to lift his mark directly into her face. "I'm just like you, brought here to rot. Mother suddenly accusing me of having no respect for authority, after all the bloody centuries of doing her dirtiest, most humiliating commands. And Father cursing Antonia, me, anyone within reach, then coming here and cursing Arlen with such… rage… never have I seen him lose that much control. And somehow his rage built a wall with more power than he's ever shown, and scored marks upon all who live inside its boundaries."

The Voice in Charlotte's heart begs her to listen. *You know this is truth! You've seen his thorns, his storms. You know his scent. Smell his shame and the truth of his surrender to you!*

But Anna whimpers behind the tree. Ash and berry splash and bus funk flood the air as a scream pierces all of Charlotte's senses and freezes her heart: **"He's a liar, Charlie, a LIAR! What do you do with liars?"**

This time, Liam follows Charlotte's gaze. He catches but a glimpse, but it is enough: more worms, perched against the tree's bark, hissing black smoke that trails like locks of hair. Its sulfurous scent suffocates and burns the lungs. "Charlotte, what do you see there, please, tell me… what… you… see?" His words grind to a halt.

A crown of worms wriggles down her forehead and settles just above her eyebrows in a numbing ripple, so cool, like puffs blown over birthday cake candles. Her eyes are full of little candles. The Voice in Charlotte's heart hears the worms' darkness nesting inside her mind, preparing to feed on her heart and soul.

Charlotte's breath reeks of death as she speaks in a low, deliberate voice, accenting each word: "I. See. A. LIAR."

She aims for Liam's jaw, and swings with all her might.

34

Compromise

Liam ducks his head just in time. His heart's fire ignites a bright light, sending power through his bones to keep them whole, but how long can he withstand such an attack? "She's not here, I tell you! Anna's not here."

Liam reaches for Charlotte's legs to hold her in place, but she slides back and brings her fist down, making full contact with his temple. Liam slams into the sand, vision blurred, hearing shaken to the point that Charlotte doesn't even sound like herself but instead like a wicked hag: "I'll break every lying bone in your whole body!"

Oh, by all in Aether's Fire, I did not want this. "I swear to you, your sister is safe," Liam spits the words out with the sand from his mouth. "She is no longer in River Vine. And she has a mark that protects her from any velidevour hunting outside the Wall." He pleads on his knees, arms moving to keep pace with Charlotte's feet and fists flaying his head, his torso, his hips. All he can do is roll, and hope, and swear his darkest storms upon Orna. *Orna, you bitch, you've built the stage, opened the curtains, and set that damned marionette dancing through her mind, and you tied its strings to me, you damned bitch.*

"Always so jealous." Another swing, another shot of pain

through Liam's arms and into his heart. Liam's inner wings beat against his ribs as he crawls through the sand like a whipped dog. "I swear, I did not touch her." *No, my lady, no! I just—I just wanted her to not be so important to you—I just, I wanted to be the one more important in your heart.* "Please, Charlotte, please, stop!"

The Voice hurls itself up from Charlotte's heart, cuts through the darkness to a doorway lying deep inside her, the door that is always sealed tight.

It smashes the lock.

The door opens to a shadow. A shadow with a belt. The leather cracks like lightning, a perverse light against the worm's darkness. The worms don't know what to do.

"No one's ever gonna like a lying little mouth like yours, you pathetic," kick, "mangy," punch, "WHORE!" The word spews out of Charlotte's mouth as a hag's voice and a man's voice, superimposed and vying for attention, both churning in Charlotte's ears. The belt's lightning cracks inside Charlotte again.

Her vision plummets into the darkest of pasts: "*Uncle Mattie, please, stop!*" A cowering figure, arms hugging its head, back torn open, scraps of skin dangling from the belt's buckle.

The belt in Charlotte's hand: "*This buckle's gonna tear that lying whore mouth off your face!*"

Blood and flesh fly with the screams.

The Voice shoves the shadow back through the doorway and slams the door shut.

With a final crack of leather-lightning, Charlotte's eyes burn back into reality....

Liam, cowering, hugging his head, eyes fearfully peering between his blackened arms: "Please, stop, Charlotte!"

"The bird is grounded. Good. Take his blood dagger and strike him."

The dagger's hilt is within easy reach, perched in its sheath on Liam's back. Charlotte can see herself reaching, fingers closing around… her knuckles, every one of them, split and bleeding.

"Take his blood dagger now, while you have the upper hand. Take it NOW."

Oh god, what am I?

A chorus screams into her head. **"You are a righteous avenger and a protector of the weak! Take the dagger and strike him! Cut him down!"**

Charlotte gulps air soaked in violence and shame. The cool numbness along her forehead suddenly stings, pounds, beats. She claws at her hair, her temples, feels a slime—it will not come off. Hair and tears fall in a scattered circle about her as she spins, sobs, yanks to get *It* off and out.

Liam pulls himself up to his feet and holds out his hands. Several fingers are already swelling. A vine of purple roses blooms from wrist to temple on both arms, yet his voice bursts with relief. "Charlotte! To Arlen, and quickly."

Charlotte's eyes water as Liam swims into focus: "I did that to you, oh, god, Liam, no, I didn't…"

Words drown as Charlotte's body convulses with the worms' resumed shrieks in her mind: **"STRIKE, STRIKE, STRIKE!"**

"Charlotte—" Liam pleads.

"Get away from me!" Charlotte bolts off the beach and into the forest, Liam's voice still sending her name up time and again like the desperate warning flares of someone lost, marooned, and alone.

Charlotte tramples bluebells and violets as she runs, tears trailing in her wake.

The Voice grabs Charlotte's heart and blocks the worms' endless needles prodding Charlotte's mind. *This darkness can never take you, not completely.*

But I beat Liam, I did that—

Because you let fear silence your strength. You've lived under evil's belt for ten years, and not once in all that time did you strike your sister. Now, silence the fear!

Charlotte runs blindly, and faster. "Fuck off, get the fuck OFF!"

But the chorus only grows louder, the needles sharper. **"Go back and fight the liar! STRIKE HIM DOWN!"**

She stumbles on a withered tree root and falls to her knees. *Oh, Liam, I'm so, so sorry. I can't, breathe anymore. I can't, do this anymore. I don't, know how to fight anymore. Help, please.* "Help, please," her weak cry echoes through the green stillness.

The Voice gathers together all the love it can still find: the laughter and music, Christmas trees and skating on frozen lakes, climbing the heights, storied stained glass and skipped stones. The Voice knots them fast between itself and Charlotte, and counts down. *Three, we're doing this... two, together... one, NOW.*

Charlotte takes what she's sure is her last honest breath. "Shut UUUP!"

The bellows blow as hurricanes, swelling Charlotte's love into a white-green fire that surges in one monumental pulse through every extremity *and outward.* The worms transform into putrid ash. Charlotte's hands drop to her hips, free at last, and she falls on her side into a wilted clump of ferns. The pulse sprints across all of River Vine, its laughing light invisible to velidevour but not to the plants, nor to the Wall that absorbs its power.

"Charlie."

Charlotte blinks, sees green threads spread inside a yellow fern leaf. Her skin tingles all over, as if she'd rubbed her entire body on carpet and gotten the static shock of her life.

Charlotte breathes. Rot. Ash. Pain. Anger.

"Charlie, you're so close."

A name whispered, struggling to reach her.

Liam? Anna? She lifts her head just above the ferns.

There a couple dozen feet away: a few wisps of red hair.

Her mark begins to itch, then burn. By the time Charlotte comes to a small clearing, body and mind both reel from exhaustion.

It's a strange clearing she's come to. Even the black tree has a little growth around it, trampled though it might be. Here, however, life is petrified: every tree bordering this place is rock hard and barren. The dirt is more sand than soil, black sand like cold crushed lava. A single broken log splits the clearing in half. Draped across it is Anna, quiet and still.

"NO!" Charlotte scrambles forward and drops to her knees to feel Anna's neck—such a weak pulse, such cold skin. So frail and thin, as if she had been starving for days.

Someone calls Charlotte's name, but she doesn't answer. Yelling is… difficult, especially when thorns coil their way around her arm, inching up toward her shoulder and neck. In spite of the pain, she squares her shoulders: she will not let Anna go, never again. "Anna, it's Charlie, you're going to be okay. Please hold on," she pants, pulling her sister off the fallen trunk and into her arms.

Anna's eyelids flutter open. "Charlie?" she whispers hoarsely.

"Yes, Anna, it's me, Charlie. You're going to be all right," Charlotte cradles her close.

"I thought I'd never see you again." Anna limply raises her hand and takes hold of Charlotte's right arm.

"I thought I'd never see you again too."

Then Charlotte realizes: Anna didn't say that. Something else...

Anna's eyes finally open.

Black pits of stars.

Her hands grow clawlike. Her hair turns pale gold, her skin nearly white. And the Lady of the Pits, her face inches from Charlotte's, smiles. Fangs. And black painted teeth.

The Lady digs her claws in tightly around the thorns, driving fresh spikes of fire through Charlotte's right arm. Charlotte screams as the Lady rights herself and flips Charlotte onto the ground. "You dare come here and steal him from me?" she spits into Charlotte's ear, saliva burning like hot oil, dripping onto her neck. "You are nothing. Your kind is nothing. And when I am through with you, you will beg to be one with the dust beneath my feet."

Cackles and whooping calls: Incomplete velidevour surround them, veins pulsing through translucent flesh, animal jaws snapping, grinning.

Orna has Charlotte pinned to the ground: wrists pinned on either side of her head, both legs pinned by Orna's bony knees. "Lady, it ain't my fault you don't give as good as you get. Now: Where. Is. My sister?"

The Lady scoffs and rises to a standing position, dragging Charlotte up with her. Orna's black claws clutch the mark on her wrist, squeezing and causing the thorns to dig deep into her flesh. "You're in no position to issue demands, human," she taunts.

"Where do you think she is?" Orna asks. "Inside these

walls, beneath this ground?"

Charlotte winds up for a left hook, the mark burning worse than the granach's blood inside her: thorns puncture muscles, tendons, and veins, and blood seeps out between Orna's claws, dripping down Charlotte's right arm.

"That particular human is gone, too far from my reach. How fortunate that your lack of trust has allowed my dreams to blossom inside you so quickly, so easily." Thorns twist Charlotte's shoulder out of joint, pulsing at her neck, when—

"Come to me, Orna. And leave her be." Liam, alone, steadfast among the dust swirls and the death-shrieks cracking through the air.

The Lady laughs, wrenches Charlotte's wrist to the breaking point. "But how boringly predictable you are, darling."

Through fallen hair, Charlotte sees Liam: fireborn, battleborn, his right arm shaking. *His mark, oh FUCK, his mark. This was a setup. And I fell for it. I've already beaten him to shit. God, what have I done?* "Get out of here, Liam, save the others!"

But the trap springs shut: Incomplete surround them, their bodies filling the gaps between the trees.

Liam says nothing, eyes only for Orna and Charlotte. Even the panting breath of the velidevour behind him does not shake his resolve.

"Come to me, my beloved, and destroy this thing that divides us." The Lady's grip tightens, but this time, Charlotte does not scream.

Liam slowly steps over the dead log. "I was willing to let you oversee the Pits on the condition you never touch this human. You broke your promise. Now I shall have to break mine."

Orna yanks Charlotte up by the hair and opens her mouth wide, very wide, black pits for eyes and mouth, pointed teeth ready to pierce Charlotte's throat.

"No!" Liam lunges forward and almost falls face-first to the ground. Incomplete laugh around him as he staggers back into balance.

Charlotte struggles to scream "Fly outta here!" but the Lady has her neck, her breath.

Liam focuses on Orna, forces himself not to look, not to think, on the Lady Charlotte's pain. He levels his voice, cools it: "Surely, Orna, we can arrive at a mutually beneficial compromise."

"Compromise?" Cein, followed by Campion, breaks through the ring with a large bag slung over his shoulder. "This is our compromise."

The bag falls with a sickening thump.

"Choose which human joins your new tree and which one is set free."

Campion opens the bag.

Jenny.

Princeborns Unite

Jenny. Unconscious but alive. Her breathing is shallow and rapid. Her glasses are cracked, and the faint scratch on her right wrist is visibly spreading and darkening: the mark has claimed her.

Charlotte's heart beats fury. "What the FUCK did you do to her?" She struggles against Orna's grip on her neck with such ferocity, she bashes the Lady's face with the back of her head. Black oil trickles down the Lady's nose. "I'll... do... t-tree.... Just let her... g—agh!..." is all that Charlotte manages to choke out.

The Lady's tongue burns Charlotte's neck, accentuating her pulsing veins. Then she releases her grip and Charlotte collapses beside the dead log, coughing and wheezing for air.

Liam's eyes flash, the hurricanes growing strong, stronger. "You dare manipulate the Lady Charlotte into an assassination attempt on my life with my own dagger? And here I always thought you a more self-sufficient woman, Orna."

Orna leers. "On the contrary, beloved, I've merely given you but a taste of my abilities. Should you return to your place by my side, where you belong, we can at last realize our full potential. Yours, and mine."

Liam kicks at the dirt. Pulls some lint out of his pocket.

"And were I to refuse your, shall we say, odorous offer?" he asks with a slight grimace, since lint is apparently more offensive than cursed worms and acidic snake tongues. "Surely you cannot think yourself capable of destroying me. Tsk-tsk, Orna, your vanity will bring your downfall. The house of Artair will not stand for such defiance against the Borderland Covenants, let alone an attack on their son."

Cein's grin widens. "Oh, we don't have to destroy you, pretty boy. We just gotta hurt you. You learn the proper pecking order, son, and we'll get along juuuust fine, right boys?"

The Incomplete's ringing laughter sets Liam's eye twitching.

Campion kicks Charlotte out of the way, stepping over the log, and approaches Liam's side. He folds his arms and shakes his head in mock understanding. "You know, it's a hard thing, watching your power and all you care about taken away. Believe me," he rests a hand on Liam's shoulder, "I know how painful it is." He nods like a television therapist.

Someone please kill me or shut this bastard up.

You need not die today. The Voice in Charlotte's heart kicks the ice between her ribs.

Thank god, I thought you were gone. And now she doesn't mind as two of Orna's thugs take hold of her arms and pin them down on the ground. She's been in this position before, and against hard, gritty asphalt, not this soft forest floor. Why, she's practically reclining on a mattress.

"When the border man found my mate, found my children, he didn't just shoot them—he *burned* them like diseased rats." Laughter and tears flow too easily, too freely. "I thought my life was over. But dear, sweet Orna, our true leader, who has proved her regard for our welfare, showed me a new life. And I couldn't be happier."

Several Incomplete applaud.

Charlotte struggles with her arms, only her arms, because

she doesn't want them to know: they've left her legs free. "Let me go! I'll take the tree, Liam, don't listen to them!"

Cein chitters and keckers, then slowly slaps his badger-like hands together.

Campion bows, over and over, until he reaches Charlotte. "Well, howdy! Still up for a hot dog?"

Charlotte spits whatever phlegm she has in his face. "I hate you most of all, frickin' flea-bitten squirrel."

Campion gives a dapper smile. "Aw, you're sweet like that." Then grabs one of Charlotte's fingers and snaps it backward.

Charlotte screams.

Liam's inner wings will burst if he doesn't do something, but too many targets, too many weaknesses, too damn many—

"Now, don't interrupt me again." Campion elbows Orna's thugs aside and rams his knee into Charlotte's stomach.

Charlotte curls into a ball, screaming in pain. A ruse. *Idiots let me go. Ha!*

Campion nudges Jenny's unconscious body with one foot and laughs again. "Now that border man, now *he* knows my pain. I have taken his son and his daughter. The rest of the world, even his pathetic mate, has forgotten them, but not him. Never. All thanks to a special lady, the true master of River Vine."

And the cheers so fill the air that Liam realizes: *they don't see the shadow that circles high overhead.*

Orna's hands lift gracefully as she thanks them all. "But let us show we are merciful to those who deserve it, my people. Liam is velidevour, a powerful princeborn. He has a power that can see us past the Wall and to lands ripe for feasting, if," she saunters closer to Liam, "he but chooses to embrace his potential."

Liam's eye twitches. He dares, he must—he looks down on Charlotte, writhing in so much pain... and inching closer and closer to the unconscious border girl.

Campion has not noticed.

"Now, beloved…"

Focus on Orna, you idiot! Don't let her see what's in your head.

"It is time to choose. Which human will live, forever free of us? Choose!"

Screeches pierce the air: Devyn reveals himself in the treetops.

Cein looks up. Grins. "There you are, beaky. Campion, how 'bout you scurry up there and bring him down here, would ya?"

"Mmmm, happy to."

"Choose, Liam," Orna reiterates.

Liam must keep Orna focused on his mouth, teasing her with feigned indecision, barely moving for a second or two, just holding her attention as Campion transforms—and Charlotte hurls herself onto Campion's tiny squirrel body. With one quick fist, she flattens his rib cage and throws him before he can bite her. Dust explodes as Campion lands in human form against Cein and some Incomplete, cursing, screaming.

"Get her out of here, Devyn!" Charlotte tries to grab Jenny.

The Lady turns, holds up her ring hand—and remembers she has no ring. Panic. She looks at Liam. He strikes her face full force with the dagger's hilt and then leaps over her crumpled body, calling, "Charlotte, run!"

Cein leaps clear of the tangle of bodies and slams into Liam's side. "You disrespecting bastard, you're gonna *die* today. Commoners, to me!"

Incomplete hobble, run, jump into a dog-pile on Liam's back. He's quickly buried in half-human torsos, jaws, and flesh.

"NO!" Charlotte screams, gets up, can't leave Jenny, can't get them off, can't do—

Arms grip, teeth clamp on Charlotte's leg, toppling her: Campion, astride her chest, veli and blood dripping between broken teeth. He smiles. "No more pretty tricks for you, Sweet C." He punches her, dislocating her shoulder.

Charlotte screams but will not cry, she will not—

Orange light whizzes by. An Incomplete screams and cups its bloody eye. The orange blur zips again, another Incomplete screams and disengages, effectively disarmed.

"Get, that, bird, she's NOTHING!" Cein calls as he waves his badger paw around his head.

The shadow dives from on high and talons slash at an Incomplete's hand before it can pluck Ember from the air. Devyn transforms with a snarl.

The mound of Incomplete begins to shake.

Campion's knee presses on Charlotte's chest while he fights to bring her hand closer to his mouth. "Hope you don't mind, I'm still hungry." He breaks another of Charlotte's fingers, determined to pull it off completely, and is rewarded by another scream of pain.

Over Jenny leaps a mass of night, one blue eye hot as the heart of a flame and the other a stone-cold emerald. But this is not just D or Dorjan: this wolf lands with such force that the earth cracks beneath him. His fur is not fur at all, but black fire flickering around star-bright teeth. His tire-sized paw bats Campion clear over the Incomplete pile. His howl sets the Incomplete shivering, screaming.

"Get *back*!" The pile weakens just as human-Devyn strikes Cein's jaw.

A raptor shriek swells, swells, and a flare of sunlight erupts, throwing the pile of Incomplete across the clearing: Liam. Whose every vein pulses fire.

Dorjan sniffs Jenny, whimpers.

Charlotte hacks herself upright, sees the mark on Jenny's

wrist: "What do we do?"

Campion scream-laughs and pounces onto Dorjan's back. "That's *my* revenge, dog!"

Dorjan's howl echoes. His body of black fire flashes white hot. Campion's skin smokes and blisters.

A roar rumbles through the air, shaking the petrified trees.

Charlotte stands. She has to. Those Incomplete are getting up. Ember cannot keep pecking away at eyes. Devyn cannot block Cein forever. She needs... "Liam, help!"

Liam runs to reach them—and claws dig into his foot, tripping him.

"You *dare!*" Orna's tongue, long and forked, slides along his toes, burning skin, but he will not scream for her, never for her. "You, dare, defy, me?"

Liam sees a new shadow strike one Incomplete down. "Always."

An old leather boot kicks squarely against Orna's temple: Arlen, never so welcome a sight. "You must take the girl's mark, and quickly."

Another ROAR, closer.

Devyn screeches in pain when two Incomplete grab his arms and a third kicks his belly. Cein's claws and teeth are growing as he advances on Devyn.

"Dorjan, help Devyn!" Liam says as he runs by the fire-wolf.

Dorjan leaps over them, butts Cein in the back, and whips his massive tail around to knock the two Incomplete off Devyn's arms.

Liam slides to Charlotte's side. "Are you—"

"Get HER!" Charlotte puts Jenny's wrist, her growing mark, in Liam's hand. He presses the dagger's tip to her skin—

"NO!" Campion's shriek is high-pitch frenzied as he runs at them, leaping into the air—and wood strikes his throat hard.

Arlen. With his trusty spoon.

Campion staggers as he chokes, gasping for breath. Blood gives him a clown's face. He coughs, blood spraying out of his mouth as he rasps, "That's the last time you humiliate me, old man."

Arlen spins the Spoon of Might at his side. "Doubtful."

Campion lunges sloppily. Arlen dodges, slams the spoon's handle between Campion's shoulder blades.

Jenny's mark slips into the blood dagger, vanishing from her wrist. Charlotte gasps, barks a laugh, and kisses Liam's knuckles before he can think a moment on the softness of her lips. "Liam, you did it!"

"Not quite." Liam turns to see Orna's wrath transform her own white skin into a freakish blue. "Devyn, Ember! Get the border girl to safety!"

Ember pierces one last Incomplete eye, Dorjan's hurls one last Incomplete through the air, and Devyn runs, transforms before Cein can grab him. Cein roars and grows in size as he did in the Pits, mouth frothing. The remaining Incomplete band behind him, behind Orna, whose tongue slithers in, out, in, out.

Arlen kicks Campion in the chest, blocks a retaliatory strike, slaps him with the spoon and stabs his temple with the handle.

Liam holds Jenny's limp form in the air as Devyn's talons close in. But Cein barrels toward them—desperate to reclaim his prey.

Charlotte steps between Cein and Liam, the Voice in her heart so warm, alive: *Never again will this darkness take the light.*

Charlotte's got a fire in her like wings shaking themselves free. "You ain't catching shit, Burly Man."

And before Devyn can grab Jenny, before Liam can help, Charlotte launches herself at Cein's claws—

ROAR! Trees collapse in clouds of dust: The She-Bear

plows into Cein and slams him into a petrified tree.

"Take the girl, Devyn!" Arlen's voice breaks through the chaos. Devyn's talons find Jenny's shoulders, and with a final screech, he and Ember fly over the forest canopy with Jenny, southbound. To safety.

Dorjan shakes himself free of black fire and stands on two feet. When his eyes open, the blue shines with righteous fury, the green with giddy vengeance.

The She-Bear growls and licks its lips. Any Incomplete left standing stumble back and flee as it pounds after them.

Dorjan turns his eyes upon Campion.

Campion merely laughs, turns to run—only to be hauled up, over Arlen's head, and body-slammed. Again. A final whack of the trusty spoon on the temple, and he's out cold.

"A spoon, Uncle? Really?"

Arlen twirls it, western-pistol style. "I'll not have my pruning knife ruined, thank you very much."

Dorjan turns to Liam. "Do us all a favor and take care of your ex, will you?"

Liam smiles as Cein's eyes dart between him and his dogged ally. "And here I thought you hated *me*."

"Hate's not quite the word I would use to describe how I feel about you." Dorjan smirks at Liam with wolf teeth and he leaps high into the air, a mass of black fire.

Cein readies his claws but cannot block both of Dorjan's front paws—just one knocks him all the way across the clearing —again—cracking bone and teeth and god knows what else. Rivers of blood, oil, and veli trickle down Cein's body.

"*You*, however," Dorjan's wolf-fire extinguishes, but the predator's grin remains. "Hate only begins to describe how I feel about you."

The She-Bear's roars still rumble in the distance as Arlen holds out his hand to Charlotte.

Can't I stay for Liam? But no, she can't: out of the clearing into the green stillness, Charlotte's too damn close to the Wall. Her thorns quicken their march up her shoulder toward her neck.

Then a sudden strike. Beady, coal-black eyes, black painted teeth, black poison: it all rushes at Charlotte. The Lady holds her: by her dislocated shoulder she's caught, by a python's mouth, by dagger-length fangs, forked tongue slithering and burning her flesh.

Then a strangled gag as wood fills Orna's mouth: Arlen shoving his trusty spoon in as deep as he can. Fangs disengage and Charlotte is freed. "Come with me, and quickly!"

Charlotte commands her lungs to breathe, her legs to walk, while Arlen limps as badly as she. Both escape Orna's reach before her viselike jaws shatter the spoon to splinters.

Liam breathes deeply and flexes his thorned arm as though he bears no mark at all. He grasps the hilt of his blade with his hand. He pulls it out, out, out: a long sword, broad, double edged, longer than his arm and lined with blood-infused feathers—an extension of himself. Outstretched, the tip dances within inches of Orna's mouth.

The Lady's vicious teeth hide behind a delicate smile, her look almost playful. "Silly princeborn. You will not kill me. You could never kill a lover, darling."

Dorjan and Cein snarl, strike, and scream behind Arlen and Charlotte, Charlotte who burns with a light so bright that no poison can extinguish it.

Fire flashes like lightning through storm clouds. Liam's body grows feathers, yet doesn't. His arms become wings, yet don't. He is an eagle, but more. He is flying fire, shooting flames. He attacks.

The Lady bobs, weaves like a python, sinuous and mesmerizing, while Liam arches his arms—no, wings—no, arms—and screams an eagle's battle cry. She lunges forward, all claws and fangs, while he soars upward and then dives down, completing a dizzy vertical loop, then rips directly toward her, before disengaging and executing a barrel roll off to one side, and then re-engaging.

They connect: The Lady catches the sword with her mouth, her fangs crunching down upon it as though she would eat its power. She grabs Liam's right wrist with her right-clawed hand and digs her talons deep into his mark, driving the thorns into his flesh and turning them rich and wet with the oil that brought the granach to life. Her hold on the ground is too much for Liam—he screeches, pulls, but cannot escape.

Fly, Liam, God, please FLY. Get away!

Then Liam jerks his sword sharply downward, sliding it free from Orna's abomination of a mouth. And in a quick, fluid motion, he swipes his blade in an upward arc to slice off the Lady's face. Like an expert butcher filleting a fish.

Charlotte hides her face against Arlen's chest.

The Lady's body seizes and spasms, a faceless puppet dancing a herky-jerky jig before its strings are cut. She screams a wordless scream, grips the limp, flaccid mask that had made her so beautiful, now hanging by a thin patch of flesh at her hairline. Oil and lavender pulse and stream over her exposed facial muscles. Stars bleed out of her lidless eyes. Toxic black fumes curl out of her severed nose. Teeth overtake her entire face.

Liam, now in human form, stands over Orna, the veins of feathers in his sword dripping with his own blood. From his pocket, Liam pulls out the purple stone that once adorned Orna's finger. He palms it, and holds it over Orna. "How you came by this power I do not know. But you will never, *never*, poison this world or its inhabitants again." He pockets the stone, grips his sword with both hands, and pounds it full-force into the ground. Earth gives way like sand, swallowing and claiming both Campion and the Lady of the Pits: they sink with a sigh and a whimper.

Cein darts into the clearing, chittering, keckering, and wailing—such infantile sounds from such a big, bad badger. He jitters left, then right; up, then down—and comes to the sad realization: he is alone. His putrid eyes twitch inside his half-badger skull when they spot Charlotte. "I knew I should have killed you on the bus, right then. Your own sister would've forgotten you. Course"—chitter, nervous chatter—"she's forgotten you now. Like you never were."

Enough. Charlotte balls the fingers she can into a fist, but Arlen holds her back, the shadows clinging to his form, taking shape. "Your venomous rein over River Vine ends today, Cein."

"There you are!" Dorjan's humanlike self appears from behind Liam and grins, death wickedly happy in his blue eye. "Do you mind?" he asks Liam with all the politeness due a matron with a teapot, short and stout.

Liam bows his permission and limps toward Charlotte and Arlen, his own thorns receding.

Charlotte wants to reach for him, but not yet. Not when she must see the bastard Cein pay. For the bus. For her sister. For all the sisters, brothers, strangers. For everyone.

"You princeborns are all alike," Cein spits blood and bile and drool. "Think you're so much better than the rest of us. Orna deserves the title ten times more than you. She understands the meaning of power. The kingborns would have loved her in a heartbeat."

"What a pity they killed themselves off." The frame of Dorjan's body smolders.

393

"And you," Cein barks, "sympathizing with humans. They'd have ripped your heart out. Allow me the pleasure." He lunges, claws drawn.

But Dorjan dodges with ease, grabbing each wrist and bending Cein's arms upward. He's still a human, but a wolf howl swells within his throat as he kicks Cein with a resounding crack: Cein's spine snaps. "No. Allow me." And Dorjan plunges his hand clear through Cein's ribs.

The shriek ripped from Cein's lips turns Charlotte's insides to jelly, but she makes herself watch Cein grapple with Dorjan's arm. His teeth gnash air. Nothing stops Dorjan, his face cold and calculating as he wrenches Cein's heart out.

The heart beats once, then flutters and stills, and the creature once known to Charlotte as Smith the bus driver blows away in a foggy ash. His eyes collapse upon themselves like coal hollowed by fire. The heart beats one final time, and then it turns to stone.

With a flick of the wrist, Liam sheathes his blade as all the blood drops fly clear away and it becomes an innocuous, mundane dagger once again. Well, if such a dagger can ever be construed as mundane. "Are you all right?" he asks Charlotte and Arlen, but mostly Charlotte.

Charlotte shrugs with her good shoulder. "I feel nothing, no pain. Probably adrenaline, or delirium. One of the two." Her functional fingers touch Liam's mark: the oil is gone, the thorns already receding. But not the bruises of her creation. Her gut lurches as a sob climbs up her throat. "Liam, I—"

His thumb finds the center of her lips, gently presses her lips closed, and cups her jaw, her head in his hand. "How did you once put it: Can we just agree we were both asses and move on?"

A little laugh—and a lot of snot—burst from Charlotte's face. Liam wipes her clean with his own sleeve. "And now you owe me a bath."

Charlotte allows herself a smile. "Hush, you. Dorjan, are you okay?"

Dorjan drop-kicks the heart into a tree trunk. "Feeling pretty good, actually. At least better than you three look. Now, give me that rabid squirrel and let's call it a day."

"He's down below, giving succor to Orna. There's been enough bloodshed today, I think," Liam says. "Besides, the injuries you all inflicted will keep Campion from crawling out of the Pits for a long time. The border child's safe."

"He was mine," Dorjan growls.

"If we're lucky, Orna will save us the headache. She has little tolerance for failure."

Now it is Dorjan who studies Liam and says, "You have changed."

"Agreed." And for the first time in what feels like ages, Arlen's mischief is back. "You all fought with such bravery —I could not be more proud than I am in this moment. Liam, I mean this with deepest respect…" Arlen takes Liam by the shoulders and draws his face close: "You grow less and less like Bearnard every day."

Liam smiles, smiles wider. *He's proud of me. I've not seen that expression on his face in so many damn centuries.* And so Liam continues to smile, especially as Charlotte wraps her arms around him and rests her head upon his good shoulder. *Her lips touched me this day. Amid all the chaos, she still reached for me. Me.* His smile grows ever wider.

Arlen approaches Dorjan. "We have so much to be thankful for in you," he says, hugging his nephew tightly and beaming.

Dorjan's body relaxes as he returns Arlen's embrace. Eyes wet, he coughs and gruffly says, "Well, yes, I should think so, Uncle."

395

Then Arlen leans in to whisper to Dorjan so quietly that Liam does not hear, for he's too focused on Orna's stone ring to notice: "Do not run far. Blessed news to discuss."

"I was tempted to try its power against her," Liam says as he shows the stone to the others, "but thought it unwise, considering how long it has followed Orna's direction. How in Aether's Fire could she have possibly lain her hands upon it? I thought the creation of all stone rings was carefully recorded and protected."

Arlen's face falls at the sight of the stone. His hand drops from Dorjan to reach for it, but shrinks away at the last minute. "Yes... but come, this place is dead to everything but sadness," he says with a shudder. "Charlotte?"

Liam looks, expecting that burning pride she held for him during the battle—but it isn't there. Instead she gazes upon that log where an apparition called itself family. *Chide her? Coax her? Damn the wench—box her ears?*

A quick tug on a curl: Dorjan, who quietly says: "Let her mourn."

And words Charlotte said long ago whisper in Liam's mind: "*You didn't let me say goodbye.*"

Liam nods to Dorjan, and remains silent. At last, he understands: ghosts cannot depart without grief.

So he picks Charlotte up and carries her as though she is a child, the little warrior queen exhausted from protecting her land from monsters. And Charlotte, so relieved and tired and saddened that the Anna was a hoax, sinks her head into his chest and breathes in.

Safe with Fire

Charlotte wakes to the sound of fluttering pages. The smell of roses. Knitbone. A few other scents she does not know. It's the night of a new moon, and the world is dark.

Wilted flowers flutter on a bedside table as Charlotte, still prone in bed, stretches both arms above her head, flexing her fingers. She wriggles her legs. No pain. Her fingers fumble on the nightstand and find the lamp switch.

The whole room glows: something in the green, blue, and gray paint catches the light and reflects it as a warm, natural twilight. The ceiling depicts Cairine, garden and cottage, the shore just on the periphery, the sun rising. The wall behind the fireplace and desk depicts a mountain range blanketed by storm clouds and besieged by lightning. The remaining walls are covered with pictures and blueprints of planes, jets, helicopters—anything capable of flight. Charlotte squints at the hand-scrawled queries and question marks that litter the blueprints.

I'm in Liam's bed. Charlotte rolls out so fast that she takes the blankets with her.

She listens. He isn't here. A sigh of relief, and curiosity overtakes her. Layers of clothes and books litter the floor: bell-bottom pants, a red flag with golden hammer and sickle,

Fitzgerald, Hess, suede coat, a metal helmet, Dickens, Heaney, high-top sneakers, an old motherboard, Jones, and—was that Roger Ebert? The desk, a grand thing of rich finish, bends under the weight of books and scribble-filled notepads— Gaelic mostly, but also Latin, French, Greek, and English: "The earth revolves around the sun? Why do the Celestine allow mankind to uncover such secrets?..." And a slew of other unintelligible scribbles.

On top of one pile is her phone. On. Two bars. Anna, Aunt Gail—her contact list is untouched.

But... does she want them here? One call, that's all, and Aunt Gail would come flying to her rescue in her red Bell 429 helicopter, with Anna riding in the passenger seat— although Anna would probably care more about the gold and glass in the dining room downstairs than about Charlotte, but that's beside the point. They would be here, where they should not be, and Charlotte would want them to understand how some velidevour are nice and some aren't and to ignore the house's dream-draining soul-sucking-apparatus and don't go upstairs to the third floor and don't go downstairs to the basement and...

You know that cannot be, the Voice inside her heart reminds her gently.

The swarm around Jenny, their appetite for her death... no. Charlotte would rather remain less than a ghost than bring Aunt Gail and Anna within sight of this place. Besides, Aunt Gail would shoot Arlen just for being a better gardener.

Anna's safe with Aunt Gail, the only family left who cares. Anna's safe.

You now know who deserves your trust.

Where are they, anyway? Charlotte wraps a blanket tightly 'round herself and opens one of the doors bookending the room. She finds herself in her lucky bathroom. *If Liam took away my quarters, I am going to scream.... Nope.* Through the bathroom, she arrives at the foyer, her own room lying just down the hall.

She enters her quarters, proceeds through the partition, and then opens the door... to find herself in the ever-responsive bathroom again. *House, your customer service is amazing.*

Muffled voices float down the hall, and a door on the right is open just a sliver: the library. Light flashes like a lightning storm, only there is no thunder. Just lots and lots of clicks.

"And it never requires matches or oil?"

"For the dozenth time, Liam, no. But you *will* need a new lightbulb if you don't knock it off."

Crash. End of the flashes. And the room goes dim.

"Well done, Dorjan. Pray tell, how does this prevent the need for a new lightbulb?"

Dorjan's mutterings are indecipherable, but a few clinks, a clank, and *one* click later, the light returns. "Now just let it— NO! Don't touch it! You'll get electrocuted—I mean a nasty juddering. By the heart's fire, you're worse than a human toddling about in diapers."

Charlotte's mouth tightens to keep the snickers in. She really shouldn't eavesdrop, and don't they deserve some privacy? She's certainly not been quiet about her own need for space.

"Suit yourself. I wager Jenny never created the likes of this."

Shadows dance along the door's edges. Lights flicker, but not from clicking.

Oh, one last look, then I'll go. Charlotte crawls to the library's door and peers down.

Liam faces a great stained-glass window that spans nearly

half of the wall. Firelight flashes at his hips as his empty hands reach out, up. Glass and iron: they creak, moan, bend, break, shatter, again and again. Shards of colors move, slide, from inside vines of copper that twist, grow, branch out. Within Liam's vitreous canvas, colors shift and transmute at his bidding, and sunshine turns his dark world into day. And shapes: a sea of greens separating water and sky, a lake of a thousand blues, tiny white waning moons tilting and dancing on the water—skipping stones.

Outside, the sun fades, and night returns to the world, dimming and obscuring the vision in glass. Liam sits, studies his work in the darkening light.

"Nicely done," Dorjan says somewhere—under the stairwell perhaps. He's out of Charlotte's sight. "It's even better than the bit of Cairine you did in the herbarium."

"Thank you."

A weird silence settles in. Do they know Charlotte's listening? No: "You have to let her go." Pause. "Look, you've got enough on your hands. So does Arlen. River Vine wasn't safe for her before, and now it's a guaranteed death trap. You know I can get her to safety." Pause.

"You feel *something* for her." The words from Liam's mouth hit the floor, one at a time, like gloves thrown down for a duel.

"Not in the way you're thinking." Dorjan's boots clang upon the iron stair. "I just think this place has ruined enough families. Let the poor girl go home."

Liam can really send me home, even with River Vine's claim on me? I could really leave? I could go and hug Anna and Aunt Gail and tell them everything. And then what? I miss them, but do I really want to leave and never return? And I can't bring them here. I can't bring Liam to them either. Here and there are just too far apart. Gah, I hate this straddling.

"Uncle, a blessed sight and even more blessed smell.

400

Please tell me that pie's not for the patient upstairs."

Arlen walks into view and sets a steaming blackberry pie on the table near Liam's window. "Do try to be clean about it, both of you."

The boys sit at either end of the table, but only Liam picks up a fork. Dorjan's hand makes a deep scoop through crust and filling and empties the lot into his mouth in a surprisingly impressive manner. Crude perhaps, but impressive.

"What in heart's fire happened to your manners?" Liam asks before shrugging and tossing his fork aside and going wrist-deep himself.

Dorjan snickers a light spray of crumble crumbs at Liam. "Oo cahnt haf manerz ihn da wihld."

"*Mac an donais*, but you make this look so easy. Am I allowed to eat what I've dribbled off my shirt?"

Charlotte has to bite her cheek to keep from laughing.

Arlen apparently doesn't mind the two stuffing their faces, as he sets tea cups near their purple-spotted table places and hangs a kettle in the fireplace. "Devyn and I have been to the Pits."

Dorjan sucks a finger clean. "And what a happy visit that must have been."

Arlen ignores him. "We healed everyone we could, but they're of one mind. You will not receive forgiveness, Liam, not from a single Pit dweller."

"They broke my law."

"*She* was their law for a century," Arlen speaks with deep urgency in his voice. "You cannot expect them to be taken with you so quickly."

"Especially when you have Ember limping about," adds Dorjan as he wipes his hands on the nearby curtain. "A perfect reminder of your pretty Master Bloody Prince self."

"I'm not proud of that."

But Liam's cold gaze does not keep Dorjan from asking, "Does Charlotte know what you were like? *Really* like?"

Liam leaps from the table, growls and Gaelic curses on his lips, but Arlen catches Liam and knocks him into a chair instead, and scolds the both of them. (*Damn, sir, that was fast. Even the pie plate stays put.*) "You will not lay a hand on each other in this place, do you hear me?"

But Liam's not listening, his eyes alive with lightning. "You say one word to her and—"

Dorjan picks up a plate of yarrow and yellow marigolds and tips them into the boiling kettle. "No, I won't. But *you* should."

"I've already told her about Antonia." He slams the name down like it's the only one that matters.

"Pfft. So all the escapades you carried on with your brother, those are, what, just the stuff of bloody and depraved exaggeration?"

Even from her hiding place, Charlotte sees Liam's hands twitch into fists, his lips into a snarl. "Don't, you—"

"Then if you really don't want her to know, you know what I think you should do," Dorjan snaps back.

"I think," Arlen forces himself into their locked stares to break the silence, "Charlotte's fate is not only Liam's decision, but hers as well. As she isn't here to speak her mind, let us return to the danger brewing underground."

Charlotte risks a quick sigh. *Not a question I want to answer now, anyway.*

Liam nods absently and kicks up his feet to rest on the table. "If Dorjan remains on the grounds, we have two princeborns that can battle the mob beneath."

"*Three* princeborns," Dorjan says.

"You cannot include me." Arlen shakes his head. "I no longer have such strength."

Arlen? Arlen! Of course he's a princeborn! He lives on veli like all the velidevour but doesn't have the crazy-glowin' eyes like the commoners. Why doesn't he ever change like Dorjan and Liam? Is he supposed to be that old? Gah, too many questions!

A darkness settles on Dorjan's face and he looks ready to transform and bite Liam. But he continues to sit, eyeing Liam like prey.

"It's not my fault he lost his spoon," Liam says.

Dorjan sneers. "This isn't about bloody kitchenware."

Slam! Arlen smacks the table with such force it cracks in two. (*What is it with you and tables, sir?*) Teacups and saucers roll off scot-free. "Leave it be, Dorjan, for Charlotte's sake." Arlen turns to Liam. "The Incomplete and other Pit dwellers no longer trust you, for they no longer *know* you. They *knew* Orna, and now they know you humiliated her for the sake of a human."

Liam exhales slowly. "You think they will demand reparation despite the example I gave them with Orna's face."

"We did not see Orna, but we could hear something of her crying through the tunnels. Campion is her voice now. And that, I think, is answer enough."

They sit in silence, oblivious to the smashed table and pie leftovers littering the space between them. Then Arlen walks to the sideboard table to pour tea from a copper kettle, adding velifol to each earthenware mug, which he quietly serves to Dorjan and Liam.

Dorjan's eyes speak, the green of envy, the blue of anger, but his lips remain silent.

Liam stares back defiantly at both and, setting his mug down on the floor, offers a solution. "What about this?" He digs into his pocket and retrieves the purple stone, cradling it in the palm of his hand. "No spoon, I know, but if you had this, could you help us fight?"

Dorjan looks at it and bites his lip.

Arlen stops breathing, moves forward. He reaches for the stone and closes his fist over it, eyes lost to millennia past. ... Then he slowly returns it to Liam, shaking his head. "My bloody days were few and terrible. No. I won't have a stone ring in order to drown this place in pain once again."

"And what of the scouts above?" asks Liam.

"They're working desperately to utilize the prey as much as possible, and more determined than ever to protect the velifol garden. Even Devyn has fully accepted your idea. But they are extremely worried about a coup." Arlen looks from Liam to Dorjan and back to Liam. "I don't think the young ones like Poppy can handle the trauma."

"Is the velifol old enough to be harvested?" Dorjan asks.

"You're drinking the second crop." Arlen replies.

"Then my congratulations to *Master* Liam and his plan," Dorjan toasts Liam and swallows the dregs. "Looks like you're finally doing something right. Just in time for it to be ripped to shreds."

Liam laughs sadly. "Perhaps my mercy was unwise. We'll have to harvest what velifol remains and hide it. Move the tree, even, if needed. If there's time."

"And Charlotte?" Dorjan's green eye sparks with the name.

"Hide her too, of course."

"Sure. And if you're lucky, you'll find her again."

Liam's shoulders tense, but he does not pounce. "What is that supposed to mean?"

"Am I the only one who's noticed she has no scent?"

Arlen stands to the side, drinking thoughtfully, as Liam pulls back, saying, "What are you talking about? I can smell her sometimes."

"Sometimes is not all the time," Dorjan says to Liam before turning to Arlen, forcing their eyes to meet. "I tell you,

Uncle, Charlotte's different. The mark not taking at the Wall, Cein's inability to control her, her handling—even fighting with—the blood dagger, her lack of scent. *All* humans have a permanent scent, not some sort of come'n'go nonsense." He looks to Liam. "So what's Charlotte's scent, by the way, in case I am ever blessed to catch it?"

Liam will not answer.

Dorjan looks to his uncle for support, but Arlen only shakes his head: the matter is closed.

Dorjan moves out of Charlotte's sight, but his voice is so cold she can picture the ice in his blue eye: "I could call for aid, Liam. It'd solve a lot of problems."

But Liam only turns to the fire, leaving his tea untouched, fingertips just barely holding the stone. "We're handling this ourselves," is all he says.

Dorjan grumbles, but Arlen moves out of sight to whisper a cryptic command: "To the lakeshore, for but a moment, and return." Dorjan's footfalls are staggered at first, then quicken, quicken to race out of Rose House.

Arlen moves his chair next to Liam's, and they sit, these two men, facing the flames for some moments in silence.

Then: "I feel so strange sometimes, Arlen. Like I'm two people. I can see myself doing… things… like before Dorjan was born, when I lived with my family in France. I burned a village's entire fleet of boats because a girl I sought favored a sailor over me. An entire society's way of life, all turned to ash, because I was denied a whim."

Arlen refuses to speak until Liam finishes his tea in one hard swallow. "You took after your father for a long time."

"I didn't have much choice, did I?" Storms fill his eyes. Even from her hiding place, Charlotte braces against the tension that builds, builds—

"Not much, no. And neither did I. Someday I can—"

"It's always 'someday' with you." Liam throws the mug into the fire, and its shrapnel erupts from the flames, careening all around them. "I should have killed my enemy today, as I did in the Pits when I took Orna's ring. But today..." He leans with both hands on the mantle, staring deep into the hearth. "I had no thirst for blood today. I let an enemy who deserved death, live, today. And still, today is not the time for you to explain your disappearance from my life?"

Yet Arlen's body remains quiet, arms folded. "Until I can believe one thing beyond all doubt."

"What is that?"

"That you are capable of far better, greater things than your father ever was." Arlen stands, admires the window's silver stones reflecting in the fire light. "And today, you have begun to prove just that."

The hope in Arlen's face appears to strike Liam to the marrow. The word comes before his heart can question its revelation. "Cairine."

Arlen's mouth moves open, shut, voice momentarily lost. "What?"

"When I smell her: she smells like the garden and the sea, like Cairine."

Charlotte hears Arlen's footsteps echo, following Dorjan's trail outside.

Liam returns to his chair, holding his head, watching the fire alone, after all that, still alone.

Charlotte stands up, heart too damn loud for its own good. Her toes tingle with more life than she had felt with death at her throat. How is it that she can stare down a gigantic

406

poisonous snapping turtle, a snake-woman with huge teeth, but can't step downstairs to comfort the man who's saved her life more than she'd care to count? She'd love to tell people: *Aunt Gail, you wouldn't beLIEVE what this guy can do when he's not an imp.*

The iron is hard and coarse under her big toe. There. First step always the hardest. She grips the blanket like a life vest as she floats down the spiral stairs.

Liam does not move.

The carpet is worn and soft to the touch. Silent steps, hand at her chest to quiet that drum, loud enough to annoy the stars.

He's asleep. Of course, he's asleep.

She carefully moves a soft curl from tickling his nose (interesting, his hair always looks so wiry) and drapes her blanket over his sleeping form. Which is probably silly, with a fire blazing and summer still in its prime outside. But Charlotte wants him to feel safe. He deserves that much, after all the events of the past few days.

The fire's light soothes, hypnotizes. Charlotte sits on the floor next to Liam's legs, eyelids heavy. She wonders if the scent, metallic with a touch of autumn leaves, is the scent of art's magic not quite dissipated.

Her head nestles against Liam's knee. The Voice in her heart sighs, too exhausted to notice a pounding, a drumming rising from deep, deep in the Pits.

END OF BOOK 1

Fallen Princeborn

CHOSEN
(AN EXCERPT OF BOOK 2)

Chosen

"*LIAM!*" Charlotte screams over the side. The wave churns back on itself and leaves the canoe untouched.

Campion laughs on the shore. The Lady's hissing like someone cut her tail off. The green net glows in the water like jellyfish tentacles, and it's shrinking. Surrounding Liam, trapping him, and—

Liam's going down.

Liam's going to drown.

A speck of orange shoots from the treetops over the Incomplete and high above the water toward Charlotte. Ember? But there's no time, and what can she do?

Charlotte clutches her chest, counts her breaths, *one, two, three*, takes a final gulp of air—dives.

Lake Aranina doesn't feel like lake water, doesn't look like lake water. Charlotte knows lakes are full of sand and fish, little bugs, turtles, ducks, plants, the lot.

But this lake is stark blue, bugless and fishless. A prairie of seaweed waves at her from the distant lake floor, like she's swimming through a North Dakota sky—

Two tailfins fly alongside the net. Two hands hold the net. Two heads of kelp-like hair bob steadily on the journey downward, blurring and merging with the darkening lake water. So Charlotte trains her eyes on one carrying a spear white as bone, her beacon in her descent through the deep dark blue.

Liam squirms, fights to free his arms from his sides, but the net sparks like static lightning, sending Liam's screams bubbling into the water.

Charlotte feels his pain in the bubbles as they run along her chest, strike her in the face. She wrenches her arms to swim deeper, faster.

The Voice in her heart sets the bellows to the forge inside and she is white-hot, surging, closing the distance. *We will know sky and grass again, we will not die helpless in the water—*

She kicks harder. Paddles faster. She nears the net, she's close, spitting close—

Liam's eyes flash open after another scream. The storms swirl, break—his mouth cries, "Go!"

Charlotte shakes her head and mouths back, "Like hell!" She will not listen to her lungs, she will not let some stupid thing like their need for air keep her from the net and Liam, now only a foot from grabbing distance.

Liam bends his head, struggles to lift his shoulder blades up. To bring the sheath within reach. The blood dagger's hilt peeks through the net.

Clicking, like a dolphin: a mermaid turns its head. Ovular eyes blink double eyelids: the outer set moves up and down, the inner side to side. Nose slits twitch as kelp hair hovers. Neck gills breathe. A mouth... thing... shaped like a six-pointed star...

Don't make her open that, The Voice warns.

But Charlotte's not thinking about some stupid mouth

thing. She sees the bone spear across the mermaid's chain-mailed chest and knows the blood dagger could destroy it, destroy them—

—them—

Dammit where's the other one?

Too late.

The second creature, a merman if his bare chest is any indication, swims in front of the spear-bearer and the net. His eyes go from ovals to slits as his inner eyelids close and gills flutter, sparkle. The star-lipped mouth opens—

Screams.

The force rockets Charlotte downward, spiraling, starry-eyed and lost in a water tornado of painful sound. *Jeez, to get this far only to become fish food—*

CRACK.

Charlotte sprawls on a rock surrounded by quiet, lifeless sand. There's no way in hell she has enough air to get to the surface. She blinks at the sapphire world, at the two swimmers circling above them like sharks, closing in.

Liam lands next to her. Too few bubbles leave his nose and mouth. No wow eyes evident as he still struggles in that net, too weak to scream as the sparks fly from foot to head, everywhere the net touches him.

No. Charlotte shoves her hand through a gap in the net. Sparks shower her arm, flood her vision. The Voice screams inside her chest, but she shoves her other hand in, lighting up the very veins inside her, pressing her soul into her feet. But she will stay with Liam, she will give him her final breath—

Water pulls back from their bodies, lifting above them like a tent's canvas. Air, dry and sweet and pure. They can breathe.

The net slithers away, taking all the sparks with it. Charlotte collapses on Liam's chest and he, too, is coughing up water and gulping air. The water hovers maybe a dozen feet above their heads, and just outside the perimeter of the rock they're lying on.

Charlotte lifts her head, leaving her hand on his chest. Liam's heartbeat is erratic, but not weak. His eyes still roll about as his body shudders with the aftershock of the net. "Hey hey, ease up, we're not dead yet. Here." She brings his hand to her own chest. "Stick with me. Calm it down, I need you." She uncurls his fingers so that his hand spreads out across her heart. "Stay with me, Liam."

His fingertips press through the soaked linen of her pajama shirt. His eyes stop rolling and find her face. *There they are, sweet with summer rain. Might be the last skies I see.*

His gasps, swallows air to speak, "Ch-Charlotte..."

Her whole body warms. "I'm not going anywhere."

And Liam's mouth slightly, ever so slightly, smiles. "Neither am I."

The merpeople circle down to the rock floor, and begin to click, back and forth, talking. Choosing? Planning?

The clicking slows.

The spear-wielding mermaid stops swimming just outside their air bubble's surface. Her scales begin to swirl in small, translucent whirlpools until the tailfin itself splits in half. The split runs through the scales, and the whirlpools cascade upward, leaving human-like legs behind. The torso and arms glow bright and fade into a scaled torso luminescent as a bubble in sunshine, the chainmail now hanging about her hips and thighs. Long, silvery-thin fins replace her arms. One wraps tightly round its spear.

She steps through the water-air interface and onto their rock. The fin arms turn all but invisible without water. The green kelp hair clings to her head, neck and chest. Her eyes double-blink, and Charlotte can't help but think of skipping

414

stones: there is a heavy strength polished smooth by time and water. The star-shaped mouth swims into a long, thin line that opens for a voice light and musical, like a breeze passing through a wind chime: "At last, the mighty velidevour come to us." Ting! goes the bone spear on the stone near Liam's head—and Charlotte's hand sneaking toward the blood dagger. "Don't bother with your weapon. Magic's not keen on the elements crossing."

Charlotte's hand wavers. The spearhead's as long and thin as her forearm, but her forearm isn't serrated on both sides like a giant shark's tooth. *Damn, that would have been handy.* "Look, Blinkey, we're not out to hurt any of... you..." Charlotte's ready to sweep her arms dramatically at all the merpeople, but no one is there but Blinkey and her comrade. The place looks too derelict, too deserted for life: a small collection of ramshackle huts with gutted windows and doors all overgrown with black-green weeds. "You're it? Damn, the velidevour sent, like, a giant monster and an angry mob after me. I feel I should be insulted."

A tired hand slaps her leg. "Manners, please." Liam's voice has enough strength to register his annoyance.

"I don't care. We just want to cross the damn lake and be gone. C'mon, Blinkey, cut us a break?"

Blinkey's nose slits twitch. She turns to click and buzz at the merman. He breaks off a length of the green net-rope to give Blinkey before he wraps the rest around his torso and swims back in the direction they came from. Her fin hitches the new coil to her chainmail. "I think not. The Queen shall have her answers."

"Answers to what?"

The eyes narrow again, but the mouth remains the same, "To kidnapping." She runs a fin along her spearhead's side. "To mutilation."

Liam manages to stand despite the yellow welts on his feet, hands, neck—everywhere. Something sways behind the mermaid that sets his inner talons scratching against his bones. "Kidnapping?"

Not that Charlotte notices. "Mutilation? You're the banshees who scream stuff to pieces. Who mmmf."

Liam's hand clamps tightly against Charlotte's mouth and he nudges her to look beyond the mermaid's shoulder.

A wall.

It towers above them, surely taller than Rose House. Yet it stands incomplete: the wall runs about the width of Rose House, but the lake waters continue on either side. And directly in front of them there's a large hole in the wall, as if it was built that way. Unlike the Wall above, this one allows life to grow upon it: seaweed, old and frayed as an ancient mariner's hair, yes, but still, it is something growing upon the rock around that hole. The hole has a pull to it, a current that barely touches them with soft fingertips, but it is there, palpable, and Liam's wings feel its pull. He has not known such a pull since traveling the Water Road so very long ago.... "Where does that go?"

Blinkey sneers, steps backward. "Nowhere. Everywhere."

"On pain of death, we're bound by magic to remain within the Wall surrounding River Vine—"

"Is that what you are afraid of?" Blinkey grins, displaying two solid rows of teeth shaped like little white Ws.

Charlotte feels the muscles in Liam's arm tighten as he replies, "I am not afraid."

"Think, Blinkey: your queeny can't talk to us if these cursed tattoos kill us first." Charlotte holds her wrist up actually hoping the thorns would start moving. But they don't, of course.

Blinkey lazily twirls her spear as she steps out of the air

bubble back into the water. The smile has not yet left her face.

Charlotte wishes it would.

Liam can't take his eyes off the hole in the wall, or the seaweed that fails to sway with the current flowing through the wall. The seaweed is still. Resistant. It keeps all its fronds away from the hole. The water beyond the hole, it looks... dark, unfathomable.

Blinkey uncoils her rope, and the green luminescence unfolds once more, only now it forms not a net but a bubble around Charlotte and Liam. *So this is what it looks like inside the balloons of all those dumb school projects with the glue and string*, Charlotte thinks, and eyes Liam's dagger. *Figures we've got a big pointy thing inside, of all places.*

Blinkey squeaks, clicks, tugs. The bubble lifts from the stone. Charlotte and Liam hold each other closely—they have to, what with being groundless and having only the bubble's fragile membrane stand between them and a spark-filled drowning.

Blinkey's mouth splits into its magic star, and her scream drives small and fast at the hole, like a snowball that poofs into a million scraps of light swirling through—a liquid comet tail.

Blinkey turns to them. Sneers.

A sudden lurching, and all the humors in Charlotte fill her throat, but the Voice pulls them back down: *Show no emotion. Hold tight.*

"Where are you taking us?"

Liam clenches his jaw. He's statue-still, but Charlotte smells his fear as he eyes the approaching hole filled with what... *aquatic fireflies?*... and surrounded by old, frayed seaweed. Her hand slides down Liam's wrist and into his palm. They're poised silent and motionless in their bubble of air.

Blinkey holds her bone spear outward until its tip touches the swirling fireflies.

Everything surges: A million bright threads unspool and crash together into one focal point before them, pulling eyes and bone and heart and voice and—

Their bubble-net floats, peacefully, steadily, cradled by a semicircle of small glowing lights and guided through the hole. *So we went through that shit topside to be fed to a mob of sparkly angler fish. You know, Day, I'd like to just call a do-over, please.*

But her wish isn't granted. As the lights come closer, Charlotte sees the sparkly angler fish for what they really are: bright orbs that dangle like lanterns from the bone spears of more mermaid-type people. Lots of unfriendly, blinkey, mermaid-type people.

Liam studies first his mark, then the hole behind them. Light recoils into its center. The seaweed waves around it, motile once more, like hair over a hag's cloudy eye. "We're beyond Lake Aranina. The ocean?"

A slow, double-lidded blink, then: "Lake. Ocean. Fresh. Salt. Always, you gill-less are keen to split and divide the land. No better than ruby sharks, the lot of you."

The merpeople float back with their lantern-spears, widening their circle, distancing themselves from the air bubble. An armed guard comes into view, sitting upon a floating giant shell with little tentacles sticking out the back. Blinkey tosses him the bubble-net's rope. To Liam, she says, "Here we have no tribes, no houses. We are stellaqui, and we are one people, of one water, the Undersky."

Another armed guard pulls the bubble close to the floating tentacle-shell thing, where a creepy little black eye just, stares. And stares.

Charlotte debates piercing their air-bubble with Liam's dagger just to make that thing stop staring. "Do ya mind?"

Liam's eyes dart among the net's spaces. "I've never seen a nautilus this size."

"You know what that thing is?"

"My lack of swimming skills doesn't render me completely ignorant of all matters water-folk. Nautili are to them what horses are to you."

"*The More You Know*," Charlotte mumble-sings to herself as she kneels to look through the net's biggest opening.

Blinkey dolphin-clicks orders to depart.

The lantern-bearing merfolk escort them, three on each side, each with an orb to light the way, as they maneuver through hulks of pointed metal poking up from the earth like lopsided gravestones. Charlotte counts the seconds to traverse a stretch of sandy rust. "We're in some sort of ship-wreck graveyard."

"The ocean, I knew it!" A smile grows on Liam's lips, one corner at a time.

Charlotte sniffs skeptically. "I don't think so. Shouldn't we smell at least a little salt?"

"All their cities are said to be in the oceans," Liam says, brow furrowed, "with the lakes reserved.... Damnation, what did the Kingborn histories say... something about study..."

"Well duh, studying's kinda required with history." Charlotte makes a face, but not so much over Liam's memory as over the lack of activity from her mark. No prickling, no choking or killing or whatever. This thing has always been eager to kill her before. Its apathy now makes this trip really surreal... compared to psycho heart-eating half-dead half-people.

She should probably stop thinking about that. "Why would merpeople want to hang out in a human boat graveyard?"

The storms in Liam's eyes grow blue-white: a reflection. "For study... they... study..." he breaks off, voice small, mouth unable to close.

Charlotte turns to see what's stoppered his mouth.

A dome hides among the broken hulls. Thin swirls of bioluminescence coast along its surface as though flowing in their own current. The bioluminescent dome is framed by six bone-white, curved, ridged beams that radiate outward from the center at the top of the dome and arc downward, anchored to the sandy floor.

"No. No, no no no, those can't be... spines. Whales don't get coliseum-big," mutters Charlotte, her eyes now coliseum-big.

"The ancient leviathan," Liam whispers.

Everyone halts before one of the spines. Blinkey slides the end of her bone spear between two vertebrae on the spine and turns her spear like a key.

A crack opens: a horizontal fissure between two vertebrae on two adjacent spines forms, widens, and that part of the dome slides upward, opening a square-ish window just large enough for Blinkey, the nautilus rider, and the bubble to move through. Liam catches Blinkey's smirk as their netted bubble floats by her and says to Charlotte. "The Kingborn Claudius once said, 'No bone is wasted among the stellaqui.'"

Blinkey nods with approval. "An apt truth as we arrive here, in the Library."

The spine seals behind them.

Some library. Where are the bookshelves? Charlotte cranes and swivels her neck, jerky-bird fashion, this way and that.

Angler lights hang from every other vertebra along the spines of the dome. The coliseum feel carries on inside the dome, with its wide, central atrium encircled by four open-floored levels. Each floor is securely anchored to the six leviathan spines, like inward facing ribs. Not a stairwell in sight—*sink or swim, apparently*, and they do: the nautilus, the guard, and Blinkey guide the bubble along the lowest level surrounding the atrium. Charlotte sees stones grouped together just like the wall outside the leviathan dome, but this "wall" must have fallen over, since it lies flat on its side in the center of the Library's atrium floor. The hole within it is much larger than the other, and dark. Very dark.

The bubble passes some barred enclosures or rooms shaped by bone and—*aw, jeez, that's gotta be skin.*

The levels above them are crowded with display cases, with various mermaids and mermen huddled around, observing, debating. "What, you got an art show going on?"

One stellaqui swims down from one of the upper levels with a small display case cradled in her arms. A translucent coat covers her torso, pink and wavy like a jellyfish. She dolphin-calls to Blinkey as she approaches. Their bubble slows.

"*Mac an Donias.*" Liam's face is ashen. "I thought the Kingborn's tale a dream, not truth."

Charlotte follows Liam's gaze to the case in the mermaid's arms. It's not flat at all, but like a shadow box, with something spread out and pinned open. At first glance it's no different than one of those pictures she'd paint as a little kid on one side of the paper, then folding the paper over to double the image. Or like a Rorschach test.

Then she sees the amber eyes. Together. Squashed. Bulging. At her. Diamond black pupils swollen. Muzzle and jaw outlining the split head, stretched and broken in a scream preserved. Tongue pulled out and split along one side of the muzzle. Red fur cut and peeled back like a banana to reveal muscle, and that's peeled back to show blood vessels and nerves and some whitish tissue, and *that's* peeled back to show organs, all opened, all open and stretched and open and dead and open—

421

Charlotte gasps, searches the upper levels to see some-thing, anything, that isn't a halved fox staring at her. There, a giant moth, fuzzy at the edges with long, warped wings. But it has fur. Mane. Tail. A stomach peeled back to show half-eaten meat, undigested feathers.

There's a mountain lion, split open.

A bear, split open.

A wolf, split open.

One case holds something too long for a wolf. Hairless, but with limbs. A small mouth. Fingers, winged by skin.

Ho-lee SHIT.

Charlotte rolls back against Liam's side and holds his arm before she can blink again. Her mouth hangs open, she's not sure she's breathing, but she's hearing Liam whisper so very clearly, "We will leave this place whole, or join the graves of your boats."

Not the most encouraging thing Liam's ever said, but anything sounds better than a display box.

A stellaqui mermaid person swims up to the top of the dome. Blinkey clicks to the other guard, who takes off in the opposite direction, down and out through the dark central hole. Light bursts and crashes in upon the bubble trail behind them both, and then thin green tendrils unspool from the dome's top all the way down to the hole in the atrium floor. The mermaid at the top of the dome calls down to Blinkey, and the tendrils begin to curl up, pulling the water up with it like shades on a window, providing an air pocket large enough to fill the entire atrium.

The bubble clings to the floor—coarse, a stone of sorts mottled by sand. The net twitches beneath Charlotte's calves as does Liam's biceps across her chest. He's whispering numbers, counting the merfolk on the still water-filled upper levels—"twelve, fourteen, eighteen…"

Only Blinkey remains on the air-filled ground floor. "Well, trespassers," she says as her tail splits into legs, "it is time I leave you to the librarians. Trust me when I say they are thrilled to have you here." She tugs at the net's rope, and the net splits apart and shrinks to a small coil at her hip. She pops the bubble with her spear. "You are welcome to one last meal before interrogation, if you wish. We are curious to study the stages of digestion in both human and velidevour." She smiles. Double-blinks, and bows them toward an enclosure with a wave of her fin. The walls, bench, table—all are carved from bone.

Charlotte narrows her eyes. "What do you guys make toilets out of? Turtle shell?"

Blinkey spins her spear's staff to thwack Charlotte's cheek before Liam can stop her. "*We* do not kill for single parts, unlike *your* kind."

"Do that again." Liam unsheathes his blood dagger. Sparks pulse weakly beneath his welts from the merfolk net, oozing a yellow pus Charlotte can only describe as smelling fishy. His curls limply frame his face, but his shoulders and feet are steady in defiance of all poison and pain. He wraps his fingers around the base of the blade. "Just try."

"Hey, it's *my* mouth she hit, jeez." Charlotte's still rubbing it as she slides off to the side, farther from Liam, out of reach lest Blinkey jabs at him, freeing her for a flank attack. If Blinkey goes for her, then Liam's free to strike. *Thank you, late night westerns.*

Blinkey's fins slide the spear lazily between them, but her curled mouth says she's none too pleased. "I said, inside. Now."

"Y-yeah, no." Charlotte nods to the dark hole, their one sure exit. "*That* looks good, though."

"And see your way to the Queen's seat?" Blinkey thrusts her spear at Charlotte, its serrated edges piercing right through the pathetic linen of Charlotte's shirt and grazing her skin. "I think not."

Liam's leap is perfect: he hunches back on the balls of his feet and soars several feet into the air. He is poised to summon the blood-sword out of his dagger, drive the blade through this stellaqui and the very rock beneath her feet, and send all to ash and ruin. He grips the blade, ready for the prick he must always pay to call the magic forth, he is a moment from the creature's head—

But the sword does not come.

And Liam's body crashes in a spray of his own blood, chest slamming against the kelp-head, taking Blinkey down, sliding into Charlotte, and turning the three of them into a muddled heap. Charlotte rolls off first before Blinkey's star-mouth-scream can find her. Air shivers with its power in a ball form, blowing past Charlotte and cracking the rib-bars of an enclosure.

"No screaming in libraries!" Charlotte spits the words from a smirking mouth and grabs a rib, wielding it like a weapon. Something's swimming in the corner of her vision on a floor above them, and she wishes she had paid more attention to that one scene of *Robin Hood* with the staves.

Liam rolls and swings the dagger round to find Blinkey's fin—

—blocked by the mermaid. Her spear's shaft meets the blade with a cold ting! and she thrusts it forward to meet his face—

But he is up, dagger on the defense, uncertain whether to use his free hand as a fist or as a hook on that spear, the fins too difficult to see, but his eagle-eyes follow the spear and block every thrust —the droplets of his own blood are freckles on the white shaft and blade. Blinkey's star-mouth peels back for another scream, but Liam dodges well enough so that the scream merely brushes his arm. He can't hide a wince: it feels like his arm was dragged along broken glass. He senses something above him, leaps and rolls towards Charlotte—

Green luminescence spirals out and strikes the floor.

Charlotte looks up.

Three water-folk circle above them like sharks, each with their own net-ropes.

"Could really use that sword, Liam."

He flashes his hand to Charlotte, revealing the slender trail of blood his blade left behind. "It won't come. Can't? This element—"

A battering ram—Blinkey—pummels his spine and sends him flying several feet into the middle of the atrium. Blinkey lands on her feet and turns her stony eyes on Charlotte, scraping her toenails against the ground as she prepares to kick again—

Green ropes thwip from above. Liam grabs merman, yowls through gritted teeth as sparks fly around his fingers, but he still grabs the burning rope and yanks it as hard as he can, dragging the merman out of the water and into the atrium where he falls with a flop, still tail-finned, face-down and stuck as Liam throws his weight on one foot to step on his back and strike his head with the butt of the blood dagger.

Charlotte swings the rib in front of her to block Captain's first kick, second, third. The mermaid's sneer gives way to snarls as she fails to land a strike with spear or foot. "C'mon, Blinkey, you can do better than that," Charlotte taunts as she back-steps toward the wall, or more specifically, the hole in the wall. *We take the fight to the hole, we leave through the hole. YES*, she grins.

"Fine." Blinkey's snarl swirls to form the star-mouth—

"Oooh, shit."

The short burst pummels Charlotte into Liam and sends

them both sliding to a halt into the fallen wall.

Blinkey jumps into the air, up through the water ceiling, and back down to land inches from Charlotte's hip. She grabs Charlotte's neck and lifts her close enough to touch her nose: "And that's Captain Blinkey to you, gill-less."

Charlotte readies her left hook. "And that's Charlotte to —YEOW!" *Like punching a goddamn brick wall!* She'd done that once during a fight, missing the bastard's face and punching a storage shed wall instead. She had to tape her fingers for weeks and pray the mistake didn't cost her her music.

Fucking did it again. Same hand too, dammit. "What the hell are you? Rock?"

Another rope thwips down past Charlotte's shoulder. Liam grabs it—

Captain Blinkey's star-mouth quivers like it wants to smile—

—until Liam yanks another merman down on top of her. "Now, Charlotte!"

And they leap onto the stones on the fallen wall. They looked smaller from their bubble, but up close each rock has to be a good five feet tall, and they've got to clamber up with Captain's spear slicing at their feet. They pull themselves on top at last, and look down into the hole. The pool's water is night-time muddy with a thousand trapped fireflies swimming in sync, and more bubbling up from the center.

A merman drops from the water above them, somersaulting in swirling light to land on his feet at the hole's edge next to Charlotte and Liam, who both drop in huddle-heaps just before he releases a star-mouth-scream that rattles their teeth as it flies over their crouching forms. Several deafening CRACKS behind them: two of the levels on the far side of the Library shatter and now float in the water.

The distraction lasts only a heartbeat, but it's enough: the stellaqui launch a green net large enough to encompass both Liam and Charlotte, dragging them off the wall and along the floor toward the enclosure. All is grit and light and clenching teeth as Charlotte forces her eyes to go past the sparks to see Liam cutting at the net, cutting at the net, yet the net merely sends its power through the dagger into his arm, scoring more welts, turning his flesh a putrefying yellow. "S-stop, Liam, you'll die!"

The spear stops him instead. Captain Blinkey cuts through the net, along the top of his biceps, and tings the floor.

Violet and crimson pool outward as Liam cries, his fingers losing their grip on the blood dagger.

Captain presses her foot onto the wound. "Maybe I will be so honored as to assist with your study, Princeborn, after the Queen is through with you."

No. You won't. The Voice inside unleashes such a white-hot rage that Charlotte is sure her blood could scald the fish tails above her. No spark, no spear, no scream could keep her hand from thrusting through the emerald cords to touch him, Liam, and his blood dagger one more time, one more bloody time before they become some fish ghoul's fucking science project.

And it's warm. The blood dagger is warm with him, with her, with... with life. She knows she sees its golden embers within the metal. Charlotte grips it tight and drags it across the net binding them: the flaming wing that saved Charlotte in the Pits rips the net in two, sending all its little tendrils shriveling back, hissing and frayed. Its fire is the most beautiful thing Charlotte has seen since she first caught sight of Liam's eyes.

Captain Blinkey staggers back. "That's impossible!"

Green luminescence rains down, but Charlotte throws her arm open, her own battle scream a fright as the fire mounts a wave strong enough to burn every net cord and move *through* the water, driving all swimming merfolk to the far side of the Library in a nervous panic.

The merman from the hole's edge leaps down off the wall to Charlotte, star-mouth poised to scream, but Charlotte slashes the air between them, and the wing of fire melts the lower half of his face and turns all obsidian. His mouth can no longer open: he runs his flippers over it, whining, now squeaking madly at Captain Blinkey and at the remaining two merfolk still on the atrium floor.

For a moment, all anyone can hear is Liam's labored breathing, the obsidian merman's muffled whines, and the bubbling water of the hole in the atrium floor.

A mermaid points with her fin at the bubbling water and clicks, eyes darting from Charlotte to dagger to hole and back. Captain Blinkey lets out what Charlotte can only guess are some nasty curses in dolphin-talk followed by a "the Queen's on her way NOW?"

Charlotte slides over until her foot nudges Liam's—*oh sure, now I touch his ass, with death spearing us everywhere.* "Liam?"

"I'm here." The way he sounds… barely.

"Don't you go anywhere." She sneaks a quick side-look at his arm. Blood still trickles out. *Dammit.*

The hole's water has bubbled itself into a tall tower, the fireflies floating in a waltzing rhythm round and round. The Library's edges are overrun with thousands of spinning little circles of light. Charlotte catches the panic on Captain Blinkey's face, and grins. "Aw, I didn't know the Queen's a disco fan."

Captain Blinkey chucks the spear at Charlotte and runs after it. She transforms mid-air from legs to tail, from fins to strong arms and hands that catch the spear, ready to drive it into Charlotte's chest with all possible force.

Charlotte dodges, unleashes another fire-wing as she sings,

"*Burn baby burn*, duh duh duh duuuuuh duh!" The wing burns through the spear's shaft, sending the blade down with a final impotent ting! into the floor.

But Captain Blinkey, shaft still in hand, rolls to ram the broken spear into Charlotte's ribs.

Charlotte deflects with the blood dagger's blade.

Captain Blinkey whips her shaft around for another strike and meets the dagger's blade, again.

Charlotte's grip is sure. Rock-hard. Golden flames begin to lick the bone shaft. Her eyes glow with an army's campfires in an emerald land. "*Burn, baby burn—*"

"SHUT UP!" Captain Blinkey barks. Her star-mouth-scream is fast—

But so is Charlotte. She rips the dagger free of the shaft and sets a fire wing loose, and the fire and scream crash together—

Magics collide.

The scream never reaches Charlotte's face. The fire-wing never touches Captain Blinkey. The magics meld and fall as paper-thin, silvery ash.

Disco lights fade. A voice from above fills the spaces left by silence: "Well. I can see you have the situation well in hand, Captain."

A hint of salt floats upward through the air. A dozen guards, half of them mermaids in chainmail and the other half mermen in helmets spikey like sea urchins, flank a mermaid in chainmail long as a dress, a circlet of silvery kelp braided into her hair. An amulet of pearl glows with angler light upon her chest.

A few guards ready their rope-nets, pale Liam in their sights.

"Don't you dare touch him!" Charlotte points the blood dagger at all of them as she runs, slips on Liam's blood and crashes to the floor but still clutching the dagger, and crawling, crawling until her free hand feels his clammy arm and smells despair so strong she's ready to cry herself, but by god, she ain't showing these water-freaks *shit*. "I will burn all of you, I swear!"

A torrent of clicks and squeaks flow from Captain Blinkey. The guards blink at her spear, the bone flakes, the obsidian-mouth merman.

Charlotte risks looking down. Between the nets and the fighting, Liam's tunic's all but scrapped shreds around his arm. Yellow pus bubbles where violet and crimson flow. "I gotta stop this bleeding," she says, her breaths shallow, panicked. *Will this work? I don't, I don't know what else to do, and Liam's closed his eyes and his lips look blue, please, not like this, don't, you promised to stay with me.*

The Voice fills Charlotte's fingers around the blood dagger. *It will work, if you put your heart into it.*

Charlotte counts her breaths. *One, two.* Positions the blood dagger's blade over the wound. *Three, four.* Takes Liam's hand and presses it between the blood dagger and her own. *Five, six.* Closes her eyes. Remembers:

To skip a stone, to paint a glass, to climb, to run, to hurt, to hold, to hope—

The engraved feathers shiver along the metal. Embers flare, just once, from hilt to tip. Then all is cold.

Charlotte takes a deep breath. She doesn't notice how every pair of water-folk eyes is just as fixed as her own on the blade and what lies beneath.

The yellow pus is gone. The wound remains, but is now cauterized, at least.

"Liam?" She cups his cheek, and leans close. "Liam?" she says again, her nose hovering over him, smelling for hope, eyes searching for a single twitch of muscle. "Liam, please."

Coughing. "I beg your—"

"Get back!" Charlotte whirls on her haunches, blood dagger out, and falls down with a soft thud on Liam's chest, facing the merfolk. Liam's body buckles upward on either side of her. His mouth hacks a little blood, but air moves in and he breathes, *oh please YES he's breathing*... only to change into curses when his head smacks back onto the floor.

"Heart's Fire, what—Char..." Liam's eyes open to see a tangled mess of dirty yellow hair surrounding a grimy face, snot-encrusted nose, chapped lips... and bottomless green eyes filled with flecks of a rainbow's light. "Are you... sitting on me?"

"Maybe," Charlotte says, blushing despite herself.

"One of the best battle-wakings I've ever had..."

"Hush, you."

The Queen stands quite still for being only a foot or two from the dagger's point. Her fins are folded politely by her hips. "Did *you* really do all this?"

Charlotte takes a quick look around: the cracked enclosure's buried in broken chunks of floor from above. Librarians are rescuing display cases on the bits along the edges. Obsidian Mouth is surrounded by some guards who can't stop slapping at his literal rockface while a few others corner Captain Blinkey, flipping her cheek and chin with their fins. Her nose doesn't seem to work in a watery world, but Charlotte can tell by the fallen look on Captain Blinkey's face that these "comrades" were more keen to insult than to comfort. "Your people broke the Library. And if your people don't stop being dicks I'll melt their gills shut."

Not that Charlotte knew if she could actually swing it, but Obsidian Mouth sure looks terrified at the prospect. He squeaks himself into a run doesn't stop until he's climbed the rubble to enter the water-filled upper levels of the Library.

"Hail, Monarch of Stellaqui," Liam says with halted breath and a limp motion of the hand, still stuck under Charlotte's backside. "We are, but travelers, seeking safe passage, through your element," he manages to wheeze out.

The Queen gives a slight curtsy, touched with a sneer. "Hail, Princeborn and Thief. No," she raises a fin, "please, do not stand on my account."

"Oh he ain't standing, and neither am I." Charlotte says, slowly patting the blood dagger against the palm of her hand. "You'll slice him open the first chance you get."

Stone-eyes rolling look scarier than one would think. "Quite true."

A loud grinding: one of the leviathan spines is moving up. Water falls upward around the vertebrae, flowing into the ceiling, keeping the first floor dry.

A merman lands hands first, giving his tail time to change. He flips forward onto legs, cries, "The child!" and devolves into a flood of dolphin-speak that causes even the Queen to go agape for a moment.

One guard tries to click the messenger into silence, but the Queen shushes the guard instead. "No. I made a promise. I will see for myself. Besides, I cannot study the accused before the High Sage bears his testimony. If he confirms the weapon in their possession is that which has killed my people," she bows forward until all Charlotte can see are her slender, trident-shaped teeth, "then we will most assuredly observe their inner workings as they lie awake, feeling every needle that pins their flesh." With four clicks and a defiant gaze, the Queen shifts herself upright and orders, "The High Sage will need water here. Take the prisoners to the largest study room, and seal it in air. Provide a small dose of nourishment—they must be well enough for questions, but not escape."

Acknowledgments

So there's something of a story behind this story.

Eight years ago, I became mother to a beautiful, gentle girl, Blondie. I also entered a very dark and very ugly realm of postpartum depression. Rachel Pierson, a dear school friend, recommended participating in National Novel Writing Month to help me jumpstart my creative writing again.

In one month, I felt like I was finding shards of light in the darkness. I could enjoy my daughter's sleepy smile. And the first draft of *Fallen Princeborn: Stolen* was complete.

Eight years and eight drafts later, *Fallen Princeborn: Stolen* was no longer a NaNoWriMo smackdown, but a novel hundreds of pages in length. Characters found their natures. The world found its history. My husband Bo supported me in any way he could, be it watching the kids so I could write, surprising me with books I needed for research, or hunting down music I needed to get the emotional feel of a scene. My college chum Rachel Weiss critiqued every draft of *FP:S* without a single complaint, always finding new questions about the narrative that needed to be explored.

Biff and Bash's birth took my postpartum and dragged it into depths I never thought lurked in myself. I couldn't form words around what I *felt*. Depression is like that—you who suffer it know how it just freezes you, hollows you, wraps around you and turns the rest of reality into some distant, far-off place you cannot touch. I needed heroes to help me find my way back to my children, to conquer the villains scraping me out, and fill me again with the love of my family. Only by telling Charlotte's story could I find the strength to cope with my own.

So here we are, you and I. Thanks to the bottomless support of fellow writers like Anne Clare, Shehanne Moore, the Steeden family, S.J. Higbee, and so many more, I found the courage to risk sharing *FP:S* with Aionios Books. Gerri Santiago took hold of *FP:S* and never let go, inspiring me to map out even more of the story's universe. Her editing, along with the work of Dan Primbs and Jackie Dever, helped me tune my heroes' voices into a harmony unique in their mutual struggles to find themselves in pasts smeared by pain.

And of course, more than anything, thank you so very much, Dear Reader, for picking up my book. All the tales told are nothing but words on a page without the readers' imaginations to bring them to life. You keep reading. I'll keep writing. Together we'll set the darkness on fire.

About Jean Lee

I started telling stories before I knew how to write them, filling pages with pictures and audio cassettes with words. This passion for storytelling grew every year to become not only my focus of graduate study, but also an escape from abuse and savior from postpartum depression. That savior has since transformed into the young-adult dark fantasy *Fallen Princeborn: Stolen.*

Stories are the fire that warms the soul. They melt fear, ignite hope, and spark relationships like nothing else. I'm honored you seated yourself here by my hearth to enjoy my fiction's light. Please feel free to visit often, for there are many treasures bizarre and fantastic in my imagination waiting to speak with tongues of flame. Then we can talk about the writers that refuel us, and the stories that stir us like marsh-mallow sticks poking a campfire's embers. Let's send the fire's sparks flying like so many fireflies into summer's night, and invite more out of the cold darkness.

You can reach me at **jeanleesworld.com**. Please subscribe to my email list to get updates on the *Fallen Princeborn* series, receive free e-books, and explore some cool writer stuff like inspiring music, writing tips discovered while reading, and interviews with fellow YA authors. You can find me on Twitter and Instagram (**@jeanleesworld**). And if the spirit should move you, please write a review of *Fallen Princeborn: Stolen* on Amazon.

You may also email me at **jeanleesworld@gmail.com**. I would love to hear from you, O Awesome Reader!

Read on and share on—
Jean Lee

Also by Jean Lee

Tales of the River Vine - A collection of short stories
Middler's Pride - Serialized at Channillo.com

Aionios Books

Thank you for taking the time to read this book. If you liked it, please share your thoughts on Goodreads or Amazon. If you didn't like it, that's cool too, please share your review anyway. We will use your feedback to improve our offerings.

For updates on our books and authors, please follow us on Instagram (@AioniosBooks) and subscribe to our newsletter through our website, AioniosBooks.com.

Gerri Santiago
Publisher
Aionios Books, LLC